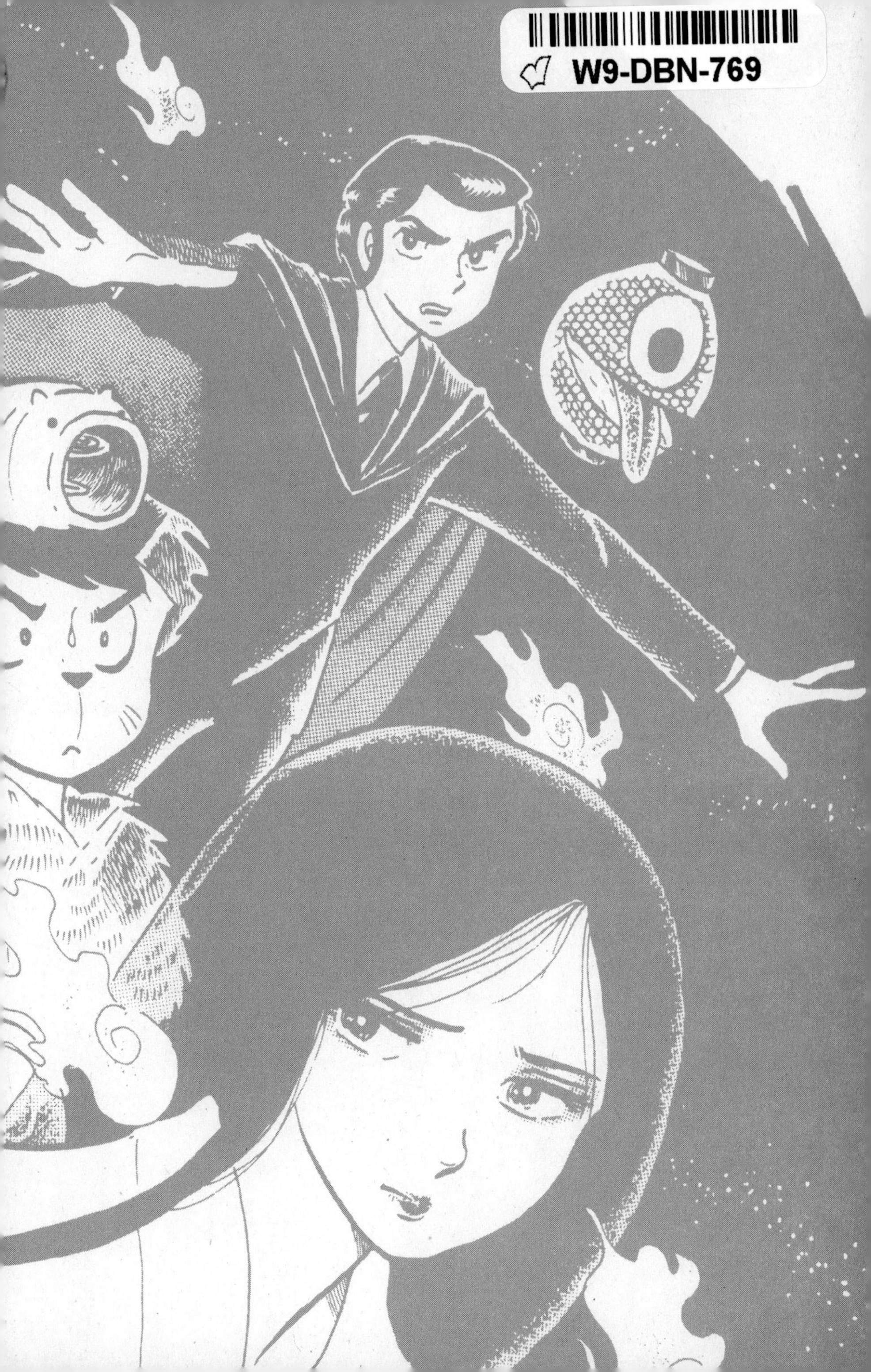

VIZ GRAPHIC NOVEL

THE RETURN OF LUM * URUSEI YATSURA™
FOR BETTER OR CURSE

This volume contains THE RETURN OF LUM * URUSEI YATSURA PART FOUR #1 through #6 in their entirety.

STORY AND ART BY RUMIKO TAKAHASHI

ENGLISH ADAPTATION BY GERARD JONES

Translator/Lillian Olsen
Touch-Up Art & Lettering/Mary Kelleher
Cover Design/Hidemi Sahara
Editor/Annette Roman

Senior Editor/Trish Ledoux
Managing Editor/Hyoe Narita
Editor-in-Chief/Satoru Fujii
Publisher/Seiji Horibuchi

Printed in Canada

Published by Viz Communications, Inc.
P.O. Box 77010 • San Francisco, CA 94107

10 9 8 7 6 5 4 3 2 1
First printing, May 1998

Vizit us at our World Wide Web site at **www.viz.com** and our new Internet magazine, **j-pop.com**, at **www.j-pop.com**!

LUM * URUSEI YATSURA GRAPHIC NOVELS TO DATE

LUM PERFECT COLLECTION
THE RETURN OF LUM
LUM IN THE SUN
SWEET REVENGE
TROUBLE TIMES TEN
FEUDAL FUROR
CREATURE FEATURES
FOR BETTER OR CURSE

VIZ GRAPHIC NOVEL

THE RETURN OF LUM *
URUSEI YATSURA™

FOR BETTER OR CURSE

STORY & ART BY
RUMIKO TAKAHASHI

CONTENTS

PART ONE   WASTE DISPOSAL _____ 7

PART TWO   RAIN, RAIN, GO AWAY! _____ 23

PART THREE   COME AGAIN SOME OTHER DAY _____ 39

PART FOUR   IT'S RAINING, IT'S POURING _____ 55

PART FIVE   WELCOME TO HOTEL GHOST _____ 71

PART SIX   UNFINISHED BUSINESS _____ 87

PART SEVEN   THE HORROR OF PARTY BEACH _____103

PART EIGHT   FUN WITH HURRICANES _____119

PART NINE   OPERATION: DATE WATCH _____135

PART TEN   CURE FOR THE UNCOMMON COLD_____151

PART ELEVEN   DOWN FOR THE COUNT _____167

PART TWELVE   BLOOD FROM A STONE _____183

PART ONE
WASTE DISPOSAL

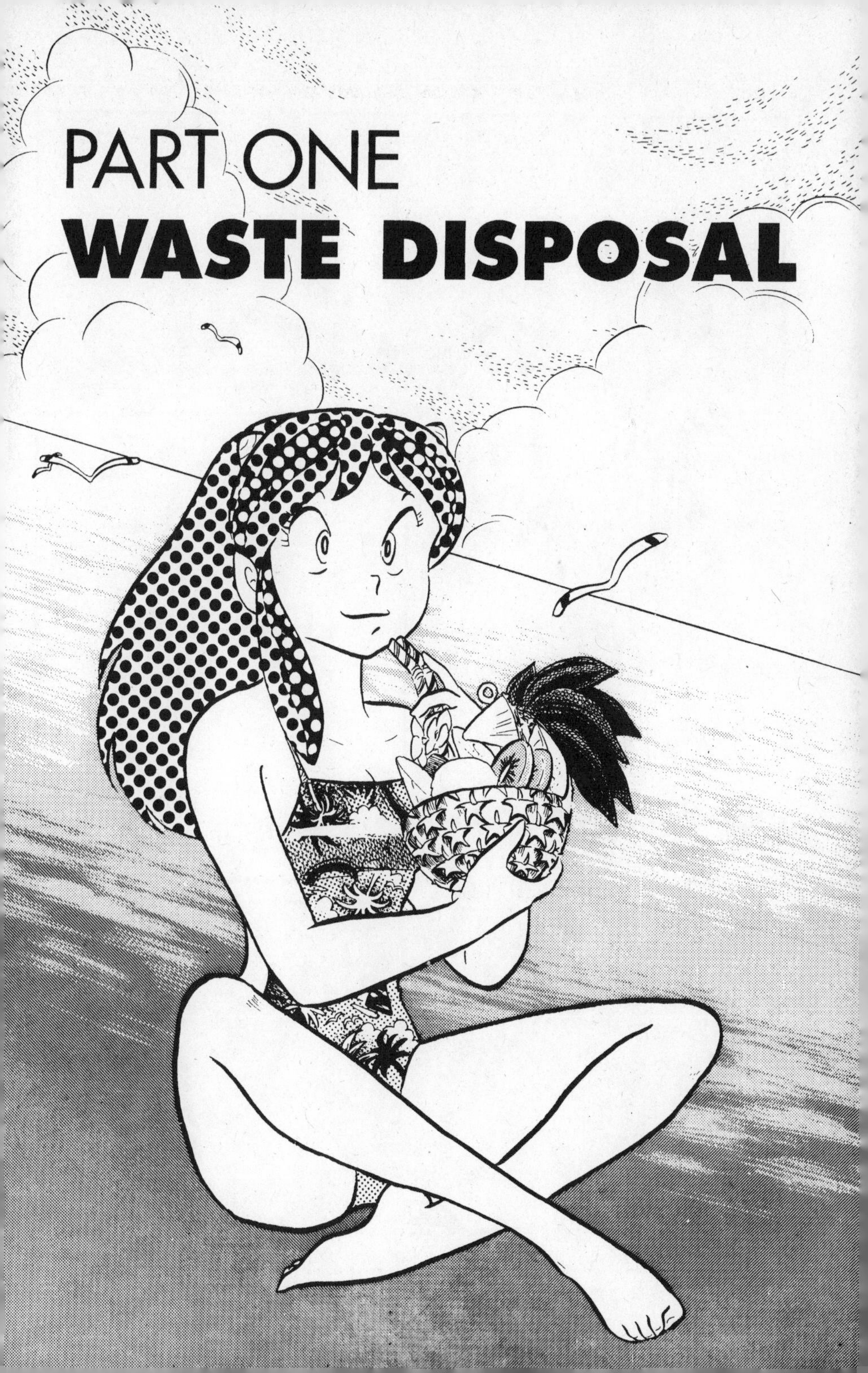

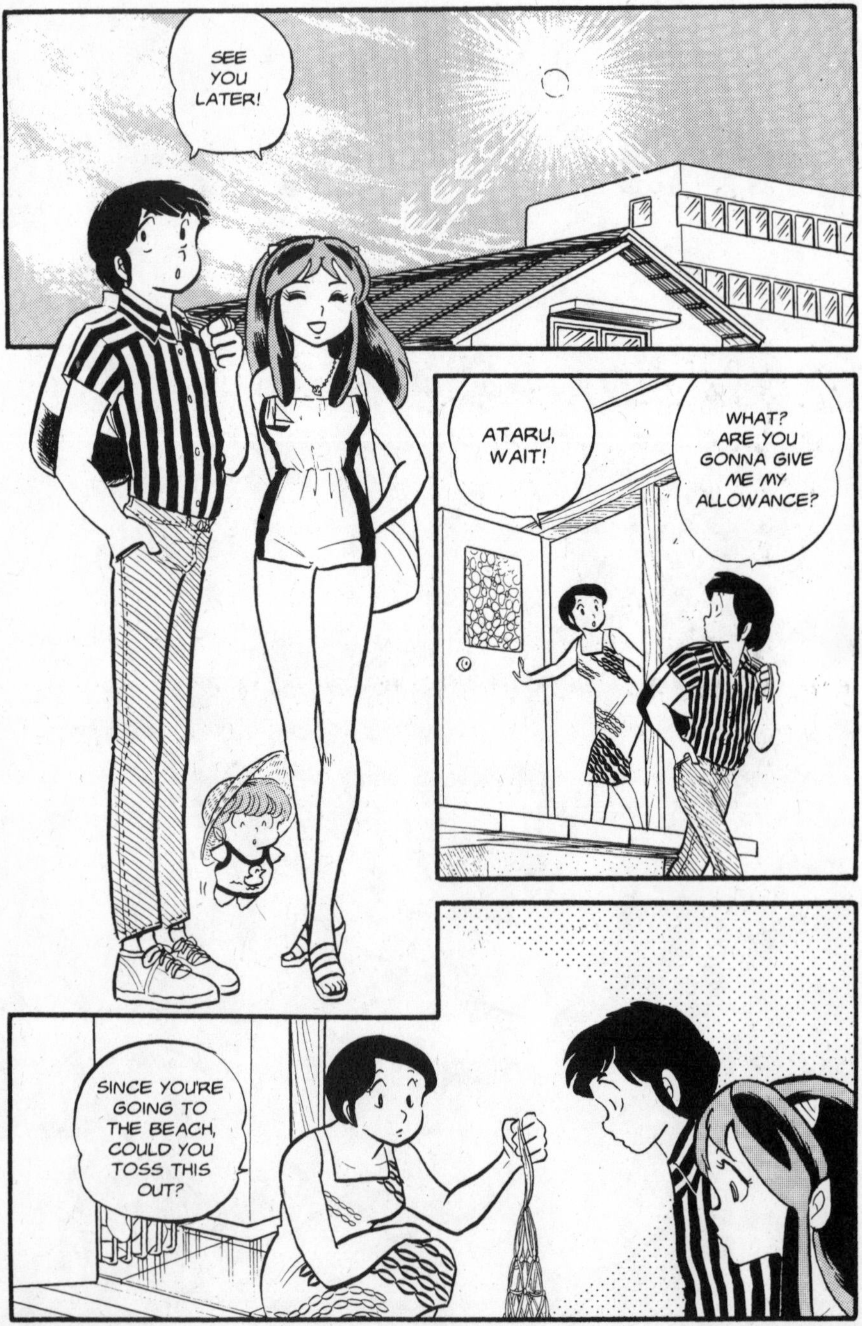
SEE YOU LATER!
ATARU, WAIT!
WHAT? ARE YOU GONNA GIVE ME MY ALLOWANCE?
SINCE YOU'RE GOING TO THE BEACH, COULD YOU TOSS THIS OUT?

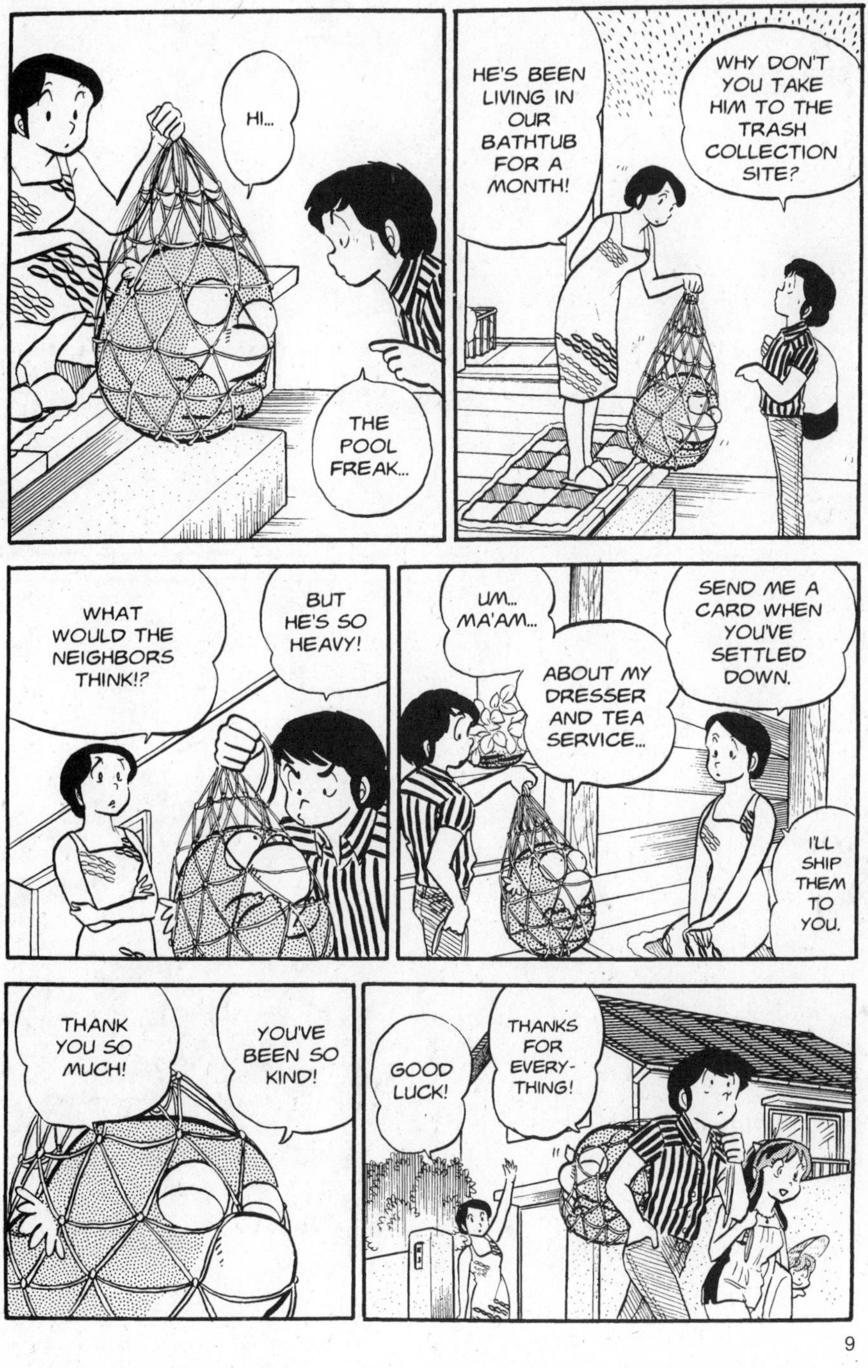
HI...
THE POOL FREAK...
HE'S BEEN LIVING IN OUR BATHTUB FOR A MONTH!
WHY DON'T YOU TAKE HIM TO THE TRASH COLLECTION SITE?
WHAT WOULD THE NEIGHBORS THINK!?
BUT HE'S SO HEAVY!
UM... MA'AM...
ABOUT MY DRESSER AND TEA SERVICE...
SEND ME A CARD WHEN YOU'VE SETTLED DOWN.
I'LL SHIP THEM TO YOU.
THANK YOU SO MUCH!
YOU'VE BEEN SO KIND!
GOOD LUCK!
THANKS FOR EVERY-THING!

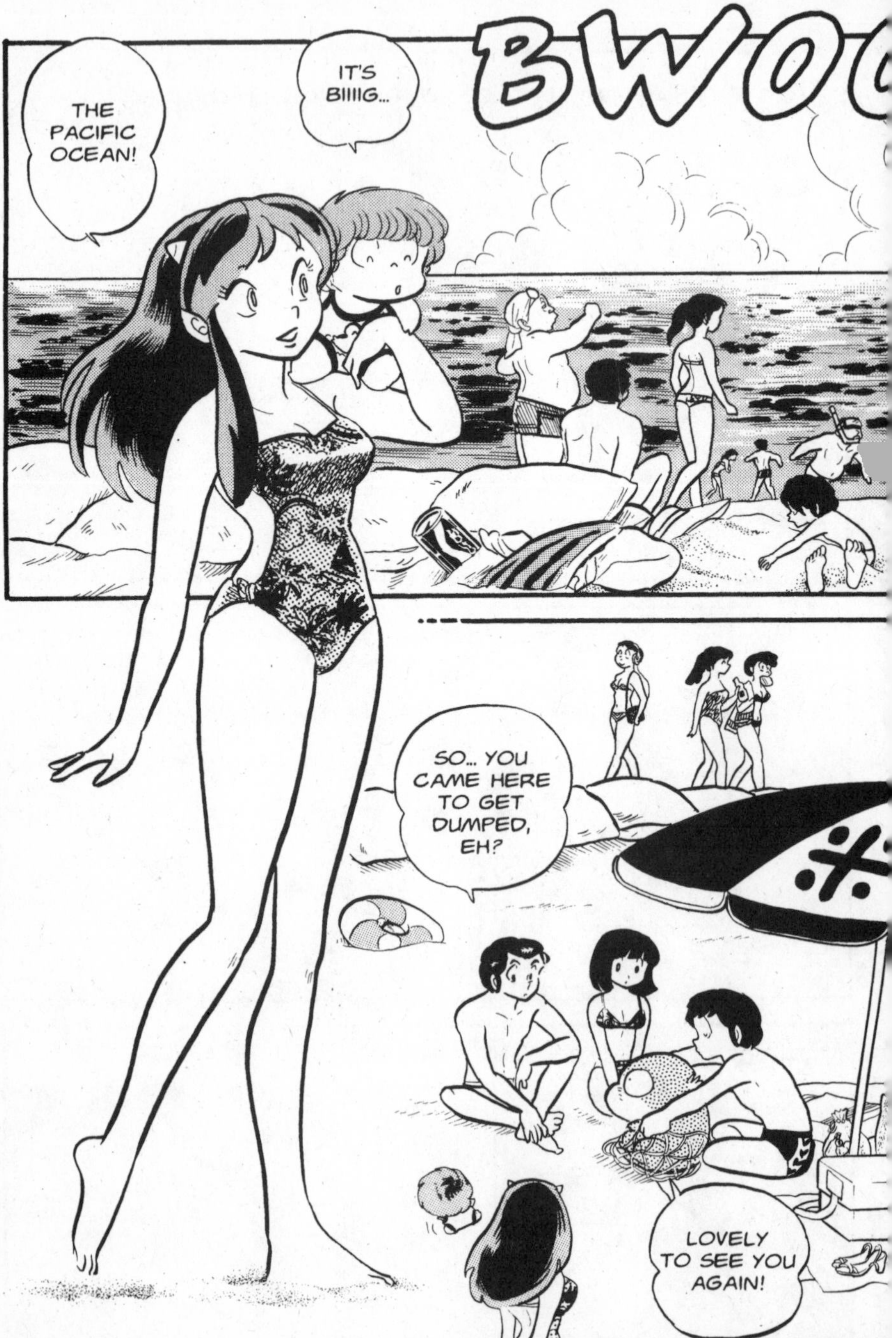
THE PACIFIC OCEAN!
IT'S BIIIG...
BWOO
SO... YOU CAME HERE TO GET DUMPED, EH?
LOVELY TO SEE YOU AGAIN!

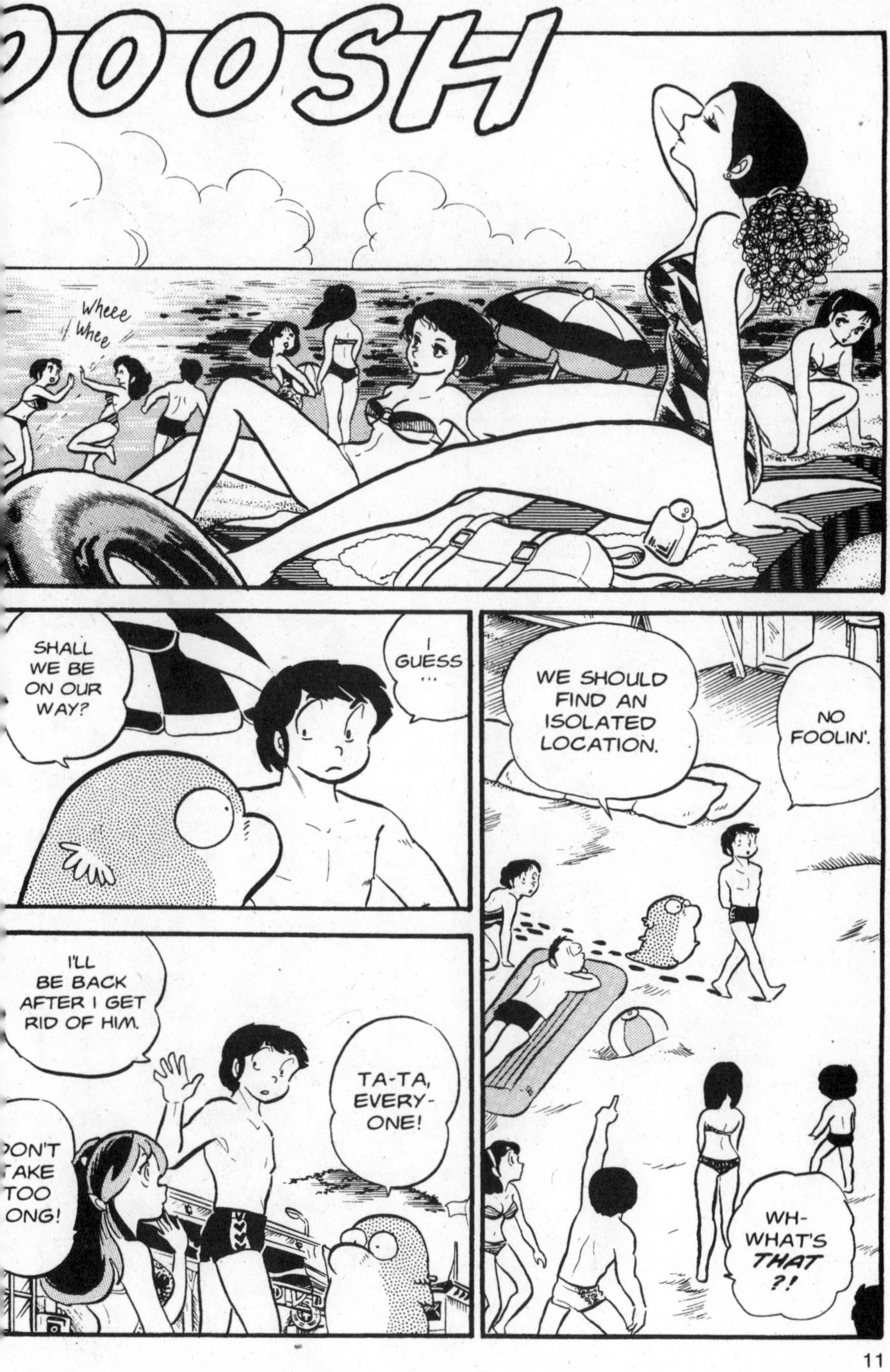
OOOSH
Wheee Whee
SHALL WE BE ON OUR WAY?
I GUESS ...
I'LL BE BACK AFTER I GET RID OF HIM.
TA-TA, EVERY-ONE!
ON'T AKE TOO ONG!
WE SHOULD FIND AN ISOLATED LOCATION.
NO FOOLIN'.
WH- WHAT'S *THAT* ?!

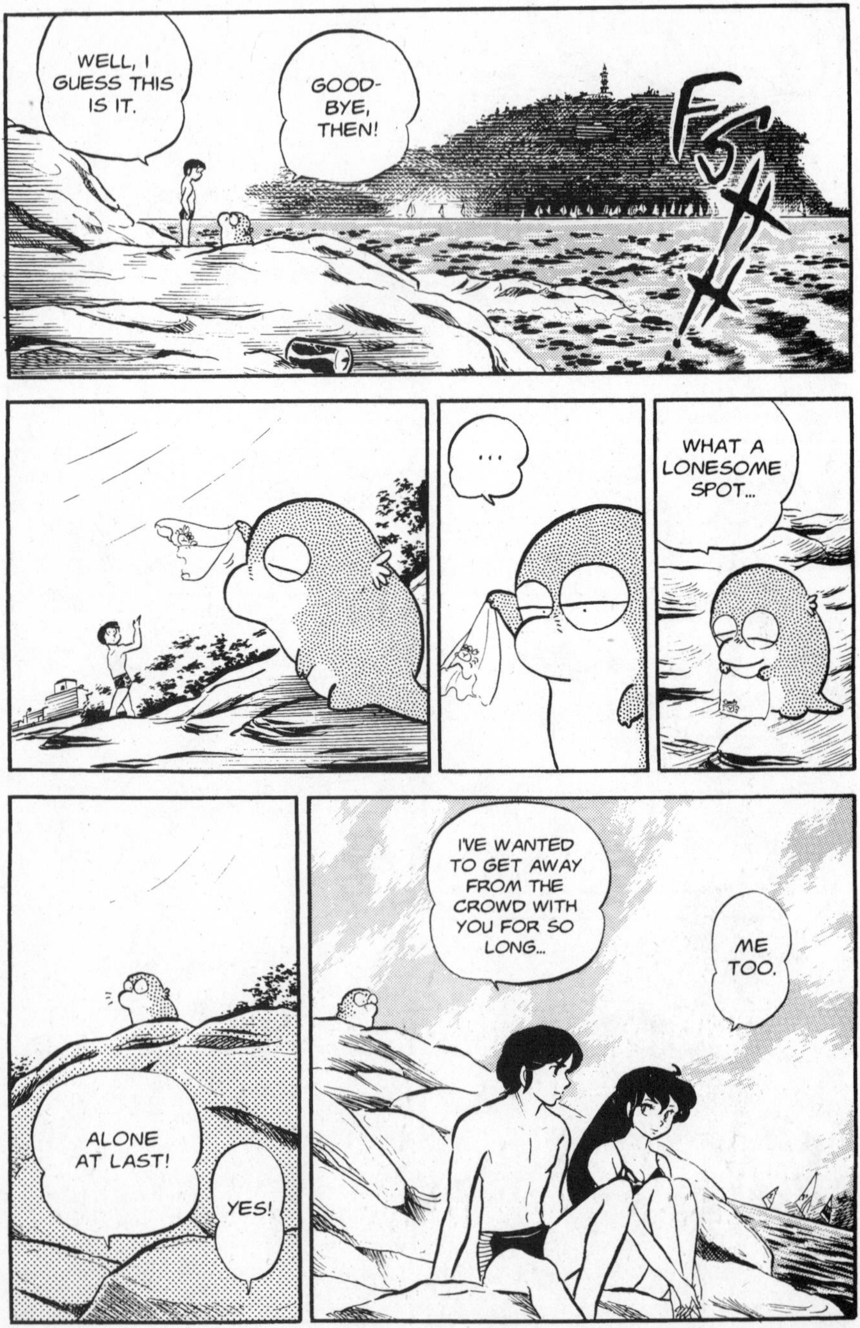
WELL, I GUESS THIS IS IT.
GOOD-BYE, THEN!
FSSHHH
...
WHAT A LONESOME SPOT...
ALONE AT LAST!
YES!
I'VE WANTED TO GET AWAY FROM THE CROWD WITH YOU FOR SO LONG...
ME TOO.

I'VE SEEN THAT WOMAN BEFORE — AT THE POOL!

NO ONE TO DISTURB US, AT LAST...

I'LL JUST SAY GOOD DAY!

GOO...

D—

mPh

ARE YOU NUTS?!

VIP

OH! YOU'VE RETURNED!

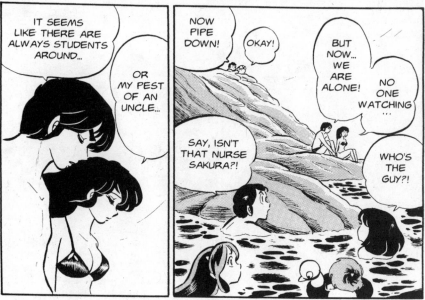

IT SEEMS LIKE THERE ARE ALWAYS STUDENTS AROUND...

OR MY PEST OF AN UNCLE...

NOW PIPE DOWN!

OKAY!

BUT NOW... WE ARE ALONE!

NO ONE WATCHING...

SAY, ISN'T THAT NURSE SAKURA?!

WHO'S THE GUY?!

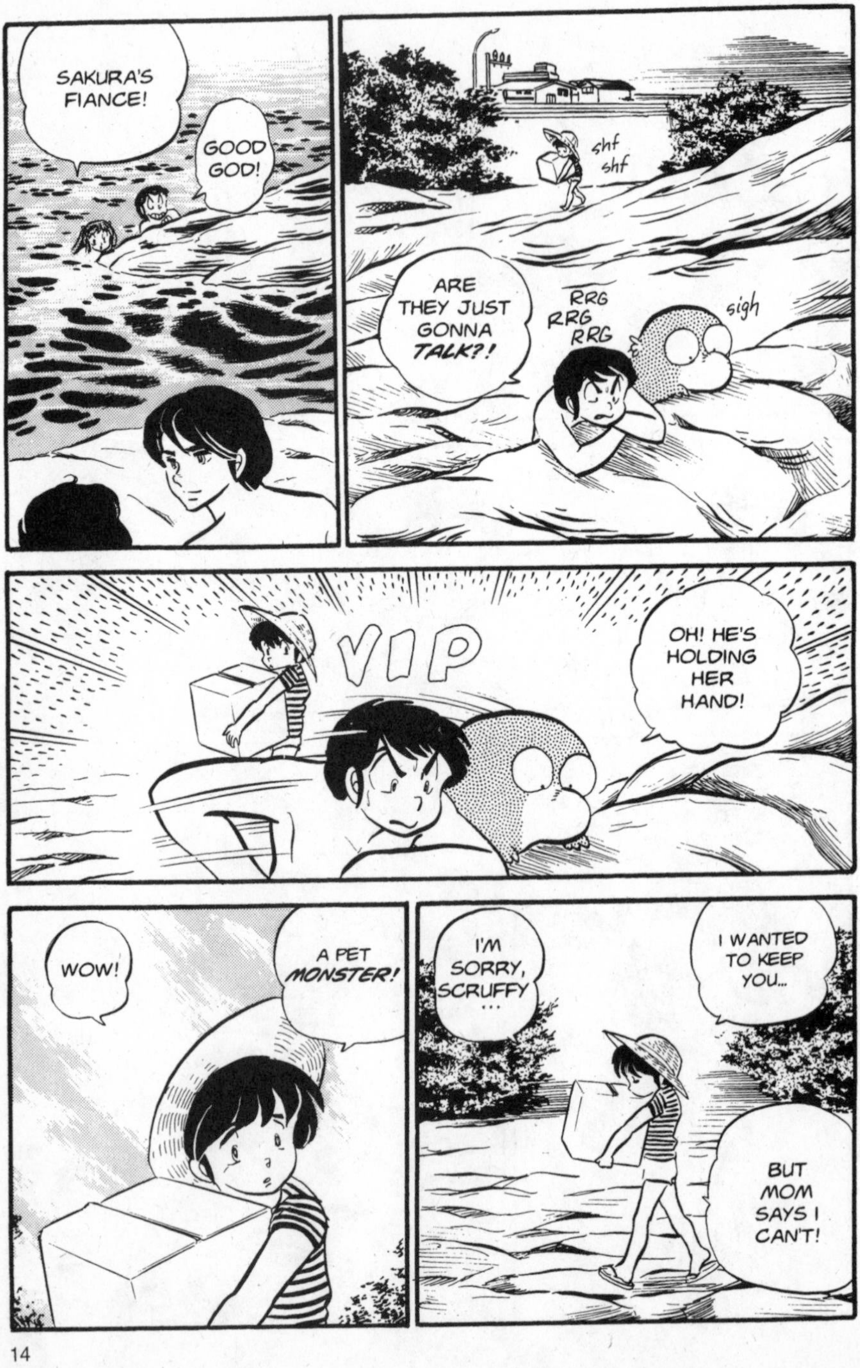
SAKURA'S FIANCE!
GOOD GOD!
shf shf
ARE THEY JUST GONNA TALK?!
RRG RRG RRG
sigh
VIP
OH! HE'S HOLDING HER HAND!
WOW!
A PET MONSTER!
I'M SORRY, SCRUFFY...
I WANTED TO KEEP YOU...
BUT MOM SAYS I CAN'T!

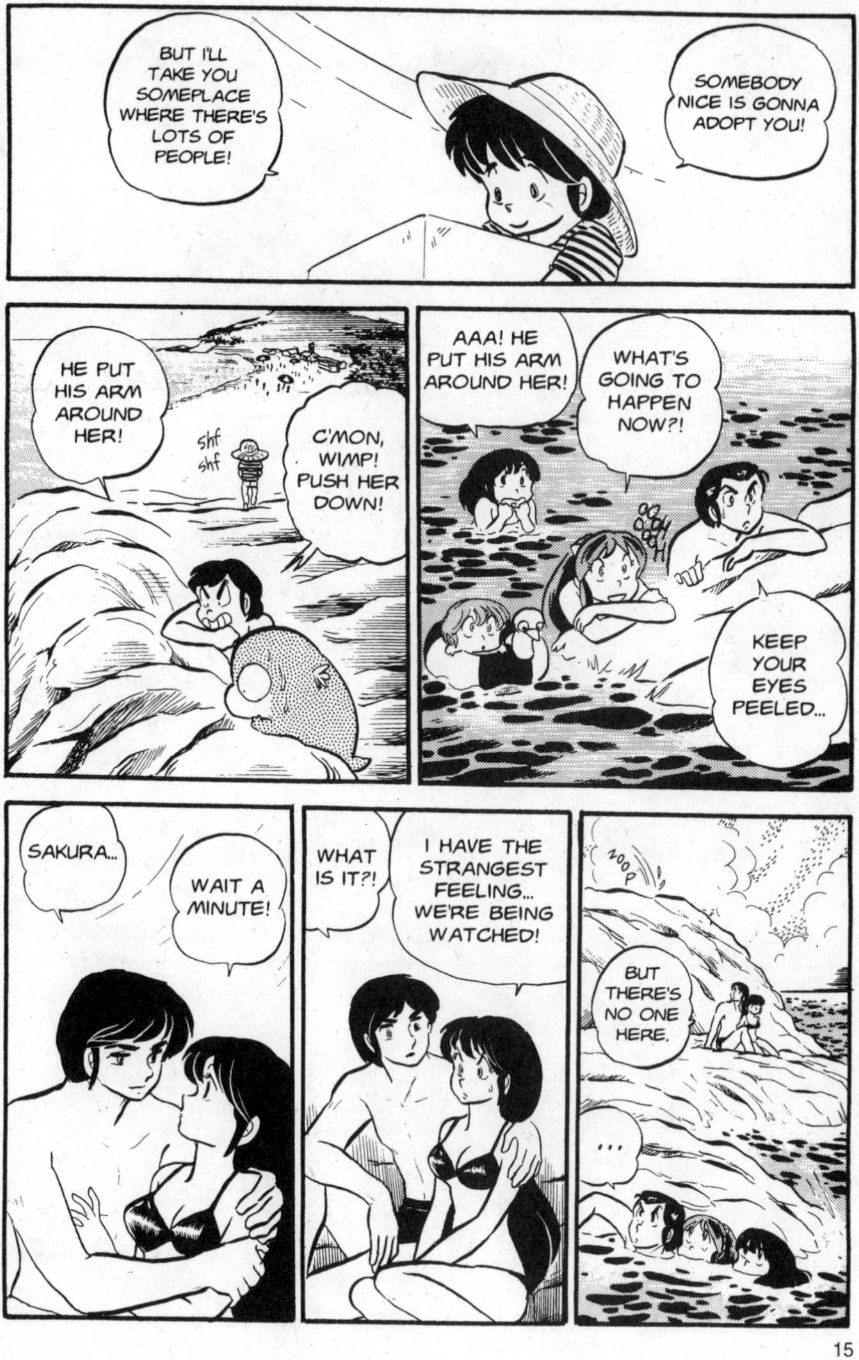
BUT I'LL TAKE YOU SOMEPLACE WHERE THERE'S LOTS OF PEOPLE!
SOMEBODY NICE IS GONNA ADOPT YOU!
HE PUT HIS ARM AROUND HER!
shf shf
C'MON, WIMP! PUSH HER DOWN!
AAA! HE PUT HIS ARM AROUND HER!
WHAT'S GOING TO HAPPEN NOW?!
KEEP YOUR EYES PEELED...
SAKURA...
WAIT A MINUTE!
WHAT IS IT?!
I HAVE THE STRANGEST FEELING... WE'RE BEING WATCHED!
ZOOP
BUT THERE'S NO ONE HERE.
...

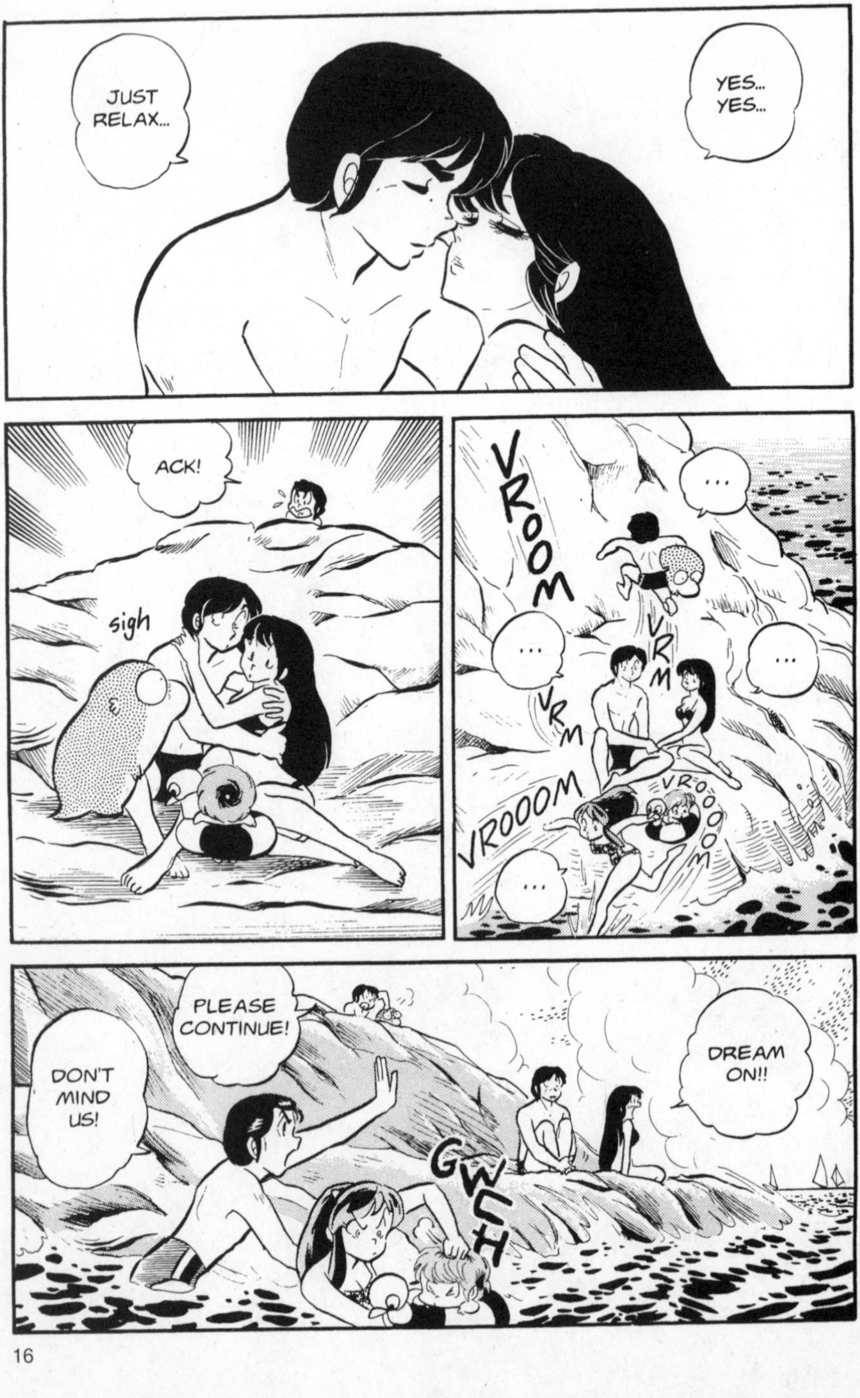
JUST RELAX...
YES... YES...
ACK!
sigh
VROOM
...
...
VRM
VRM
...
VROOOM
VROOOOOOM
...
PLEASE CONTINUE!
DON'T MIND US!
DREAM ON!!
GWCH

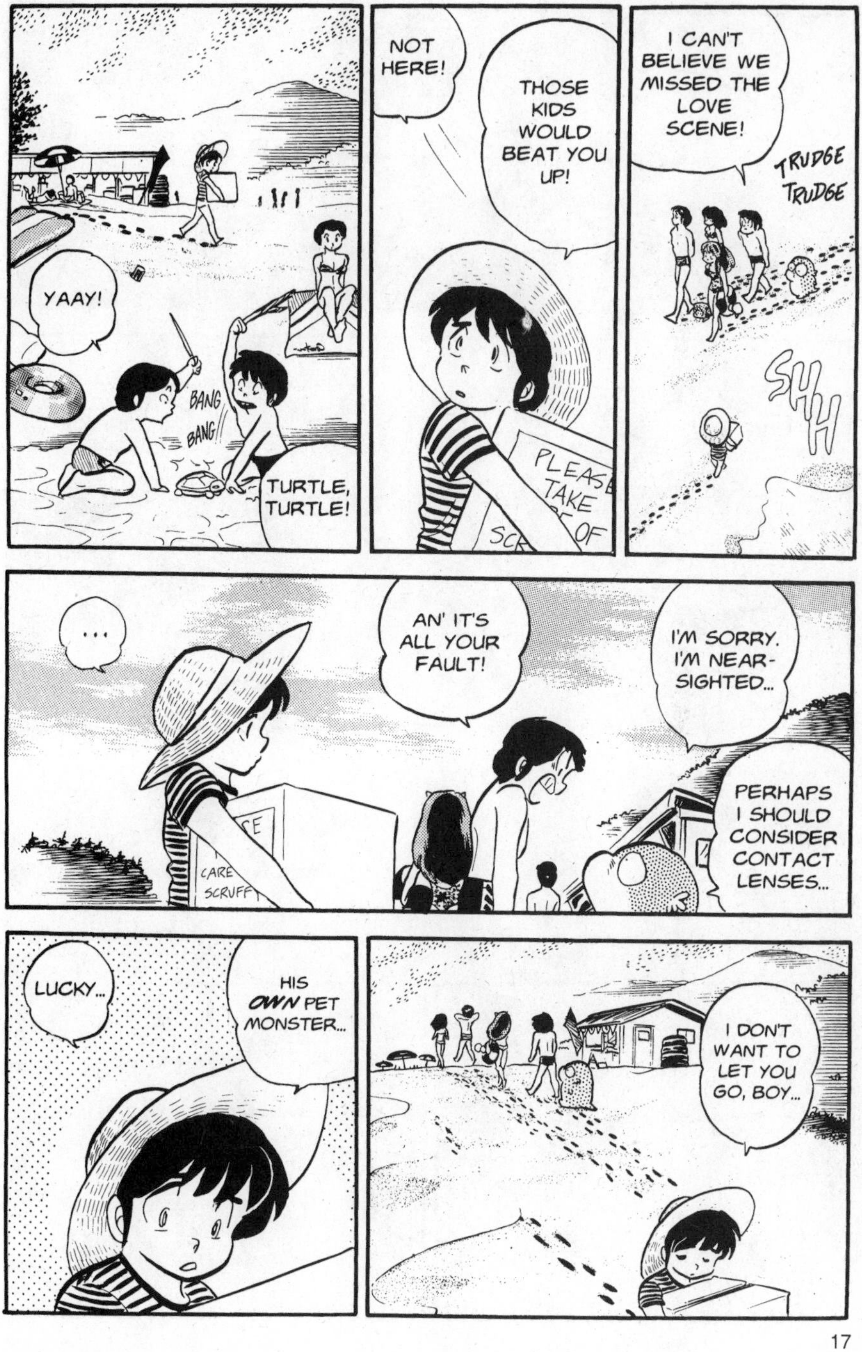
YAAY!
BANG
BANG
TURTLE, TURTLE!
NOT HERE!
THOSE KIDS WOULD BEAT YOU UP!
PLEASE TAKE ... OF
SC
I CAN'T BELIEVE WE MISSED THE LOVE SCENE!
TRUDGE TRUDGE
SHH
...
AN' IT'S ALL YOUR FAULT!
I'M SORRY. I'M NEAR-SIGHTED...
PERHAPS I SHOULD CONSIDER CONTACT LENSES...
CARE
SCRUFF
LUCKY...
HIS OWN PET MONSTER...
I DON'T WANT TO LET YOU GO, BOY...

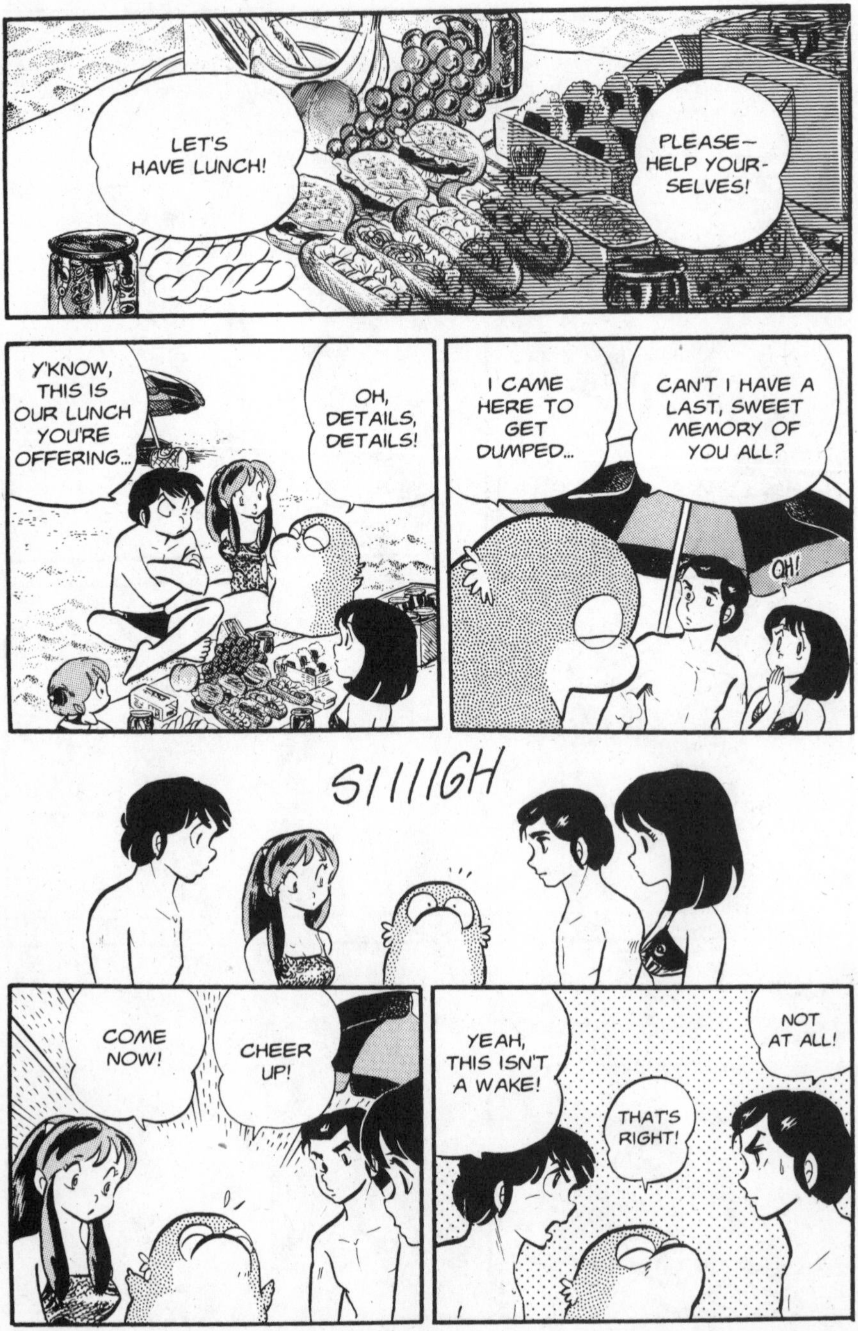
LET'S HAVE LUNCH!
PLEASE— HELP YOUR- SELVES!
Y'KNOW, THIS IS OUR LUNCH YOU'RE OFFERING...
OH, DETAILS, DETAILS!
I CAME HERE TO GET DUMPED...
CAN'T I HAVE A LAST, SWEET MEMORY OF YOU ALL?
OH!
SIIIIGH
COME NOW!
CHEER UP!
YEAH, THIS ISN'T A WAKE!
NOT AT ALL!
THAT'S RIGHT!

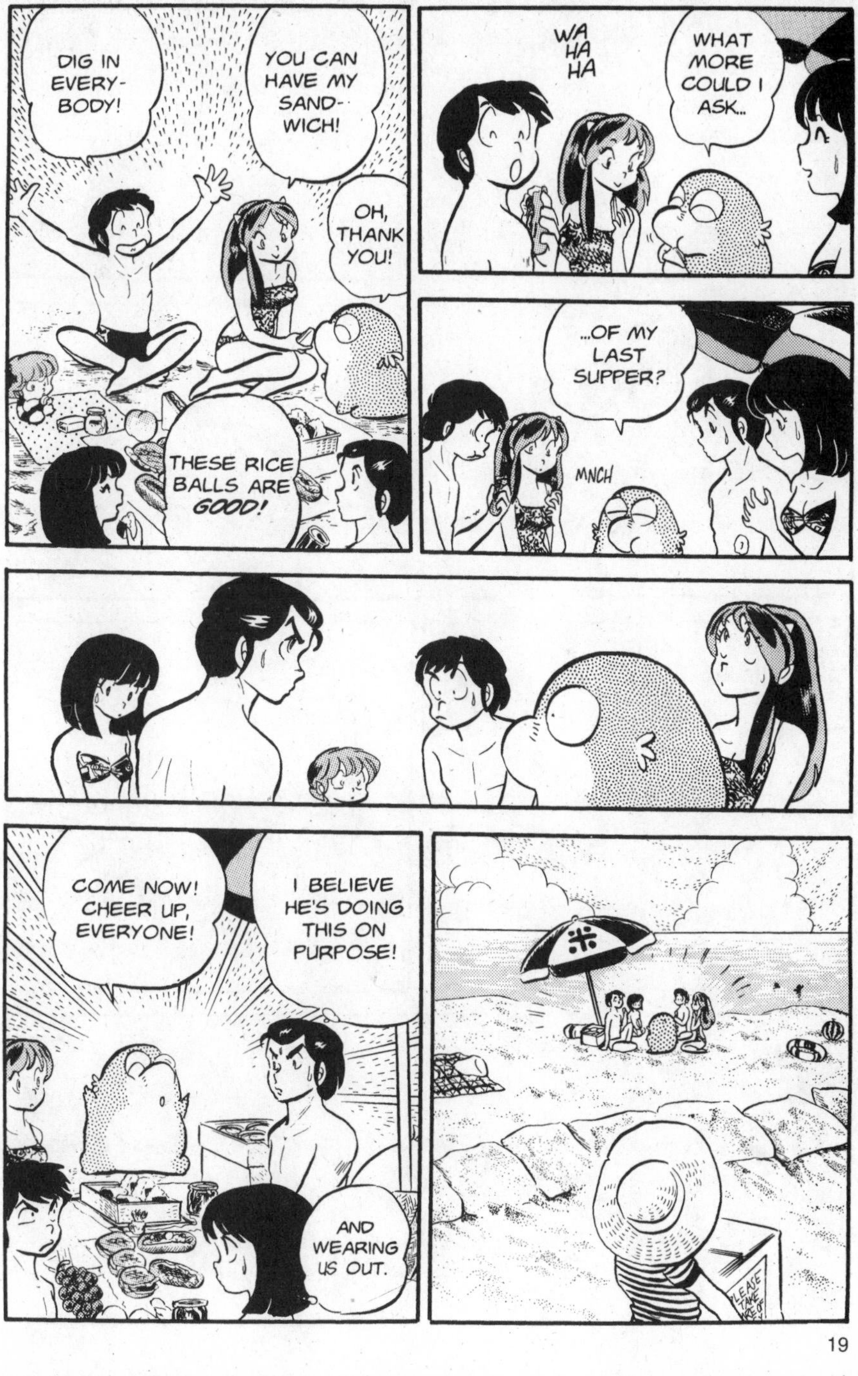
DIG IN EVERY-BODY!
YOU CAN HAVE MY SAND-WICH!
OH, THANK YOU!
THESE RICE BALLS ARE GOOD!
WA HA HA
WHAT MORE COULD I ASK...
...OF MY LAST SUPPER?
MNCH
COME NOW! CHEER UP, EVERYONE!
I BELIEVE HE'S DOING THIS ON PURPOSE!
AND WEARING US OUT.

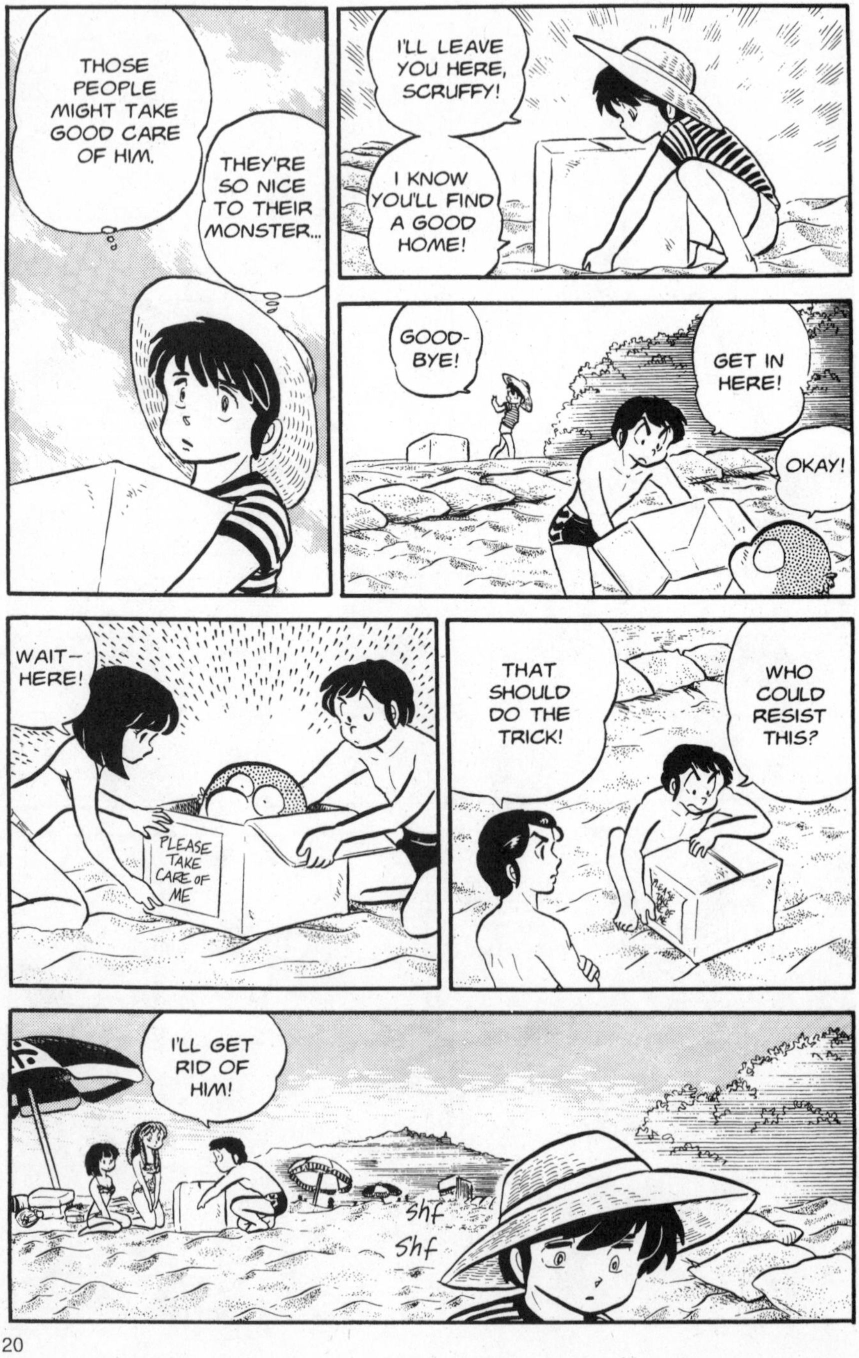
THOSE PEOPLE MIGHT TAKE GOOD CARE OF HIM.
THEY'RE SO NICE TO THEIR MONSTER...
I'LL LEAVE YOU HERE, SCRUFFY!
I KNOW YOU'LL FIND A GOOD HOME!
GOOD-BYE!
GET IN HERE!
OKAY!
WAIT— HERE!
PLEASE TAKE CARE OF ME
THAT SHOULD DO THE TRICK!
WHO COULD RESIST THIS?
I'LL GET RID OF HIM!
shf
shf

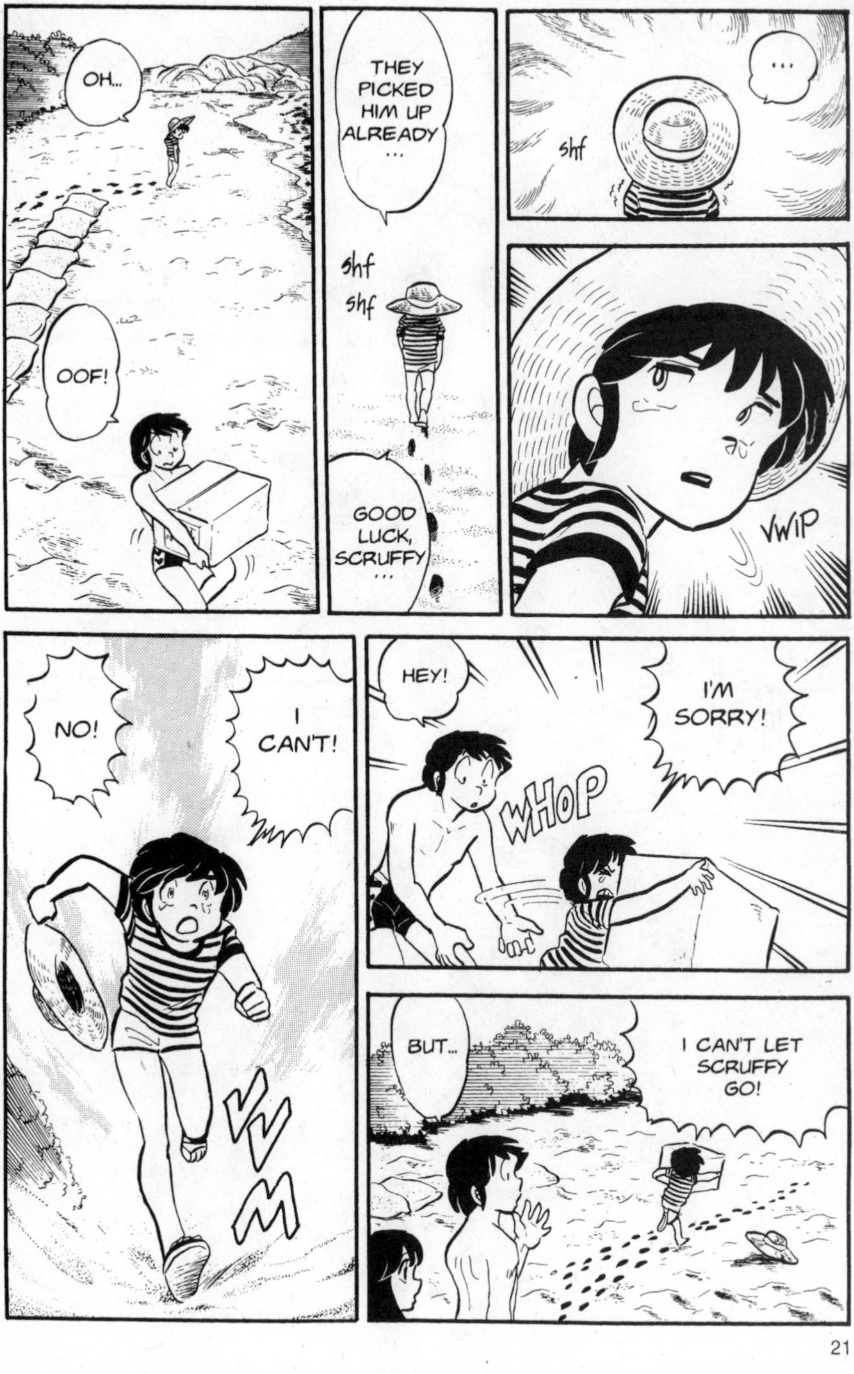
OH...
OOF!
THEY PICKED HIM UP ALREADY ...
shf
shf
GOOD LUCK, SCRUFFY ...
...
shf
VWIP
NO!
I CAN'T!
HEY!
I'M SORRY!
WHOP
BUT...
I CAN'T LET SCRUFFY GO!

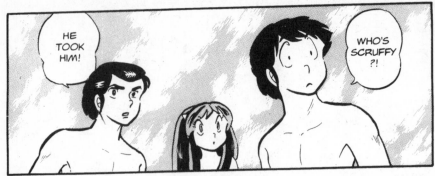

HE TOOK HIM!
WHO'S SCRUFFY ?!
LUM-CHAN! THERE'S A CARDBOARD BOX HERE, TOO!
"PLEASE TAKE CARE OF SCRUFFY."
PLEASE TAKE CARE OF SCRUFFY
HE MUST HAVE GRABBED THE WRONG BOX!
HE'LL DUMP IT AS SOON AS HE FINDS OUT THERE'S A MONSTER INSIDE!
PLEASE TAKE CARE SCRUFFY
IF HE WAS WILLING TO KEEP *THIS*... I DOUBT IT.
CHERRY...
WELL, FANCY MEETING YOU HERE!
NOW *THAT* WAS A KIND LITTLE BOY!
CARE OF SCRUFFY
I WANT *MY* MONSTER BACK!!

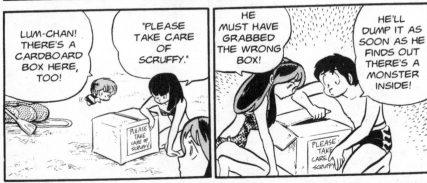

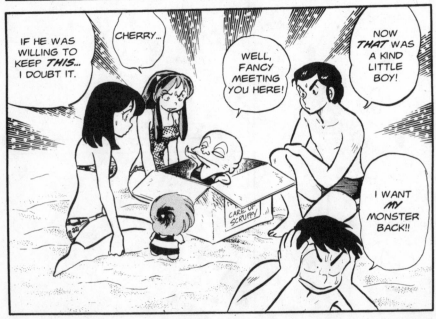

PART TWO
RAIN, RAIN, GO AWAY!

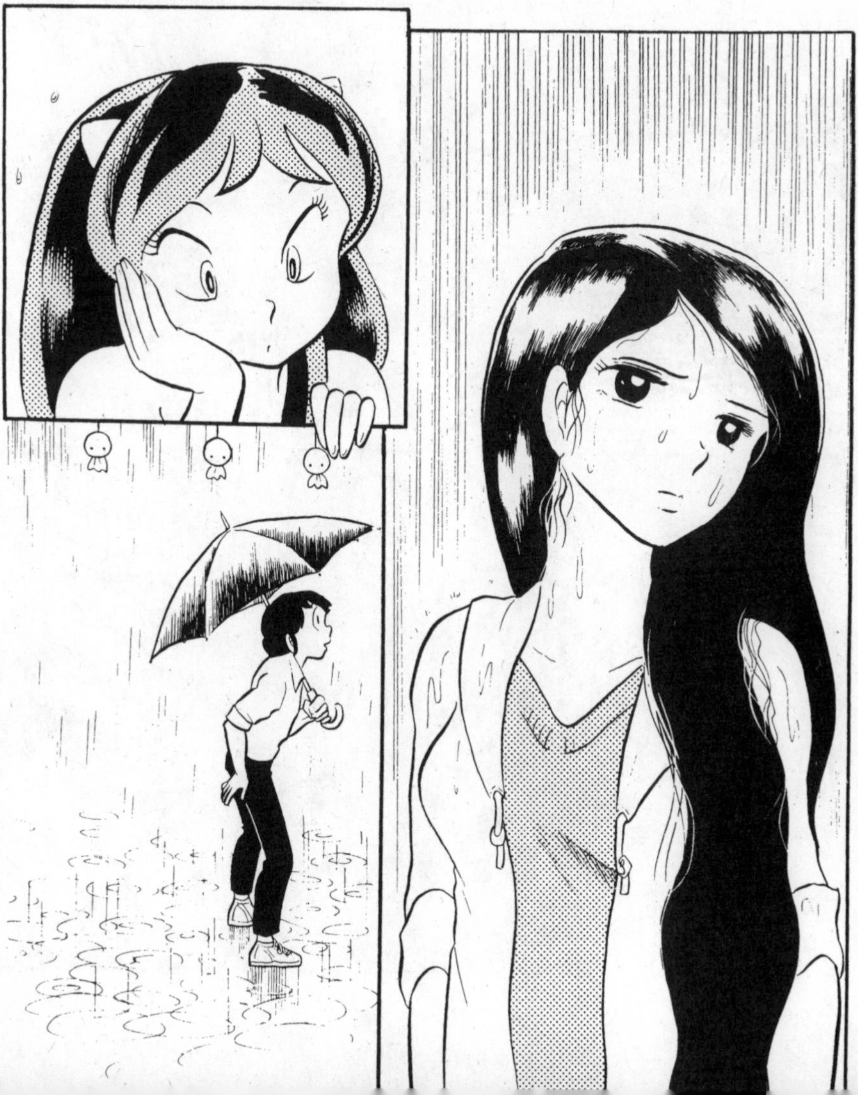

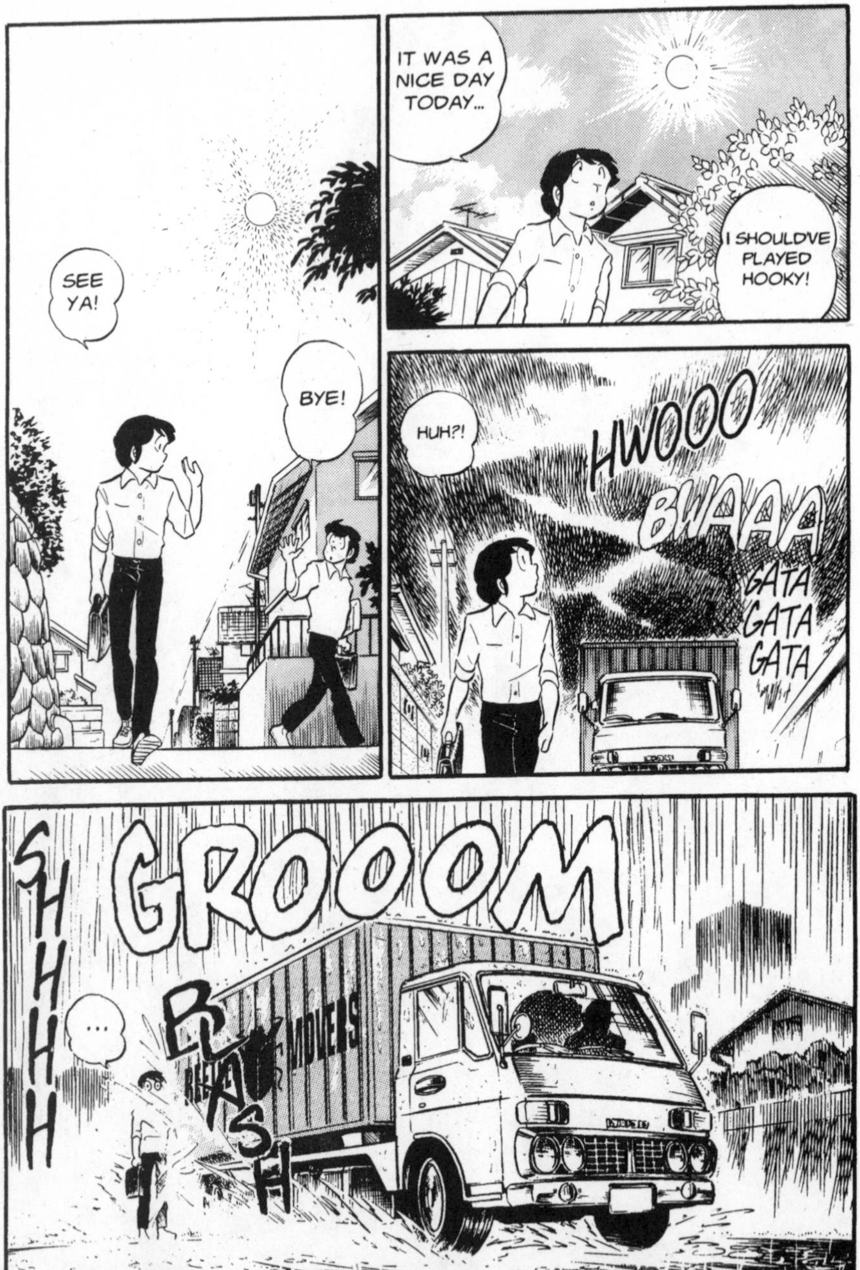
SEE YA!
BYE!
IT WAS A NICE DAY TODAY...
I SHOULD'VE PLAYED HOOKY!
HUH?!
HWOOO
BWAAA
GATA GATA GATA
SHHHHH
GROOOM
...
BLASH

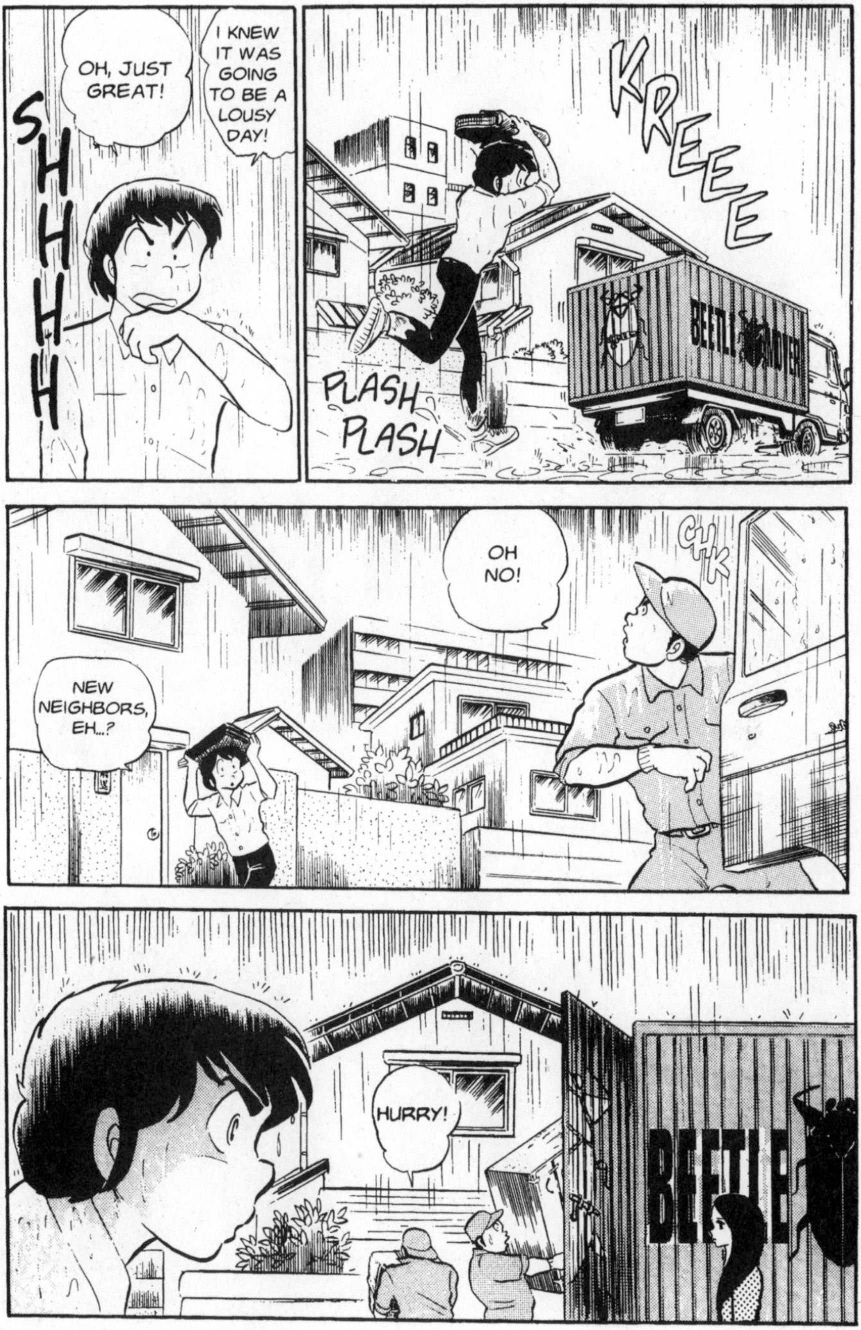
OH, JUST GREAT!
I KNEW IT WAS GOING TO BE A LOUSY DAY!
SHHHHH
KREEEE
PLASH PLASH
NEW NEIGHBORS, EH...?
OH NO!
CHK
HURRY!
BEETLE

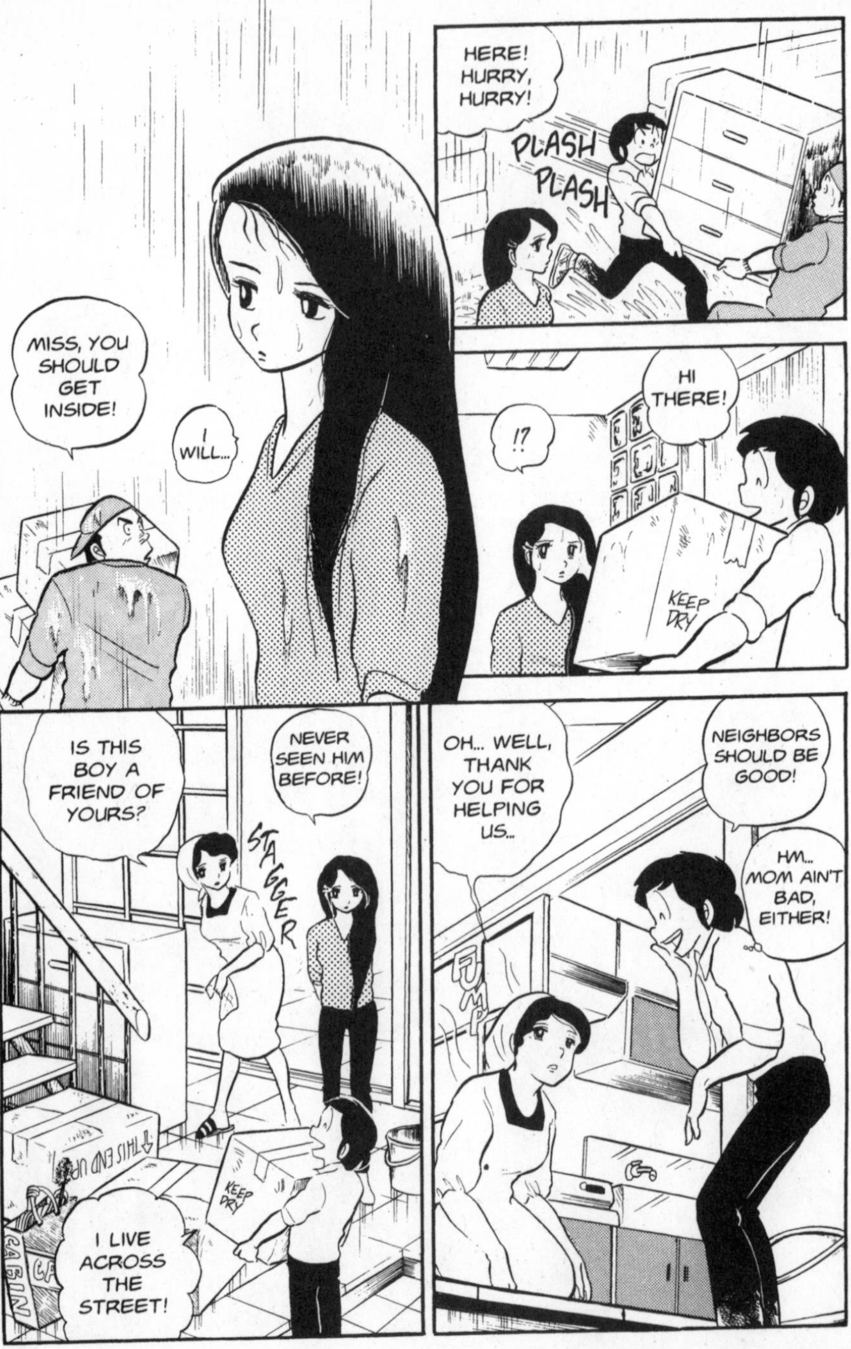
MISS, YOU SHOULD GET INSIDE!
I WILL...
HERE! HURRY, HURRY!
PLASH
PLASH
!?
HI THERE!
KEEP DRY
IS THIS BOY A FRIEND OF YOURS?
NEVER SEEN HIM BEFORE!
STAGGER
THIS END UP
KEEP DRY
I LIVE ACROSS THE STREET!
OH... WELL, THANK YOU FOR HELPING US...
NEIGHBORS SHOULD BE GOOD!
HM... MOM AIN'T BAD, EITHER!
FUMP

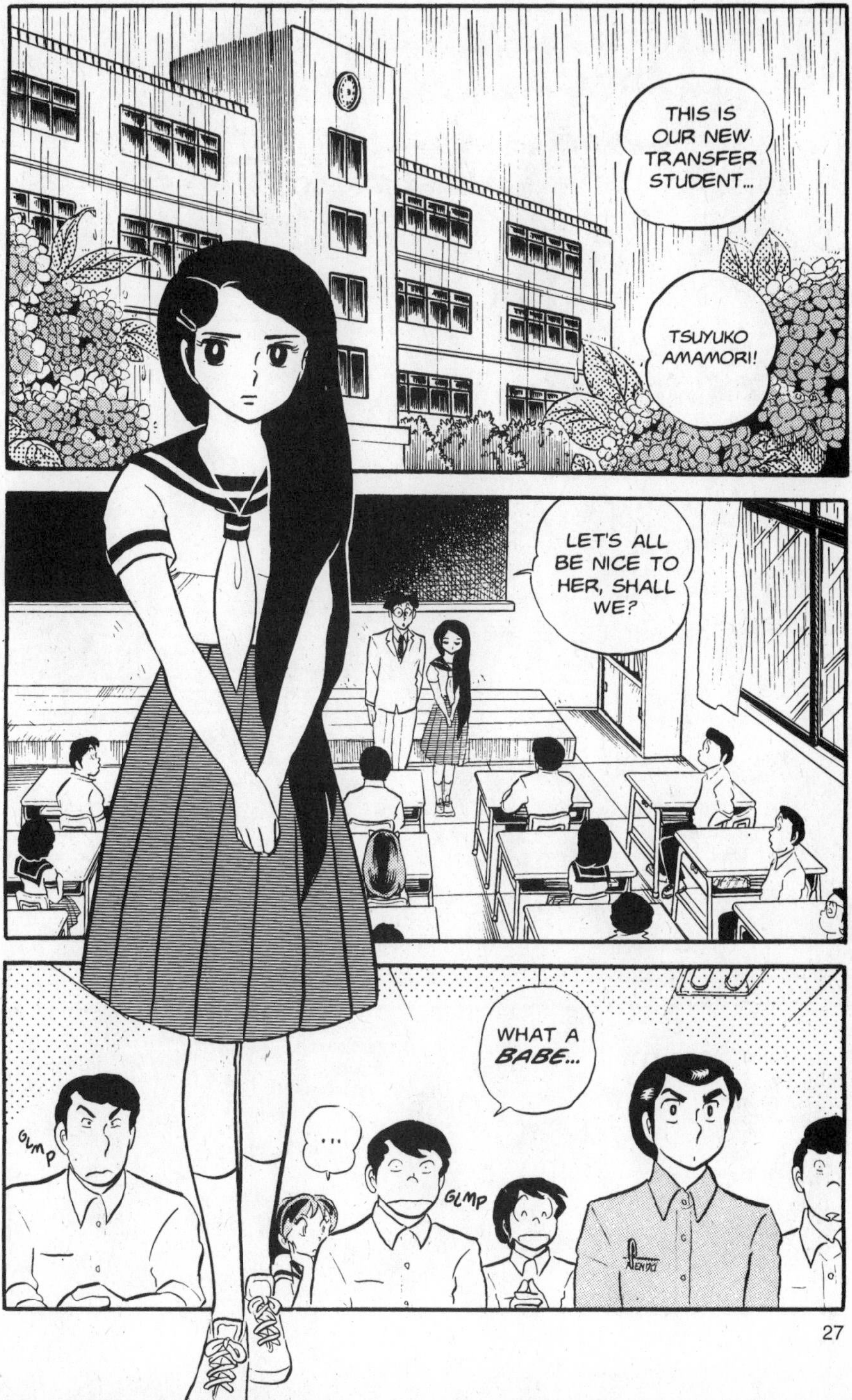
THIS IS OUR NEW TRANSFER STUDENT...
TSUYUKO AMAMORI!
LET'S ALL BE NICE TO HER, SHALL WE?
GLMP
...
GLMP
WHAT A *BABE*...

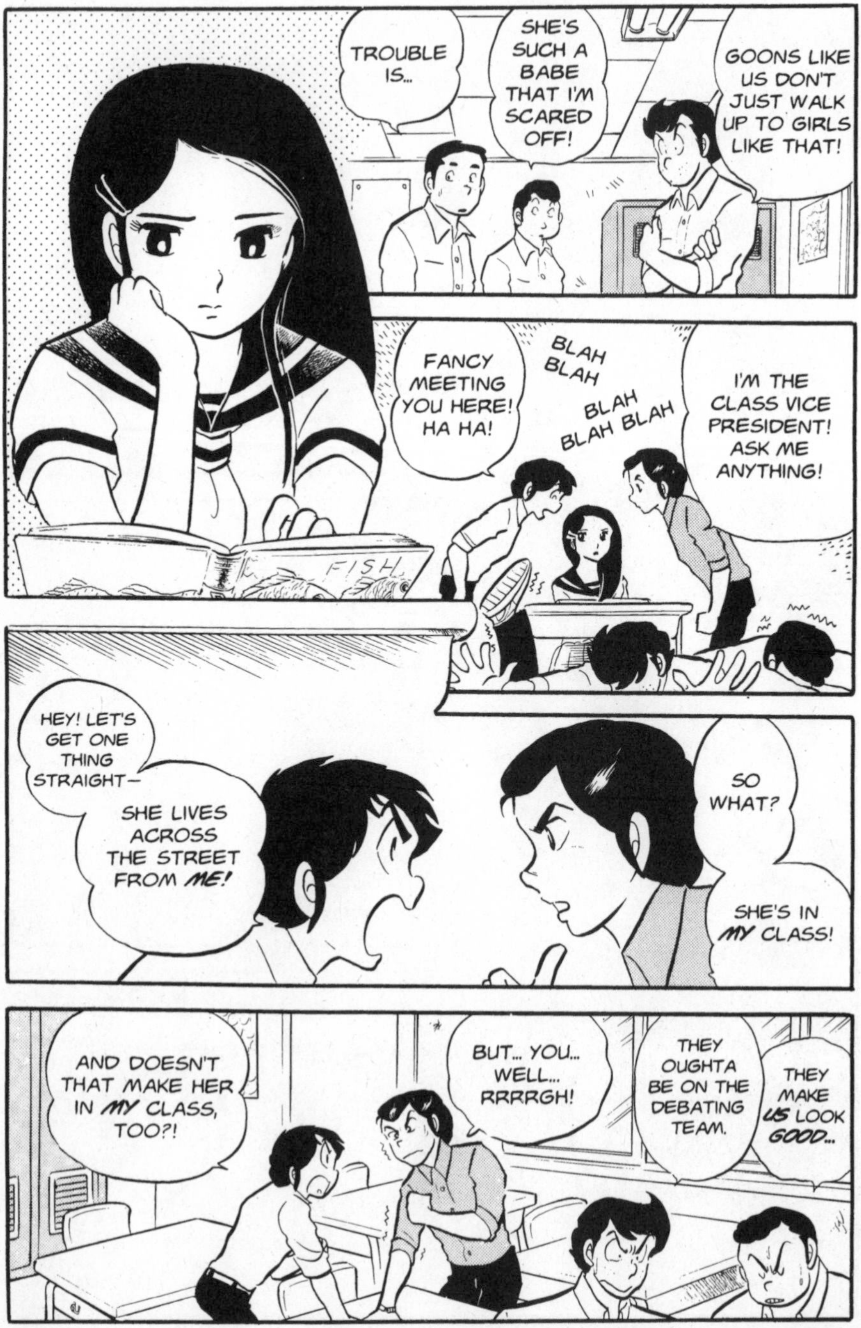
TROUBLE IS...
SHE'S SUCH A BABE THAT I'M SCARED OFF!
GOONS LIKE US DON'T JUST WALK UP TO GIRLS LIKE THAT!
FANCY MEETING YOU HERE! HA HA!
BLAH BLAH
BLAH BLAH BLAH
I'M THE CLASS VICE PRESIDENT! ASK ME ANYTHING!
FISH
HEY! LET'S GET ONE THING STRAIGHT—
SHE LIVES ACROSS THE STREET FROM ME!
SO WHAT?
SHE'S IN MY CLASS!
AND DOESN'T THAT MAKE HER IN MY CLASS, TOO?!
BUT... YOU... WELL... RRRRGH!
THEY OUGHTA BE ON THE DEBATING TEAM.
THEY MAKE US LOOK GOOD...

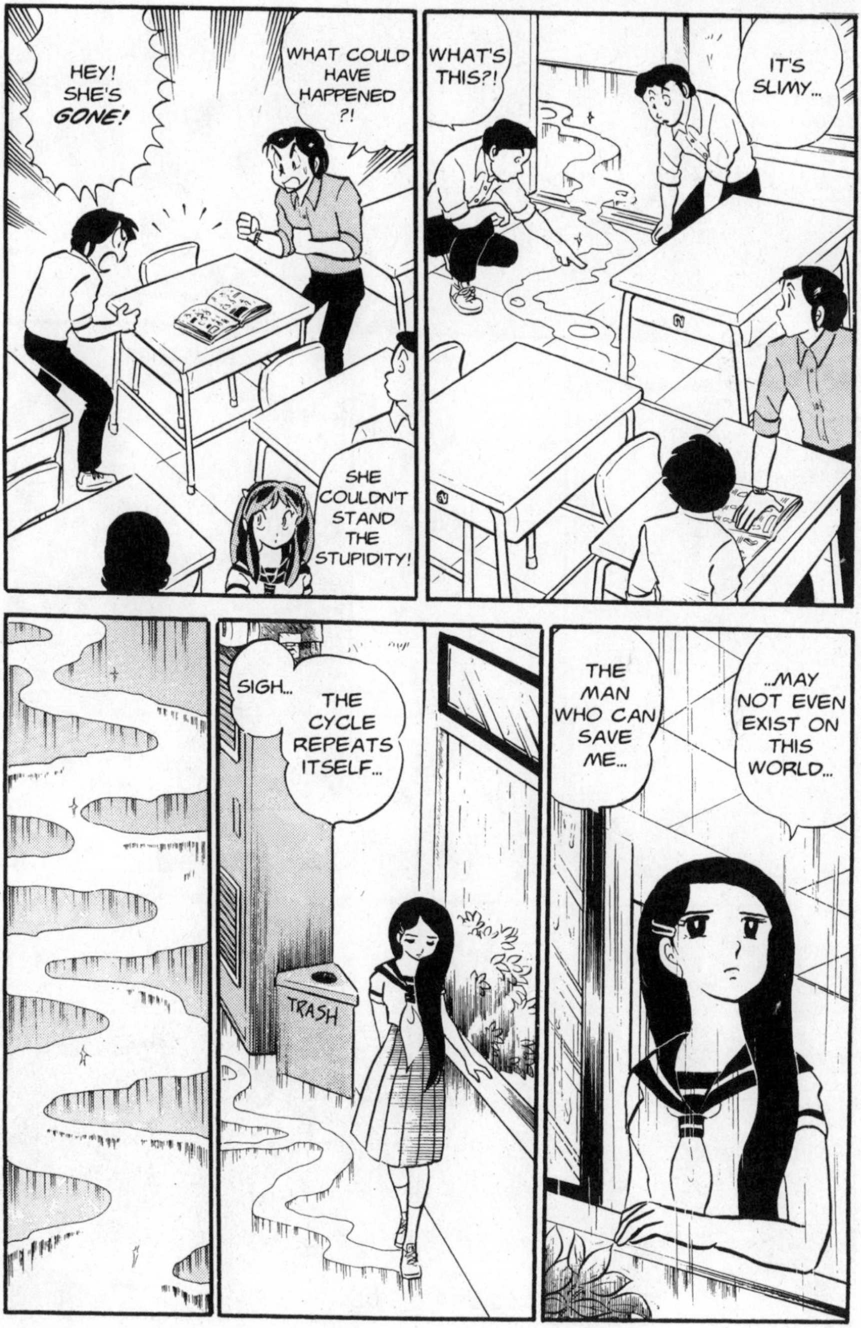
HEY! SHE'S GONE!
WHAT COULD HAVE HAPPENED ?!
SHE COULDN'T STAND THE STUPIDITY!
WHAT'S THIS?!
IT'S SLIMY...
SIGH...
THE CYCLE REPEATS ITSELF...
TRASH
THE MAN WHO CAN SAVE ME...
...MAY NOT EVEN EXIST ON THIS WORLD...

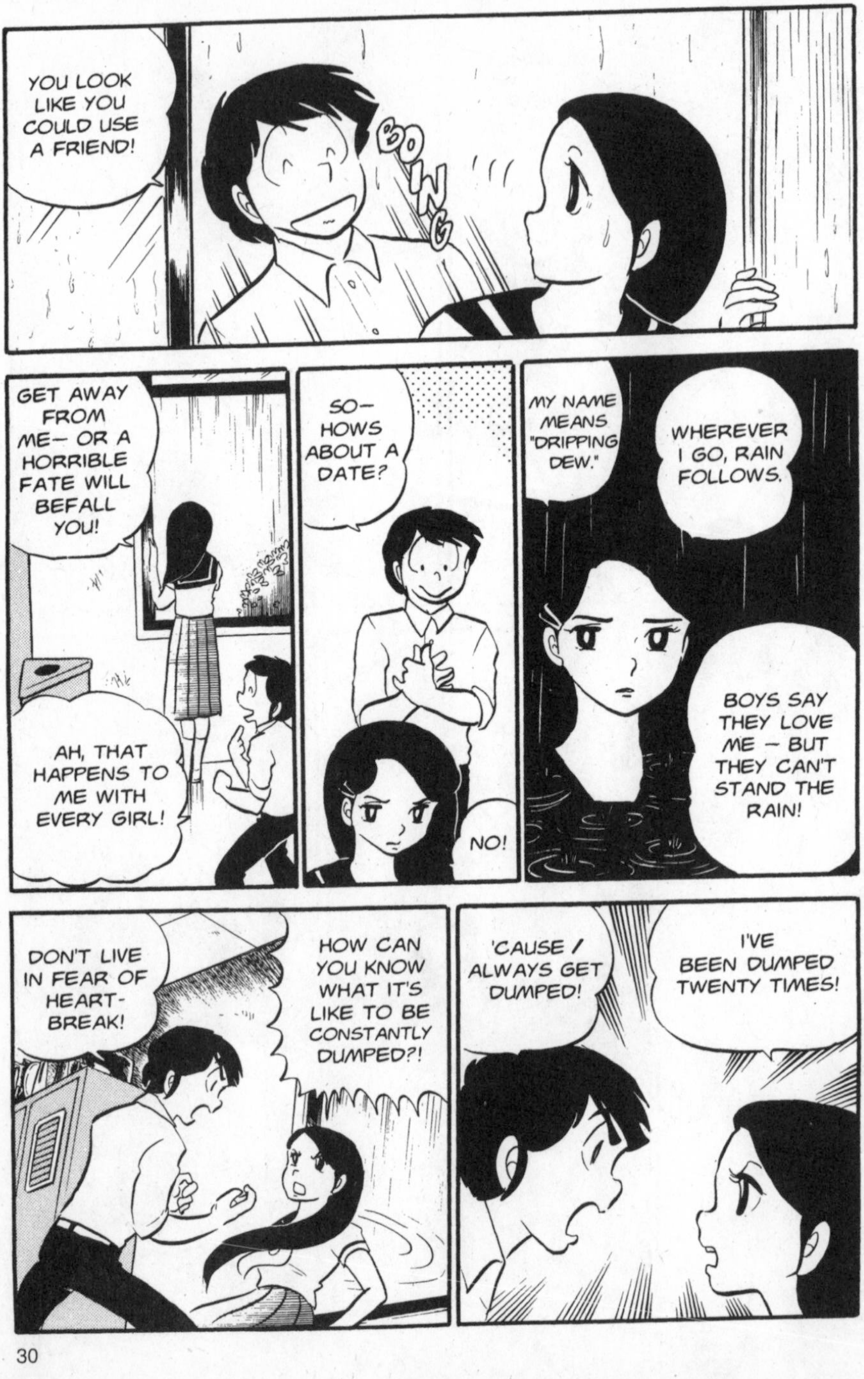
YOU LOOK LIKE YOU COULD USE A FRIEND!
BOING
GET AWAY FROM ME— OR A HORRIBLE FATE WILL BEFALL YOU!
AH, THAT HAPPENS TO ME WITH EVERY GIRL!
SO— HOWS ABOUT A DATE?
NO!
MY NAME MEANS "DRIPPING DEW."
WHEREVER I GO, RAIN FOLLOWS.
BOYS SAY THEY LOVE ME – BUT THEY CAN'T STAND THE RAIN!
DON'T LIVE IN FEAR OF HEART-BREAK!
HOW CAN YOU KNOW WHAT IT'S LIKE TO BE CONSTANTLY DUMPED?!
'CAUSE I ALWAYS GET DUMPED!
I'VE BEEN DUMPED TWENTY TIMES!

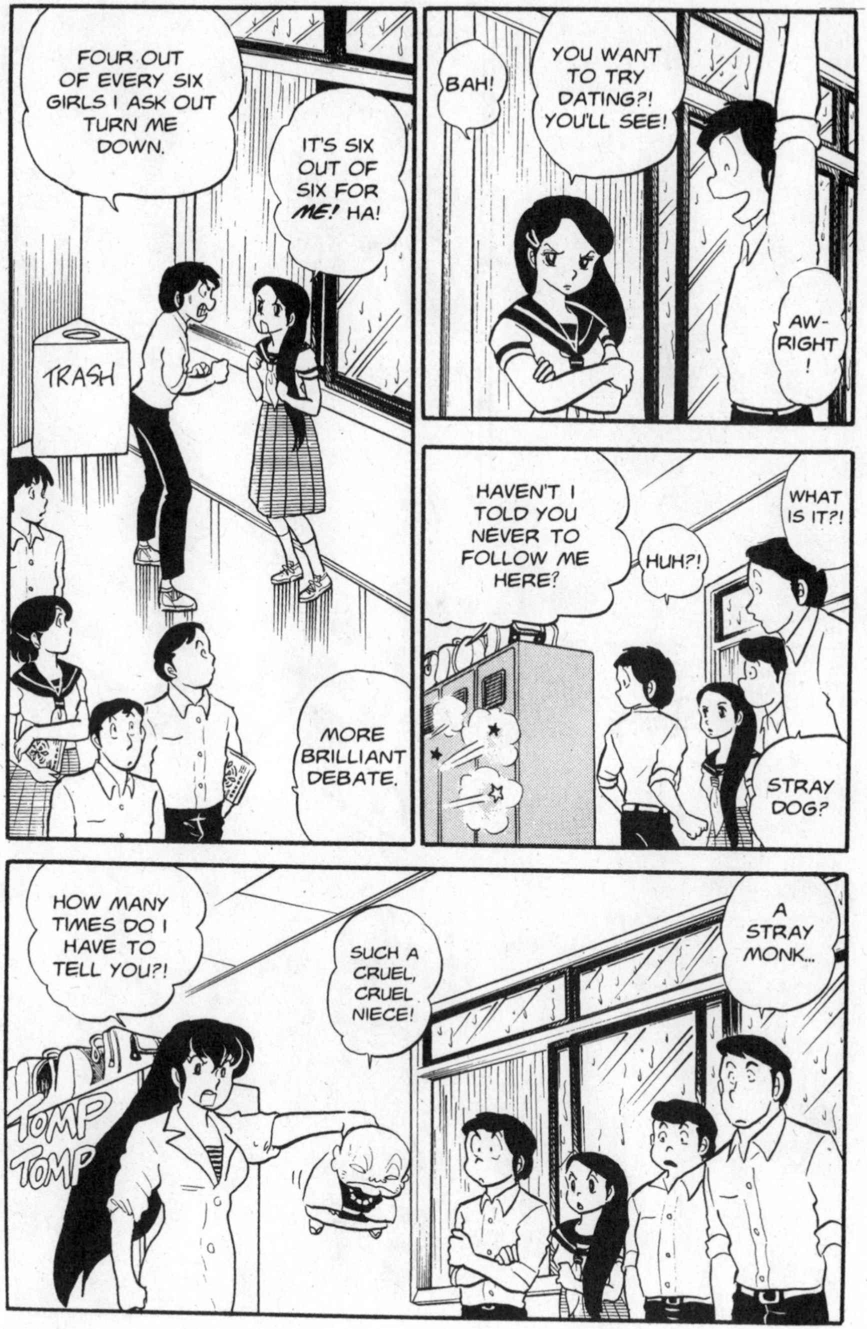
FOUR OUT OF EVERY SIX GIRLS I ASK OUT TURN ME DOWN.
IT'S SIX OUT OF SIX FOR ME! HA!
TRASH
MORE BRILLIANT DEBATE.
BAH!
YOU WANT TO TRY DATING?! YOU'LL SEE!
AW-RIGHT!
HAVEN'T I TOLD YOU NEVER TO FOLLOW ME HERE?
HUH?!
WHAT IS IT?!
STRAY DOG?
HOW MANY TIMES DO I HAVE TO TELL YOU?!
SUCH A CRUEL, CRUEL NIECE!
A STRAY MONK...
TOMP TOMP

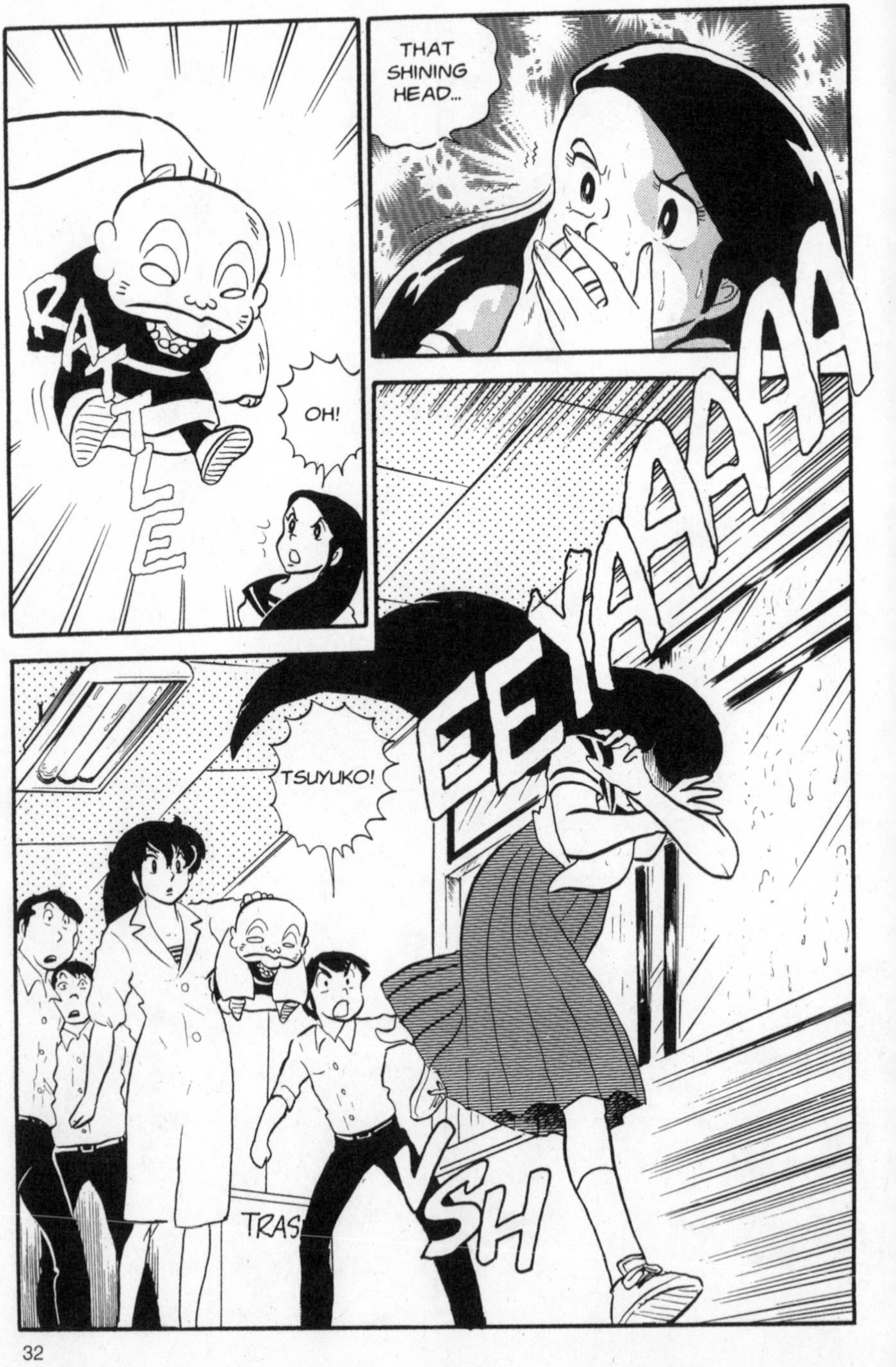
RATTLE
OH!
THAT SHINING HEAD...
EEYAAAAAA
TSUYUKO!
TRAS
VSH

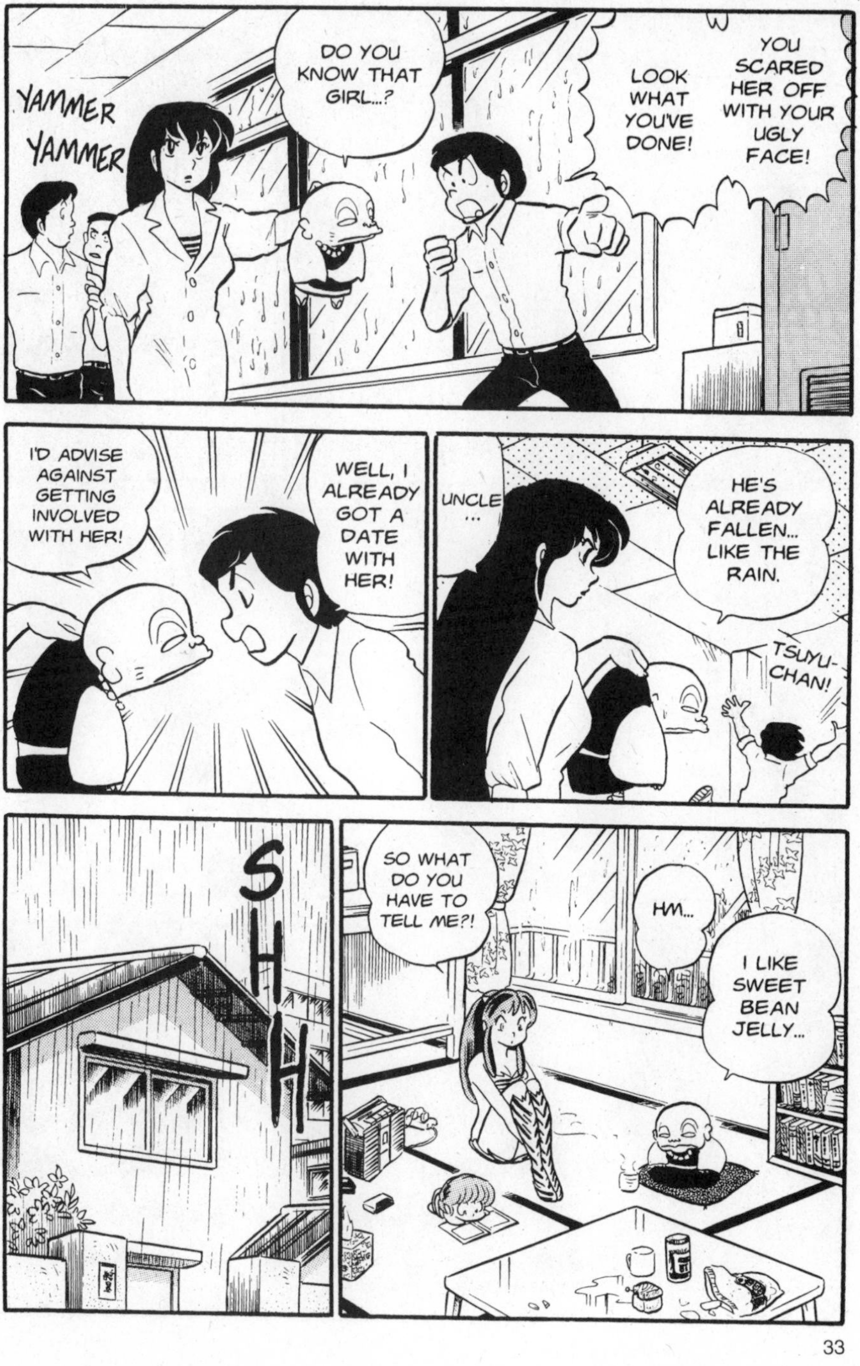
YAMMER YAMMER
DO YOU KNOW THAT GIRL...?
LOOK WHAT YOU'VE DONE!
YOU SCARED HER OFF WITH YOUR UGLY FACE!
I'D ADVISE AGAINST GETTING INVOLVED WITH HER!
WELL, I ALREADY GOT A DATE WITH HER!
UNCLE...
HE'S ALREADY FALLEN... LIKE THE RAIN.
TSUYU-CHAN!
SHH
SO WHAT DO YOU HAVE TO TELL ME?!
HM...
I LIKE SWEET BEAN JELLY...

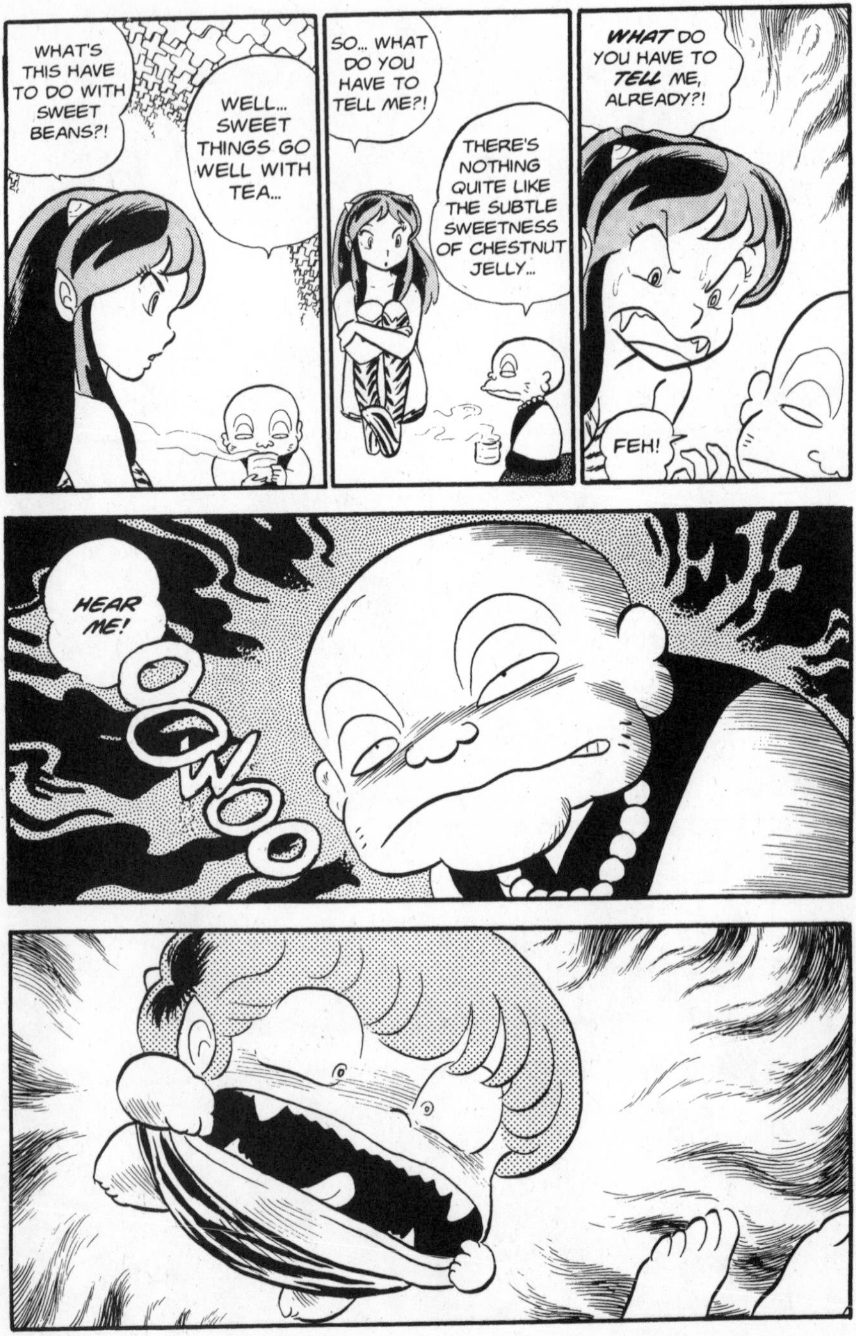
WHAT'S THIS HAVE TO DO WITH SWEET BEANS?!
WELL... SWEET THINGS GO WELL WITH TEA...
SO... WHAT DO YOU HAVE TO TELL ME?!
THERE'S NOTHING QUITE LIKE THE SUBTLE SWEETNESS OF CHESTNUT JELLY...
WHAT DO YOU HAVE TO ***TELL*** ME, ALREADY?!
FEH!
HEAR ME!
OOWOOO

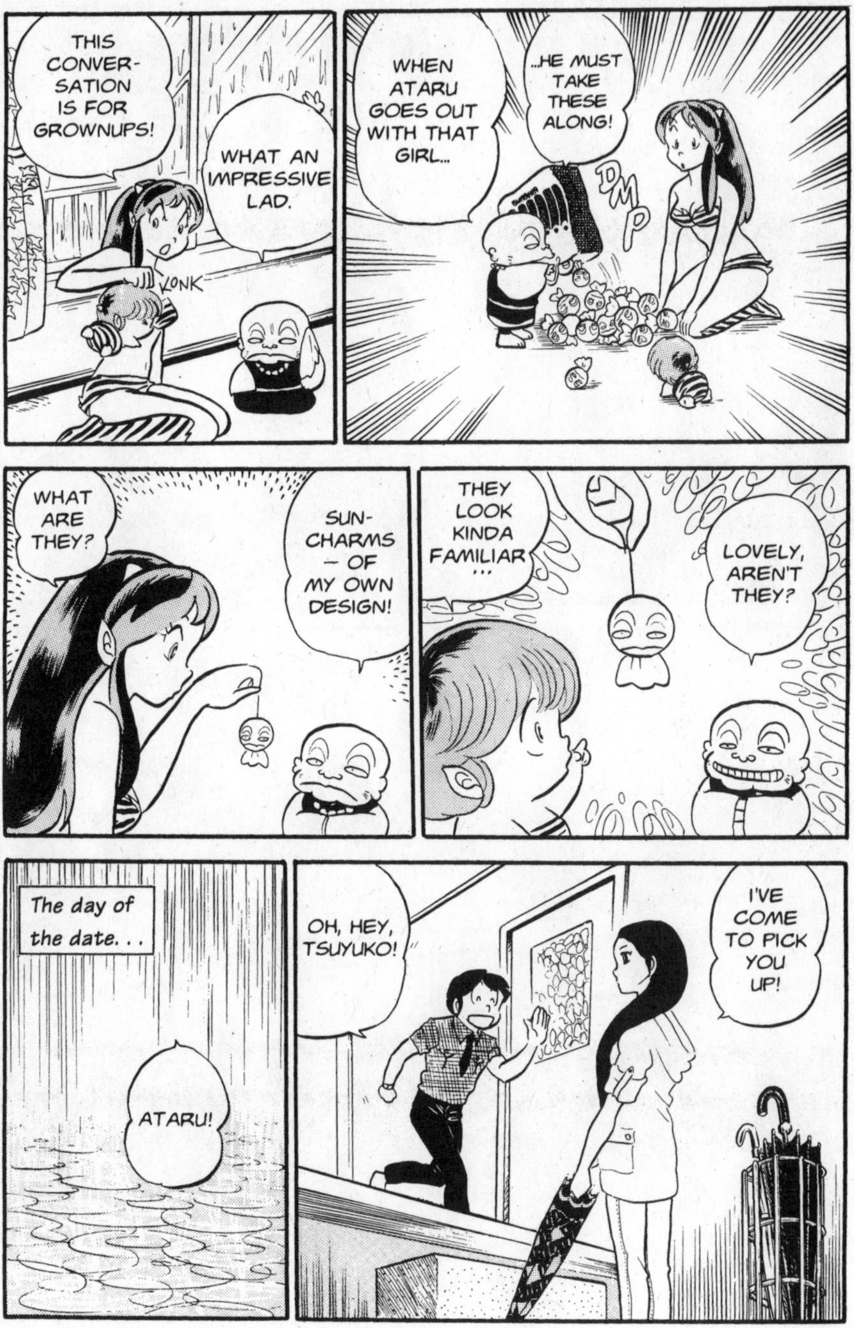
THIS CONVER-SATION IS FOR GROWNUPS!
WHAT AN IMPRESSIVE LAD.
KONK
WHEN ATARU GOES OUT WITH THAT GIRL...
...HE MUST TAKE THESE ALONG!
DMP
WHAT ARE THEY?
SUN-CHARMS — OF MY OWN DESIGN!
THEY LOOK KINDA FAMILIAR...
LOVELY, AREN'T THEY?
The day of the date. . .
ATARU!
OH, HEY, TSUYUKO!
I'VE COME TO PICK YOU UP!

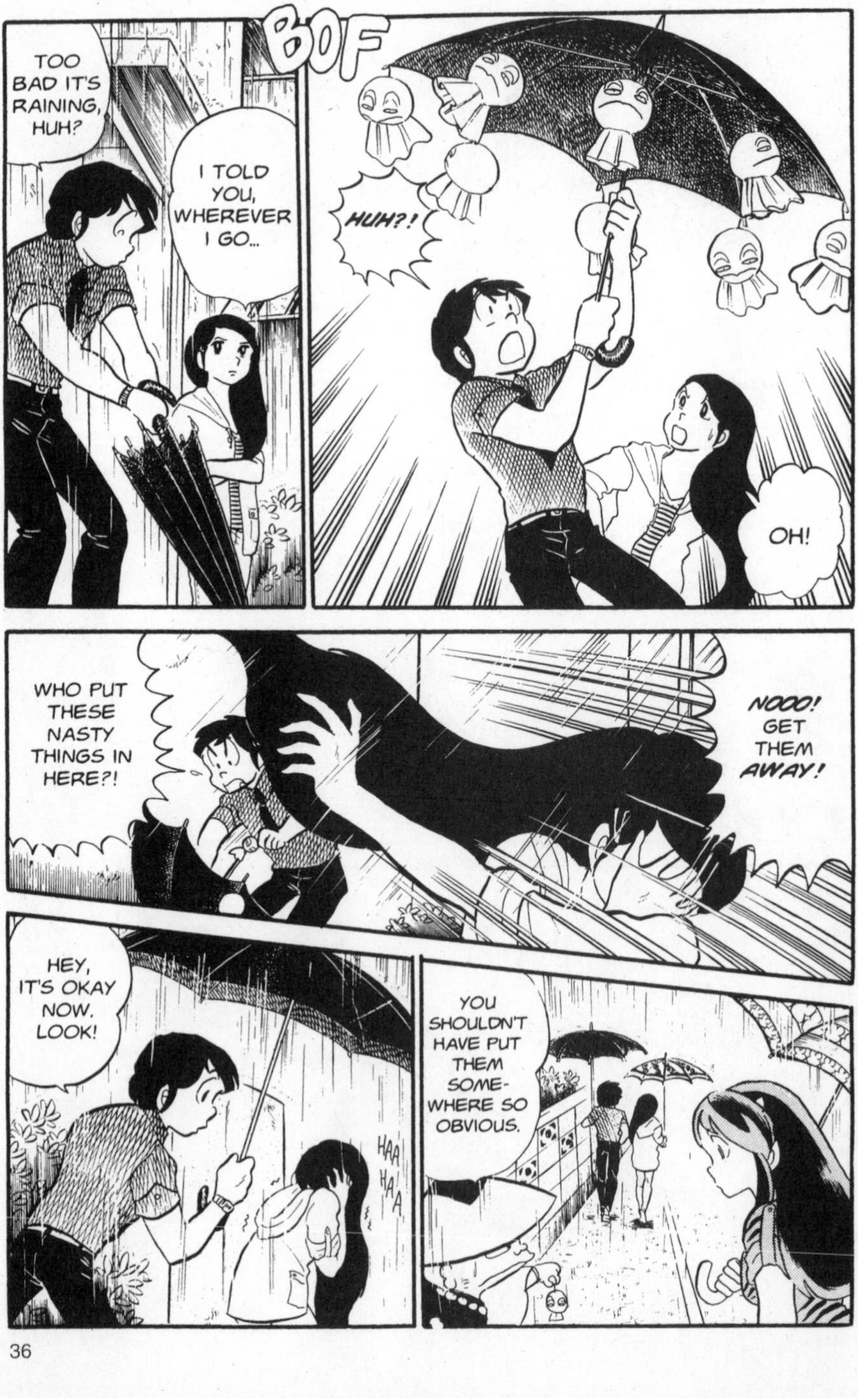
TOO BAD IT'S RAINING, HUH?
I TOLD YOU, WHEREVER I GO...
BOF
HUH?!
OH!
WHO PUT THESE NASTY THINGS IN HERE?!
NOOO! GET THEM AWAY!
HEY, IT'S OKAY NOW. LOOK!
HAA HAA
YOU SHOULDN'T HAVE PUT THEM SOME-WHERE SO OBVIOUS.

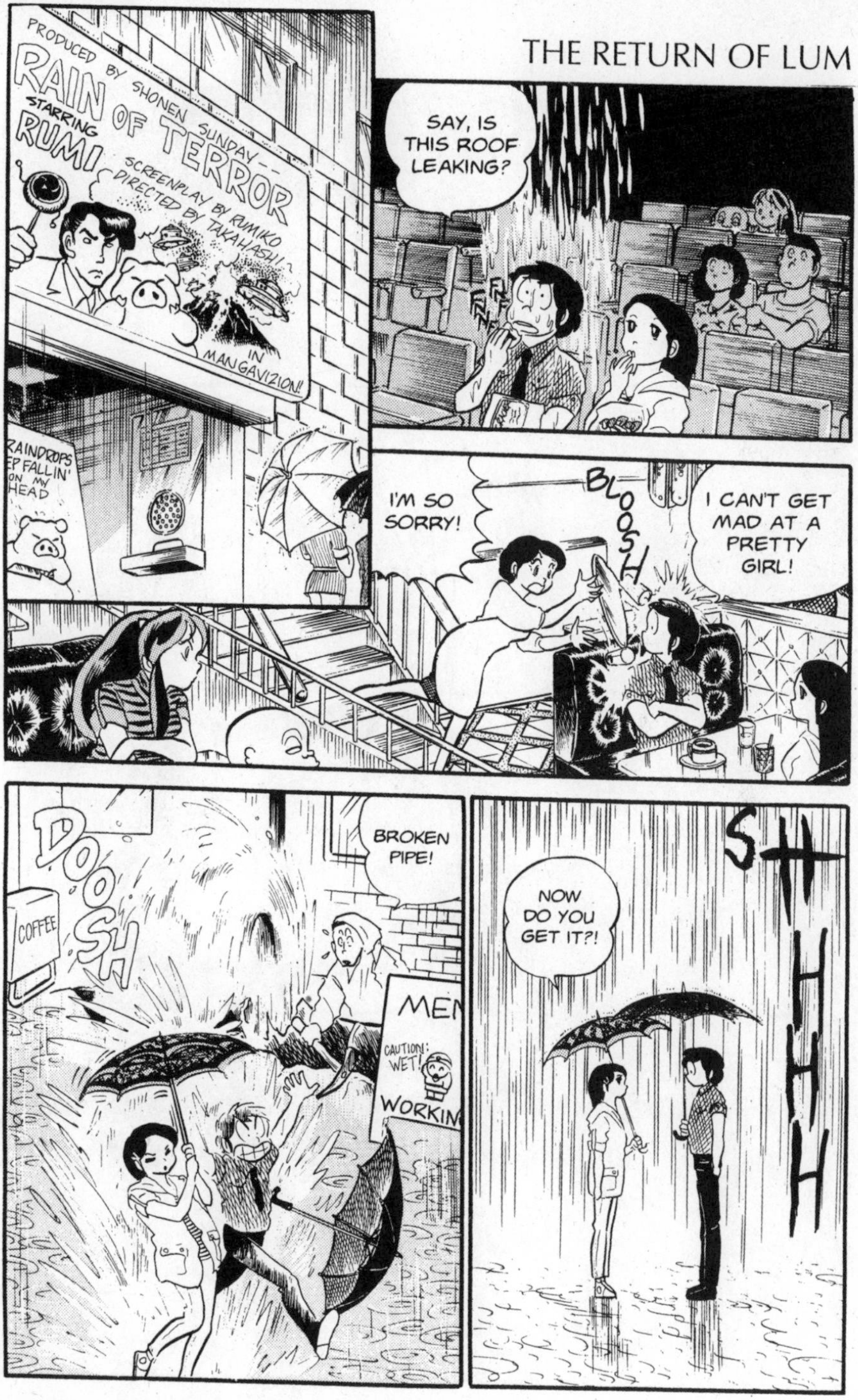
PRODUCED BY SHONEN SUNDAY---
RAIN OF TERROR
STARRING RUMI
SCREENPLAY BY RUMIKO
DIRECTED BY TAKAHASHI!
IN MANGAVIZION!
RAINDROPS EP FALLIN' ON MY HEAD
SAY, IS THIS ROOF LEAKING?
I'M SO SORRY!
BLOOSH
I CAN'T GET MAD AT A PRETTY GIRL!
DOOOSH
BROKEN PIPE!
COFFEE
MEN
CAUTION! WET!
WORKIN
NOW DO YOU GET IT?!
SHHHH

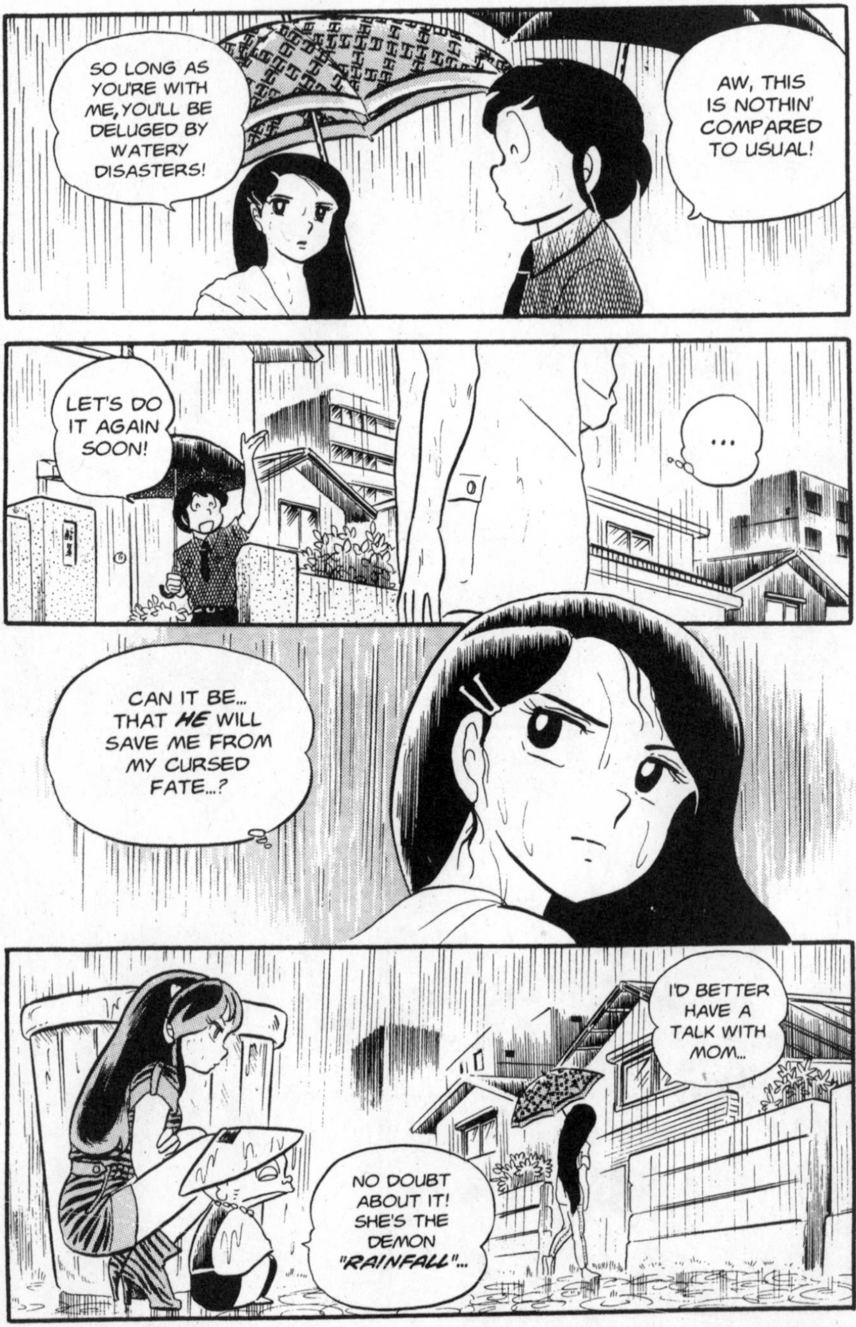
SO LONG AS YOU'RE WITH ME, YOU'LL BE DELUGED BY WATERY DISASTERS!
AW, THIS IS NOTHIN' COMPARED TO USUAL!
LET'S DO IT AGAIN SOON!
...
CAN IT BE... THAT *HE* WILL SAVE ME FROM MY CURSED FATE...?
I'D BETTER HAVE A TALK WITH MOM...
NO DOUBT ABOUT IT! SHE'S THE DEMON "*RAINFALL*"...

PART THREE
COME AGAIN SOME OTHER DAY

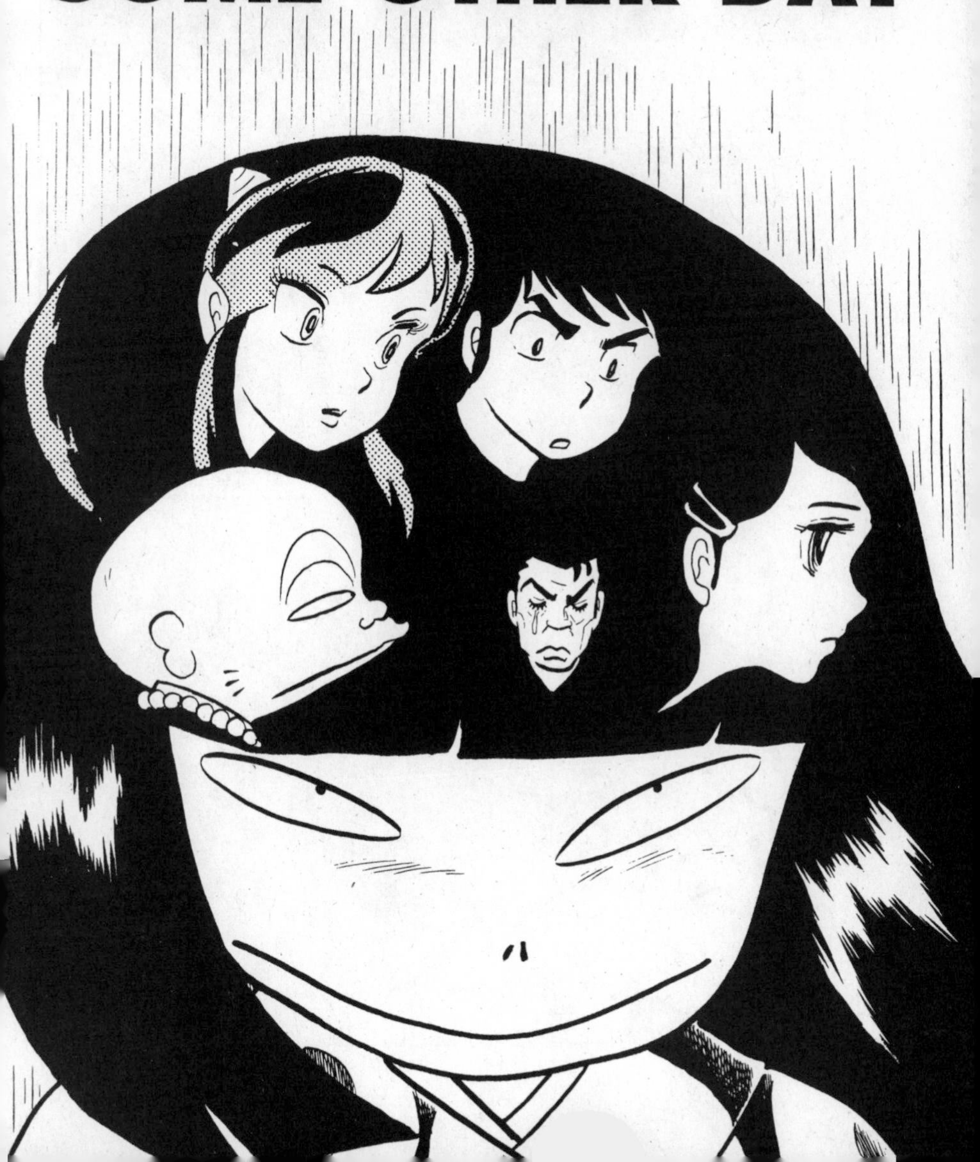

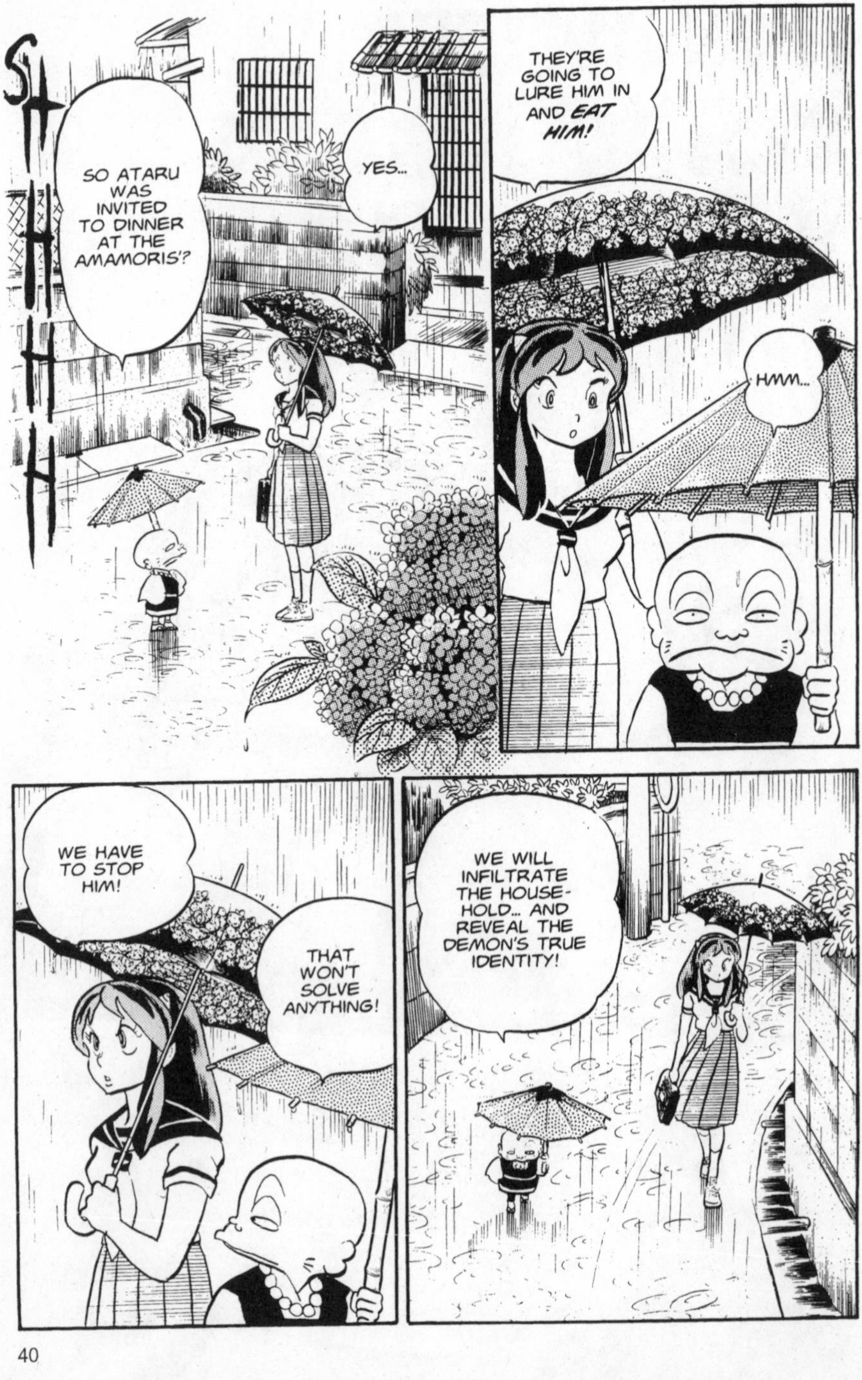
SHHHH
SO ATARU WAS INVITED TO DINNER AT THE AMAMORIS'?
YES...
THEY'RE GOING TO LURE HIM IN AND *EAT HIM!*
HMM...
WE HAVE TO STOP HIM!
THAT WON'T SOLVE ANYTHING!
WE WILL INFILTRATE THE HOUSE-HOLD... AND REVEAL THE DEMON'S TRUE IDENTITY!

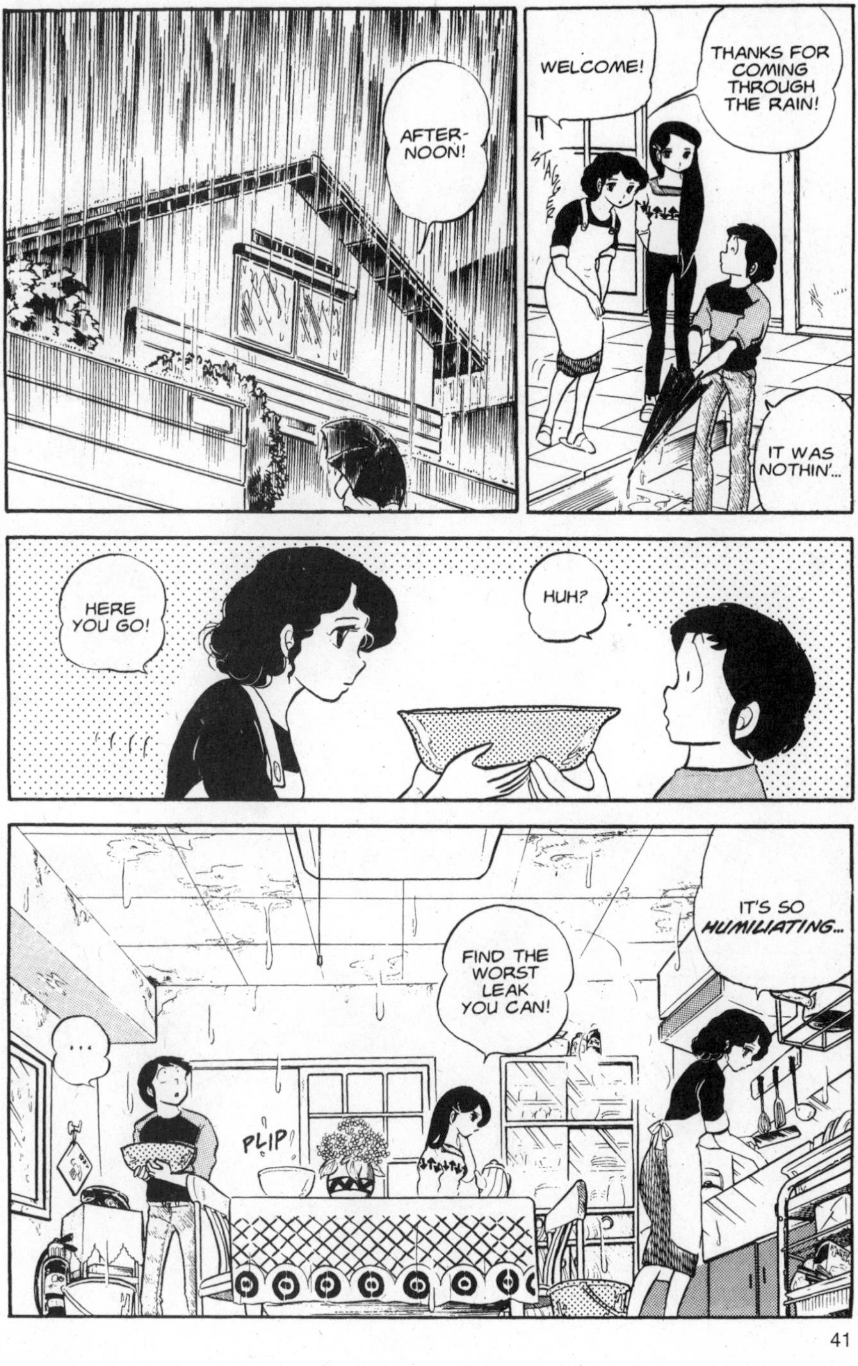
AFTER-NOON!
WELCOME!
THANKS FOR COMING THROUGH THE RAIN!
STAGGER
IT WAS NOTHIN'...
HERE YOU GO!
HUH?
...
IT'S SO *HUMILIATING*...
FIND THE WORST LEAK YOU CAN!
PLIP

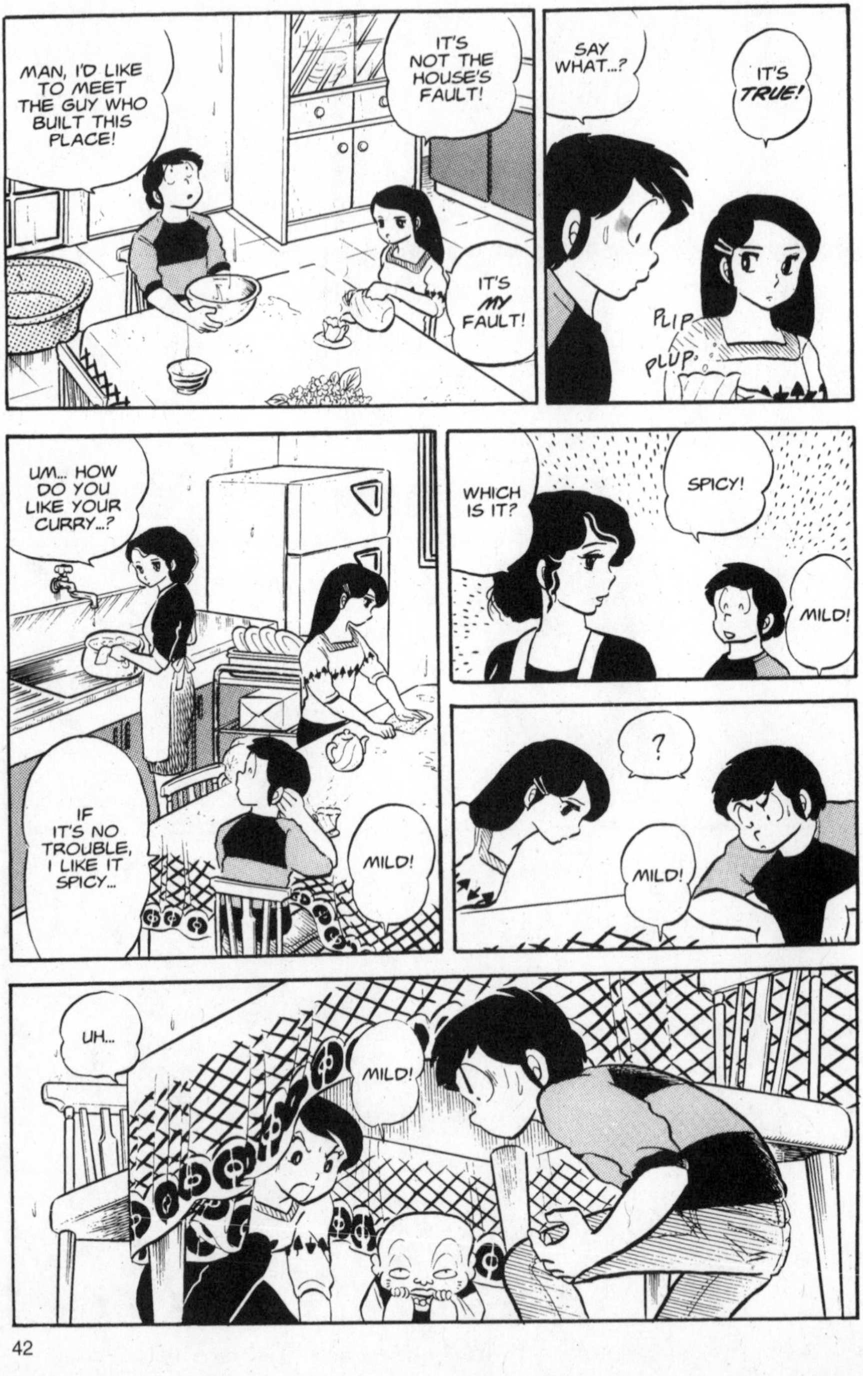
MAN, I'D LIKE TO MEET THE GUY WHO BUILT THIS PLACE!
IT'S NOT THE HOUSE'S FAULT!
IT'S MY FAULT!
SAY WHAT...?
IT'S TRUE!
PLIP
PLUP
UM... HOW DO YOU LIKE YOUR CURRY...?
IF IT'S NO TROUBLE, I LIKE IT SPICY...
MILD!
WHICH IS IT?
SPICY!
MILD!
?
MILD!
UH...
MILD!

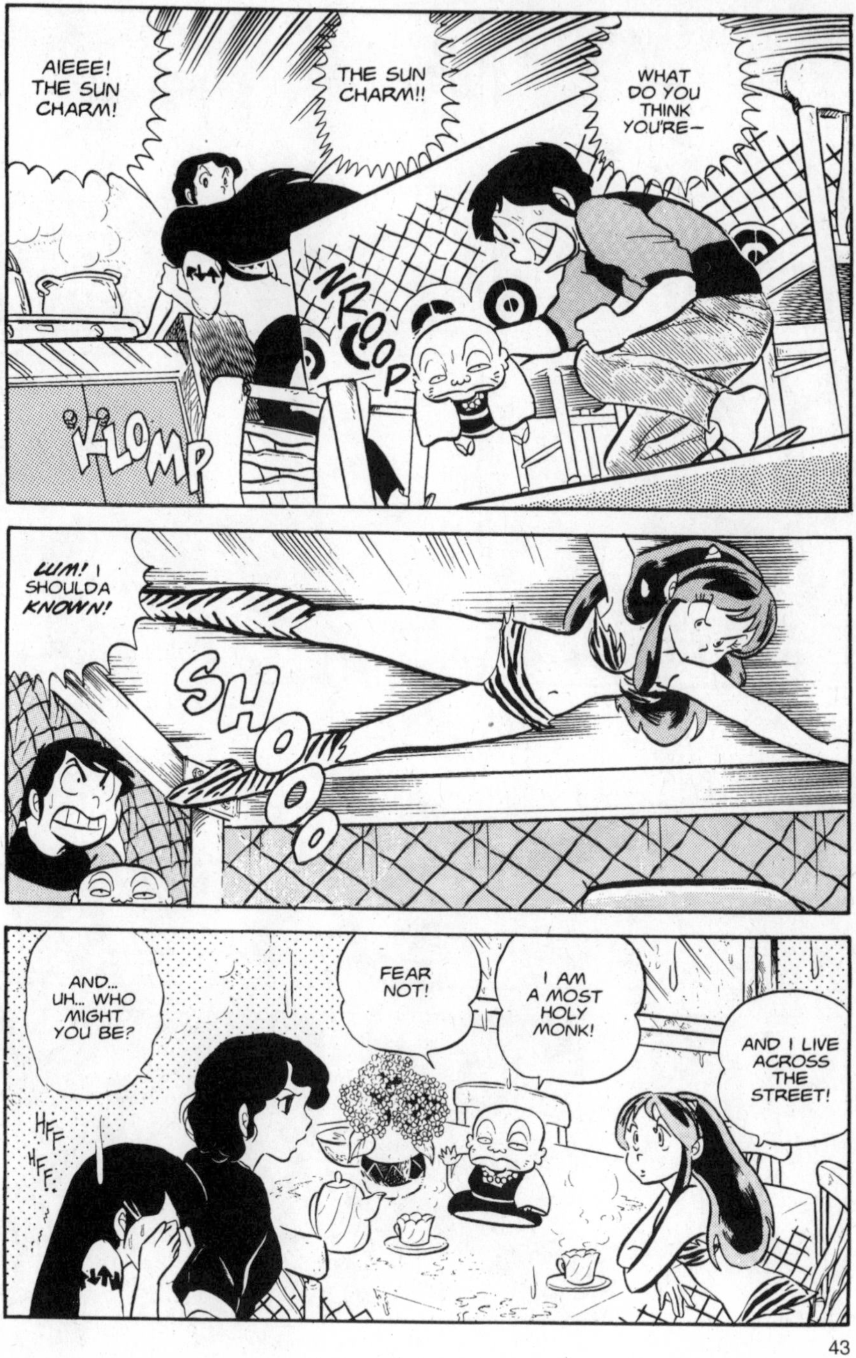
AIEEE! THE SUN CHARM!
THE SUN CHARM!!
WHAT DO YOU THINK YOU'RE—
NROOOOP
KLOMP
LUM! I SHOULDA KNOWN!
SHOOOO
AND... UH... WHO MIGHT YOU BE?
HFF HFF
FEAR NOT!
I AM A MOST HOLY MONK!
AND I LIVE ACROSS THE STREET!

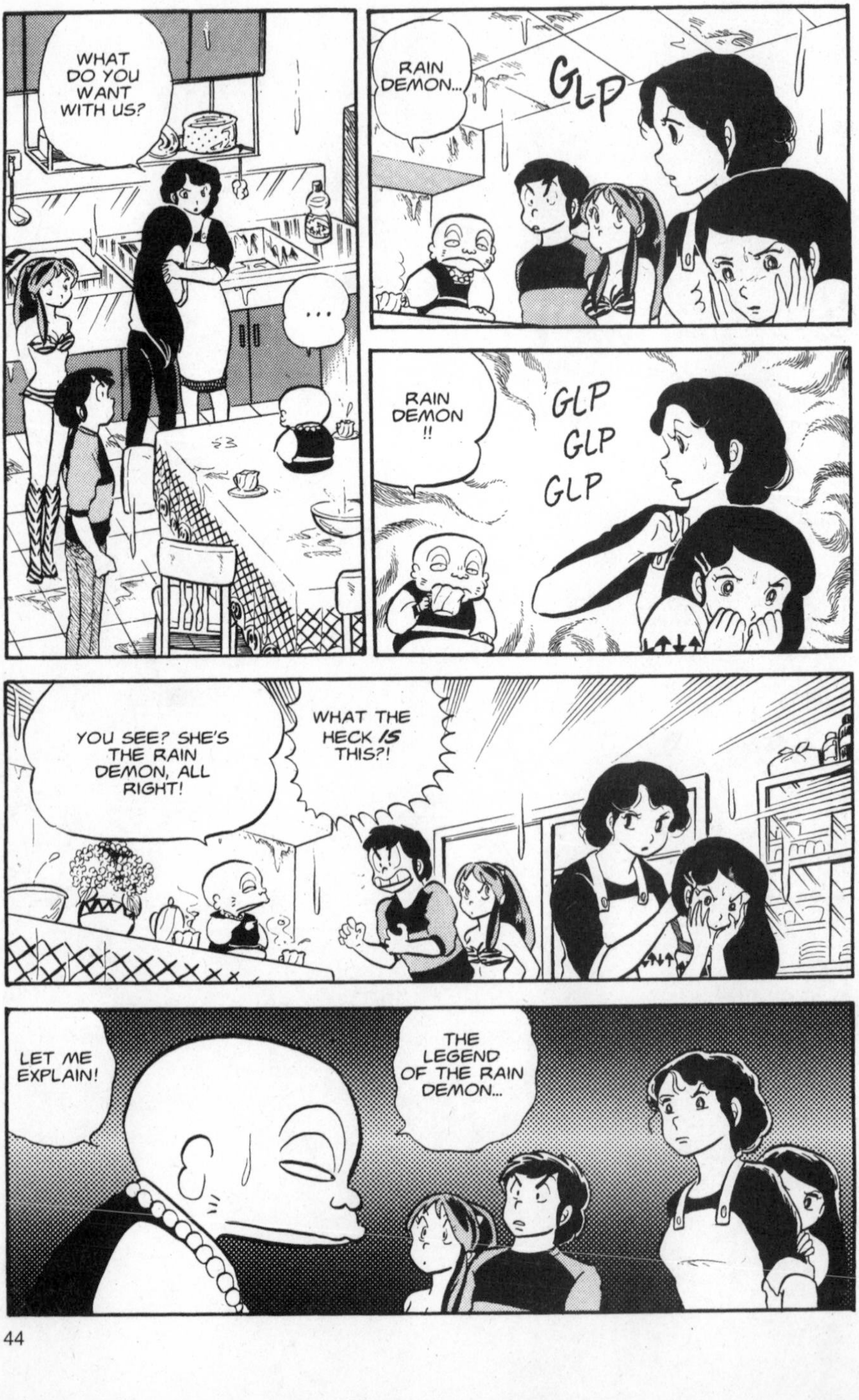
WHAT DO YOU WANT WITH US?
...
RAIN DEMON...
GLP
RAIN DEMON !!
GLP GLP GLP
YOU SEE? SHE'S THE RAIN DEMON, ALL RIGHT!
WHAT THE HECK *IS* THIS?!
LET ME EXPLAIN!
THE LEGEND OF THE RAIN DEMON...

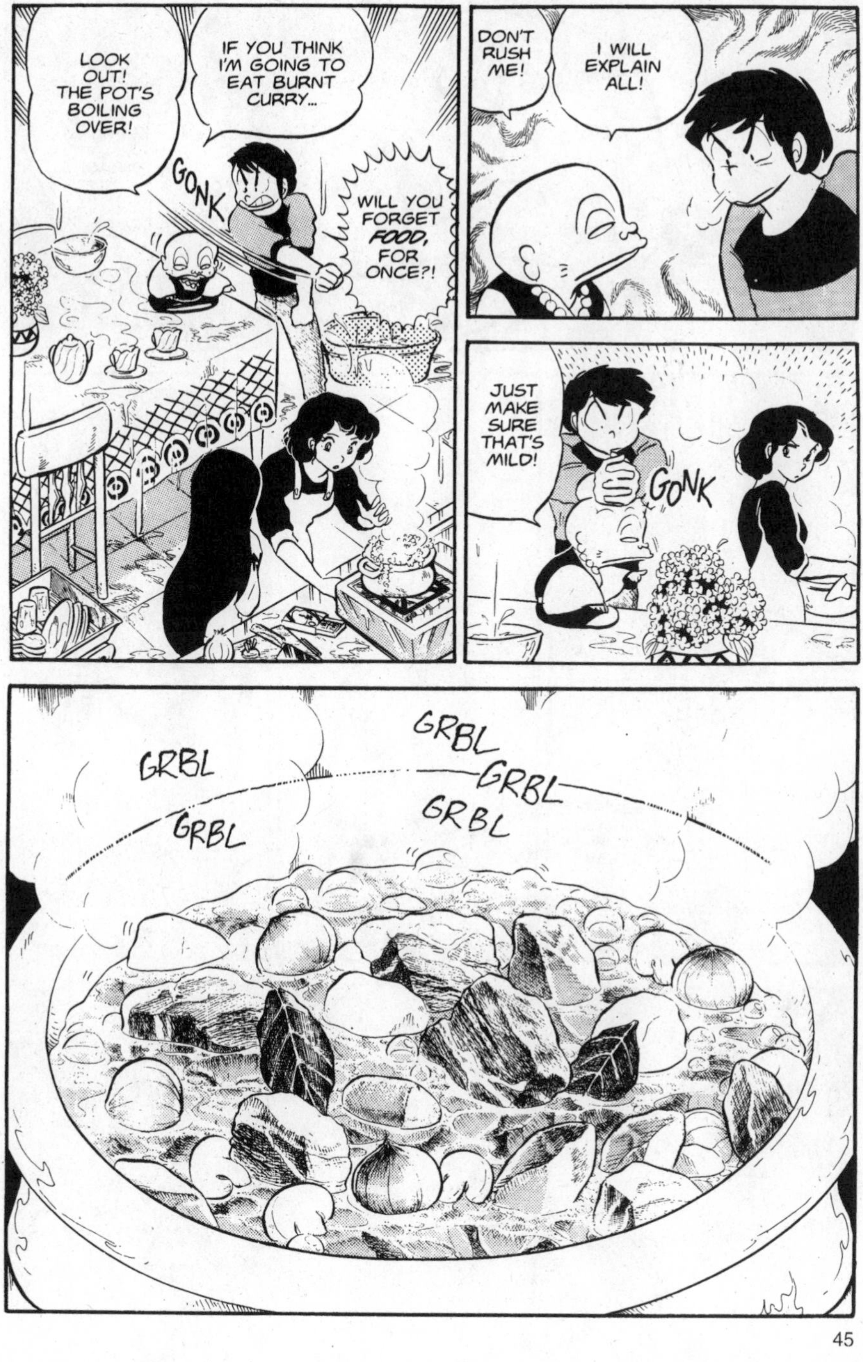
LOOK OUT! THE POT'S BOILING OVER!
IF YOU THINK I'M GOING TO EAT BURNT CURRY...
GONK
WILL YOU FORGET FOOD, FOR ONCE?!
DON'T RUSH ME!
I WILL EXPLAIN ALL!
JUST MAKE SURE THAT'S MILD!
GONK
GRBL
GRBL
GRBL
GRBL
GRBL

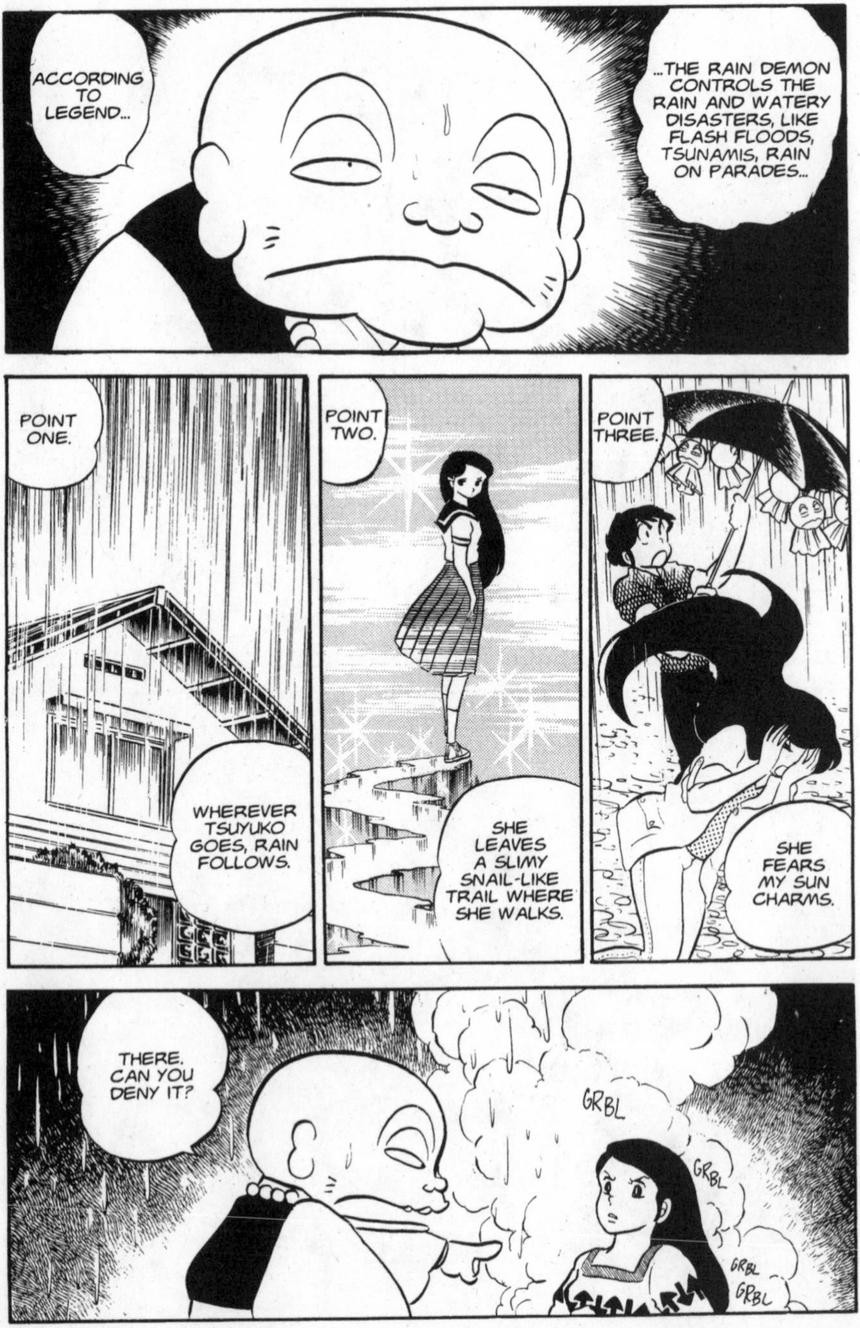
ACCORDING TO LEGEND...
...THE RAIN DEMON CONTROLS THE RAIN AND WATERY DISASTERS, LIKE FLASH FLOODS, TSUNAMIS, RAIN ON PARADES...
POINT ONE.
WHEREVER TSUYUKO GOES, RAIN FOLLOWS.
POINT TWO.
SHE LEAVES A SLIMY SNAIL-LIKE TRAIL WHERE SHE WALKS.
POINT THREE.
SHE FEARS MY SUN CHARMS.
THERE. CAN YOU DENY IT?
GRBL
GRBL
GRBL
GRBL

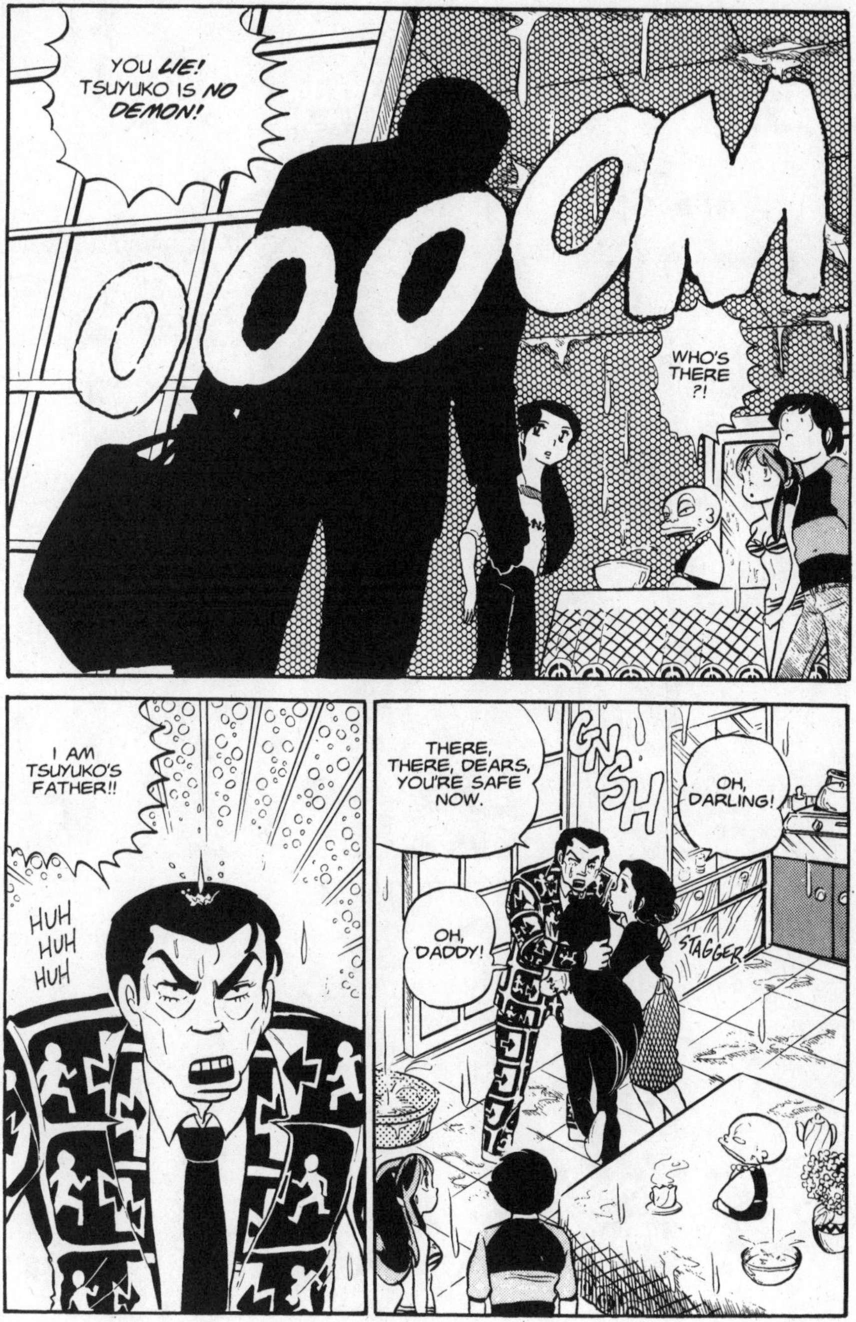
YOU LIE! TSUYUKO IS NO DEMON!
OOOOOM
WHO'S THERE ?!
I AM TSUYUKO'S FATHER!!
HUH HUH HUH
THERE, THERE, DEARS, YOU'RE SAFE NOW.
GNSH
OH, DARLING!
OH, DADDY!
STAGGER

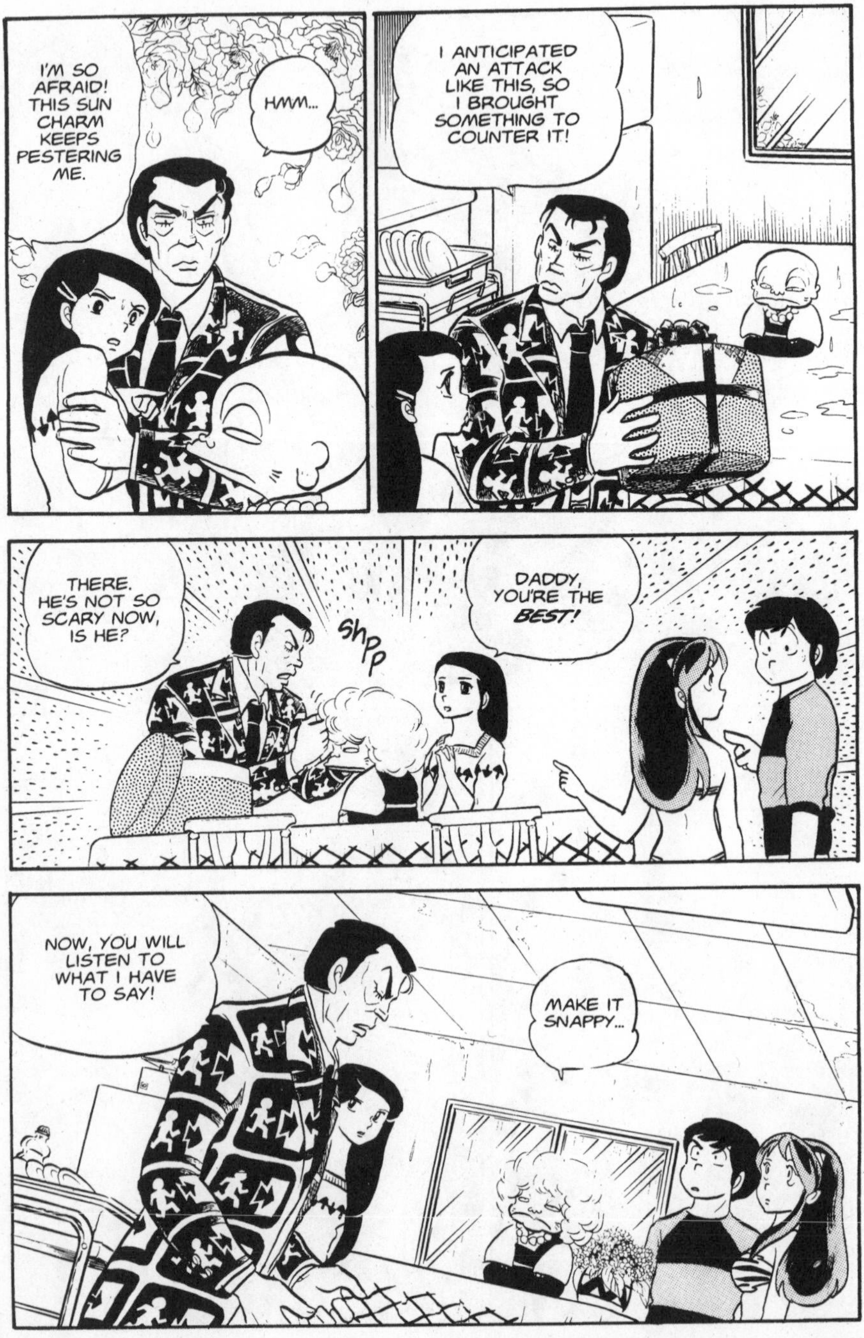
I'M SO AFRAID! THIS SUN CHARM KEEPS PESTERING ME.
HMM...
I ANTICIPATED AN ATTACK LIKE THIS, SO I BROUGHT SOMETHING TO COUNTER IT!
THERE. HE'S NOT SO SCARY NOW, IS HE?
SHPP
DADDY, YOU'RE THE *BEST!*
NOW, YOU WILL LISTEN TO WHAT I HAVE TO SAY!
MAKE IT SNAPPY...

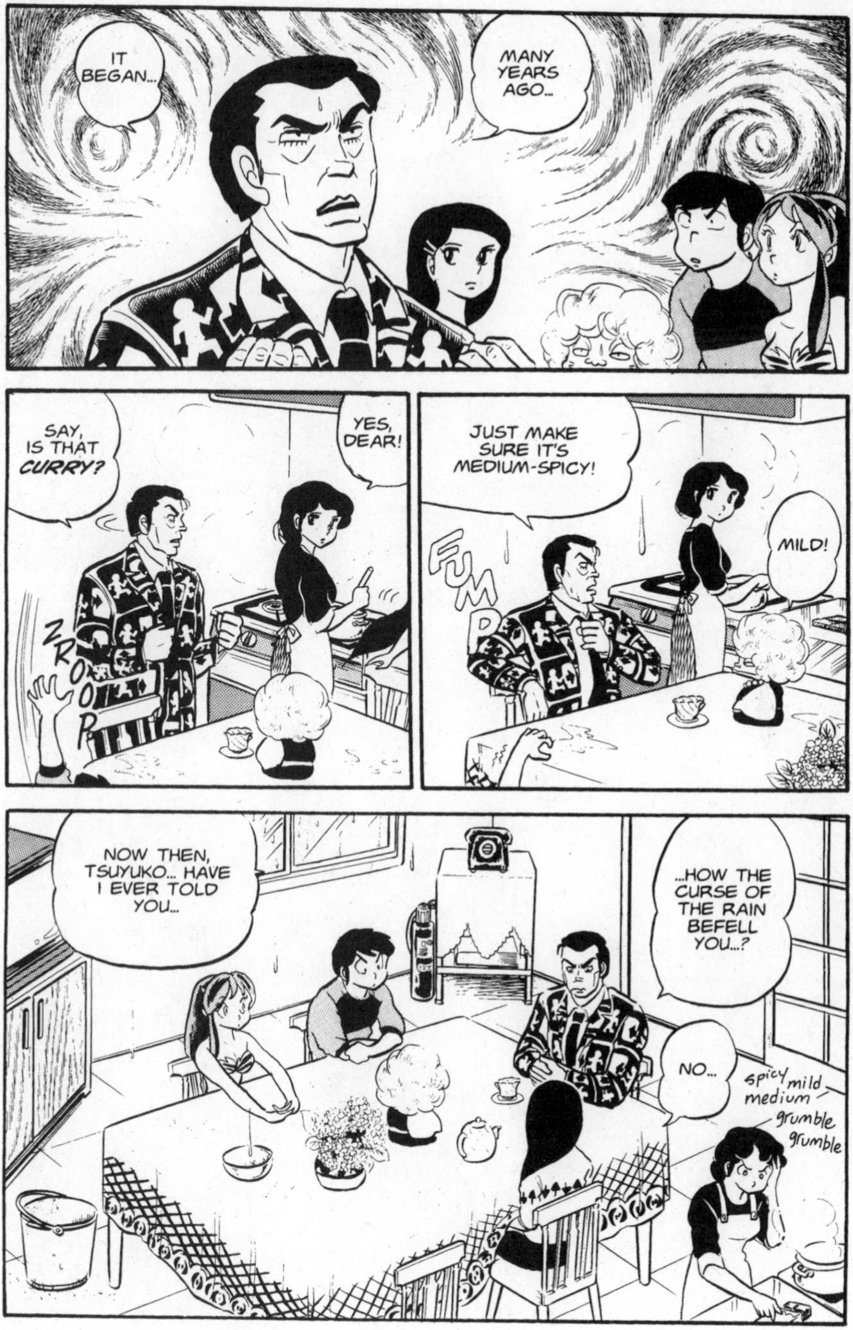
IT BEGAN...
MANY YEARS AGO...
SAY, IS THAT CURRY?
YES, DEAR!
ZROOOP
JUST MAKE SURE IT'S MEDIUM-SPICY!
FUMP
MILD!
NOW THEN, TSUYUKO... HAVE I EVER TOLD YOU...
...HOW THE CURSE OF THE RAIN BEFELL YOU...?
NO...
spicy mild medium
grumble grumble

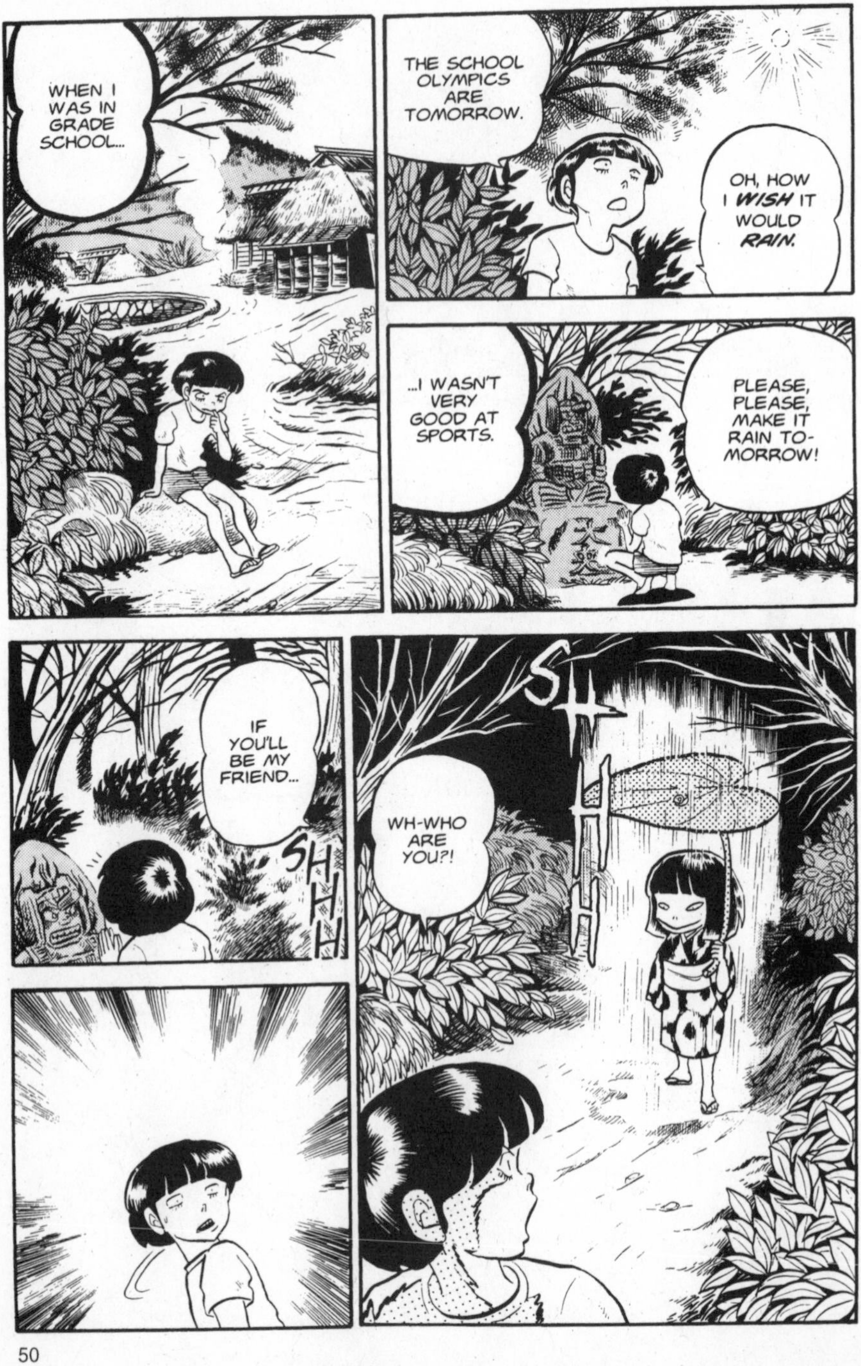
WHEN I WAS IN GRADE SCHOOL...
THE SCHOOL OLYMPICS ARE TOMORROW.
OH, HOW I WISH IT WOULD RAIN.
...I WASN'T VERY GOOD AT SPORTS.
PLEASE, PLEASE, MAKE IT RAIN TOMORROW!
IF YOU'LL BE MY FRIEND...
SHHH
SHHH
WH-WHO ARE YOU?!

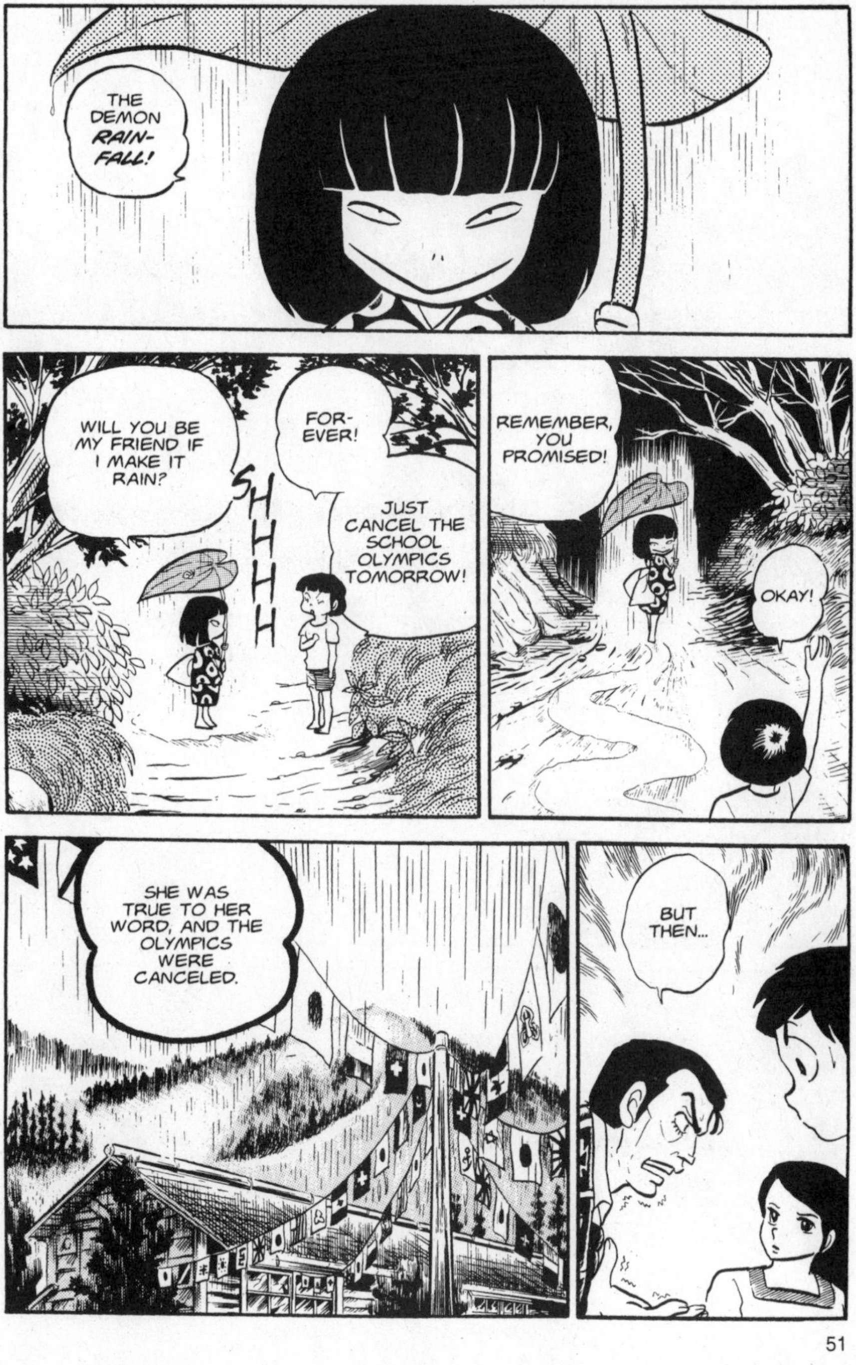
THE DEMON *RAIN-FALL!*
WILL YOU BE MY FRIEND IF I MAKE IT RAIN?
SHHHH
FOR-EVER!
JUST CANCEL THE SCHOOL OLYMPICS TOMORROW!
REMEMBER, YOU PROMISED!
OKAY!
SHE WAS TRUE TO HER WORD, AND THE OLYMPICS WERE CANCELED.
BUT THEN...

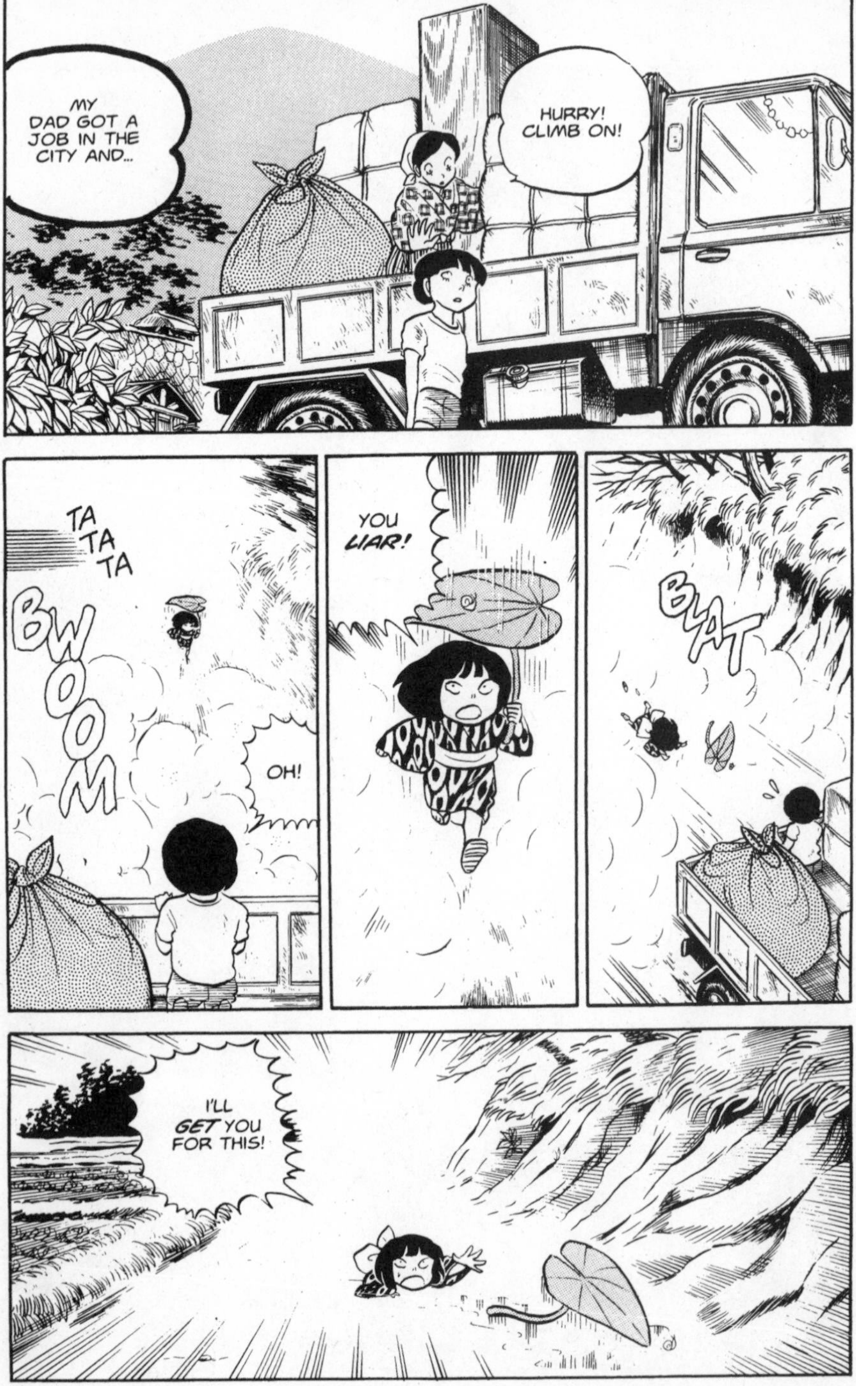
MY DAD GOT A JOB IN THE CITY AND...
HURRY! CLIMB ON!
TA TA TA
BWOOM
OH!
YOU LIAR!
BLAT
I'LL GET YOU FOR THIS!

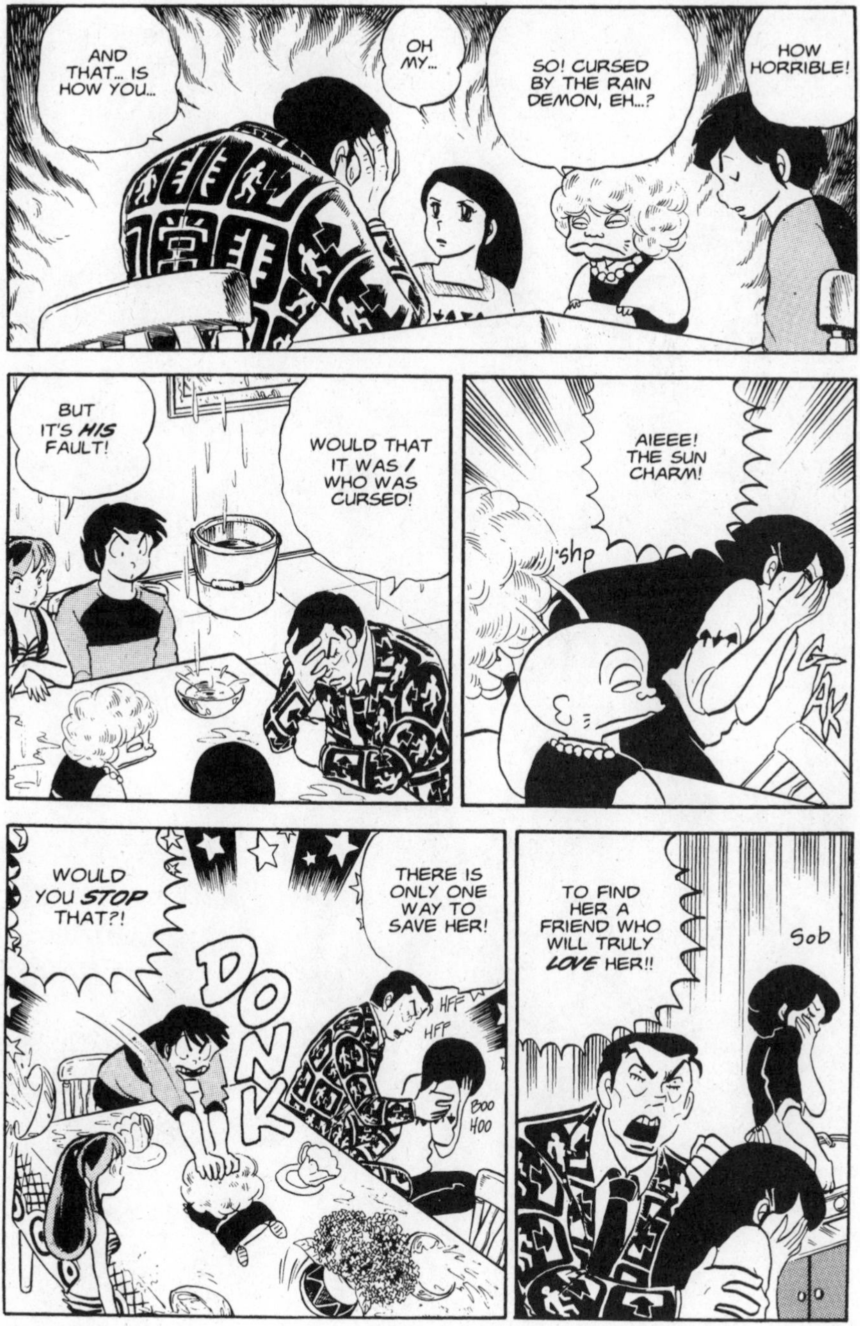
AND THAT... IS HOW YOU...
OH MY...
SO! CURSED BY THE RAIN DEMON, EH...?
HOW HORRIBLE!
BUT IT'S **HIS** FAULT!
WOULD THAT IT WAS *I* WHO WAS CURSED!
AIEEE! THE SUN CHARM!
shp
GTAK
WOULD YOU **STOP** THAT?!
THERE IS ONLY ONE WAY TO SAVE HER!
DONK
HFF
HFF
BOO HOO
TO FIND HER A FRIEND WHO WILL TRULY ***LOVE*** HER!!
Sob

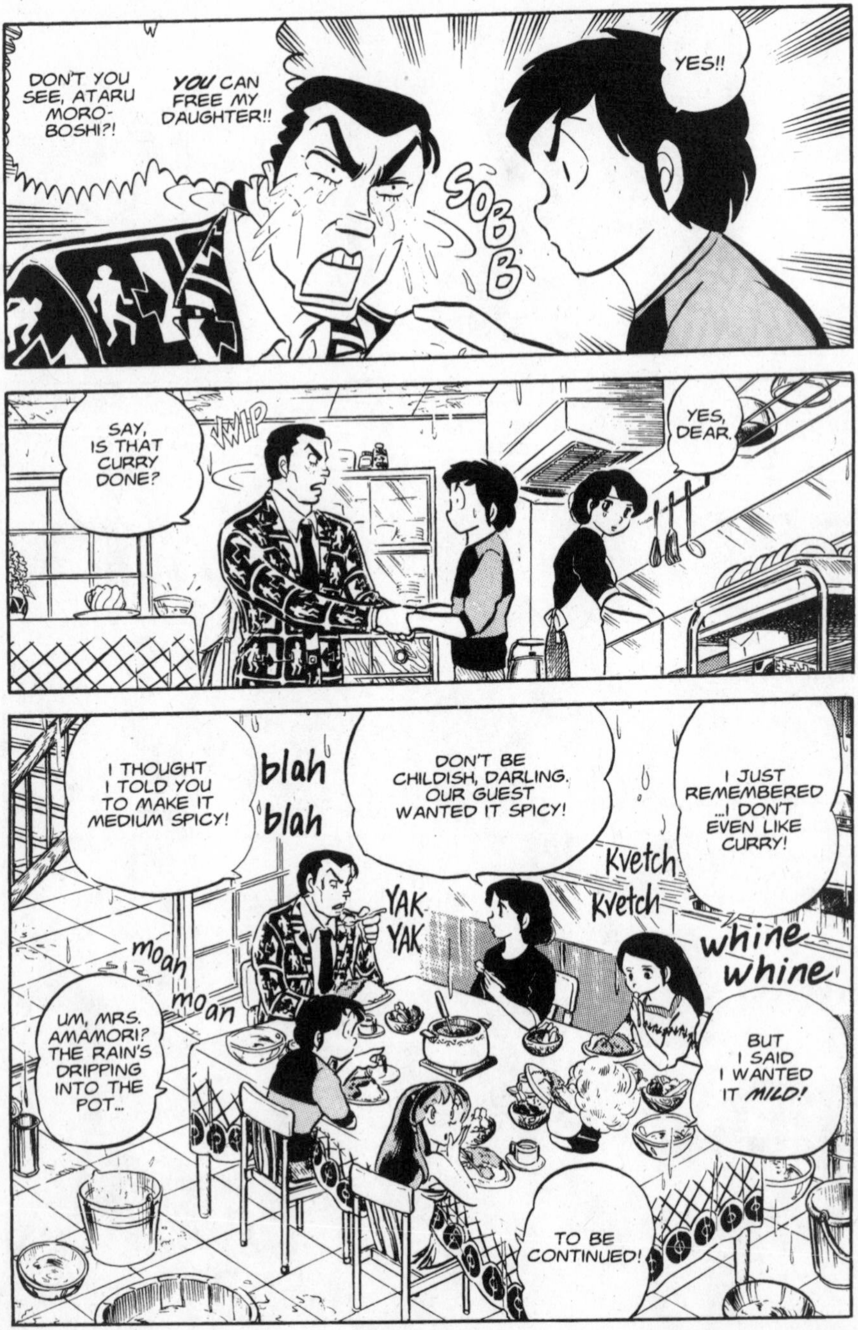
DON'T YOU SEE, ATARU MORO-BOSHI?!
YOU CAN FREE MY DAUGHTER!!
SOB
YES!!
SAY, IS THAT CURRY DONE?
WHIP
YES, DEAR.
I THOUGHT I TOLD YOU TO MAKE IT MEDIUM SPICY!
blah blah
DON'T BE CHILDISH, DARLING. OUR GUEST WANTED IT SPICY!
YAK YAK
Kvetch Kvetch
I JUST REMEMBERED ...I DON'T EVEN LIKE CURRY!
moan moan
UM, MRS. AMAMORI? THE RAIN'S DRIPPING INTO THE POT...
whine whine
BUT I SAID I WANTED IT MILD!
TO BE CONTINUED!

PART FOUR
IT'S RAINING, IT'S POURING

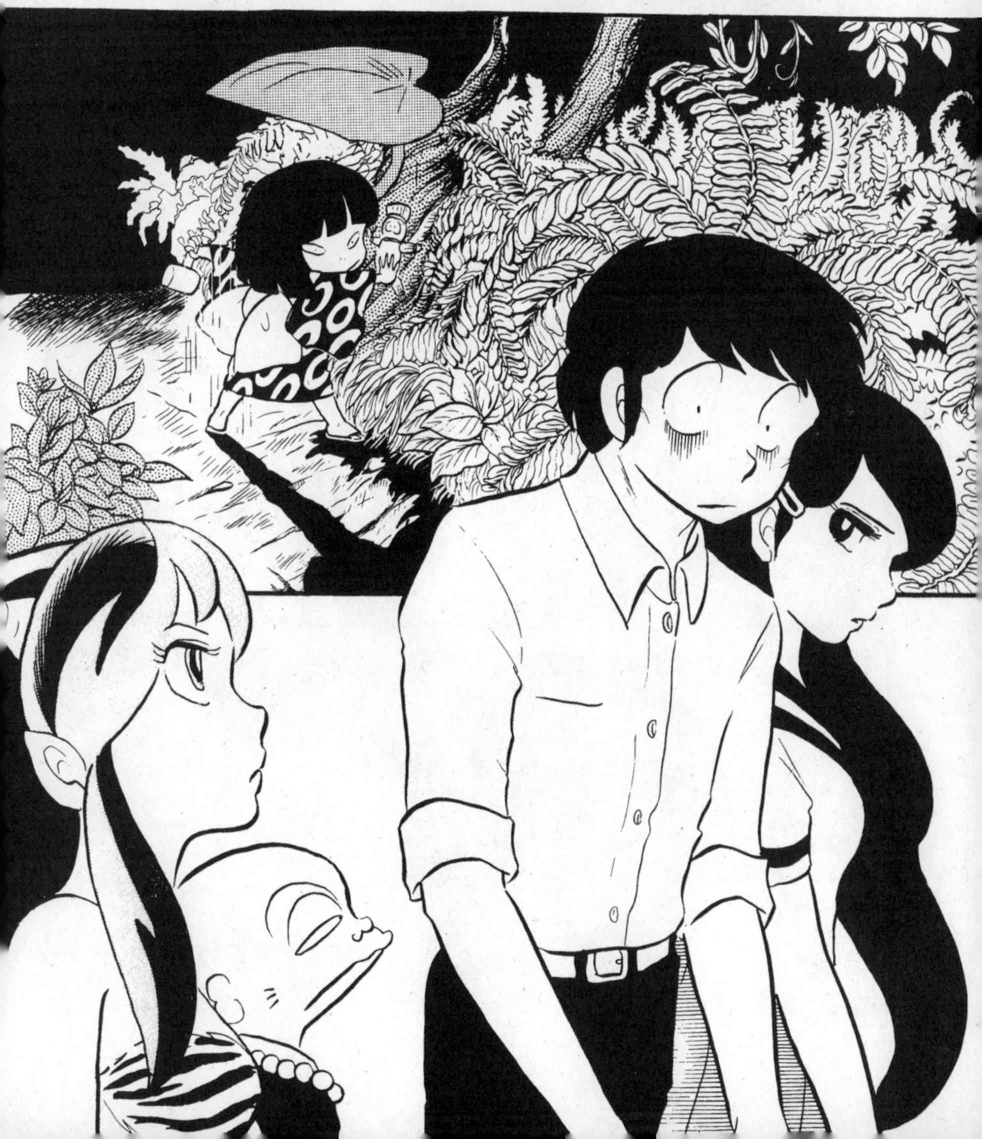

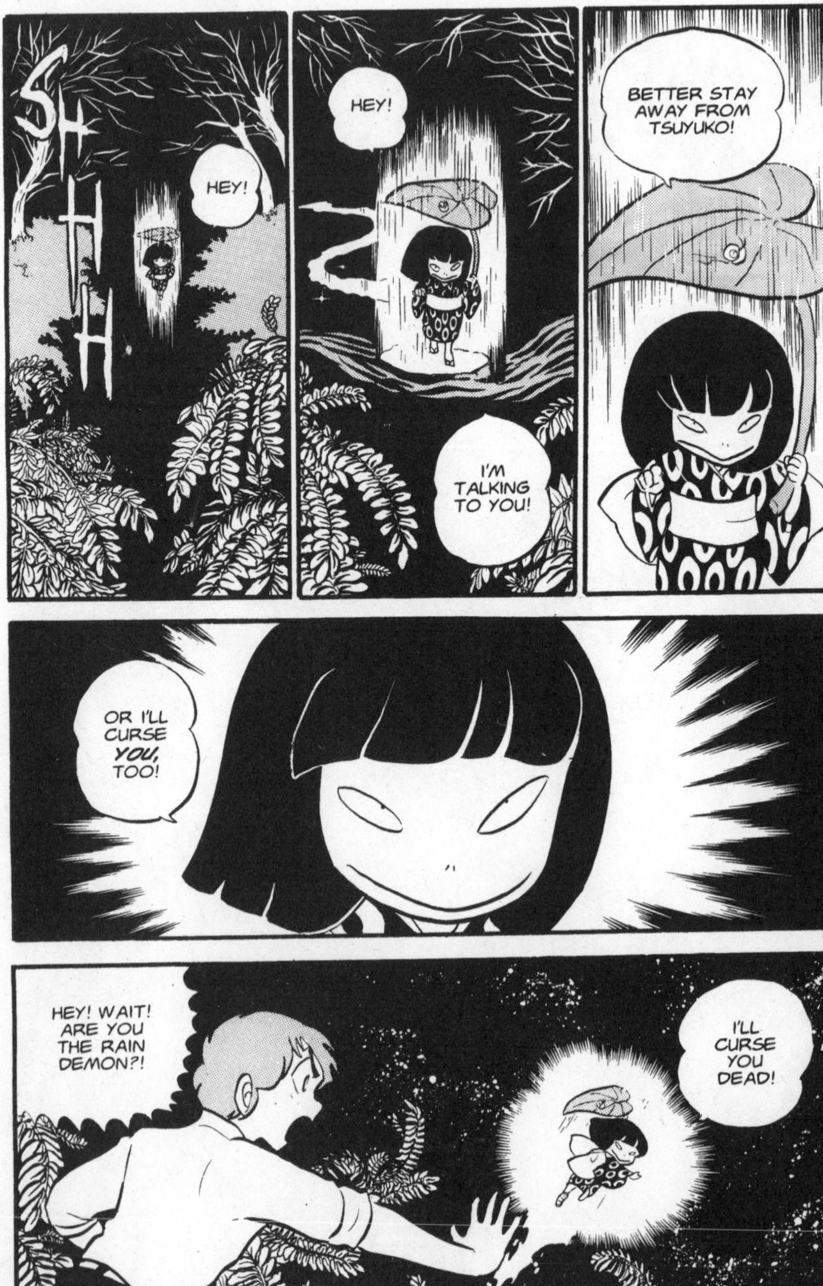
SHHH
HEY!
HEY!
I'M TALKING TO YOU!
BETTER STAY AWAY FROM TSUYUKO!
OR I'LL CURSE YOU, TOO!
HEY! WAIT! ARE YOU THE RAIN DEMON?!
I'LL CURSE YOU DEAD!

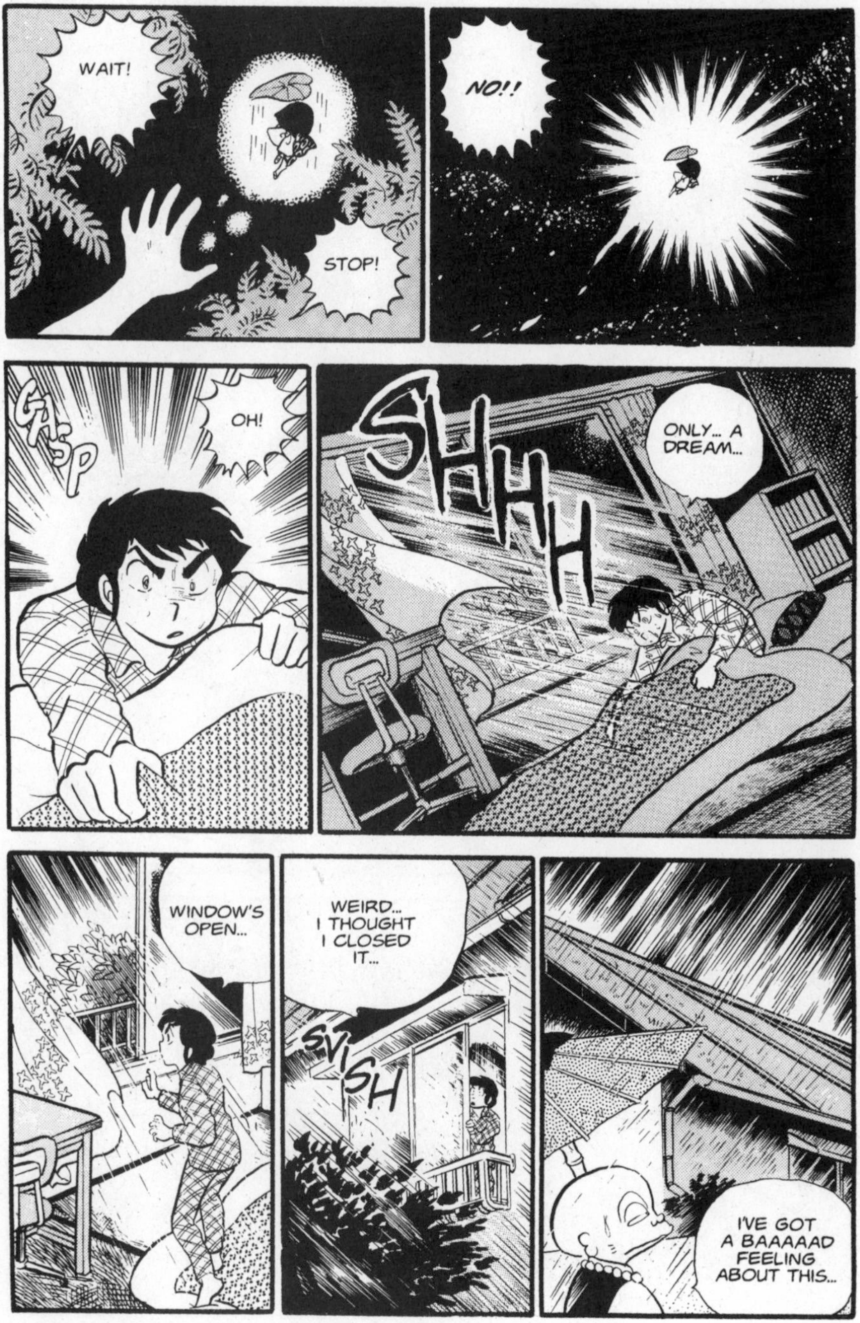
WAIT!
STOP!
NO!!
GASP
OH!
SHHHH
ONLY... A DREAM...
WINDOW'S OPEN...
WEIRD... I THOUGHT I CLOSED IT...
SWISH
I'VE GOT A BAAAAAD FEELING ABOUT THIS...

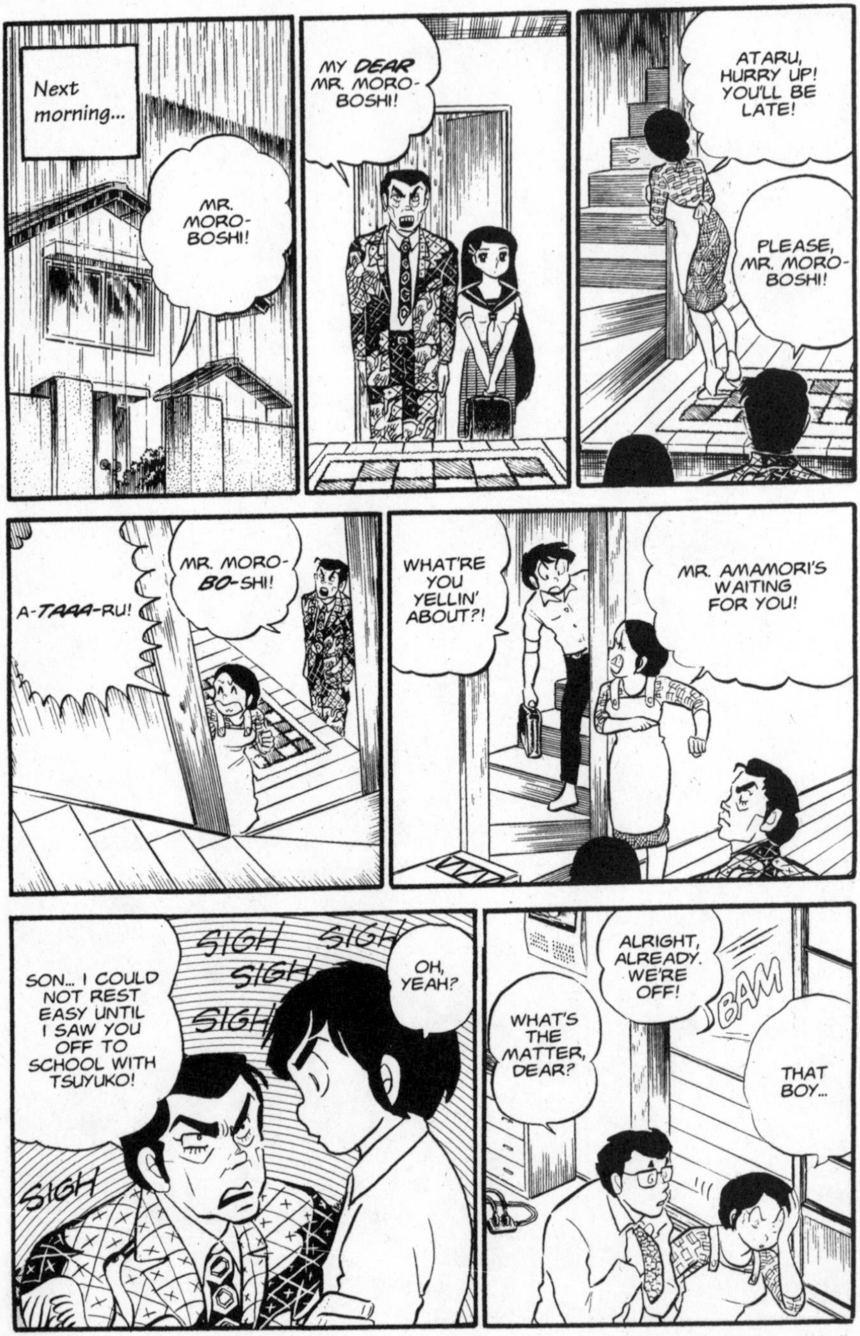
Next morning...
MR. MORO-BOSHI!
MY DEAR MR. MORO-BOSHI!
ATARU, HURRY UP! YOU'LL BE LATE!
PLEASE, MR. MORO-BOSHI!
A-TAAA-RU!
MR. MORO-BO-SHI!
WHAT'RE YOU YELLIN' ABOUT?!
MR. AMAMORI'S WAITING FOR YOU!
SON... I COULD NOT REST EASY UNTIL I SAW YOU OFF TO SCHOOL WITH TSUYUKO!
SIGH SIGH
SIGH
SIGH
OH, YEAH?
SIGH
ALRIGHT, ALREADY. WE'RE OFF!
BAM
WHAT'S THE MATTER, DEAR?
THAT BOY...

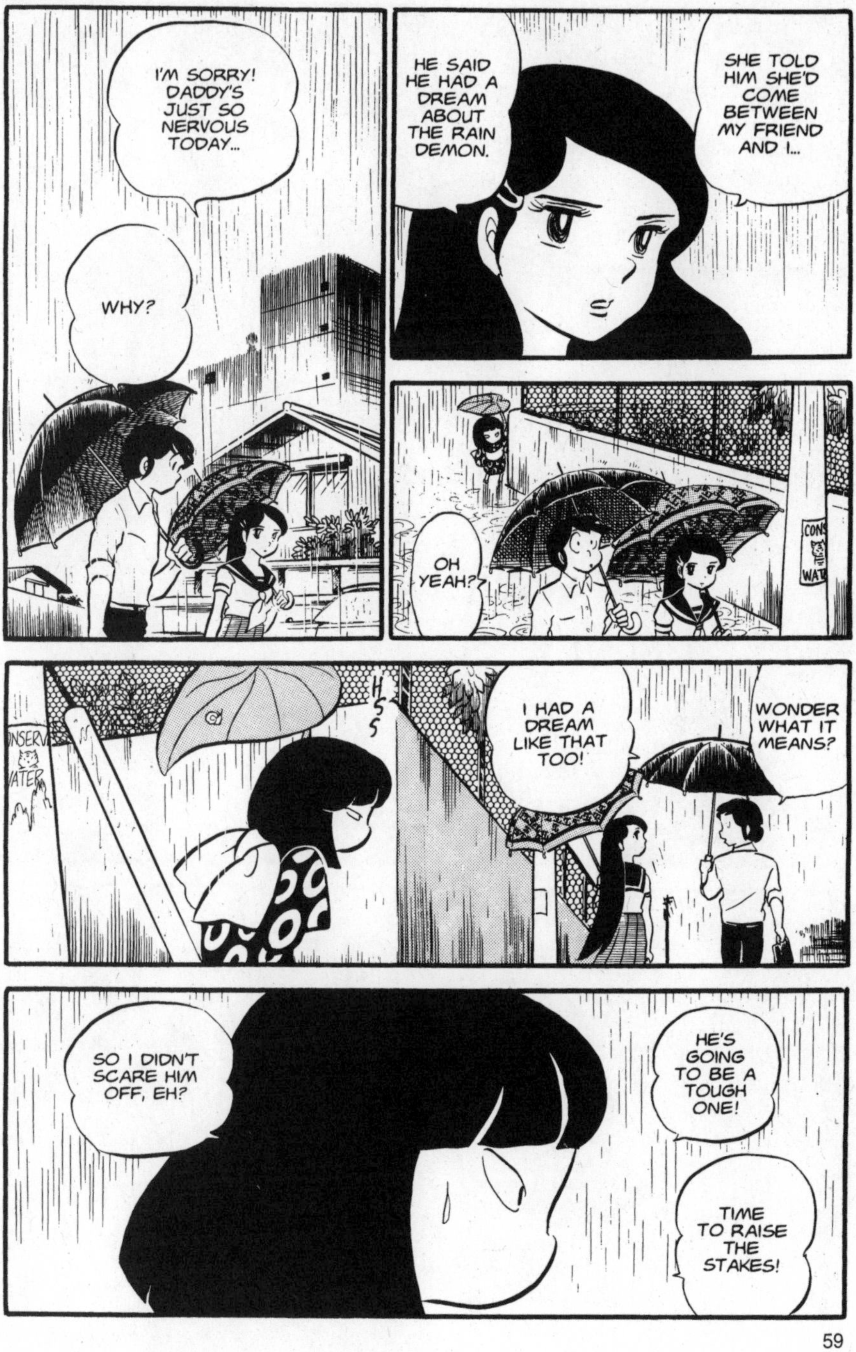
I'M SORRY! DADDY'S JUST SO NERVOUS TODAY...
WHY?
HE SAID HE HAD A DREAM ABOUT THE RAIN DEMON.
SHE TOLD HIM SHE'D COME BETWEEN MY FRIEND AND I...
OH YEAH?
HSS
I HAD A DREAM LIKE THAT TOO!
WONDER WHAT IT MEANS?
SO I DIDN'T SCARE HIM OFF, EH?
HE'S GOING TO BE A TOUGH ONE!
TIME TO RAISE THE STAKES!

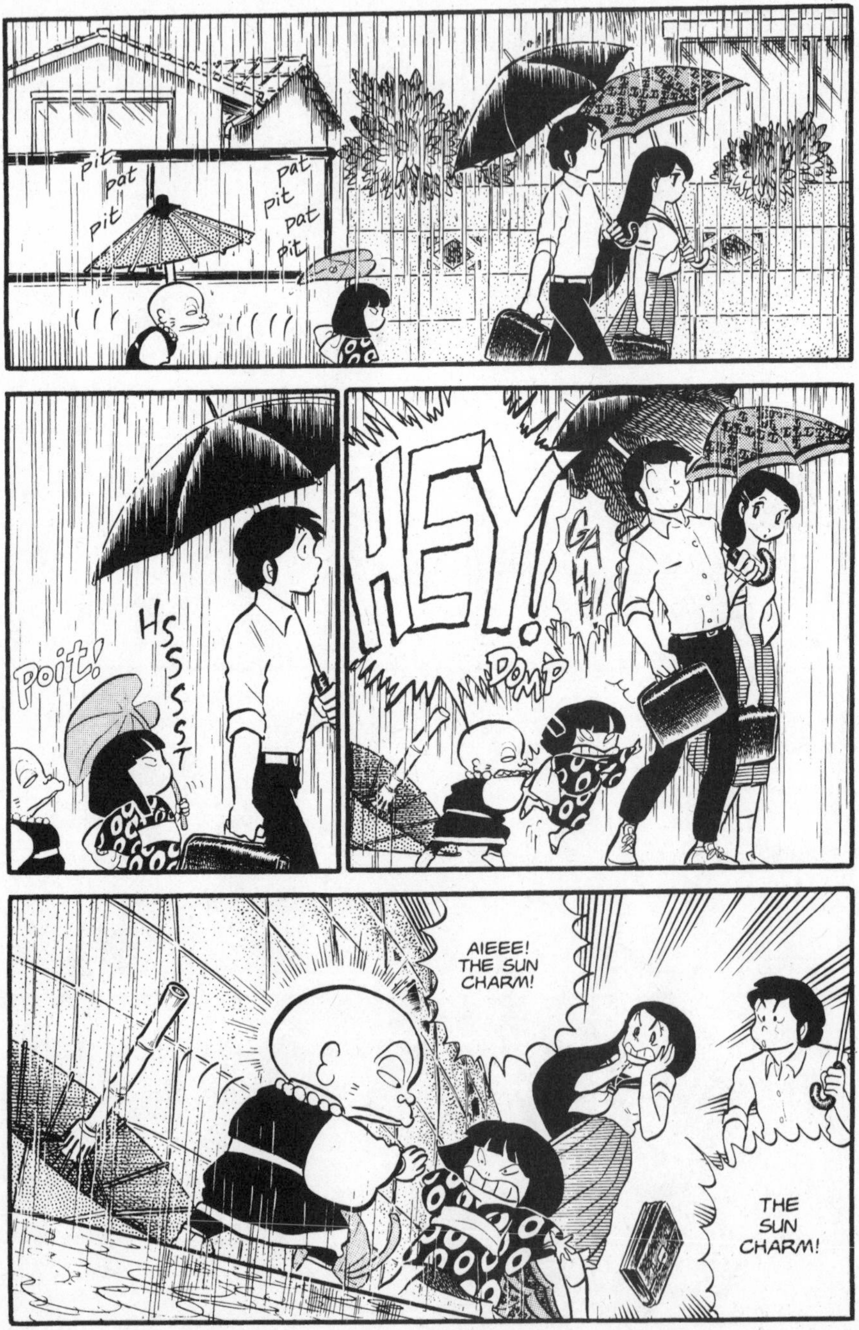
pit
pat
pit
pat
pit
pat
pit
Poit!
HSSSSST
HEY!
GAHH!
DOMP
AIEEE! THE SUN CHARM!
THE SUN CHARM!

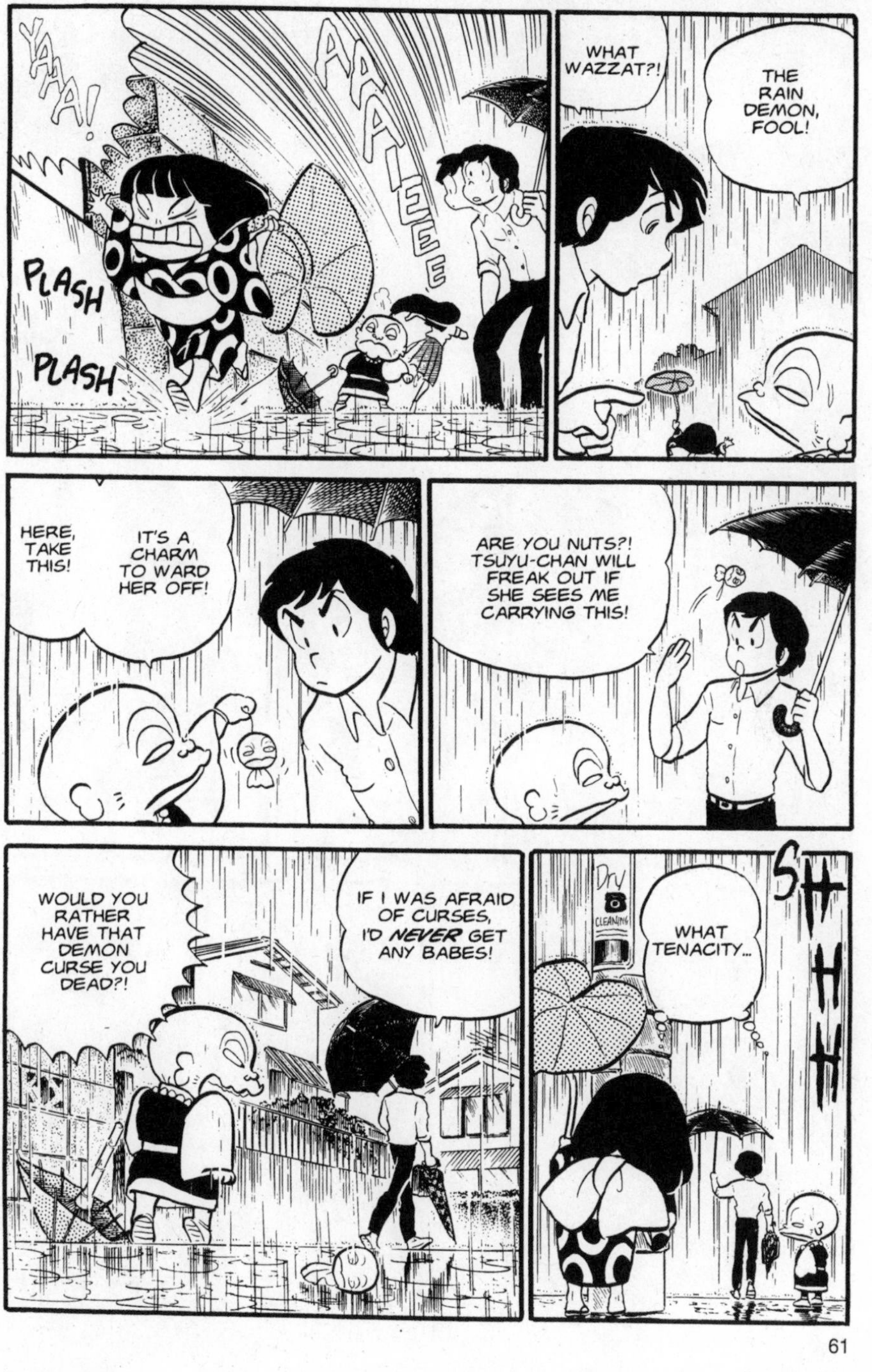
YAAA!
AAAIEEEE
PLASH
PLASH
WHAT WAZZAT?!
THE RAIN DEMON, FOOL!
HERE, TAKE THIS!
IT'S A CHARM TO WARD HER OFF!
ARE YOU NUTS?! TSUYU-CHAN WILL FREAK OUT IF SHE SEES ME CARRYING THIS!
WOULD YOU RATHER HAVE THAT DEMON CURSE YOU DEAD?!
IF I WAS AFRAID OF CURSES, I'D NEVER GET ANY BABES!
Dry CLEANING
WHAT TENACITY...
SHHHH

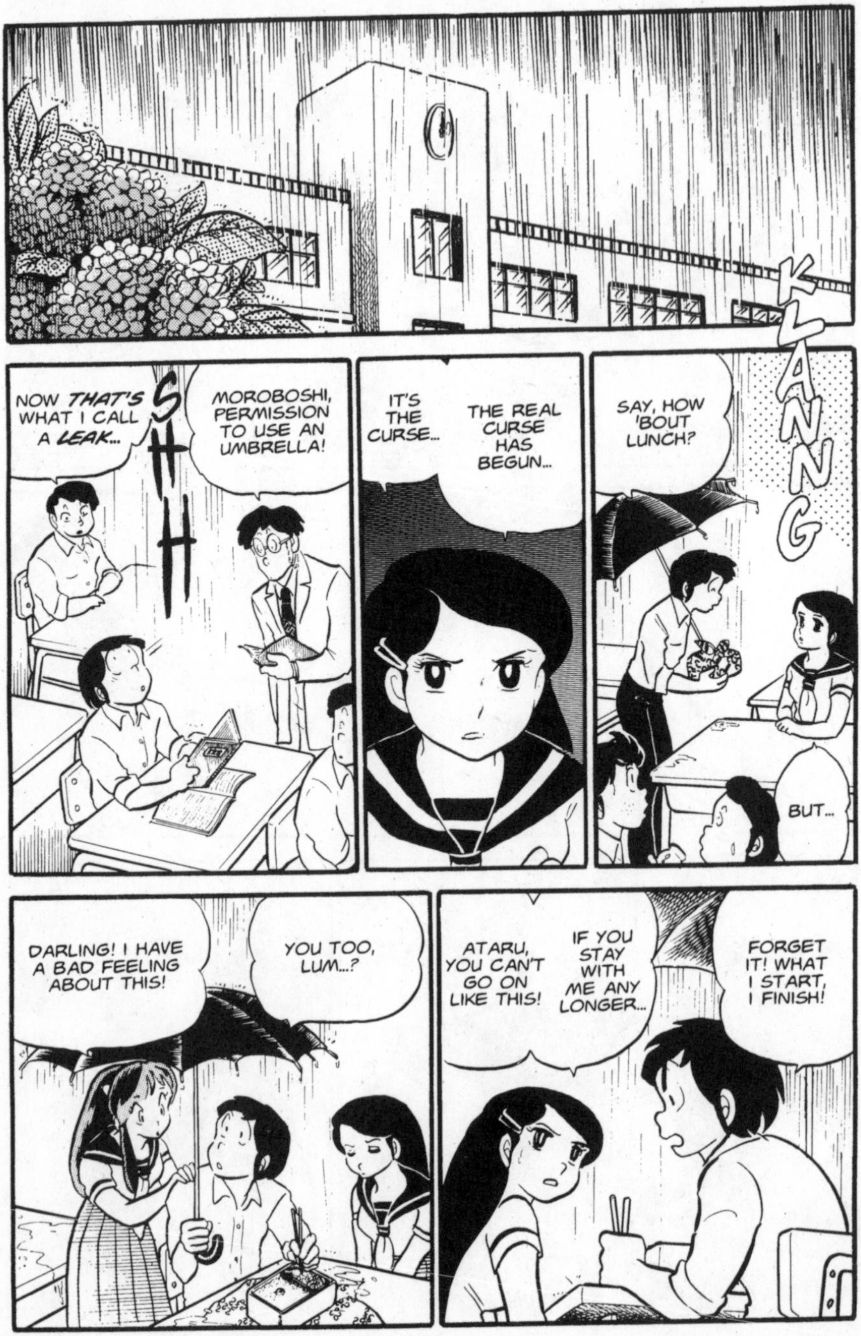
KLANNG
NOW THAT'S WHAT I CALL A LEAK...
SHH
MOROBOSHI, PERMISSION TO USE AN UMBRELLA!
IT'S THE CURSE...
THE REAL CURSE HAS BEGUN...
SAY, HOW 'BOUT LUNCH?
BUT...
DARLING! I HAVE A BAD FEELING ABOUT THIS!
YOU TOO, LUM...?
ATARU, YOU CAN'T GO ON LIKE THIS!
IF YOU STAY WITH ME ANY LONGER...
FORGET IT! WHAT I START, I FINISH!

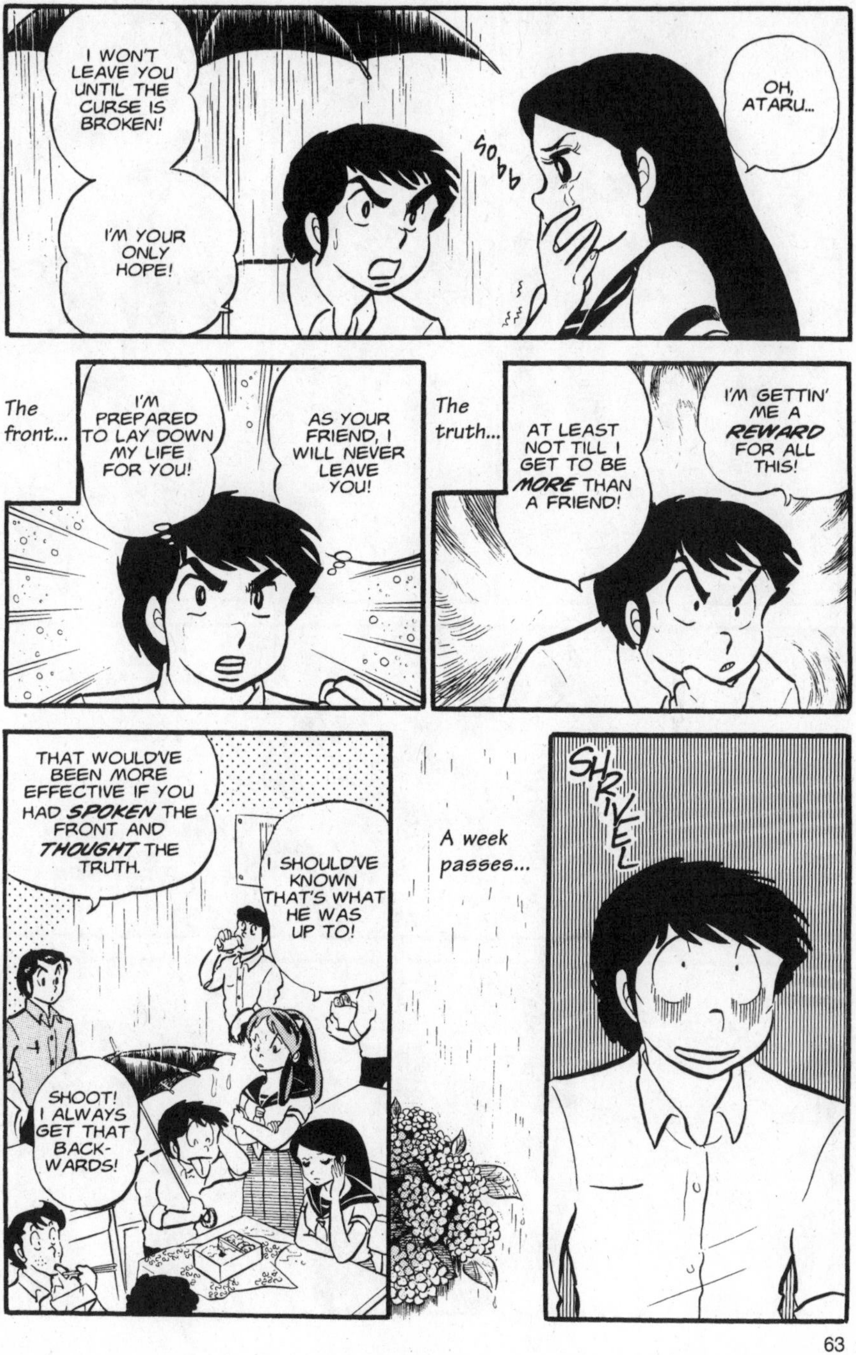
I WON'T LEAVE YOU UNTIL THE CURSE IS BROKEN!
I'M YOUR ONLY HOPE!
SOBB
OH, ATARU...
The front...
I'M PREPARED TO LAY DOWN MY LIFE FOR YOU!
AS YOUR FRIEND, I WILL NEVER LEAVE YOU!
The truth...
AT LEAST NOT TILL I GET TO BE MORE THAN A FRIEND!
I'M GETTIN' ME A REWARD FOR ALL THIS!
THAT WOULD'VE BEEN MORE EFFECTIVE IF YOU HAD SPOKEN THE FRONT AND THOUGHT THE TRUTH.
I SHOULD'VE KNOWN THAT'S WHAT HE WAS UP TO!
SHOOT! I ALWAYS GET THAT BACK-WARDS!
A week passes...
SHRIVEL

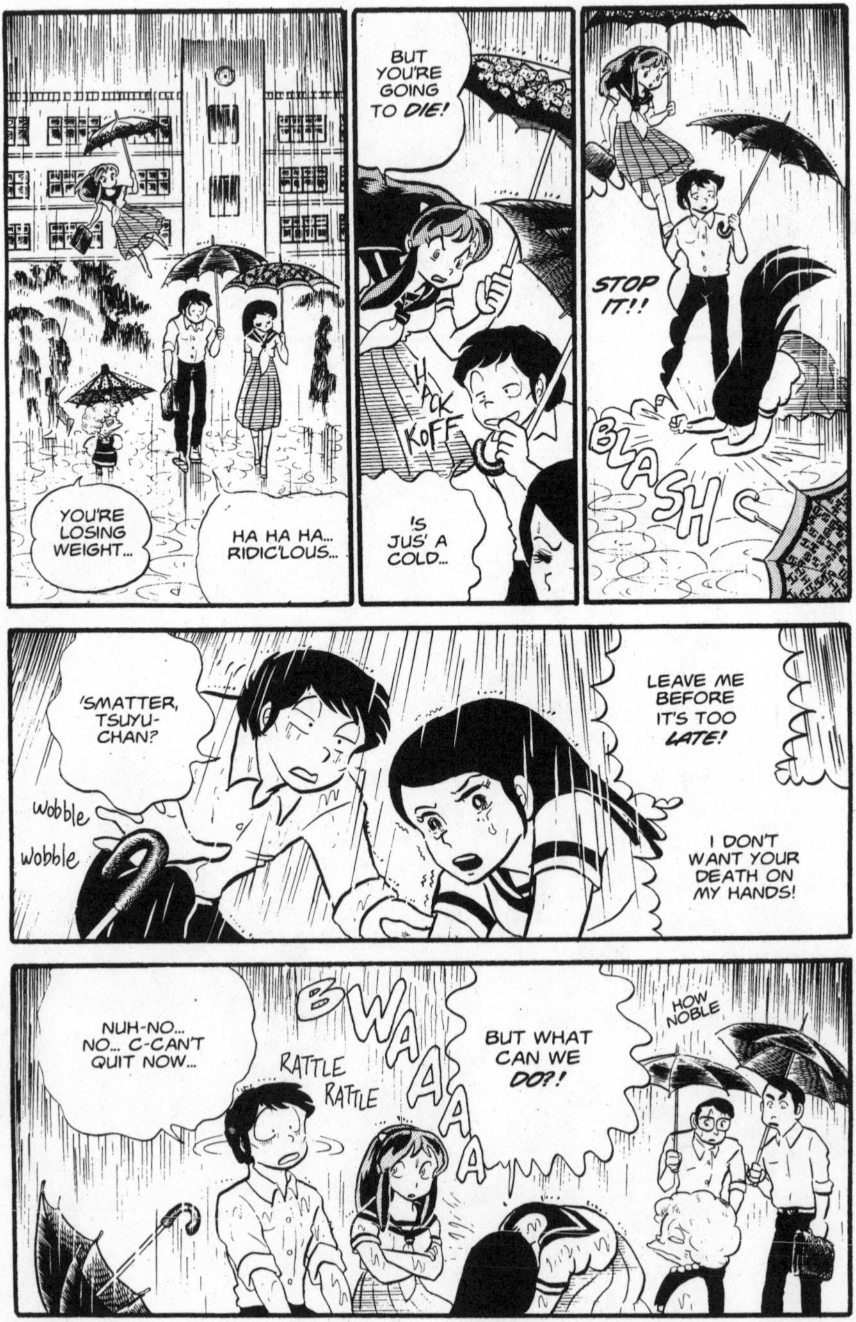

YOU'RE LOSING WEIGHT...
HA HA HA... RIDIC'LOUS...
BUT YOU'RE GOING TO DIE!
HACK
KOFF
'S JUS' A COLD...
STOP IT!!
BLASH
'SMATTER, TSUYU-CHAN?
wobble
wobble
LEAVE ME BEFORE IT'S TOO LATE!
I DON'T WANT YOUR DEATH ON MY HANDS!
NUH-NO... NO... C-CAN'T QUIT NOW...
RATTLE
RATTLE
BWAAAAA
BUT WHAT CAN WE DO?!
HOW NOBLE

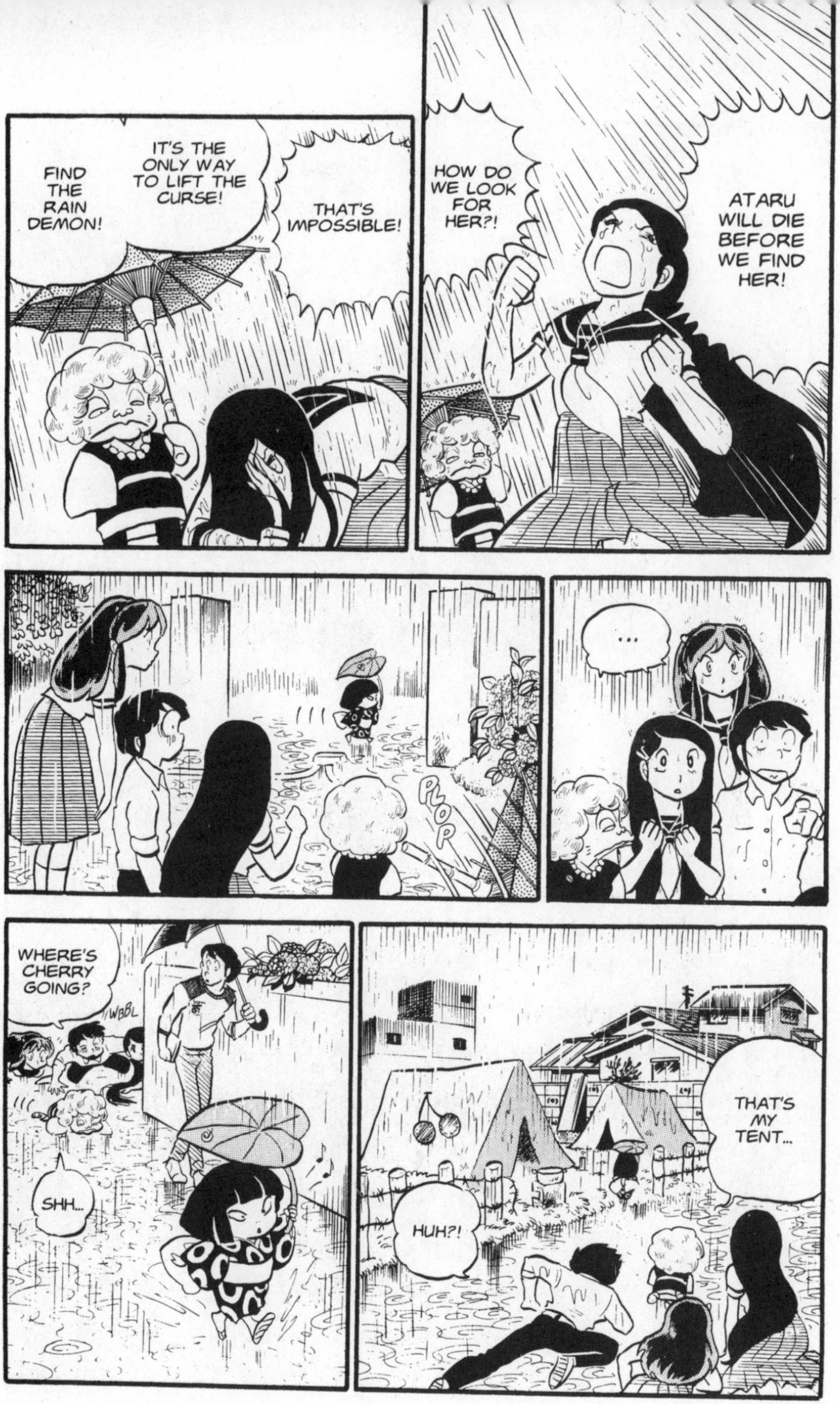
FIND THE RAIN DEMON!
IT'S THE ONLY WAY TO LIFT THE CURSE!
THAT'S IMPOSSIBLE!
HOW DO WE LOOK FOR HER?!
ATARU WILL DIE BEFORE WE FIND HER!
PLOP
...
WHERE'S CHERRY GOING?
WBBL
SHH...
HUH?!
THAT'S MY TENT...

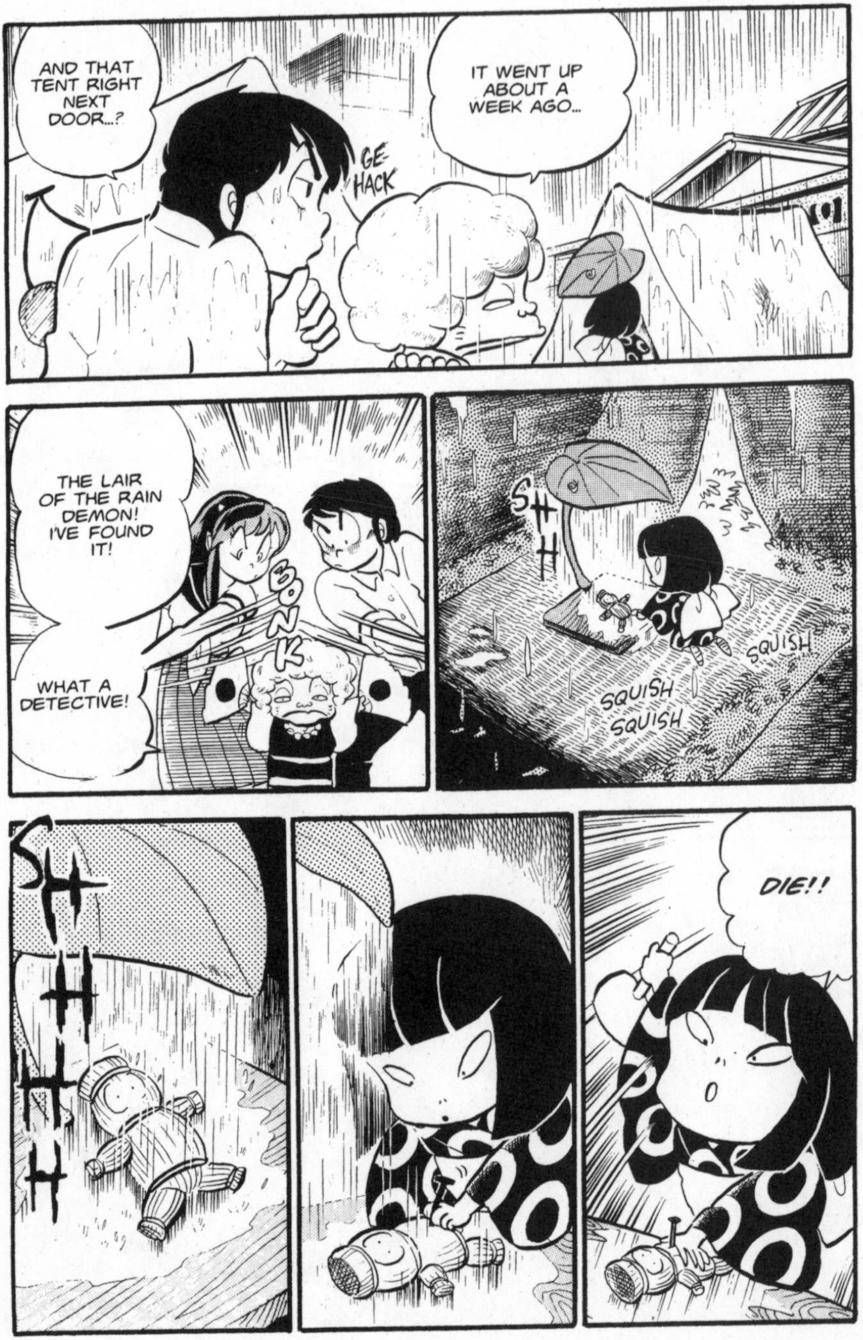
AND THAT TENT RIGHT NEXT DOOR...?
GE HACK
IT WENT UP ABOUT A WEEK AGO...
THE LAIR OF THE RAIN DEMON! I'VE FOUND IT!
BONK
WHAT A DETECTIVE!
SHH
SQUISH
SQUISH SQUISH
SHHHHH
DIE!!

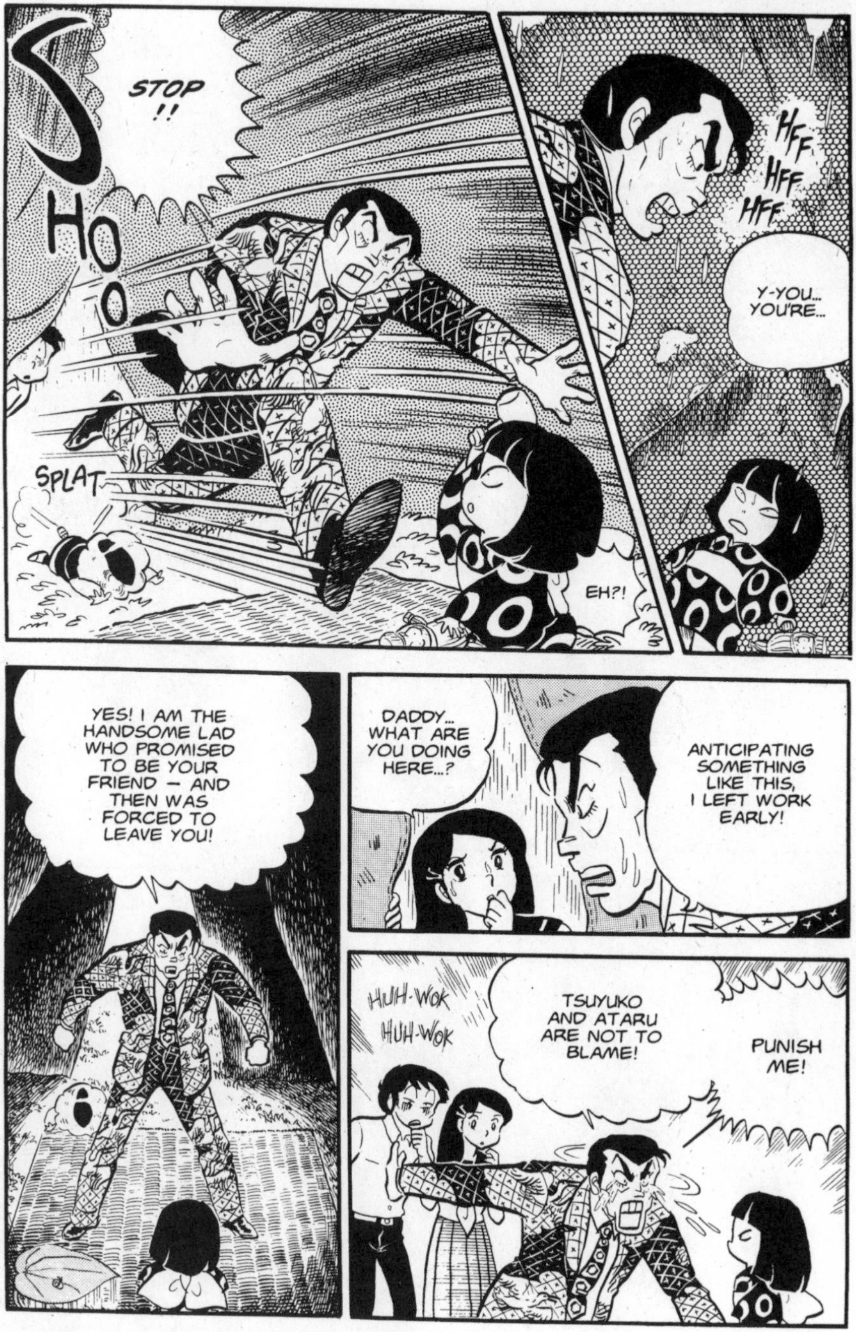
SHOO
STOP !!
SPLAT
EH?!
HFF HFF HFF
Y-YOU... YOU'RE...
YES! I AM THE HANDSOME LAD WHO PROMISED TO BE YOUR FRIEND – AND THEN WAS FORCED TO LEAVE YOU!
DADDY... WHAT ARE YOU DOING HERE...?
ANTICIPATING SOMETHING LIKE THIS, I LEFT WORK EARLY!
HUH-WOK HUH-WOK
TSUYUKO AND ATARU ARE NOT TO BLAME!
PUNISH ME!

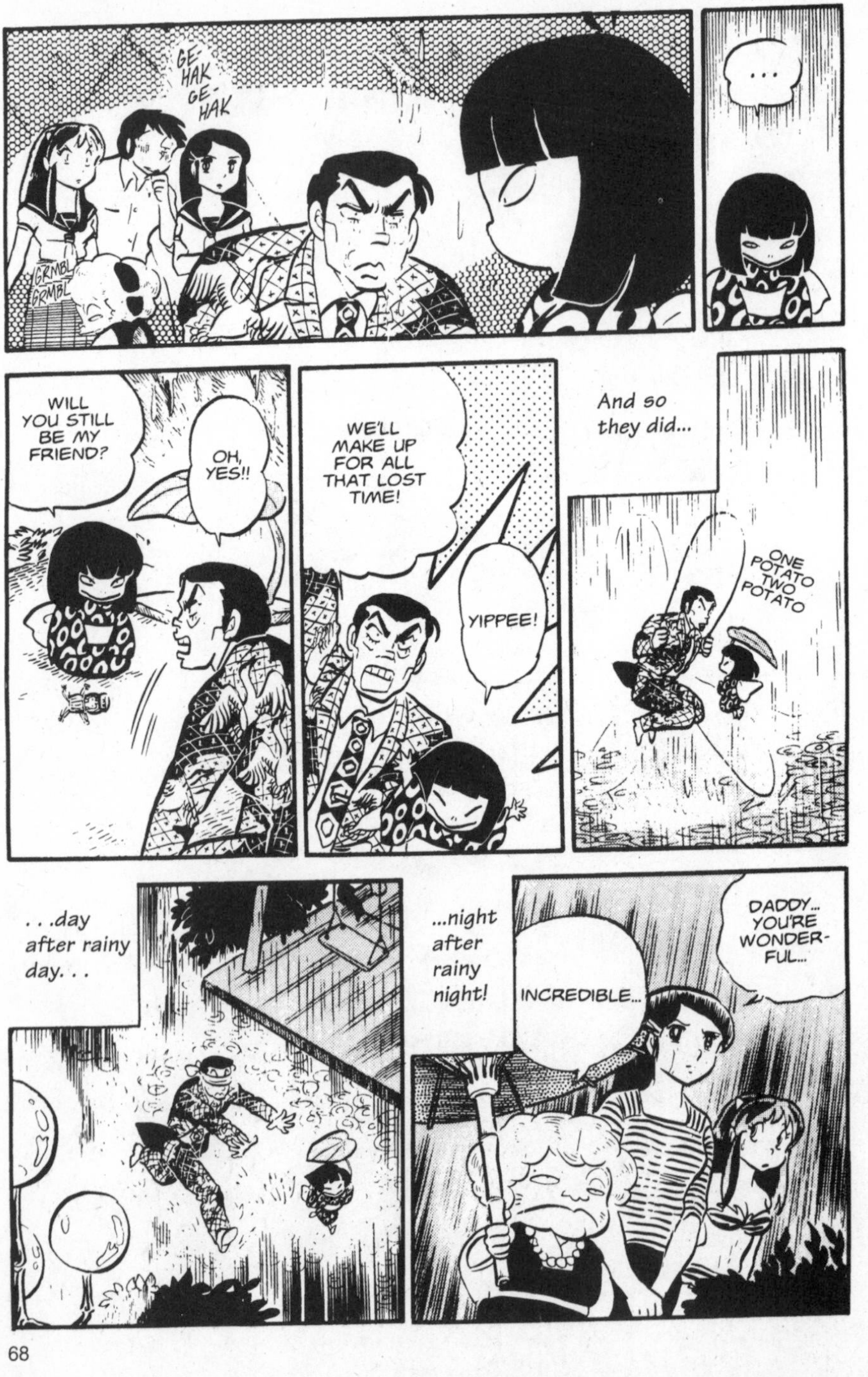
GE-HAK GE-HAK
GRMBL GRMBL
...
WILL YOU STILL BE MY FRIEND?
OH, YES!!
WE'LL MAKE UP FOR ALL THAT LOST TIME!
YIPPEE!
And so they did...
ONE POTATO TWO POTATO
. . .day after rainy day. . .
...night after rainy night!
INCREDIBLE...
DADDY... YOU'RE WONDERFUL...

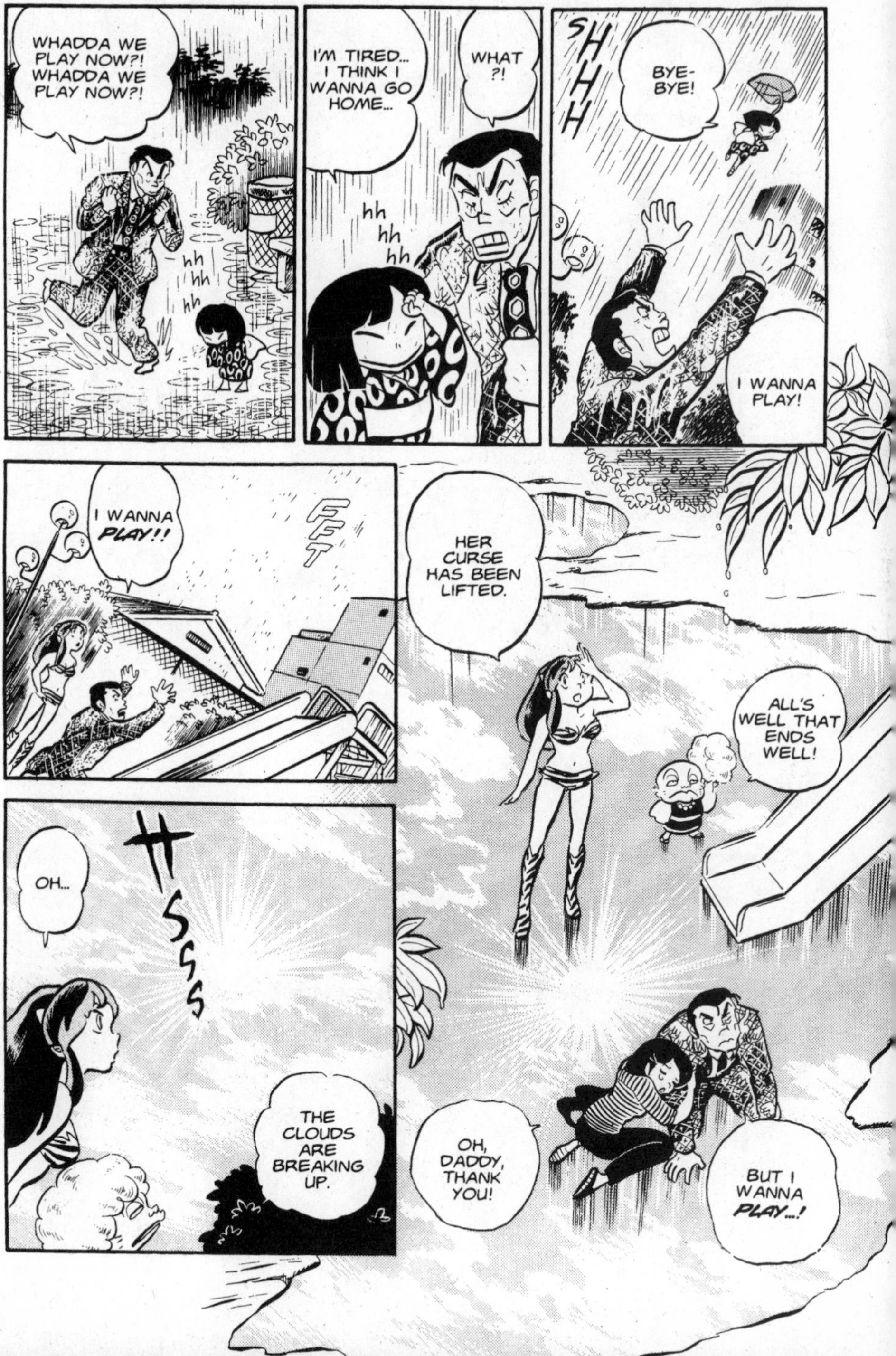
WHADDA WE PLAY NOW?! WHADDA WE PLAY NOW?!
hh hh hh
I'M TIRED... I THINK I WANNA GO HOME...
WHAT ?!
hh hh hh
SHHH
BYE-BYE!
I WANNA PLAY!
I WANNA PLAY!!
FFT
OH...
HSSS
THE CLOUDS ARE BREAKING UP.
HER CURSE HAS BEEN LIFTED.
ALL'S WELL THAT ENDS WELL!
OH, DADDY, THANK YOU!
BUT I WANNA PLAY...!

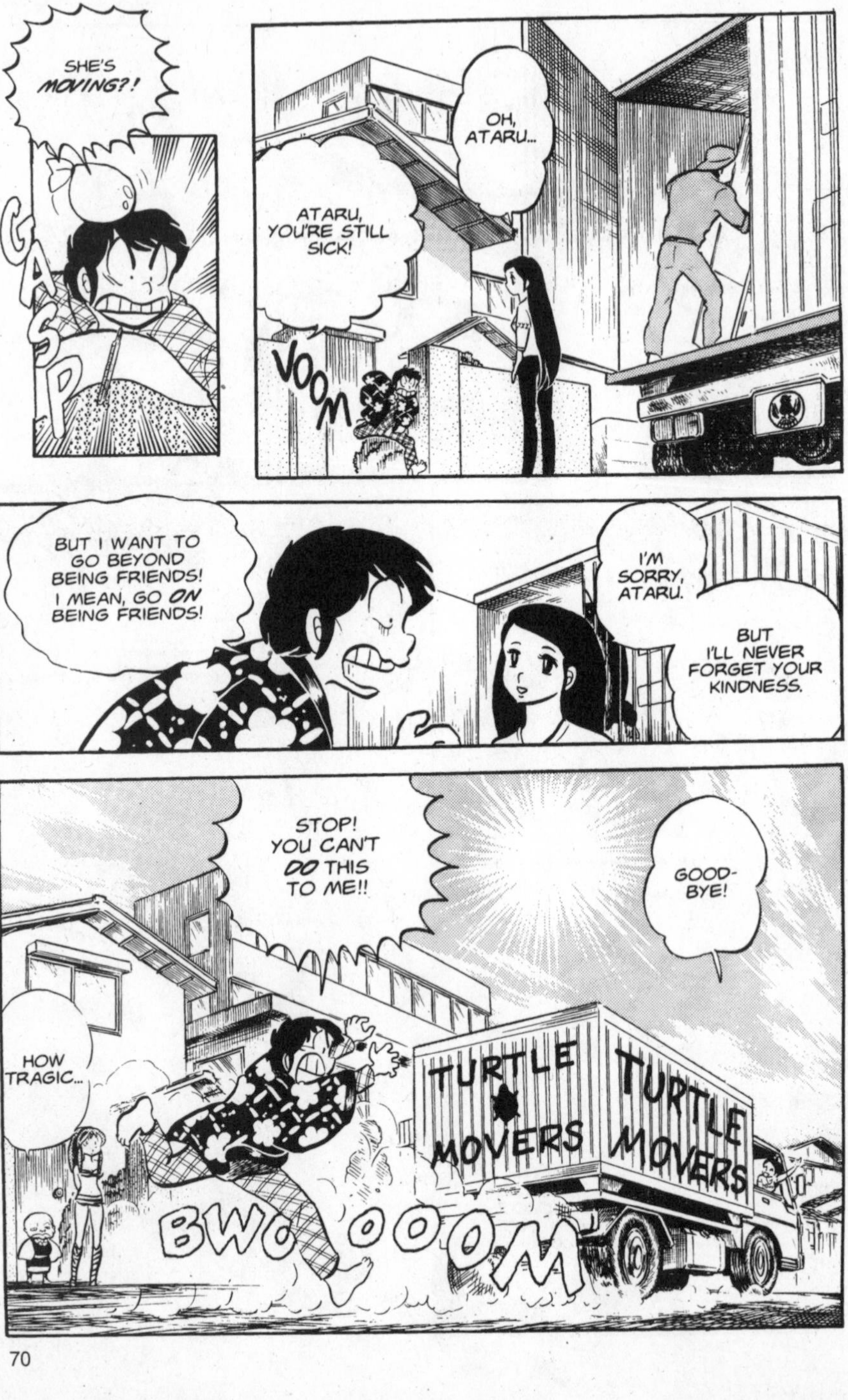
SHE'S *MOVING?!*
GASP
OH, ATARU...
ATARU, YOU'RE STILL SICK!
VOOM
BUT I WANT TO GO BEYOND BEING FRIENDS! I MEAN, GO *ON* BEING FRIENDS!
I'M SORRY, ATARU.
BUT I'LL NEVER FORGET YOUR KINDNESS.
STOP! YOU CAN'T *DO* THIS TO ME!!
GOOD-BYE!
HOW TRAGIC...
TURTLE MOVERS
TURTLE MOVERS
BWOOOOOM

PART FIVE
WELCOME TO HOTEL GHOST

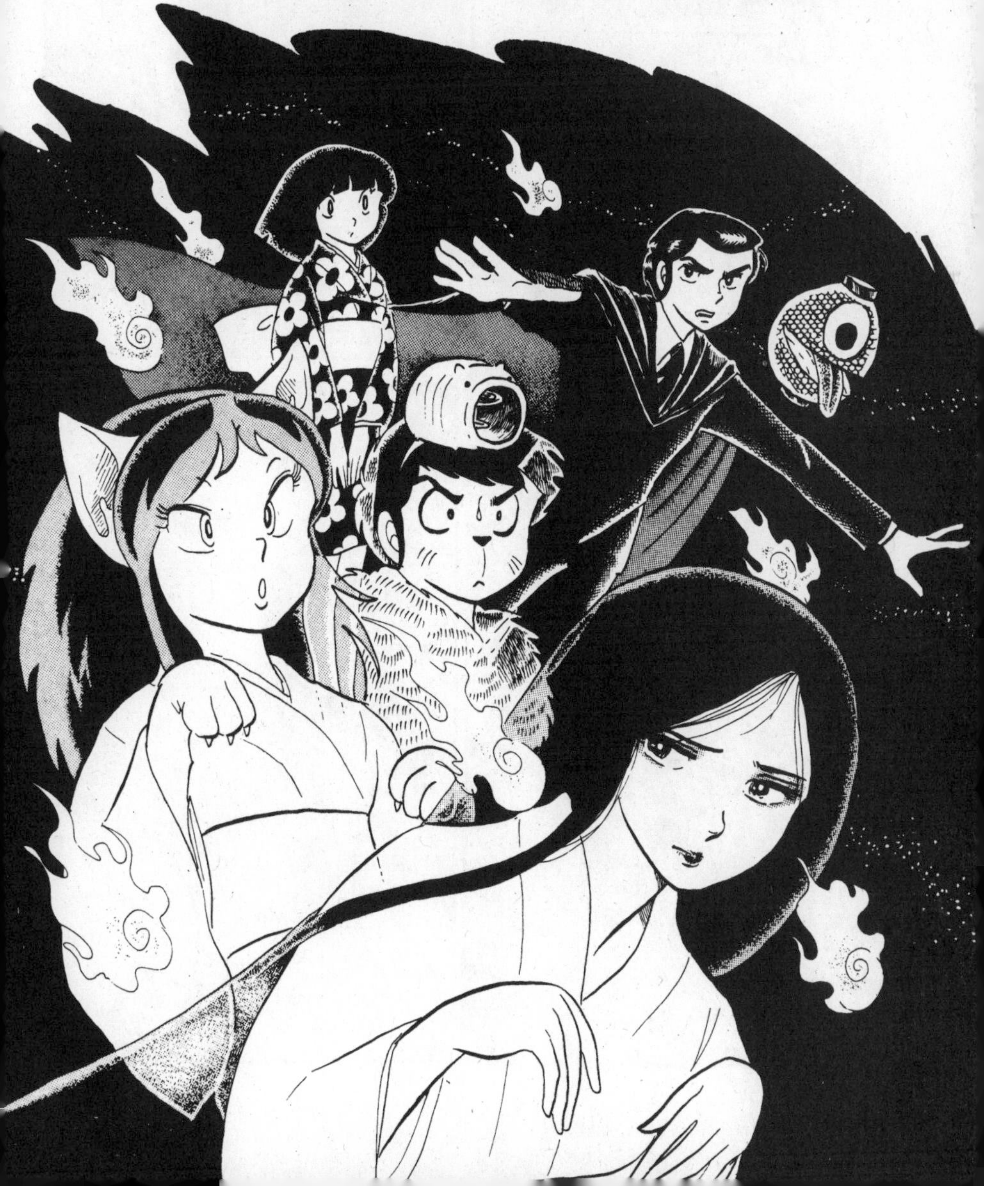

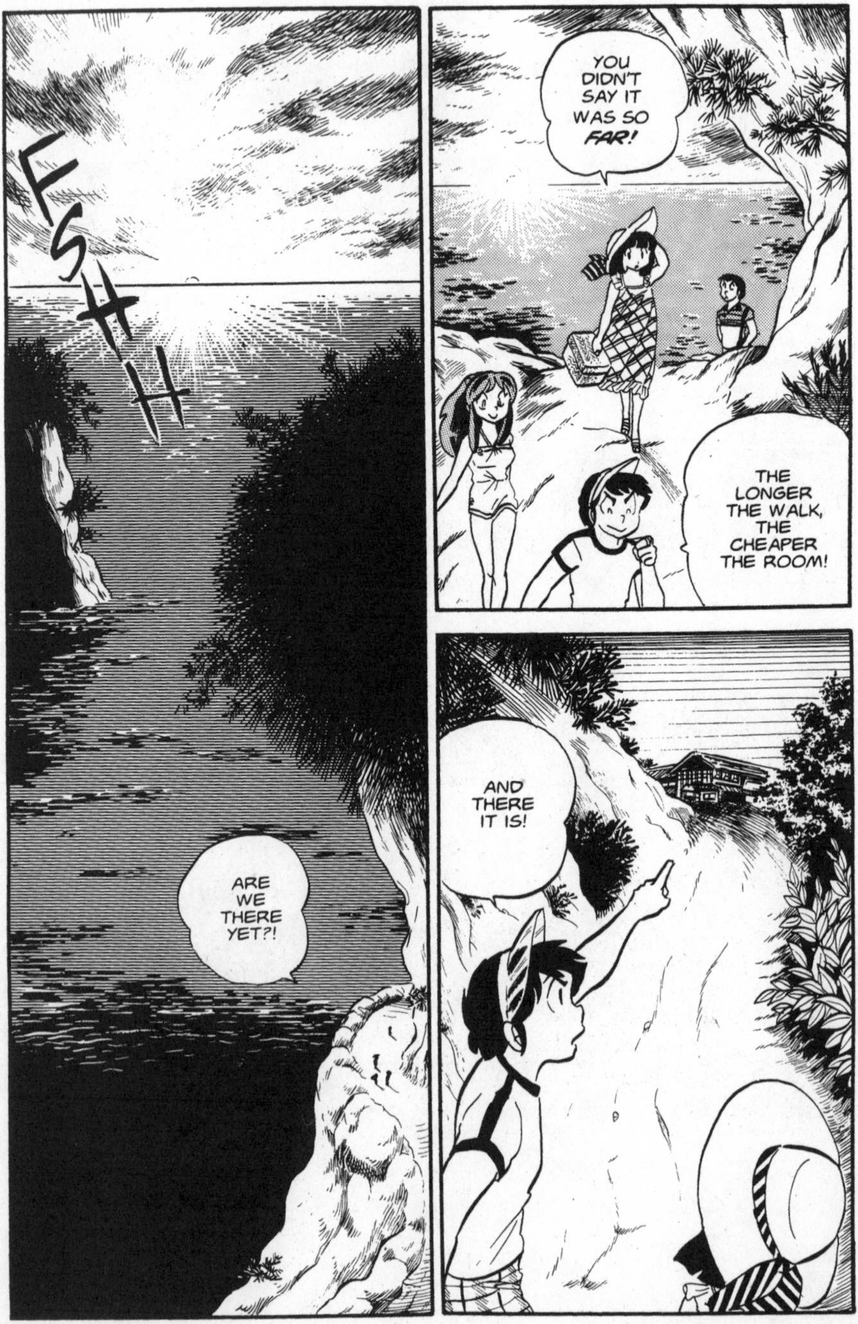
FSHH
ARE WE THERE YET?!
YOU DIDN'T SAY IT WAS SO *FAR!*
THE LONGER THE WALK, THE CHEAPER THE ROOM!
AND THERE IT IS!

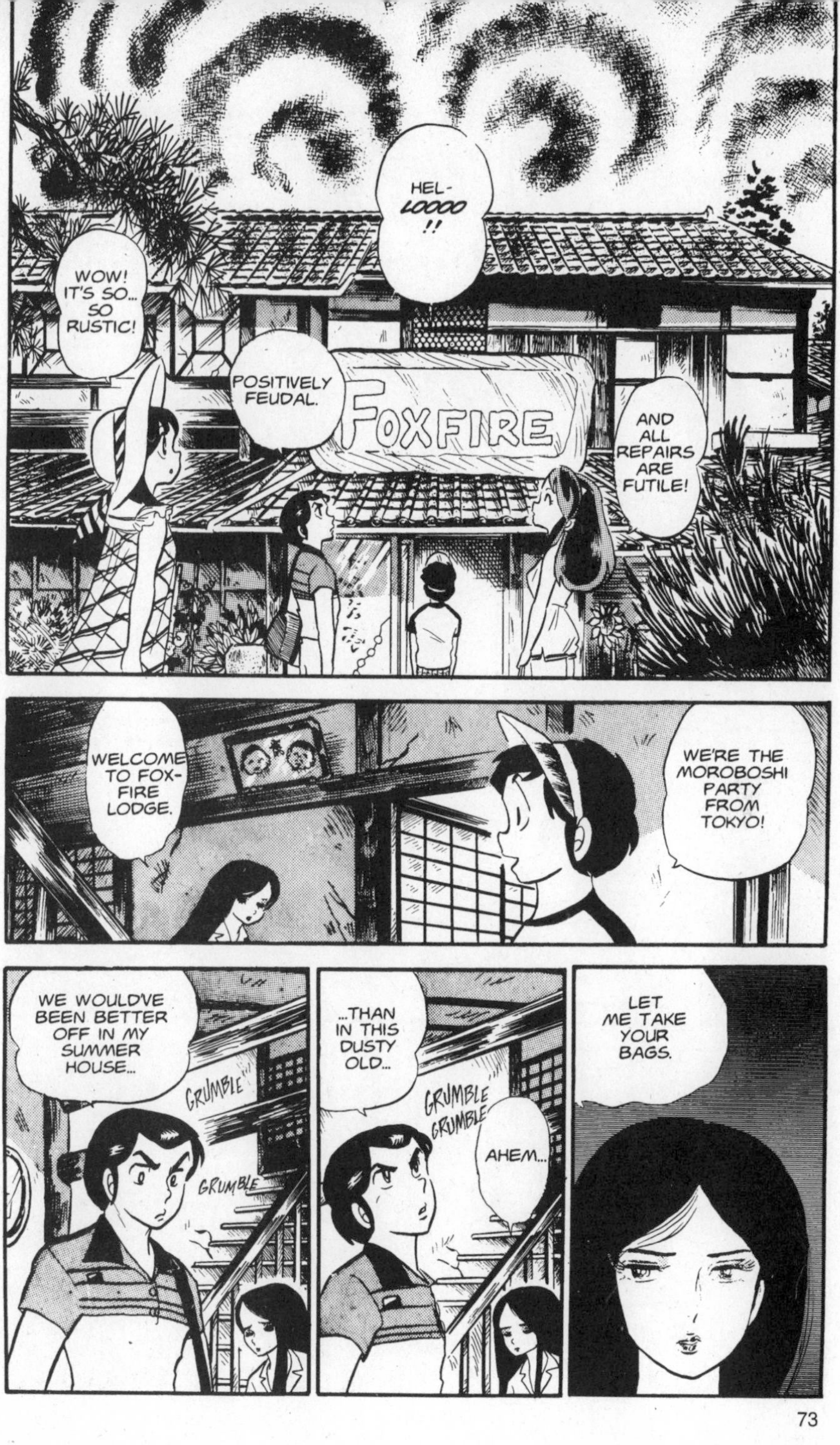
WOW! IT'S SO... SO RUSTIC!
HEL-LOOOO!!
POSITIVELY FEUDAL.
FOXFIRE
AND ALL REPAIRS ARE FUTILE!
WELCOME TO FOX-FIRE LODGE.
WE'RE THE MOROBOSHI PARTY FROM TOKYO!
WE WOULD'VE BEEN BETTER OFF IN MY SUMMER HOUSE...
GRUMBLE
GRUMBLE
...THAN IN THIS DUSTY OLD...
GRUMBLE GRUMBLE
AHEM...
LET ME TAKE YOUR BAGS.

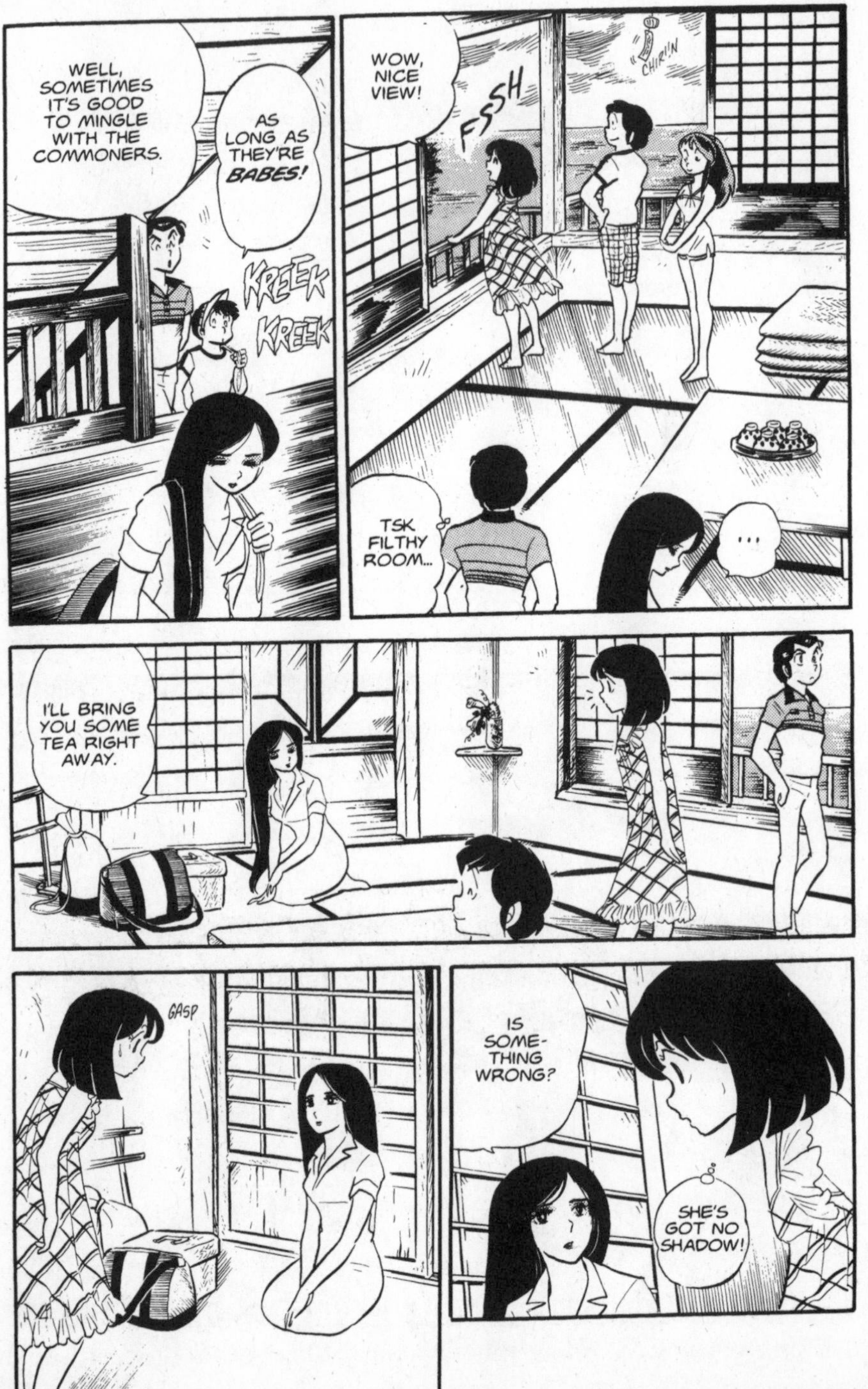
WELL, SOMETIMES IT'S GOOD TO MINGLE WITH THE COMMONERS.
AS LONG AS THEY'RE *BABES!*
KREEK
KREEK
WOW, NICE VIEW!
FSSH
CHIRIN
TSK FILTHY ROOM...
...
I'LL BRING YOU SOME TEA RIGHT AWAY.
GASP
IS SOME-THING WRONG?
SHE'S GOT NO SHADOW!

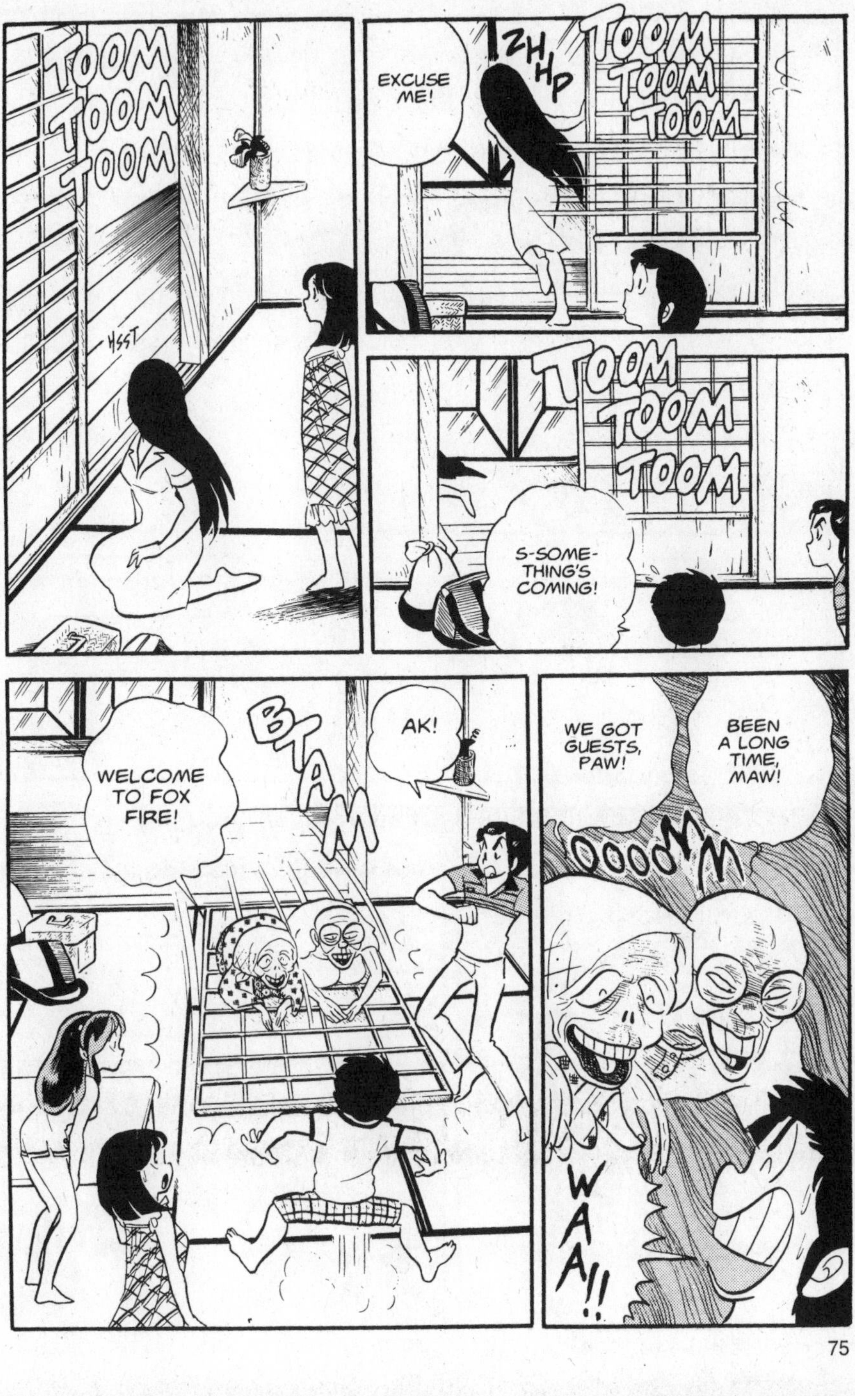
TOOM TOOM TOOM
HSST
EXCUSE ME!
ZHHP
TOOM TOOM TOOM
TOOM TOOM TOOM
S-SOME-THING'S COMING!
WELCOME TO FOX FIRE!
BTAM
AK!
WE GOT GUESTS, PAW!
BEEN A LONG TIME, MAW!
OOOOMM
WAA!!

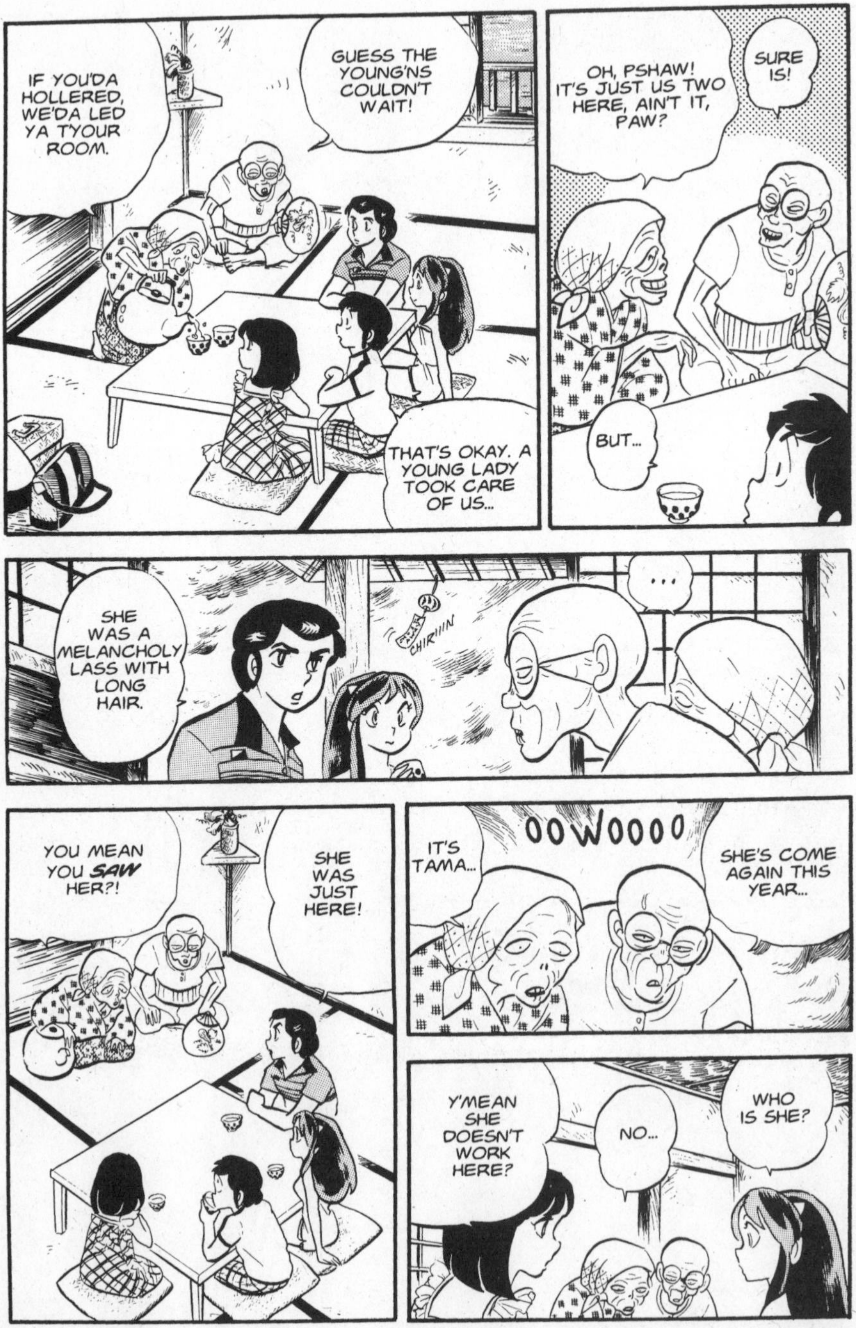
IF YOU'DA HOLLERED, WE'DA LED YA T'YOUR ROOM.
GUESS THE YOUNG'NS COULDN'T WAIT!
THAT'S OKAY. A YOUNG LADY TOOK CARE OF US...
OH, PSHAW! IT'S JUST US TWO HERE, AIN'T IT, PAW?
SURE IS!
BUT...
SHE WAS A MELANCHOLY LASS WITH LONG HAIR.
CHIRIIIN
...
YOU MEAN YOU *SAW* HER?!
SHE WAS JUST HERE!
IT'S TAMA...
OOWOOOO
SHE'S COME AGAIN THIS YEAR...
Y'MEAN SHE DOESN'T WORK HERE?
NO...
WHO IS SHE?

IT'S BETTER THAT Y'DON'T HEAR OF IT...

YEP, YEP, FOR YER OWN GOOD...

WHAT?

NOW I'M CURIOUS!

BUT, Y'KNOW, PAW...

NOW, NOW, MAW...

TELL US!

BUT REALLY, PAW!

NOW REALLY, MAW!

THIS IS GETTING ANNOYING!

SO, D'YA REALLY WANT TO HEAR IT?

YES!

WE DON'T WANT TO SHOCK YOU...

WHAT COULD POSSIBLY SHOCK US AFTER *THAT* BUILD UP?

OKAY, THEN...

TAMA IS...

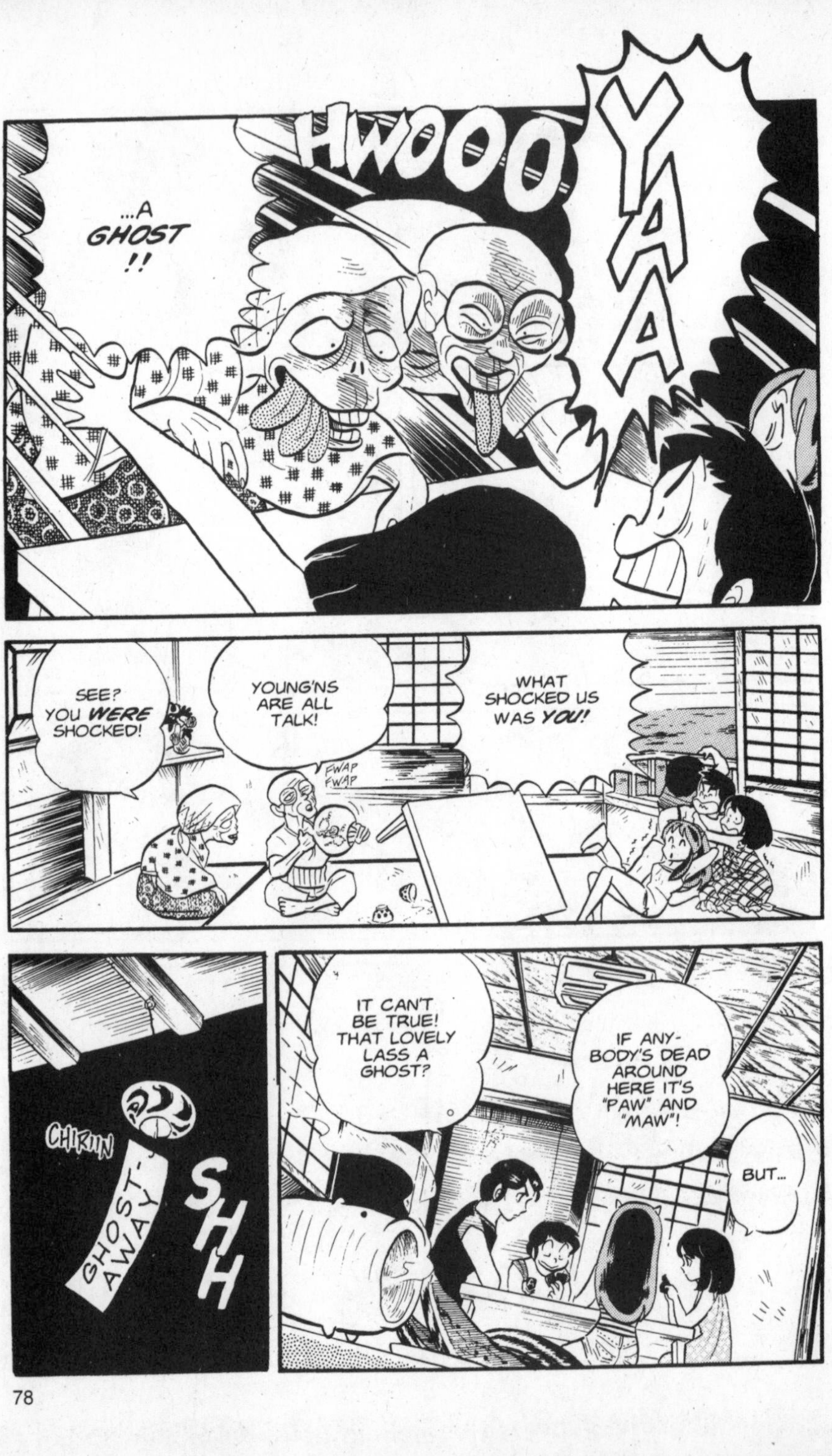
...A GHOST !!
HWOOOYAAA
SEE? YOU WERE SHOCKED!
YOUNG'NS ARE ALL TALK!
FWAP FWAP
WHAT SHOCKED US WAS YOU!
CHIRIIN
GHOST-AWAY
SHH
IT CAN'T BE TRUE! THAT LOVELY LASS A GHOST?
IF ANY-BODY'S DEAD AROUND HERE IT'S "PAW" AND "MAW"!
BUT...

TAMA HASN'T SHOWN UP SINCE, HAS SHE?

WHAT ARE YOU SAYING?

DIDN'T YOU NOTICE?

THAT GIRL DIDN'T HAVE A SHADOW...

HSSSH

SWAHH

WAK!

PUP

EEEEE!!

HWOO

OBBLE OBBLE

KYAA!!

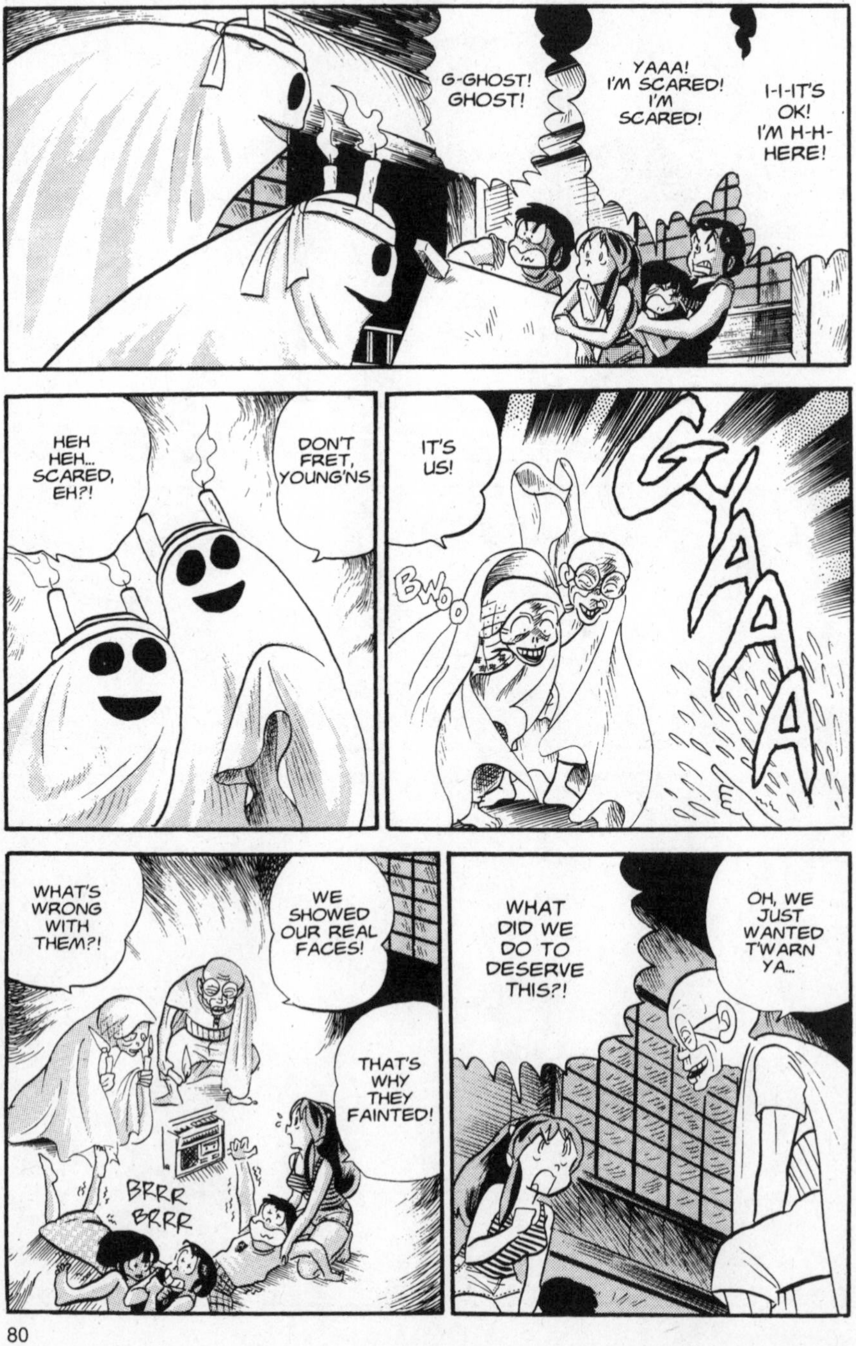
G-GHOST! GHOST!
YAAA! I'M SCARED! I'M SCARED!
I-I-IT'S OK! I'M H-H-HERE!
HEH HEH... SCARED, EH?!
DON'T FRET, YOUNG'NS
IT'S US!
BWOO
GYAAAA
WHAT'S WRONG WITH THEM?!
WE SHOWED OUR REAL FACES!
THAT'S WHY THEY FAINTED!
BRRR BRRR
WHAT DID WE DO TO DESERVE THIS?!
OH, WE JUST WANTED T'WARN YA...

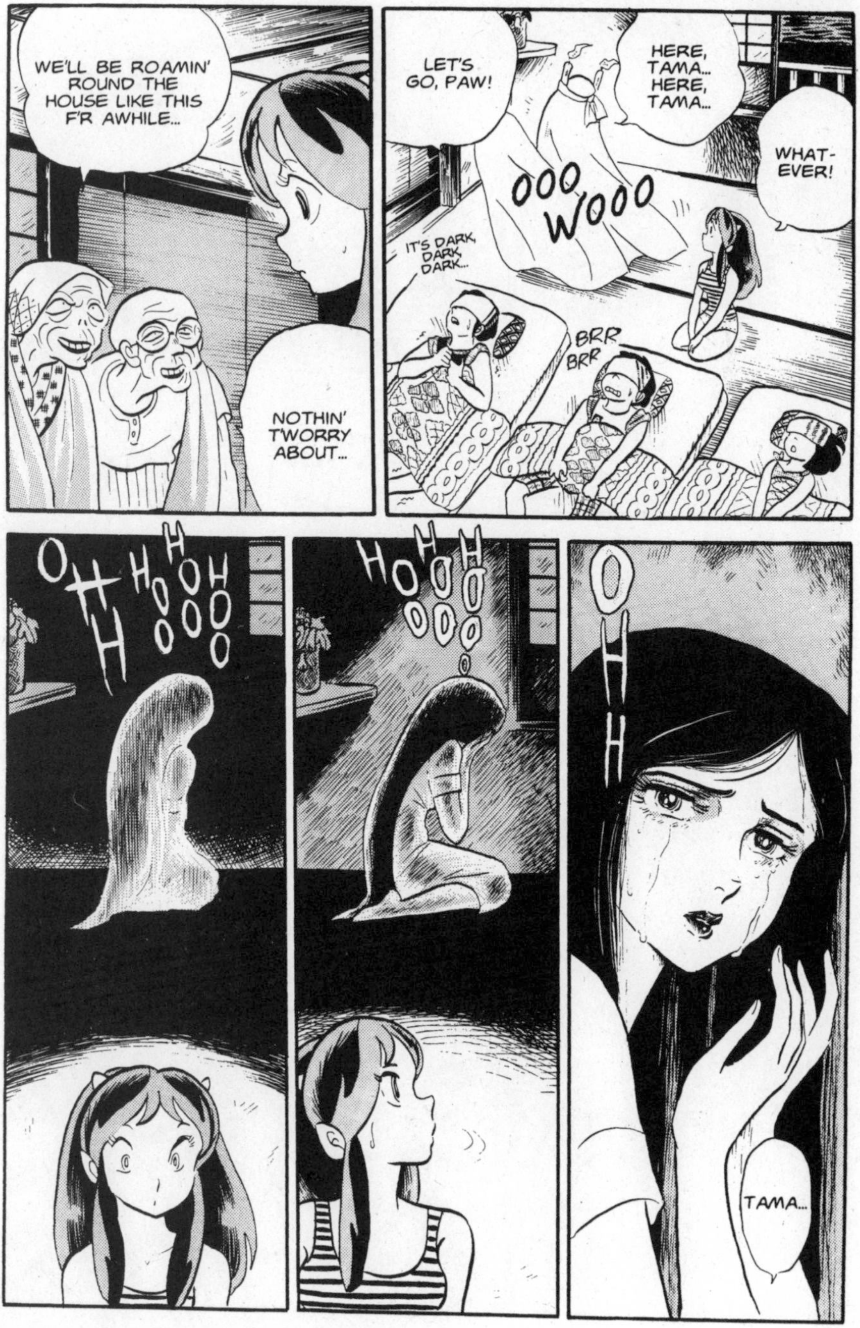
WE'LL BE ROAMIN' ROUND THE HOUSE LIKE THIS F'R AWHILE...
NOTHIN' TWORRY ABOUT...
LET'S GO, PAW!
HERE, TAMA... HERE, TAMA...
WHAT-EVER!
OOO WOOO
IT'S DARK, DARK, DARK...
BRR BRR
OHHHOHOHOHOOO
HOHHOOOOHHOOO
OHHH
TAMA...

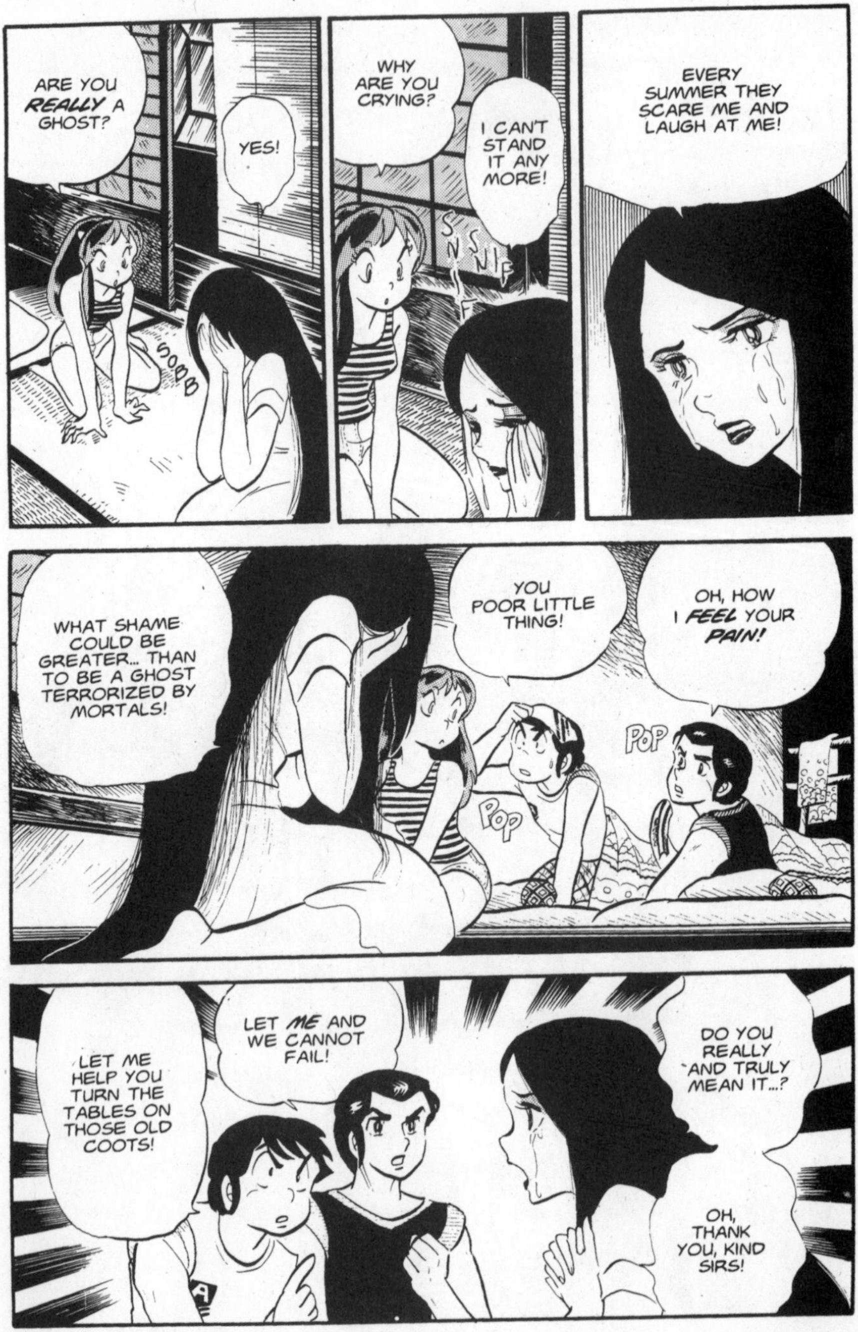
ARE YOU *REALLY* A GHOST?
YES!
SOBB
WHY ARE YOU CRYING?
I CAN'T STAND IT ANY MORE!
EVERY SUMMER THEY SCARE ME AND LAUGH AT ME!
WHAT SHAME COULD BE GREATER... THAN TO BE A GHOST TERRORIZED BY MORTALS!
YOU POOR LITTLE THING!
OH, HOW I *FEEL* YOUR *PAIN!*
POP
POP
LET ME HELP YOU TURN THE TABLES ON THOSE OLD COOTS!
LET *ME* AND WE CANNOT FAIL!
DO YOU REALLY AND TRULY MEAN IT...?
OH, THANK YOU, KIND SIRS!

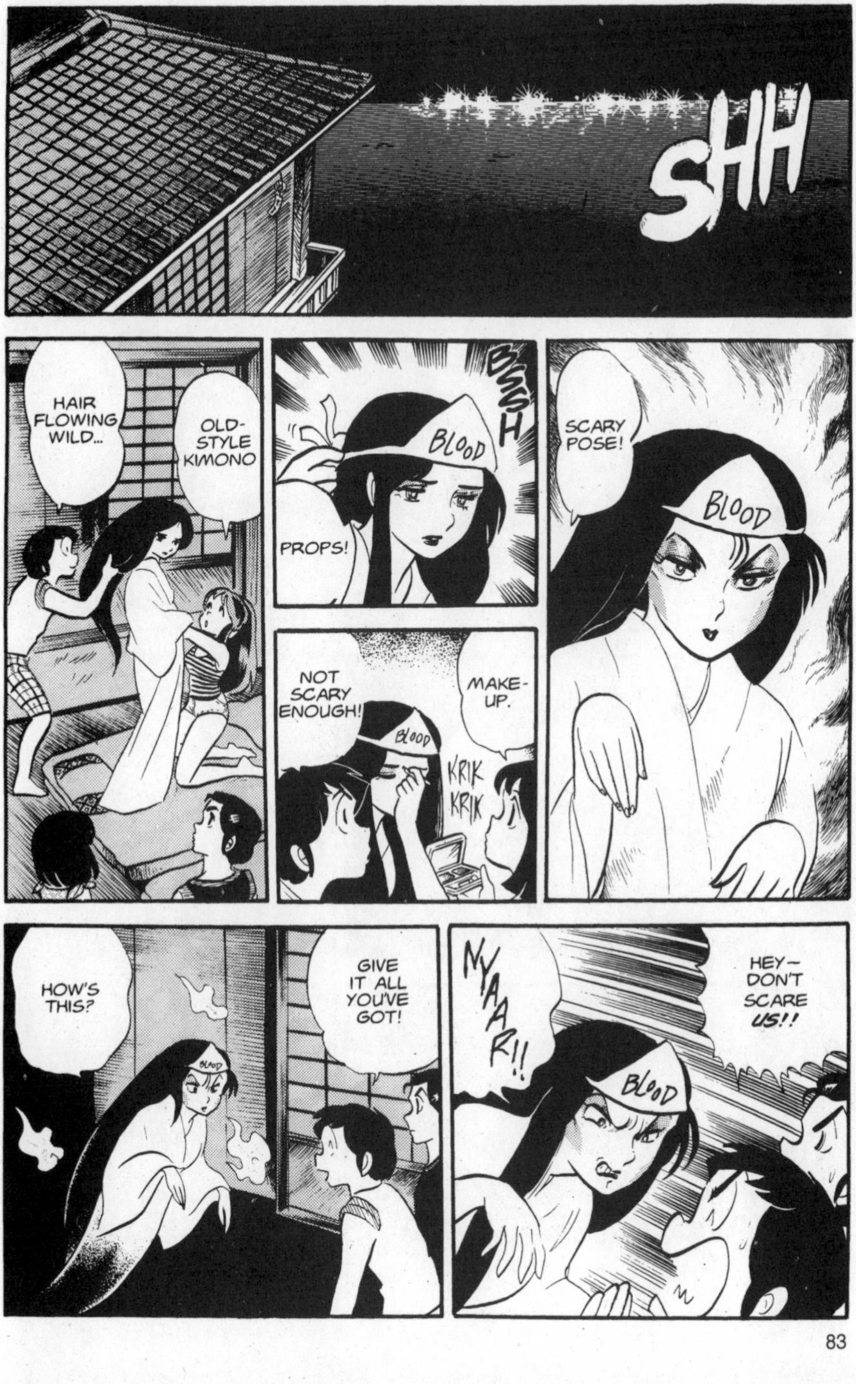
SHH
HAIR FLOWING WILD...
OLD-STYLE KIMONO
BSSH
BLOOD
PROPS!
SCARY POSE!
BLOOD
NOT SCARY ENOUGH!
MAKE-UP.
BLOOD
KRIK KRIK
HOW'S THIS?
BLOOD
GIVE IT ALL YOU'VE GOT!
NYAAAR!!
BLOOD
HEY—DON'T SCARE *US!!*

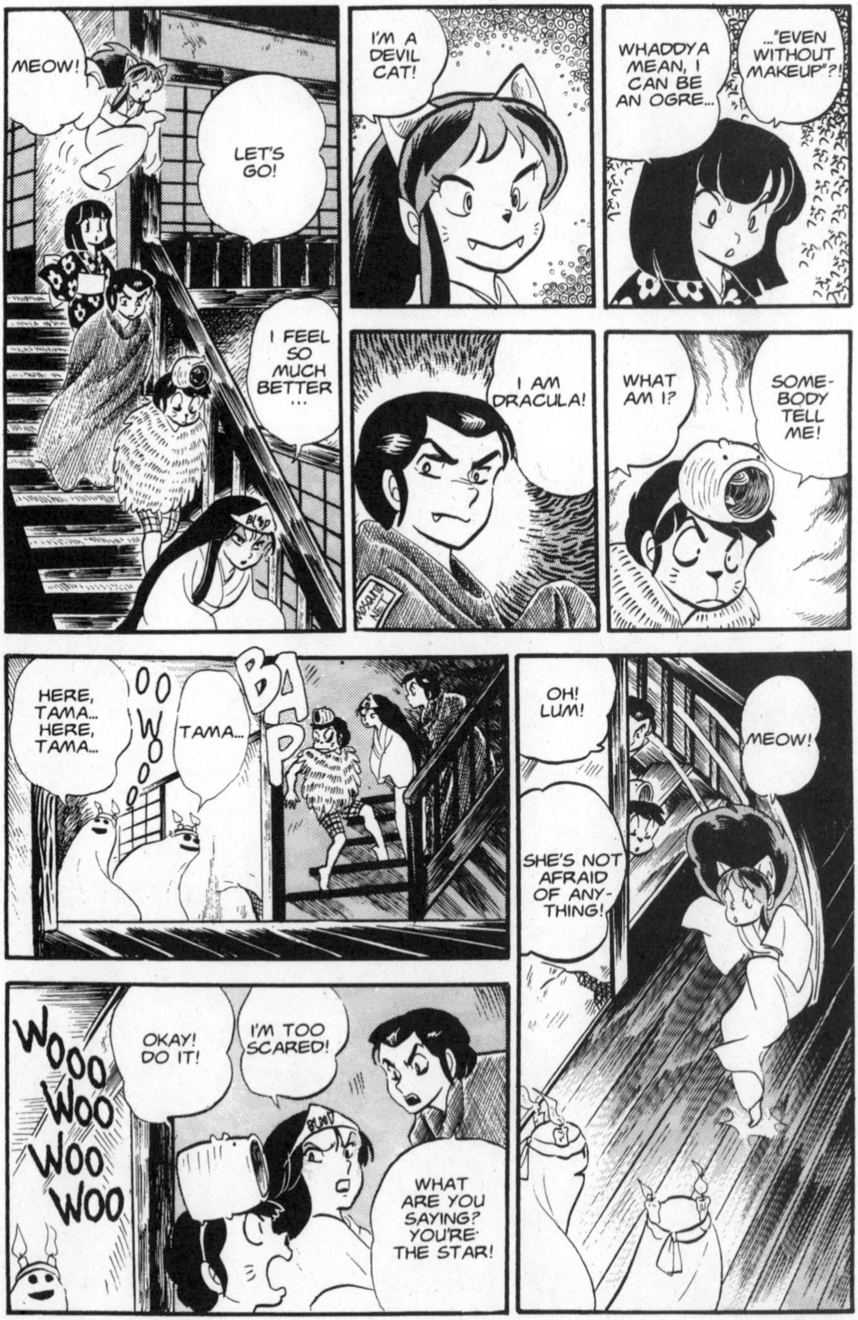
MEOW!
LET'S GO!
I FEEL SO MUCH BETTER...
I'M A DEVIL CAT!
WHADDYA MEAN, I CAN BE AN OGRE...
..."EVEN WITHOUT MAKEUP"?!
I AM DRACULA!
MOSQUITO NET
WHAT AM I?
SOMEBODY TELL ME!
HERE, TAMA... HERE, TAMA...
OOWOOOO
TAMA...
BAP
WOOO WOO WOO WOO
OKAY! DO IT!
I'M TOO SCARED!
WHAT ARE YOU SAYING? YOU'RE THE STAR!
OH! LUM!
MEOW!
SHE'S NOT AFRAID OF ANYTHING!

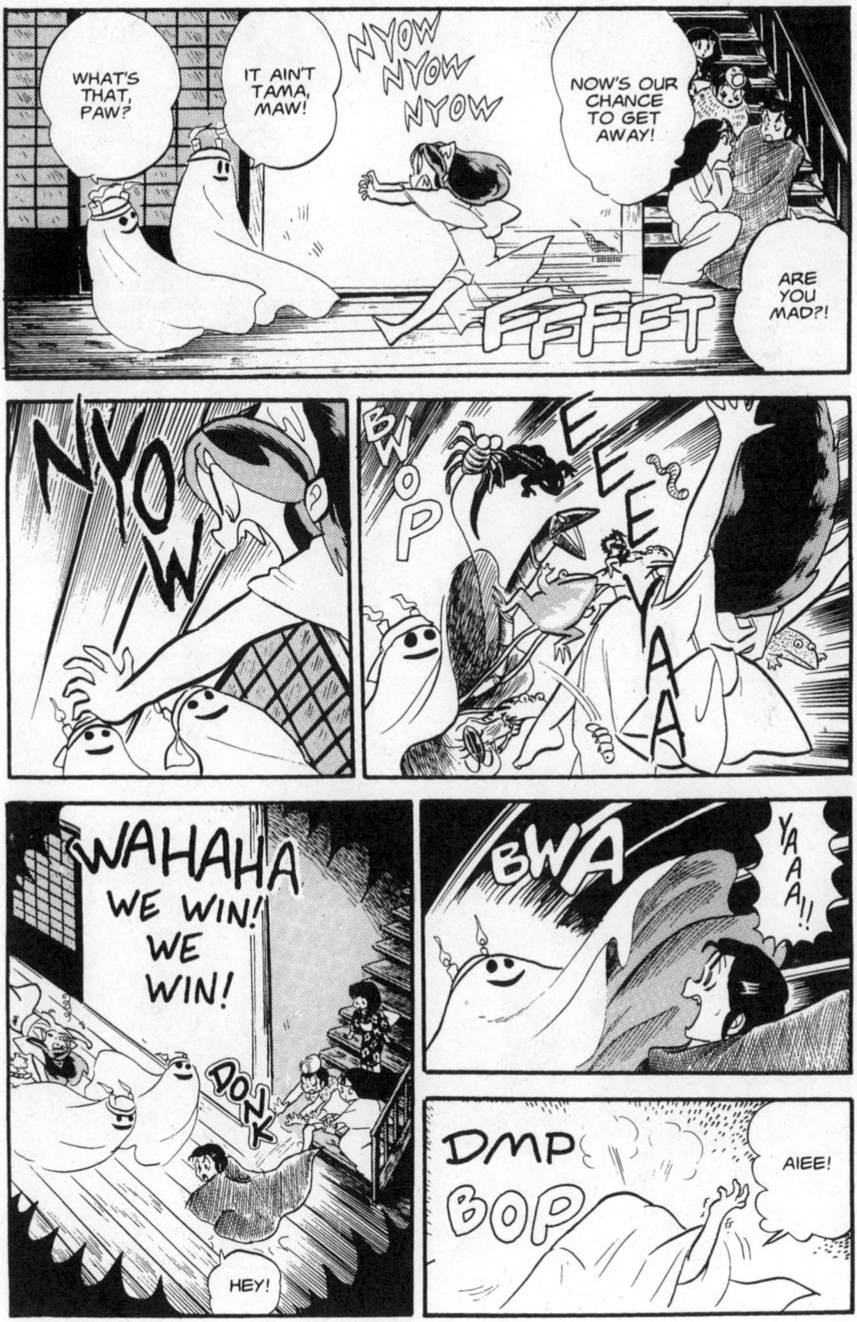
WHAT'S THAT, PAW?
IT AIN'T TAMA, MAW!
NYOW NYOW NYOW
NOW'S OUR CHANCE TO GET AWAY!
ARE YOU MAD?!
FFFFT
NYOWW
BWOP
EEEYAAA
WAHAHA
WE WIN! WE WIN!
DONK
HEY!
BWA
YAAAA!!
DMP
BOP
AIEE!

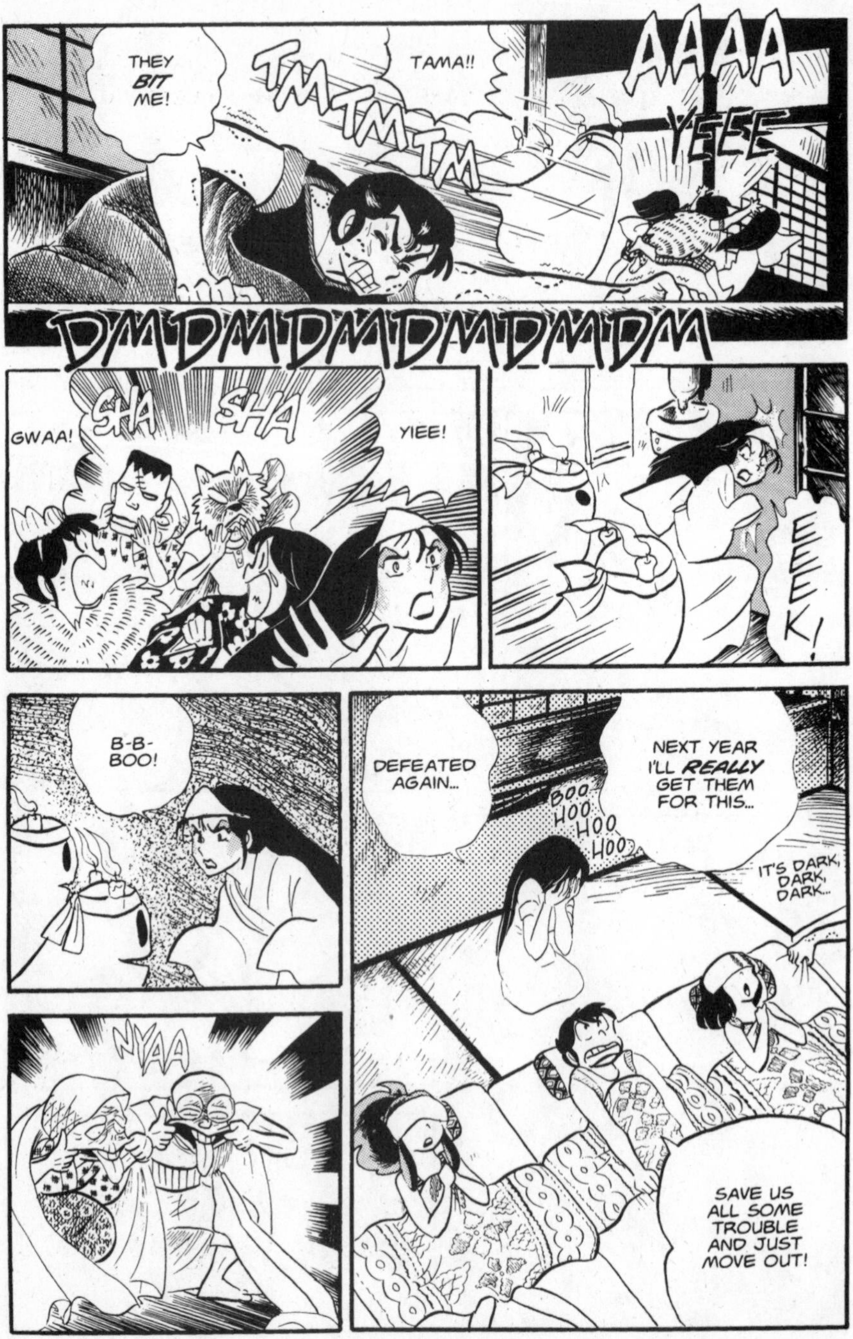

THEY BIT ME!
TMTMTMTM
TAMA!!
AAAA YEEE
DMDMDMDMDMDMDM
SHA SHA
GWAA!
YIEE!
EEEEK!
B-B-BOO!
NYAA
DEFEATED AGAIN...
BOO HOO HOO HOO
NEXT YEAR I'LL REALLY GET THEM FOR THIS...
IT'S DARK, DARK, DARK...
SAVE US ALL SOME TROUBLE AND JUST MOVE OUT!

PART SIX
UNFINISHED BUSINESS

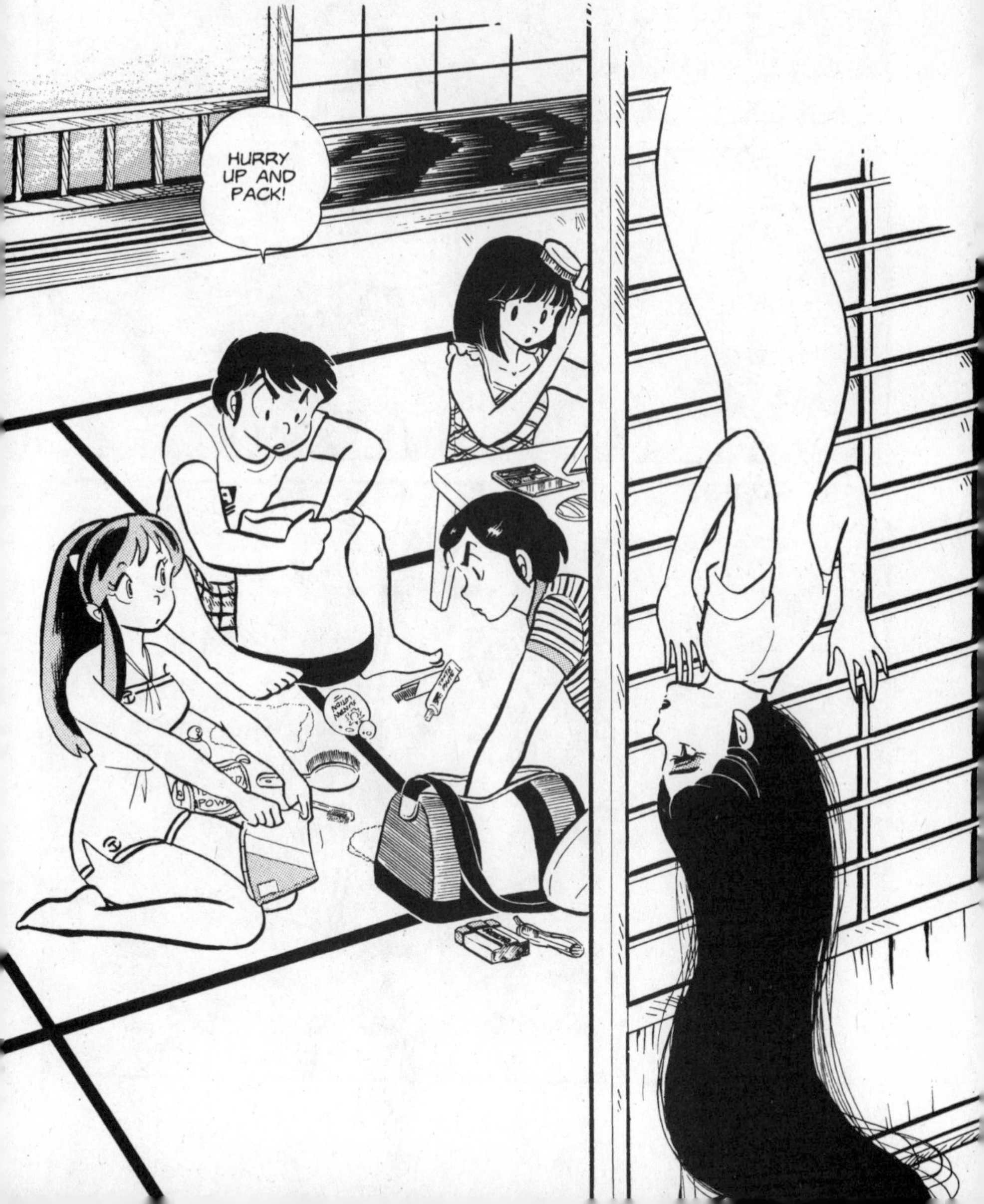
HURRY UP AND PACK!

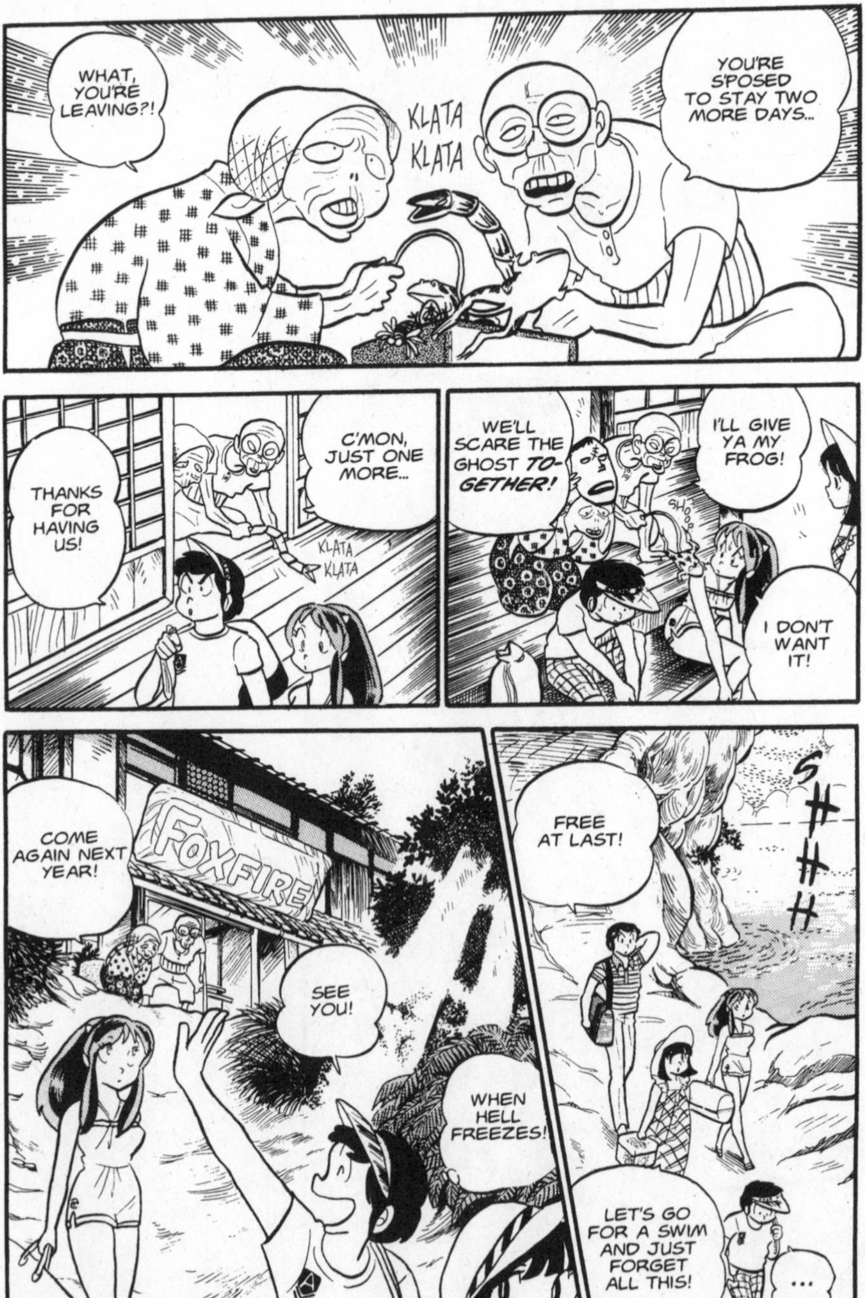
WHAT, YOU'RE LEAVING?!
KLATA KLATA
YOU'RE S'POSED TO STAY TWO MORE DAYS...
THANKS FOR HAVING US!
C'MON, JUST ONE MORE...
KLATA KLATA
WE'LL SCARE THE GHOST *TO-GETHER!*
I'LL GIVE YA MY FROG!
SHOOO
I DON'T WANT IT!
FOXFIRE
COME AGAIN NEXT YEAR!
SEE YOU!
WHEN HELL FREEZES!
FREE AT LAST!
SHHHH
LET'S GO FOR A SWIM AND JUST FORGET ALL THIS!
...

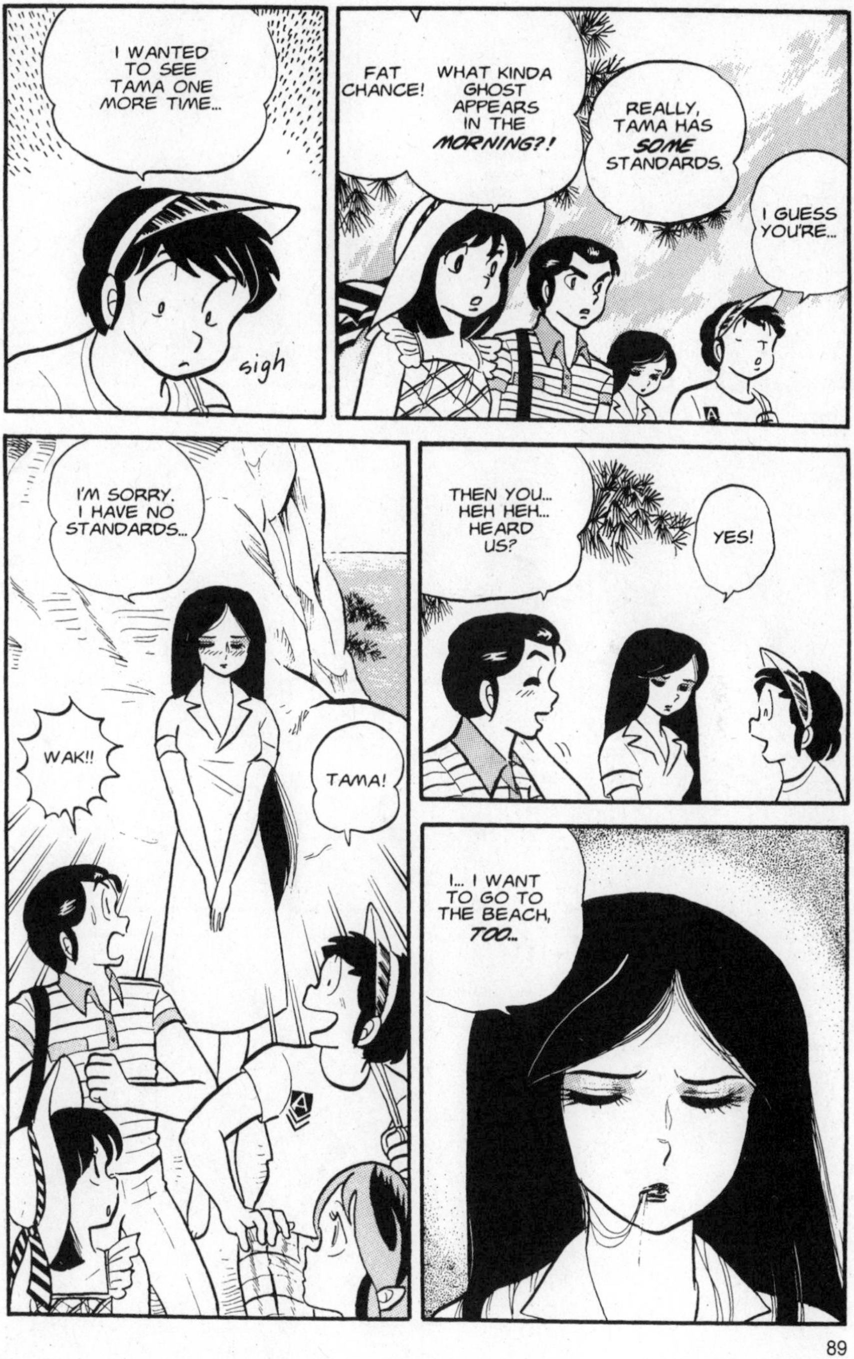
I WANTED TO SEE TAMA ONE MORE TIME...
sigh
FAT CHANCE!
WHAT KINDA GHOST APPEARS IN THE MORNING?!
REALLY, TAMA HAS SOME STANDARDS.
I GUESS YOU'RE...
I'M SORRY. I HAVE NO STANDARDS...
WAK!!
TAMA!
THEN YOU... HEH HEH... HEARD US?
YES!
I... I WANT TO GO TO THE BEACH, TOO...

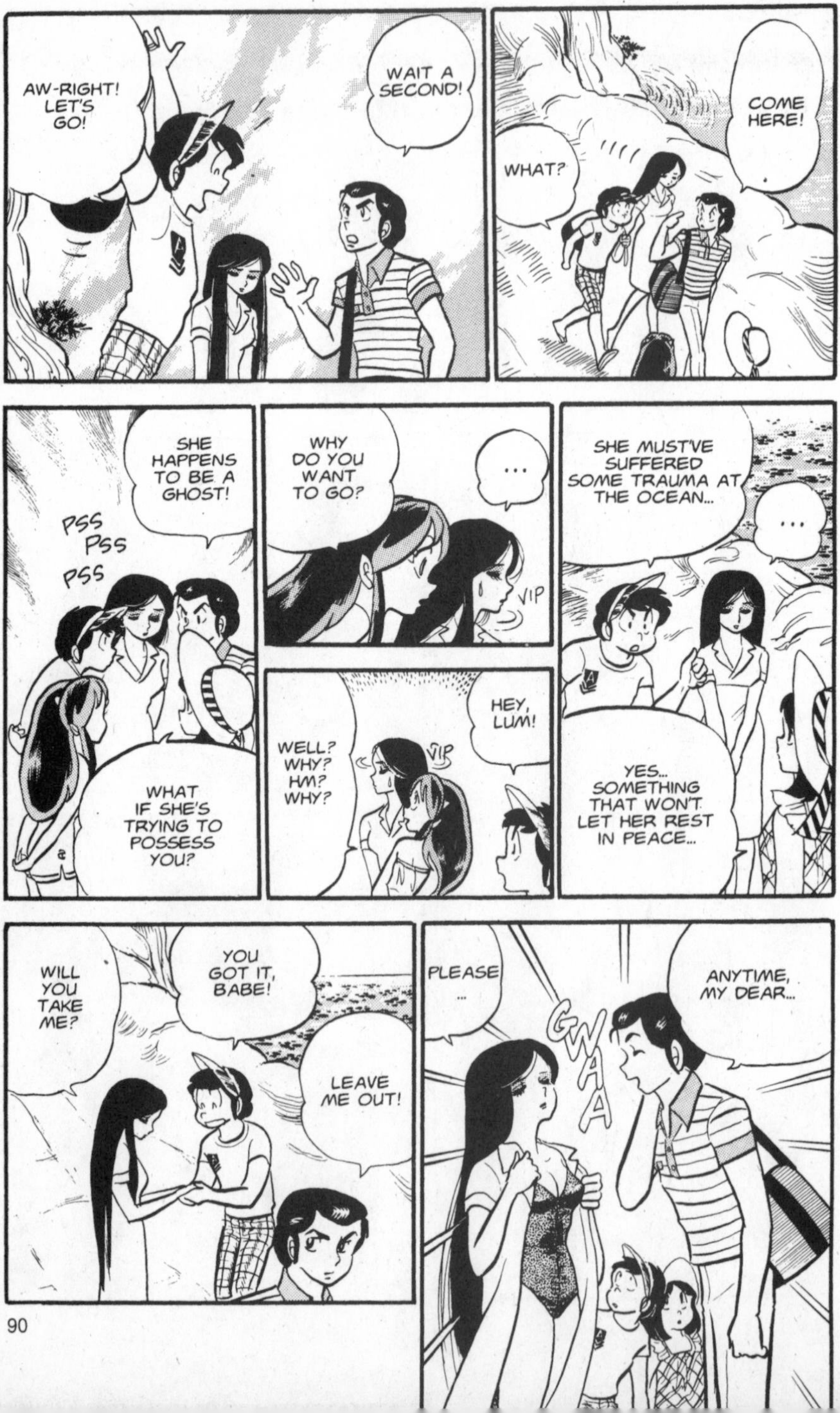
AW-RIGHT! LET'S GO!
WAIT A SECOND!
WHAT?
COME HERE!
SHE HAPPENS TO BE A GHOST!
PSS PSS PSS
WHAT IF SHE'S TRYING TO POSSESS YOU?
WHY DO YOU WANT TO GO?
...
VIP
SHE MUST'VE SUFFERED SOME TRAUMA AT THE OCEAN...
...
YES... SOMETHING THAT WON'T LET HER REST IN PEACE...
HEY, LUM!
WELL? WHY? HM? WHY?
VIP
WILL YOU TAKE ME?
YOU GOT IT, BABE!
LEAVE ME OUT!
PLEASE ...
ANYTIME, MY DEAR...
GWAA

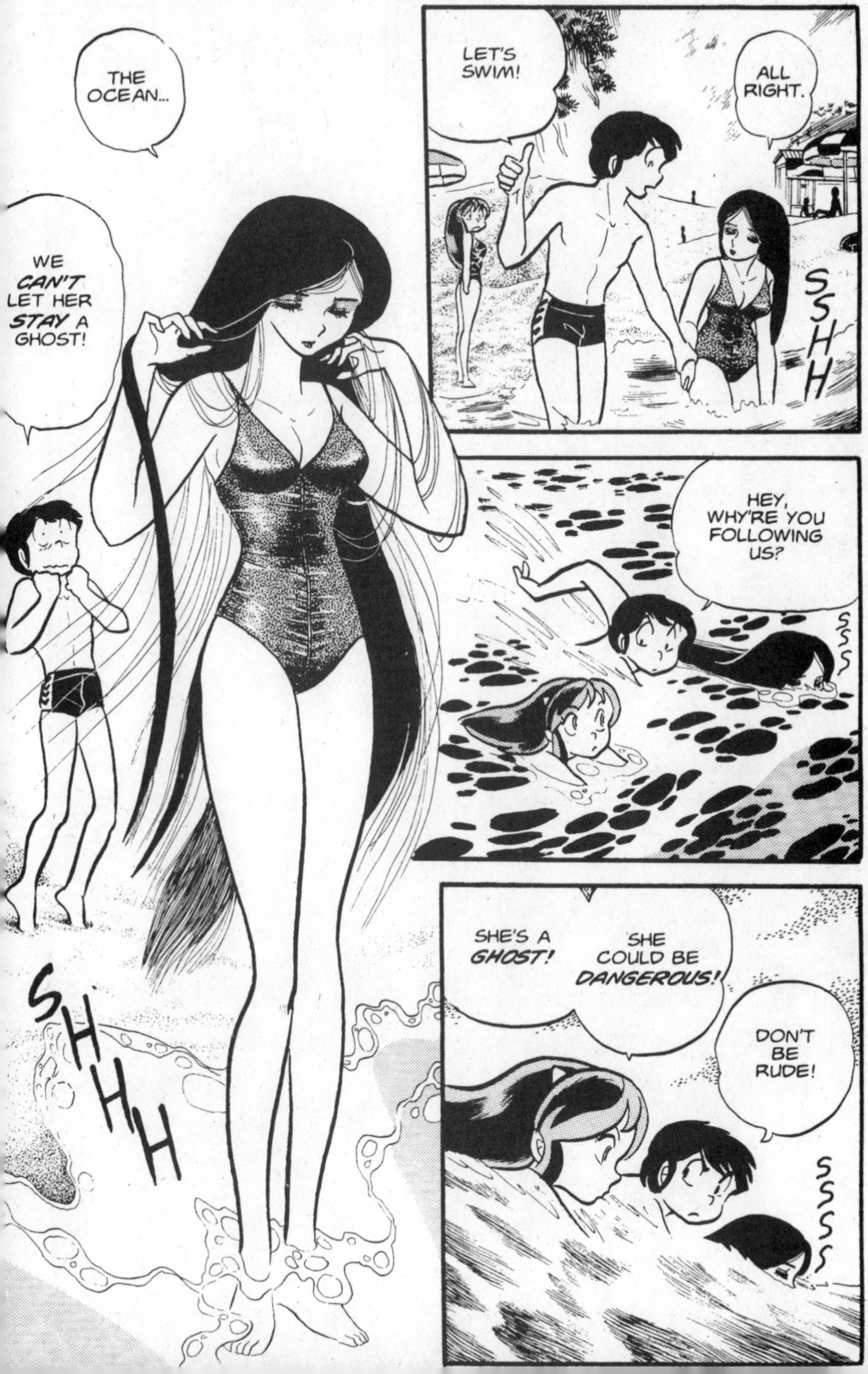
THE OCEAN...
WE *CAN'T* LET HER *STAY* A GHOST!
SHHHH
LET'S SWIM!
ALL RIGHT.
SSHH
HEY, WHY'RE YOU FOLLOWING US?
SSS
SHE'S A *GHOST!*
SHE COULD BE *DANGEROUS!*
DON'T BE RUDE!
SSSS

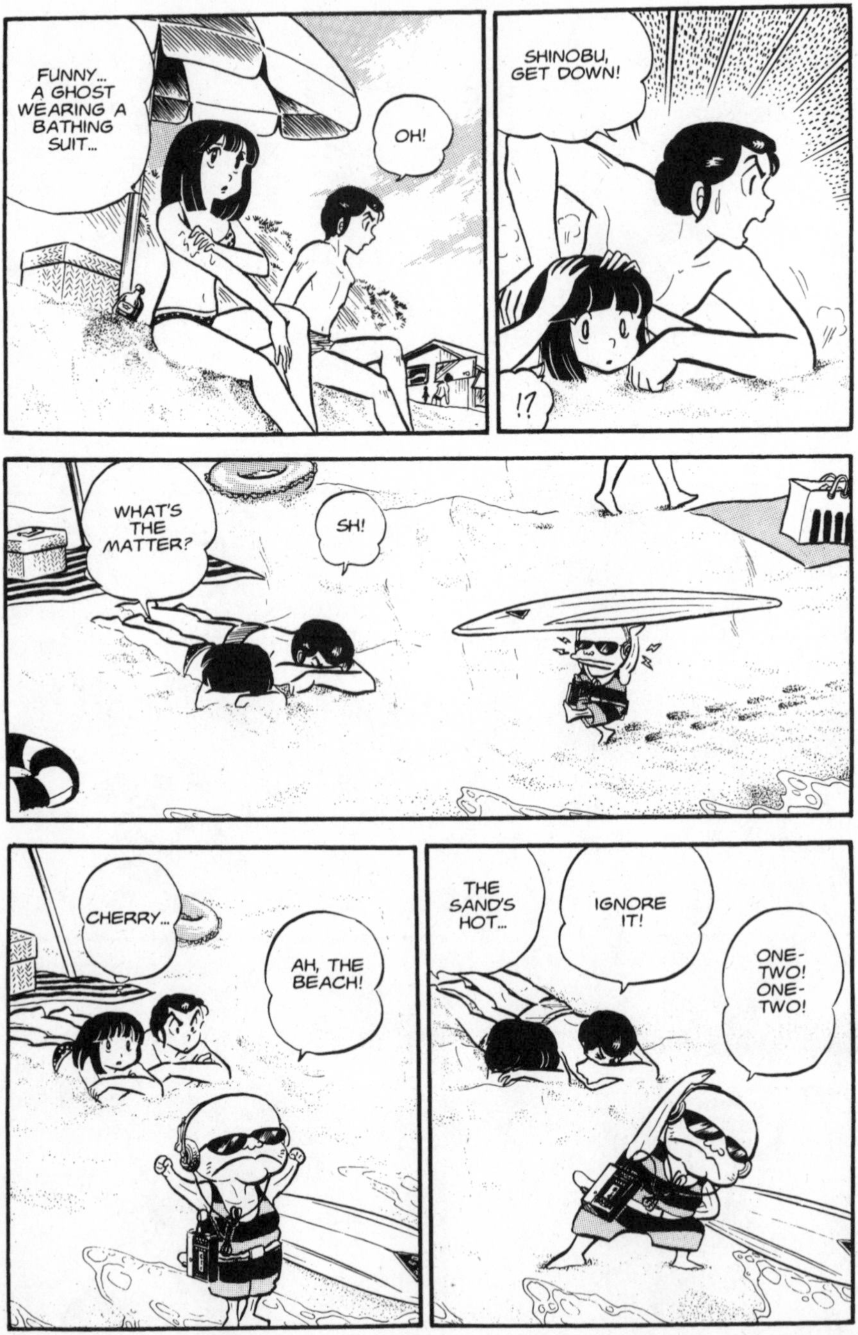
FUNNY... A GHOST WEARING A BATHING SUIT...
OH!
SHINOBU, GET DOWN!
!?
WHAT'S THE MATTER?
SH!
CHERRY...
AH, THE BEACH!
THE SAND'S HOT...
IGNORE IT!
ONE-TWO! ONE-TWO!

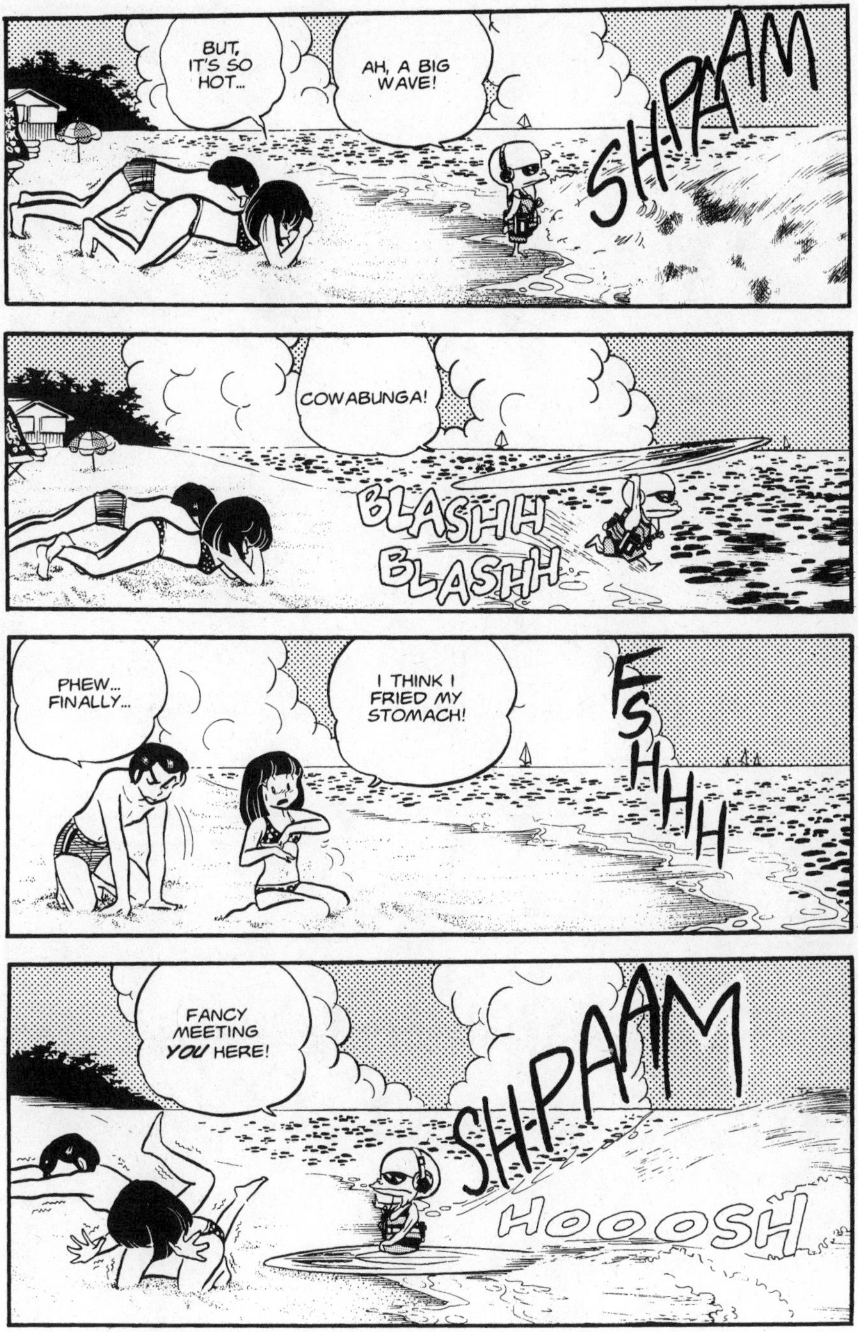
BUT, IT'S SO HOT...
AH, A BIG WAVE!
SH-PAAM
COWABUNGA!
BLASHH BLASHH
PHEW... FINALLY...
I THINK I FRIED MY STOMACH!
FSHHHH
FANCY MEETING *YOU* HERE!
SH-PAAM
HOOOSH

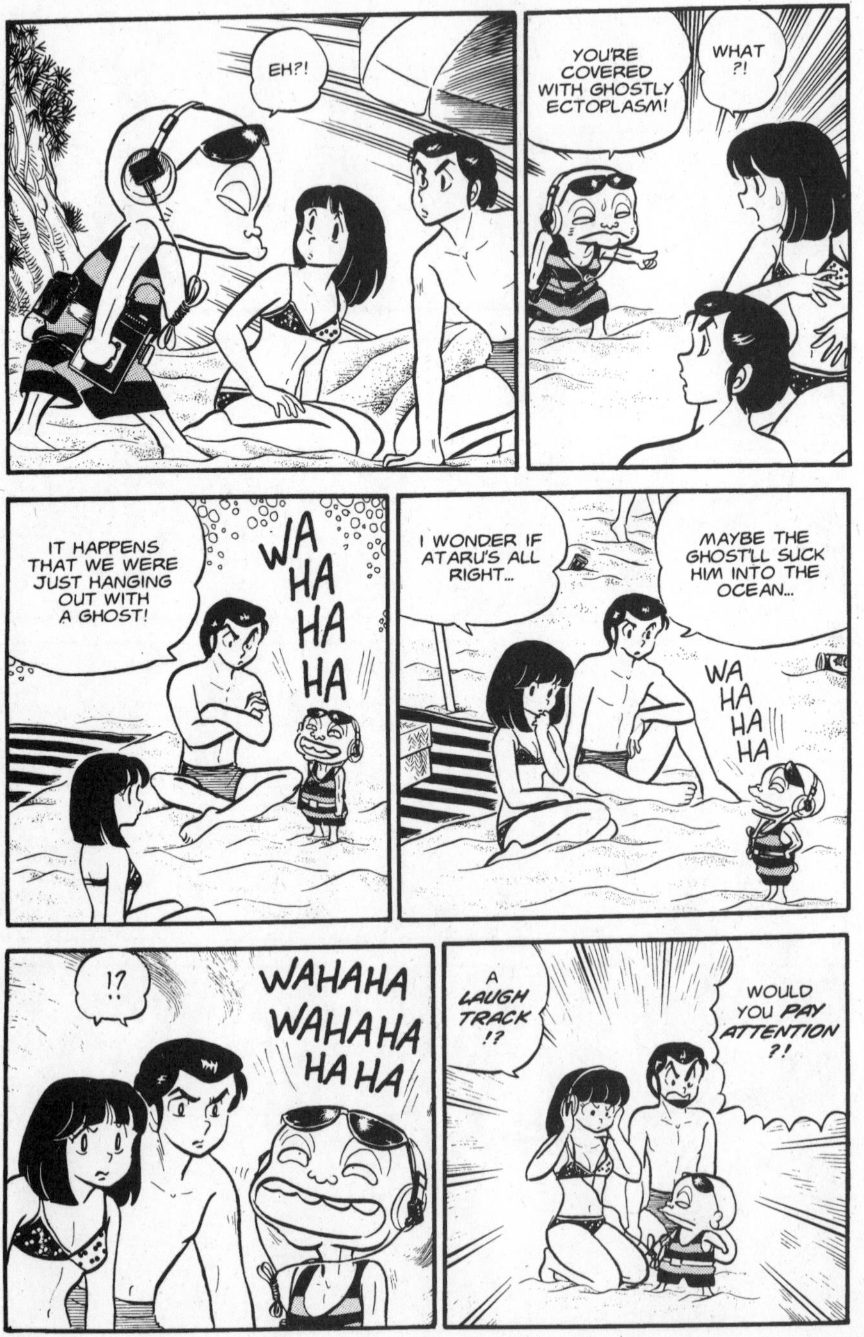
EH?!
YOU'RE COVERED WITH GHOSTLY ECTOPLASM!
WHAT ?!
IT HAPPENS THAT WE WERE JUST HANGING OUT WITH A GHOST!
WA HA HA HA
I WONDER IF ATARU'S ALL RIGHT...
MAYBE THE GHOST'LL SUCK HIM INTO THE OCEAN...
WA HA HA HA
!?
WAHAHA WAHAHA HAHA
A LAUGH TRACK !?
WOULD YOU PAY ATTENTION ?!

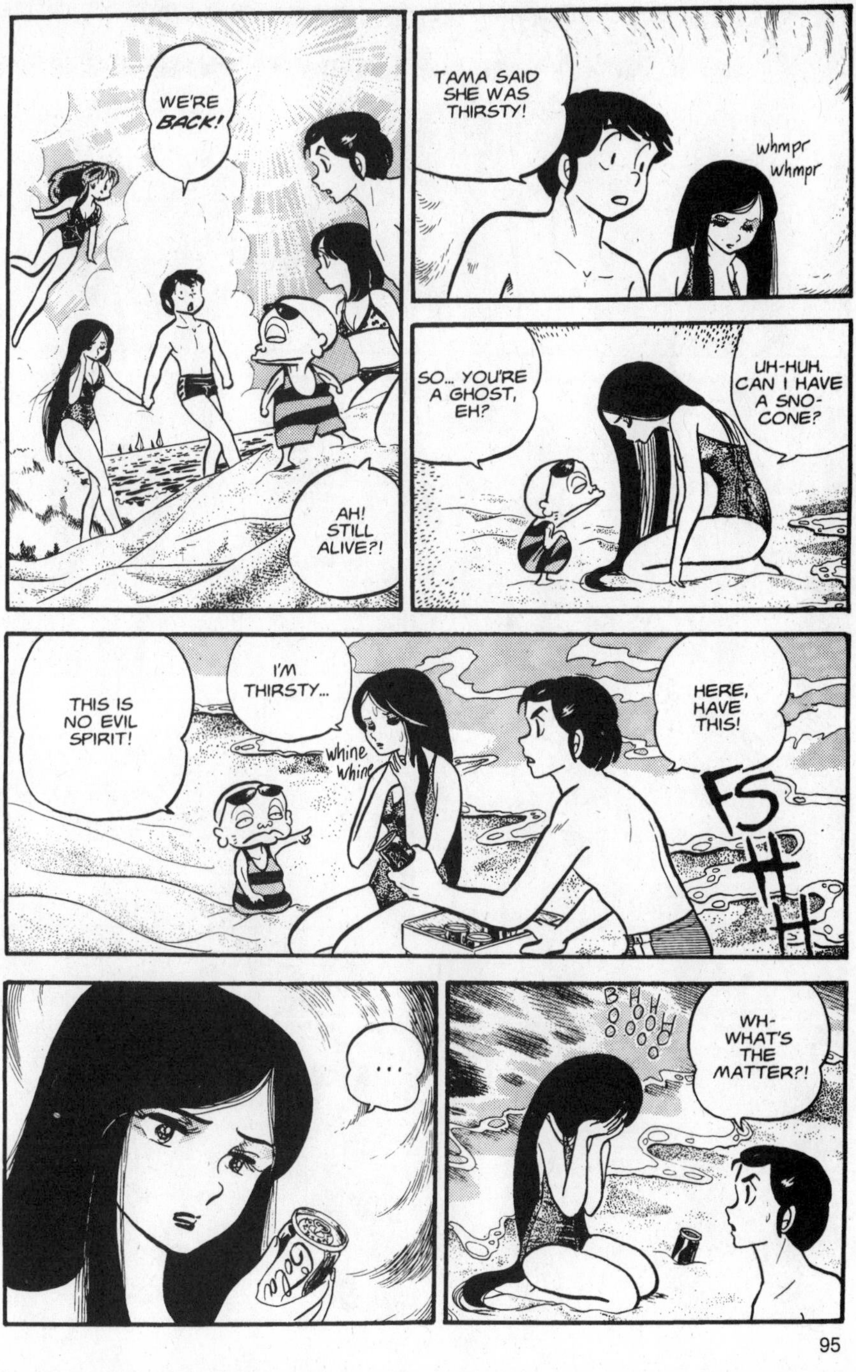
WE'RE *BACK!*
AH! STILL ALIVE?!
TAMA SAID SHE WAS THIRSTY!
whmpr whmpr
SO... YOU'RE A GHOST, EH?
UH-HUH. CAN I HAVE A SNO-CONE?
THIS IS NO EVIL SPIRIT!
I'M THIRSTY...
whine whine
HERE, HAVE THIS!
FSHH
...
WH- WHAT'S THE MATTER?!

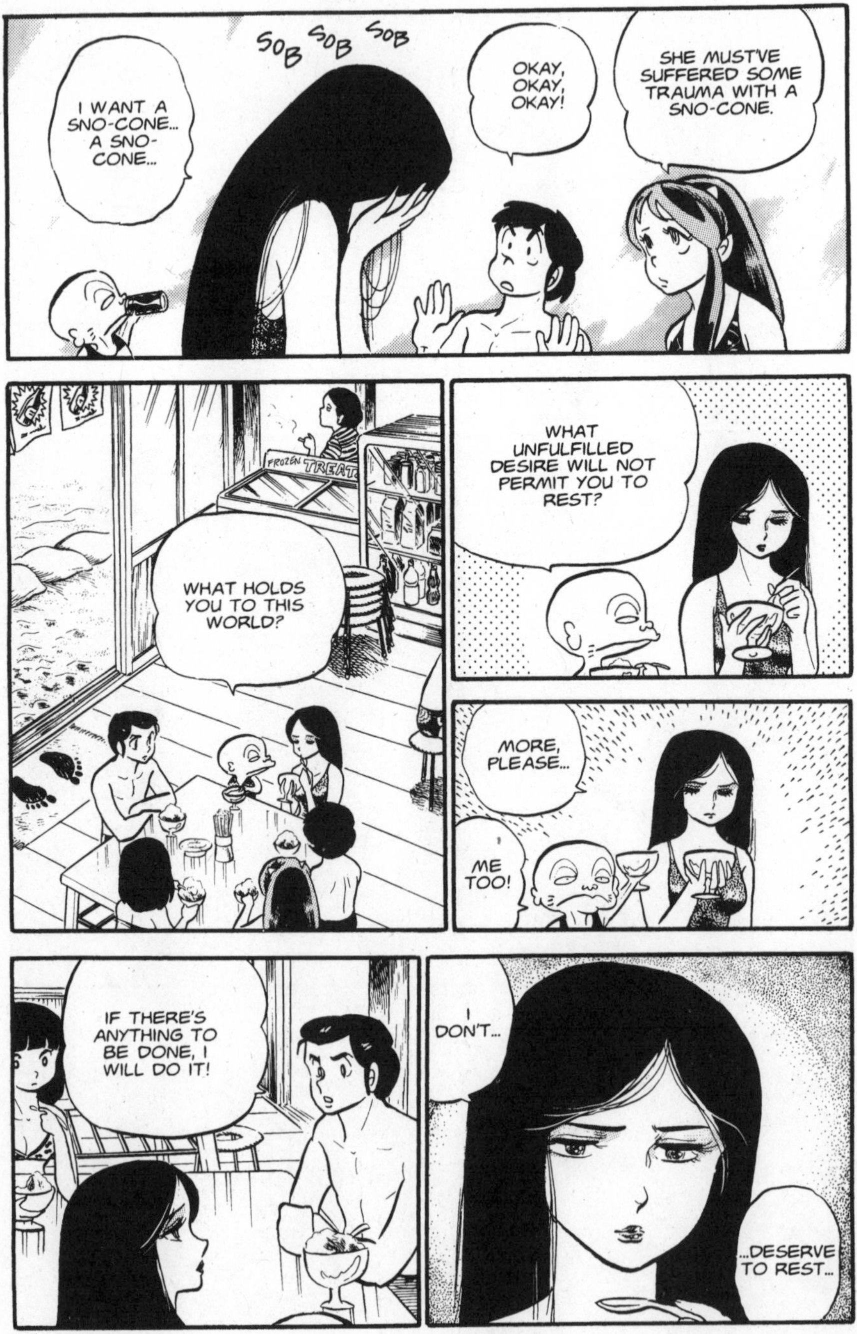
I WANT A SNO-CONE... A SNO-CONE...
SOB SOB SOB
OKAY, OKAY, OKAY!
SHE MUST'VE SUFFERED SOME TRAUMA WITH A SNO-CONE.
FROZEN TREAT
WHAT HOLDS YOU TO THIS WORLD?
WHAT UNFULFILLED DESIRE WILL NOT PERMIT YOU TO REST?
MORE, PLEASE...
ME TOO!
IF THERE'S ANYTHING TO BE DONE, I WILL DO IT!
I DON'T...
...DESERVE TO REST...

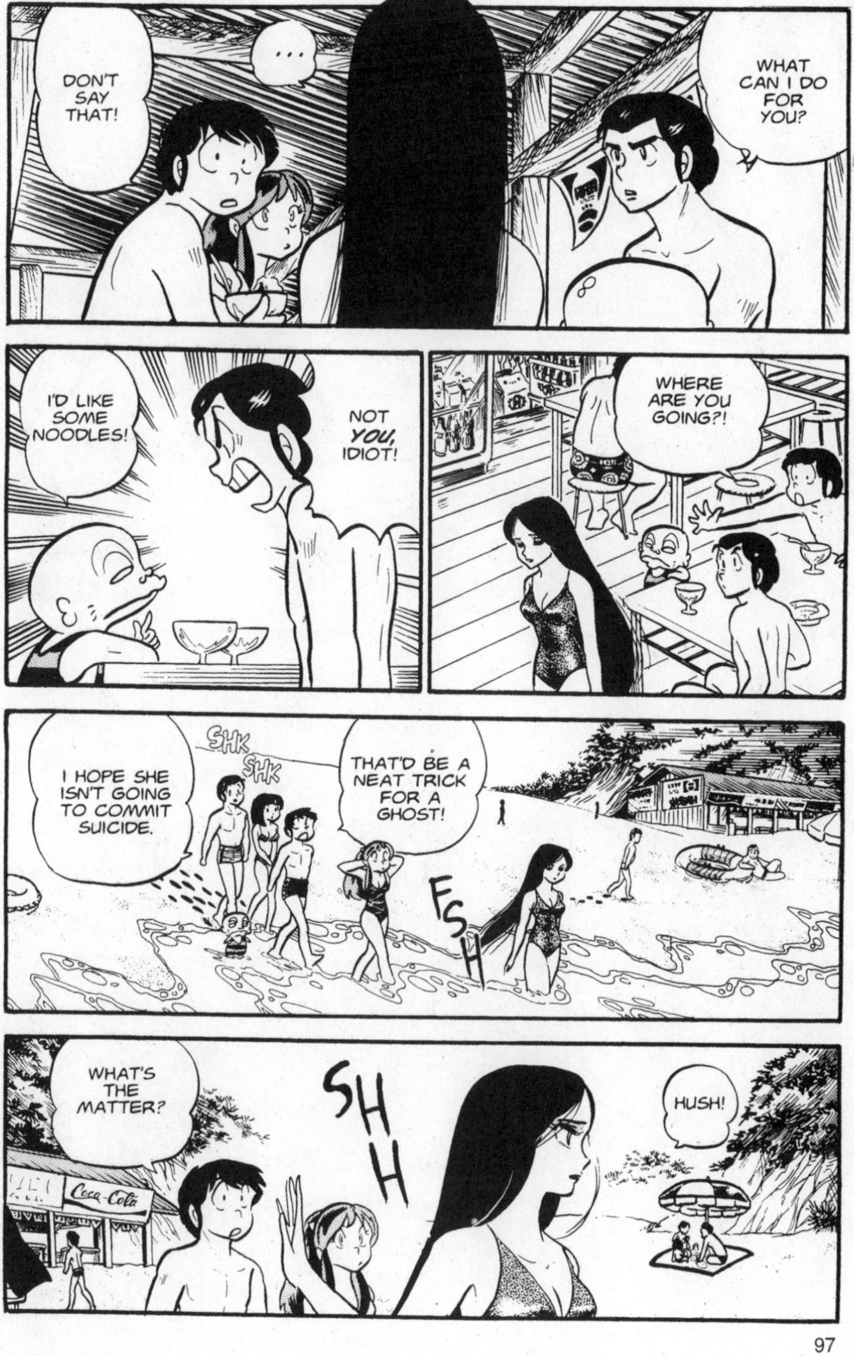
DON'T SAY THAT!
...
WHAT CAN I DO FOR YOU?
I'D LIKE SOME NOODLES!
NOT YOU, IDIOT!
WHERE ARE YOU GOING?!
I HOPE SHE ISN'T GOING TO COMMIT SUICIDE.
SHK SHK
THAT'D BE A NEAT TRICK FOR A GHOST!
FSH
WHAT'S THE MATTER?
SHH
HUSH!
Coca-Cola

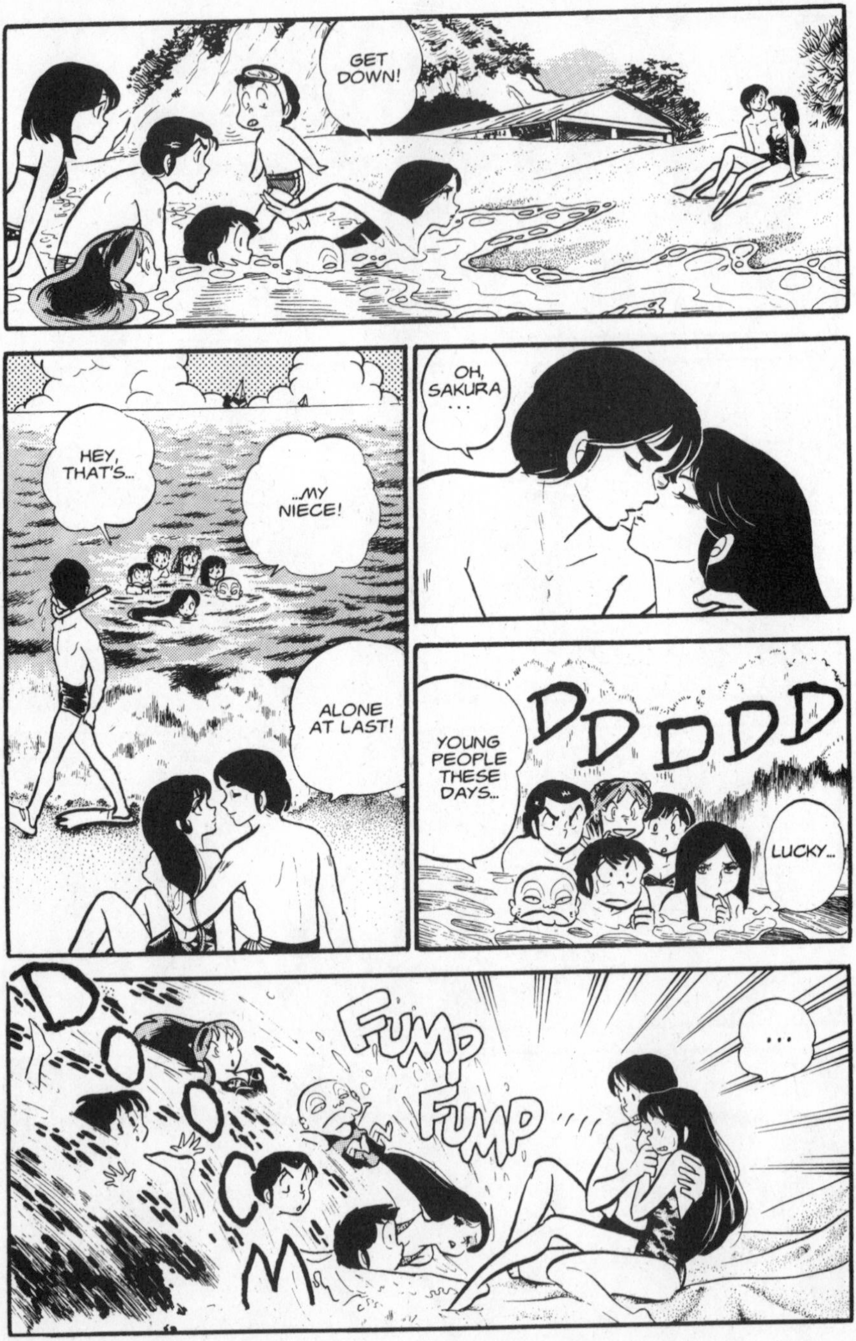
GET DOWN!
HEY, THAT'S...
...MY NIECE!
ALONE AT LAST!
OH, SAKURA ...
YOUNG PEOPLE THESE DAYS...
DDDDD
LUCKY...
DOOOM
FUMP
FUMP
...

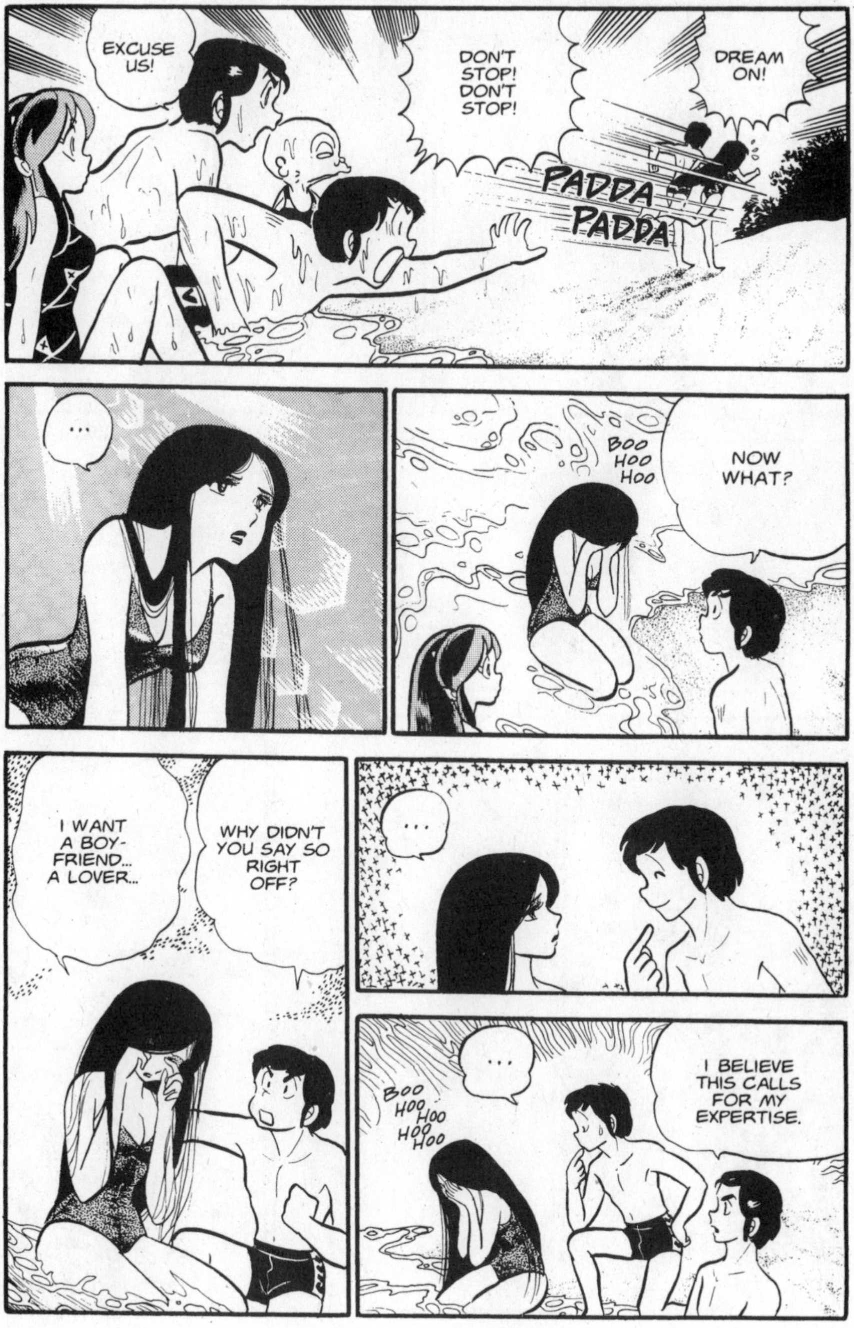
EXCUSE US!
DON'T STOP! DON'T STOP!
DREAM ON!
PADDA PADDA
...
BOO HOO HOO
NOW WHAT?
I WANT A BOY-FRIEND... A LOVER...
WHY DIDN'T YOU SAY SO RIGHT OFF?
...
...
BOO HOO HOO HOO HOO
I BELIEVE THIS CALLS FOR MY EXPERTISE.

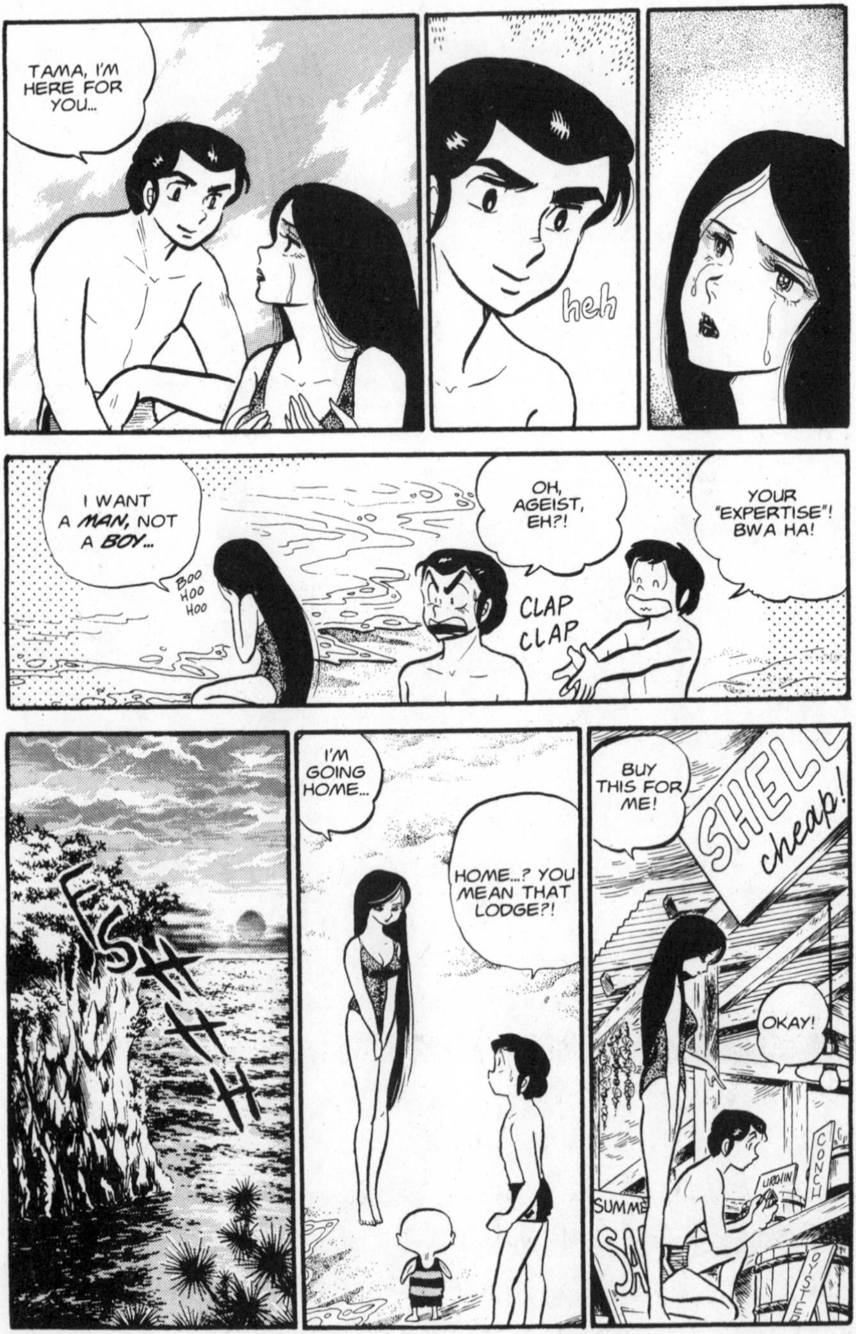
TAMA, I'M HERE FOR YOU...
heh
I WANT A *MAN*, NOT A *BOY*...
BOO HOO HOO
OH, AGEIST, EH?!
CLAP CLAP
YOUR "EXPERTISE"! BWA HA!
FSHHH
I'M GOING HOME...
HOME...? YOU MEAN THAT LODGE?!
BUY THIS FOR ME!
cheap!
OKAY!
URCHIN
CONCH

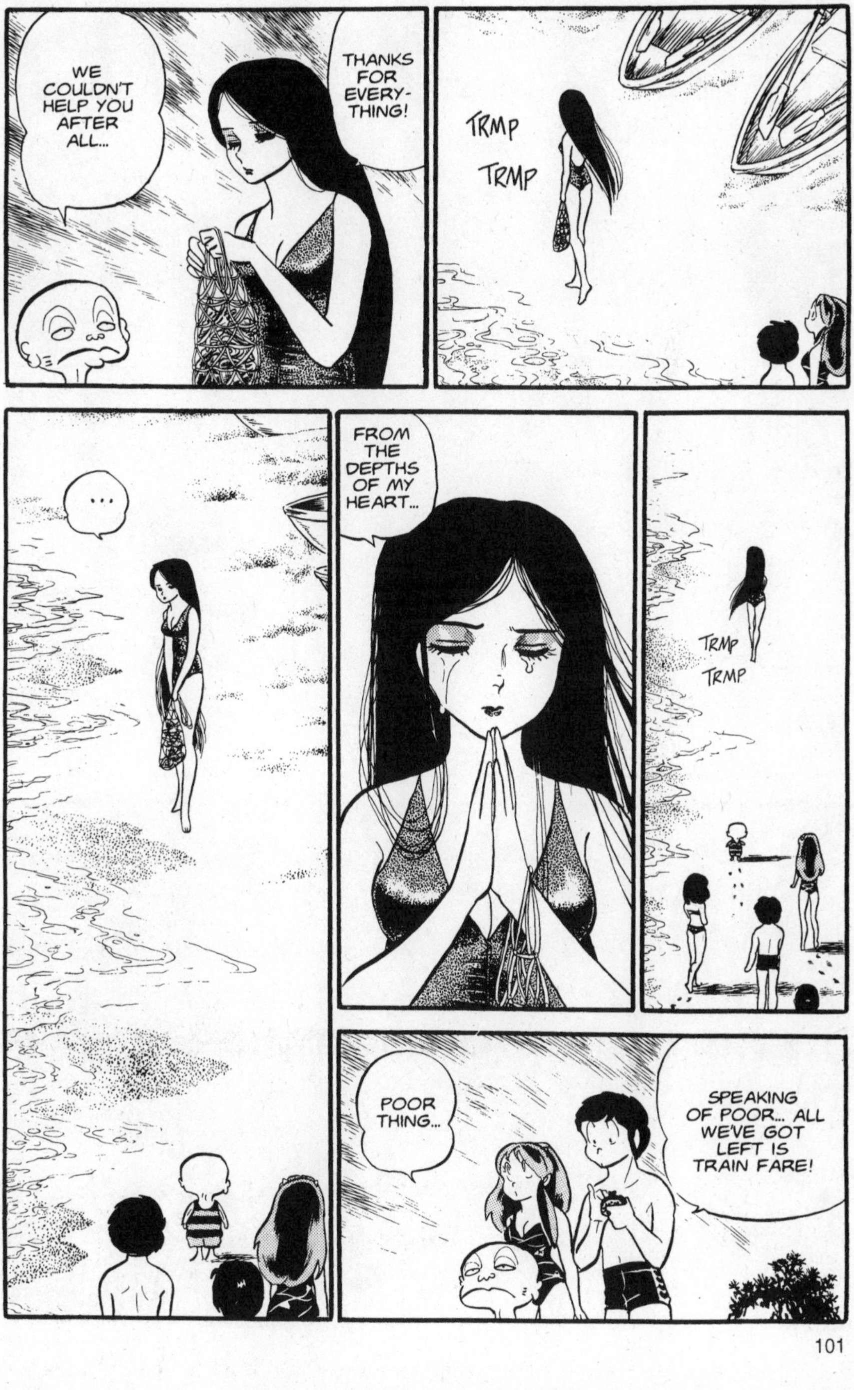
WE COULDN'T HELP YOU AFTER ALL...
THANKS FOR EVERY-THING!
TRMP
TRMP
...
FROM THE DEPTHS OF MY HEART...
TRMP
TRMP
POOR THING...
SPEAKING OF POOR... ALL WE'VE GOT LEFT IS TRAIN FARE!

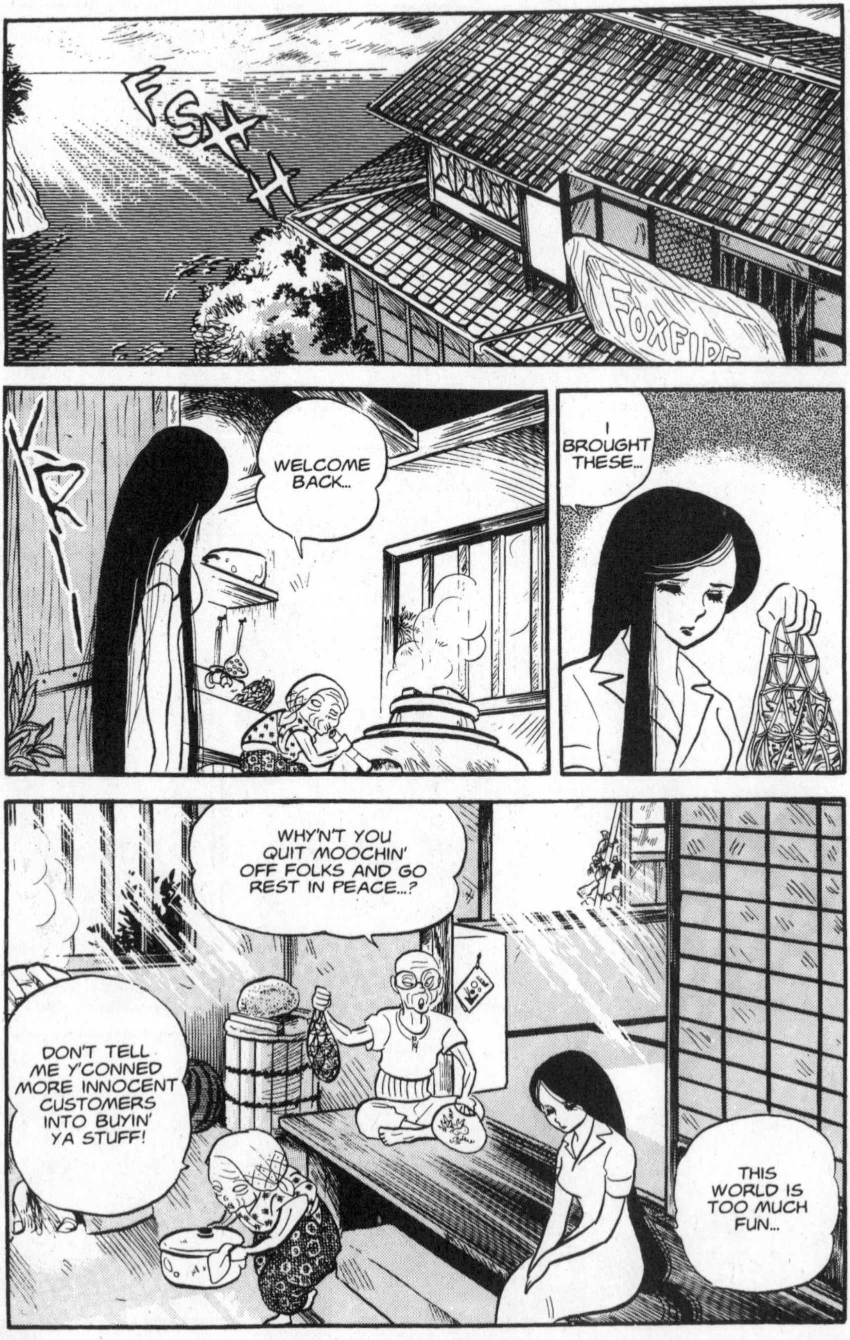
FSHH
FOXFIRE
KR
WELCOME BACK...
I BROUGHT THESE...
WHY'N'T YOU QUIT MOOCHIN' OFF FOLKS AND GO REST IN PEACE...?
DON'T TELL ME Y'CONNED MORE INNOCENT CUSTOMERS INTO BUYIN' YA STUFF!
THIS WORLD IS TOO MUCH FUN...

PART SEVEN
THE HORROR OF PARTY BEACH

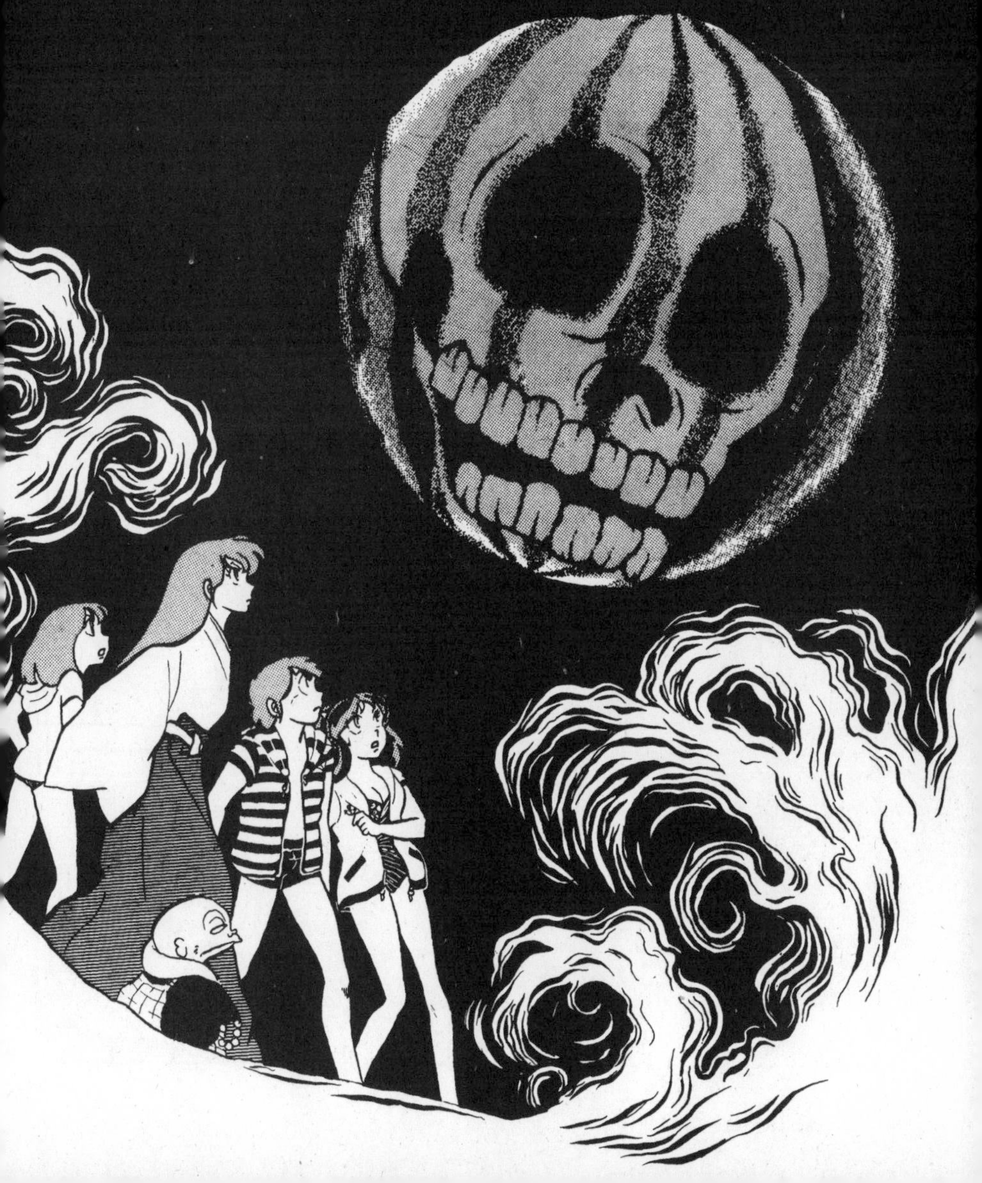

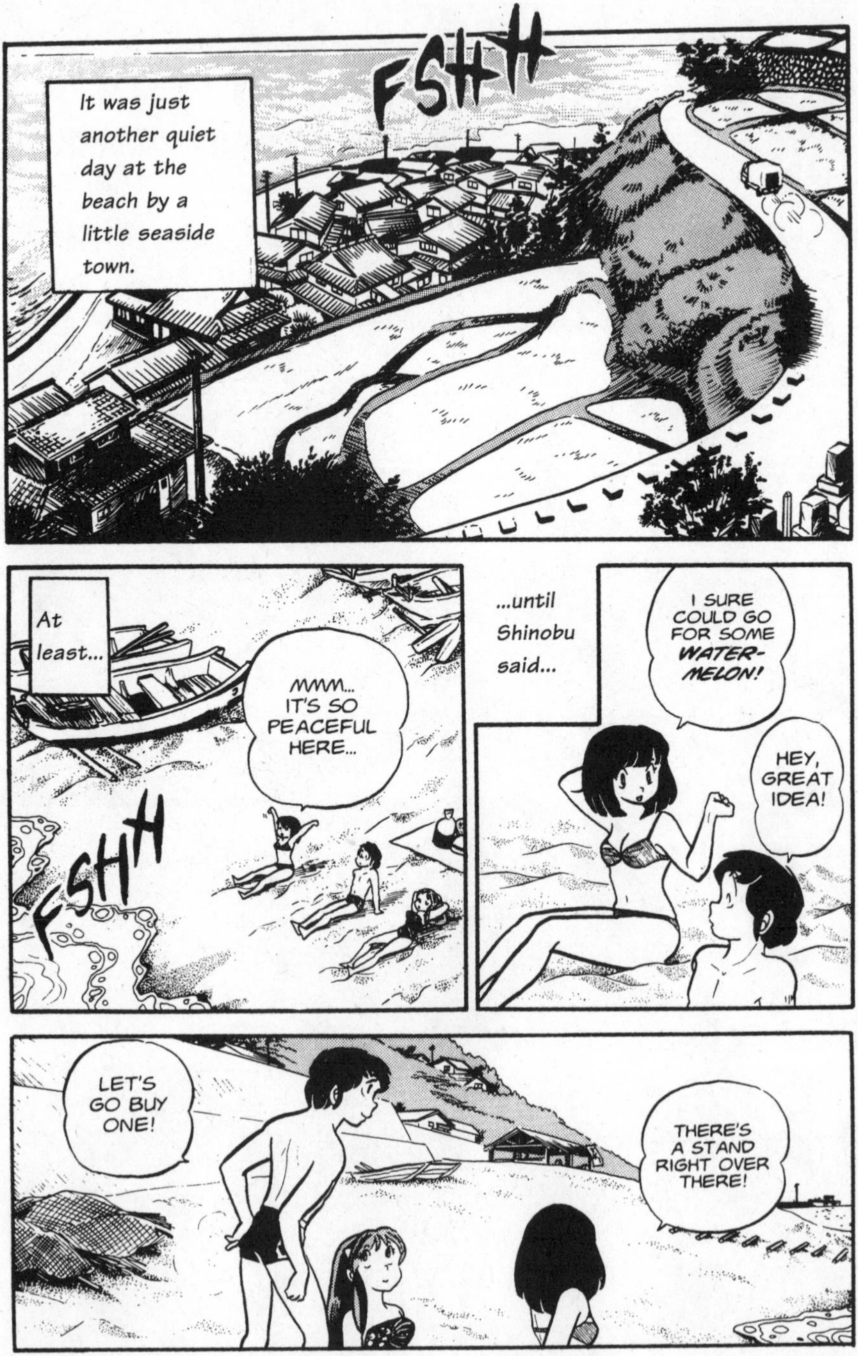
It was just another quiet day at the beach by a little seaside town.
FSHH
At least...
MMM... IT'S SO PEACEFUL HERE...
FSHH
...until Shinobu said...
I SURE COULD GO FOR SOME WATER-MELON!
HEY, GREAT IDEA!
LET'S GO BUY ONE!
THERE'S A STAND RIGHT OVER THERE!

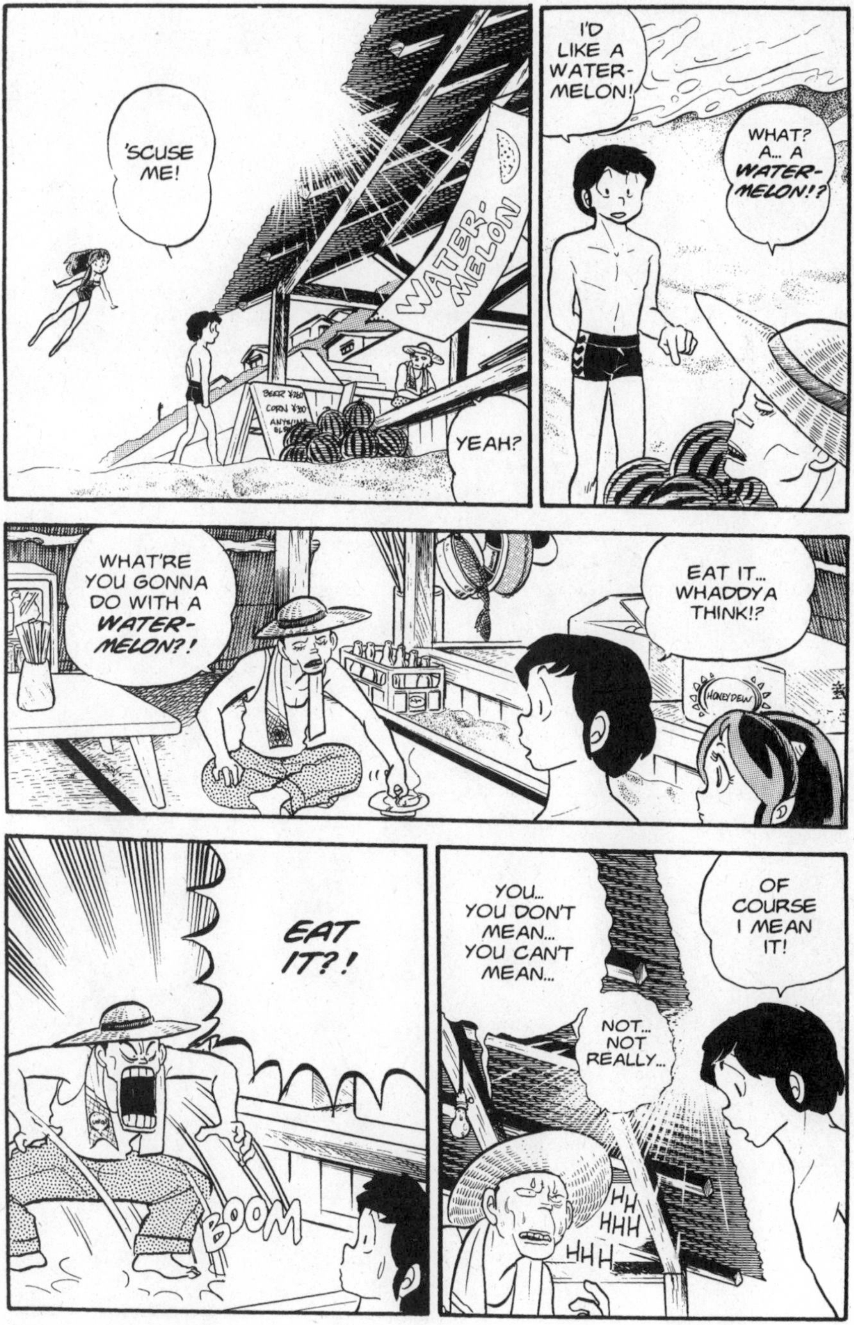
'SCUSE ME!
WATER-MELON
YEAH?
I'D LIKE A WATER-MELON!
WHAT? A... A WATER-MELON!?
WHAT'RE YOU GONNA DO WITH A WATER-MELON?!
EAT IT... WHADDYA THINK!?
HONEYDEW
EAT IT?!
BOOM
YOU... YOU DON'T MEAN... YOU CAN'T MEAN...
OF COURSE I MEAN IT!
NOT... NOT REALLY...
HH HHH HHH

beer ¥260 cola ¥120 oj ¥120 milk ¥80
CANTALOUPE
YOU CAN'T!!
DOOM
GET OUT!!
BEWARE THE GREAT WATER-MELON!
THE WHAT?!
WHY DO YOU HAVE THEM ON DISPLAY IF YOU WON'T SELL THEM?!
DON'T ASK SO MANY QUESTIONS!!
JUST STAY AWAY FROM WATER-MELONS, YOU HEAR?!
TALK ABOUT A MELON-HEAD...
HE WOULDN'T LET YOU BUY ANY?!
YEAH! AND THAT JUST MAKES ME WANT ONE EVEN MORE!

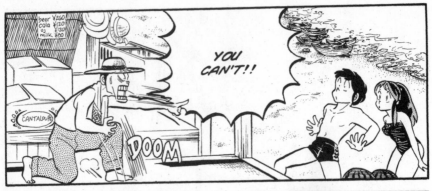

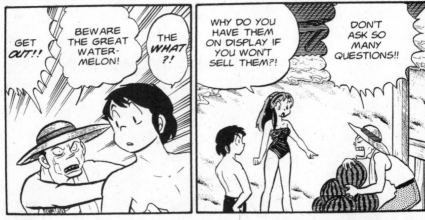

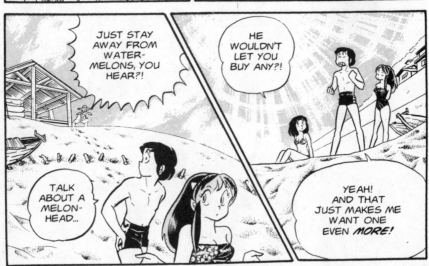

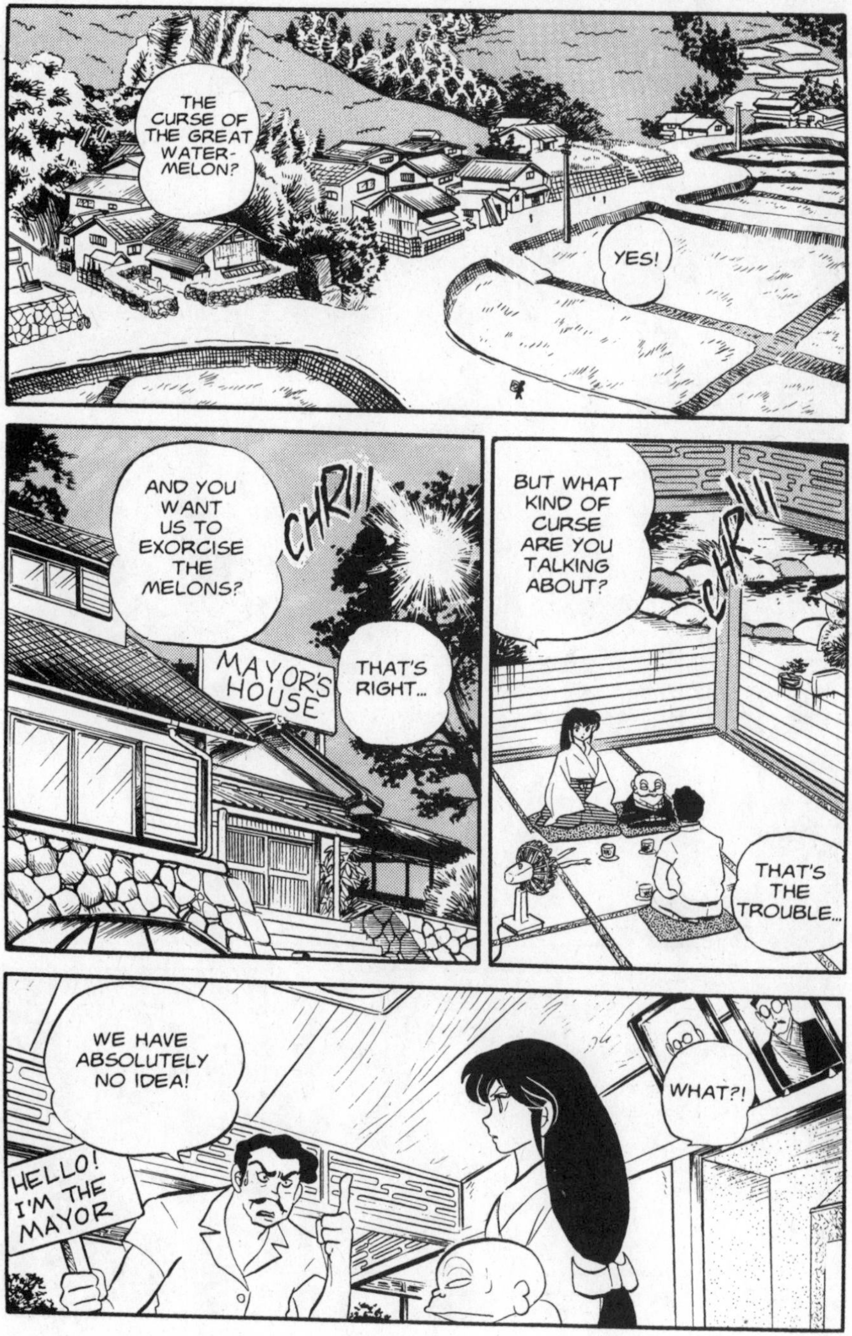
THE CURSE OF THE GREAT WATER-MELON?
YES!
AND YOU WANT US TO EXORCISE THE MELONS?
CHRIII
MAYOR'S HOUSE
THAT'S RIGHT...
BUT WHAT KIND OF CURSE ARE YOU TALKING ABOUT?
CHRIII
THAT'S THE TROUBLE...
WE HAVE ABSOLUTELY NO IDEA!
WHAT?!
HELLO! I'M THE MAYOR

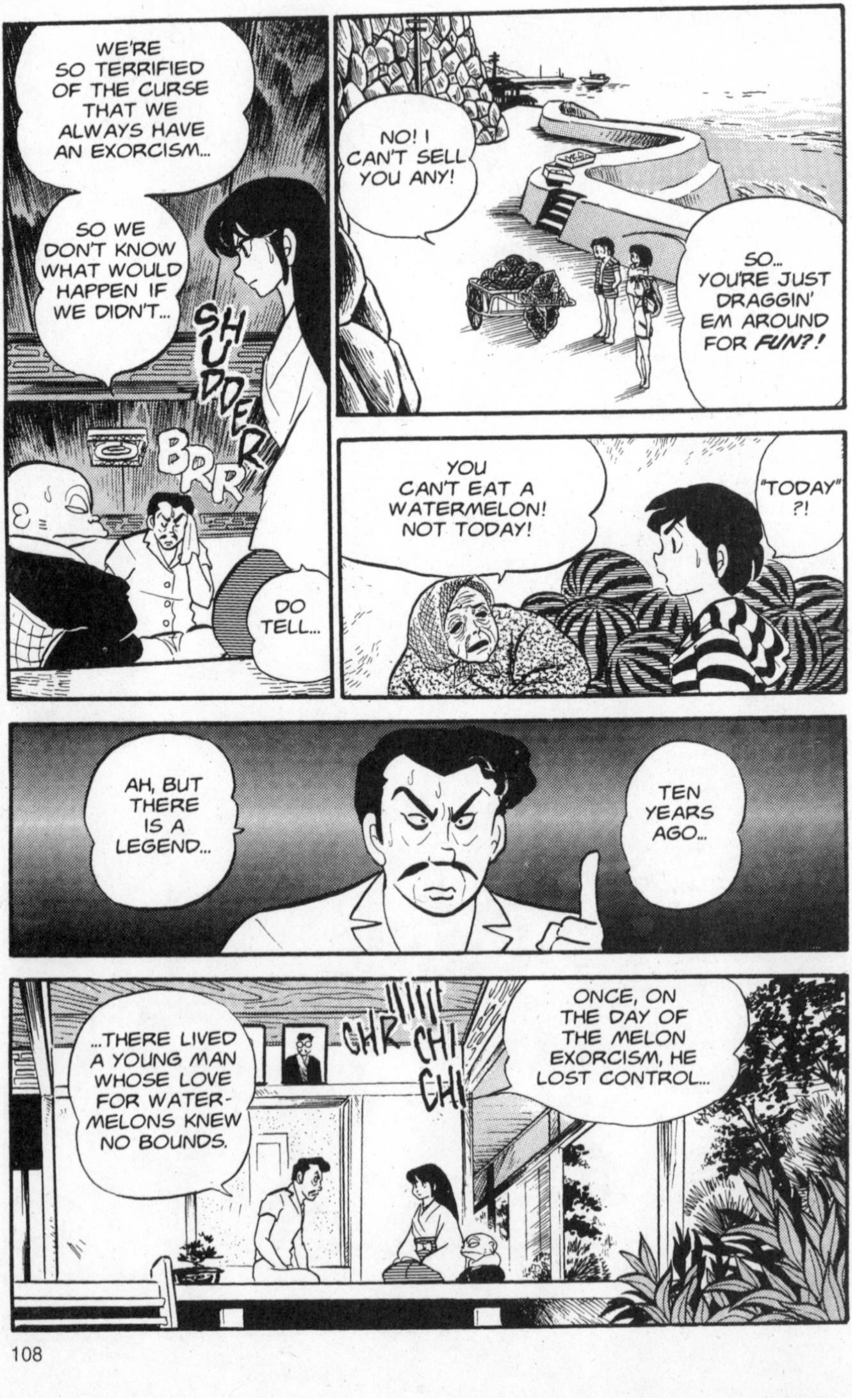
WE'RE SO TERRIFIED OF THE CURSE THAT WE ALWAYS HAVE AN EXORCISM...
SO WE DON'T KNOW WHAT WOULD HAPPEN IF WE DIDN'T...
SHUDDER
BRRR
DO TELL...
NO! I CAN'T SELL YOU ANY!
SO... YOU'RE JUST DRAGGIN' EM AROUND FOR *FUN?!*
YOU CAN'T EAT A WATERMELON! NOT TODAY!
"TODAY"?!
AH, BUT THERE IS A LEGEND...
TEN YEARS AGO...
...THERE LIVED A YOUNG MAN WHOSE LOVE FOR WATER-MELONS KNEW NO BOUNDS.
CHR CHI CHI
ONCE, ON THE DAY OF THE MELON EXORCISM, HE LOST CONTROL...

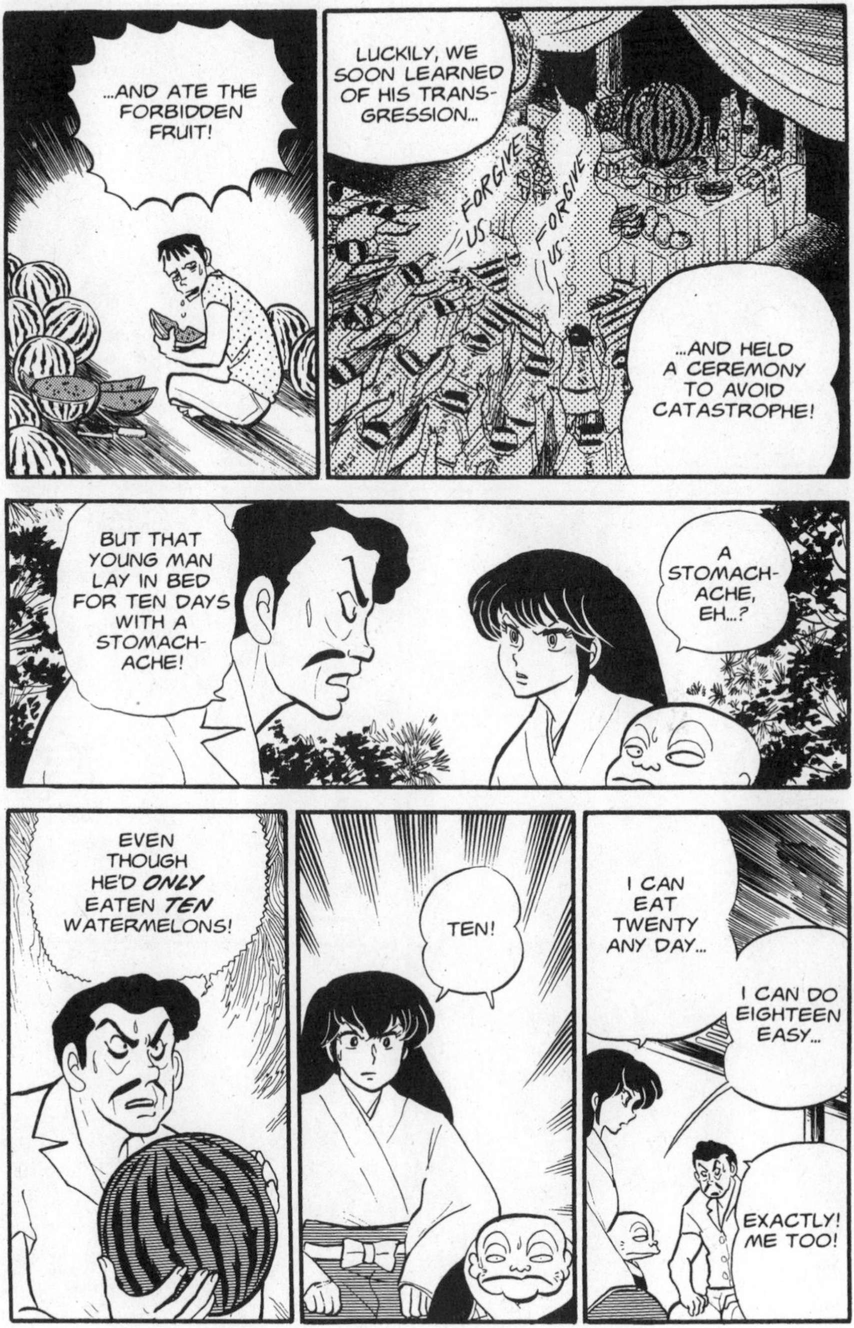
...AND ATE THE FORBIDDEN FRUIT!
LUCKILY, WE SOON LEARNED OF HIS TRANS- GRESSION...
FORGIVE US
FORGIVE US
...AND HELD A CEREMONY TO AVOID CATASTROPHE!
BUT THAT YOUNG MAN LAY IN BED FOR TEN DAYS WITH A STOMACH- ACHE!
A STOMACH- ACHE, EH...?
EVEN THOUGH HE'D *ONLY* EATEN *TEN* WATERMELONS!
TEN!
I CAN EAT TWENTY ANY DAY...
I CAN DO EIGHTEEN EASY...
EXACTLY! ME TOO!

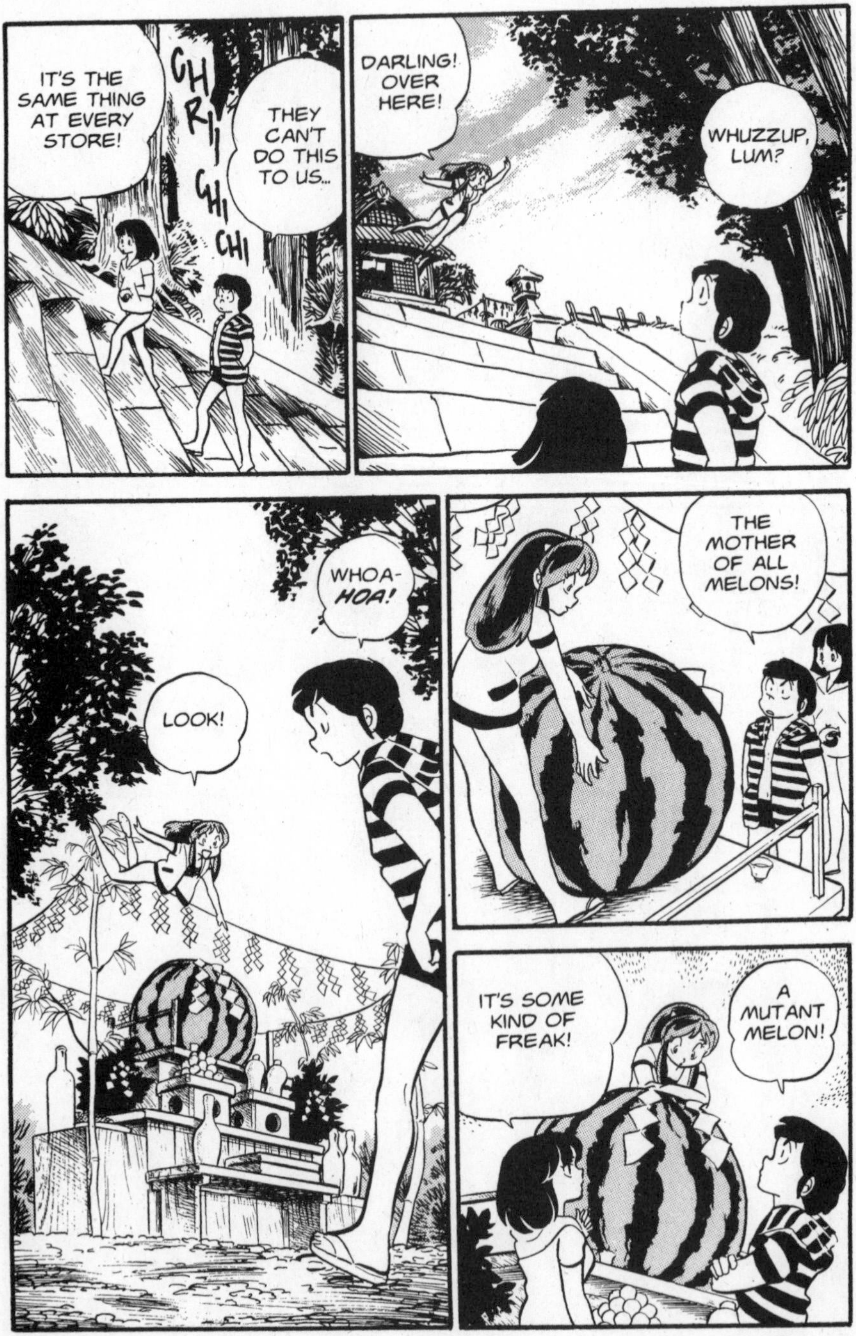
IT'S THE SAME THING AT EVERY STORE!
CHRI CHI CHI
THEY CAN'T DO THIS TO US...
DARLING! OVER HERE!
WHUZZUP, LUM?
WHOA-HOA!
LOOK!
THE MOTHER OF ALL MELONS!
IT'S SOME KIND OF FREAK!
A MUTANT MELON!

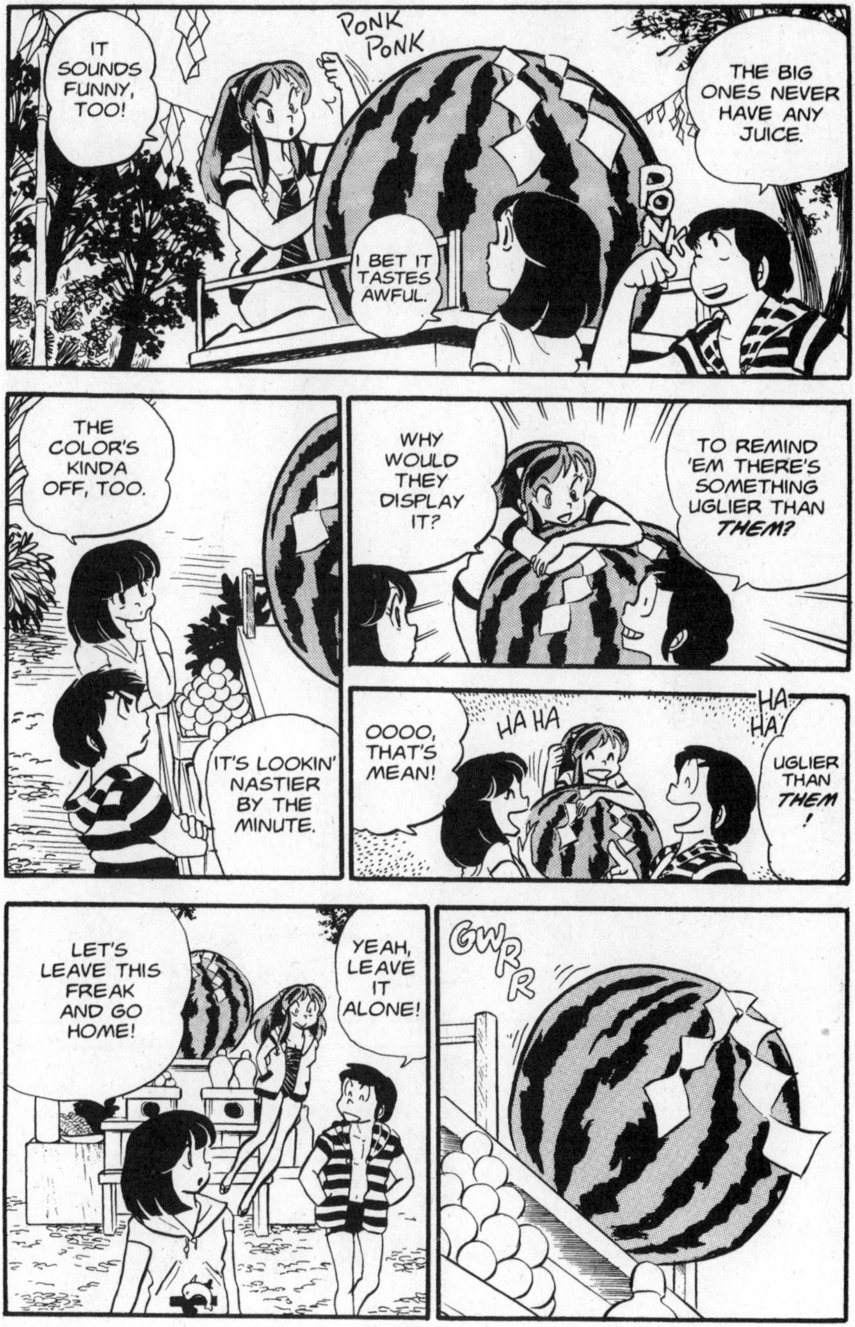
IT SOUNDS FUNNY, TOO!
PONK PONK
THE BIG ONES NEVER HAVE ANY JUICE.
PONK
I BET IT TASTES AWFUL.
THE COLOR'S KINDA OFF, TOO.
IT'S LOOKIN' NASTIER BY THE MINUTE.
WHY WOULD THEY DISPLAY IT?
TO REMIND 'EM THERE'S SOMETHING UGLIER THAN *THEM?*
OOOO, THAT'S MEAN!
HA HA
HA HA
UGLIER THAN *THEM*!
LET'S LEAVE THIS FREAK AND GO HOME!
YEAH, LEAVE IT ALONE!
GWRR

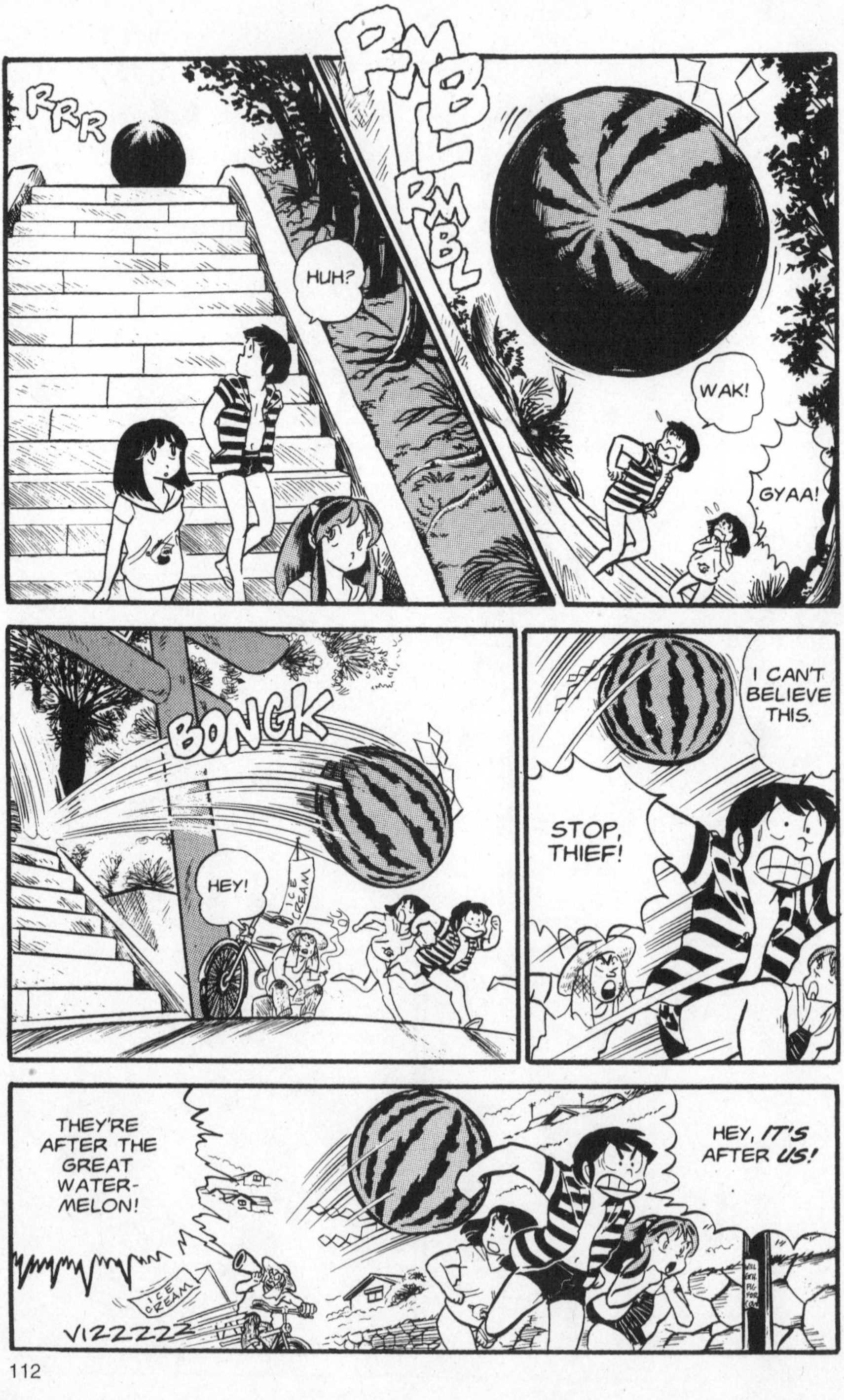
RRR
HUH?
RMBL RMBL
WAK!
GYAA!
BONGK
ICE CREAM
HEY!
I CAN'T BELIEVE THIS.
STOP, THIEF!
THEY'RE AFTER THE GREAT WATER-MELON!
HEY, *IT'S* AFTER *US!*
ICE CREAM
VIZZZZZ

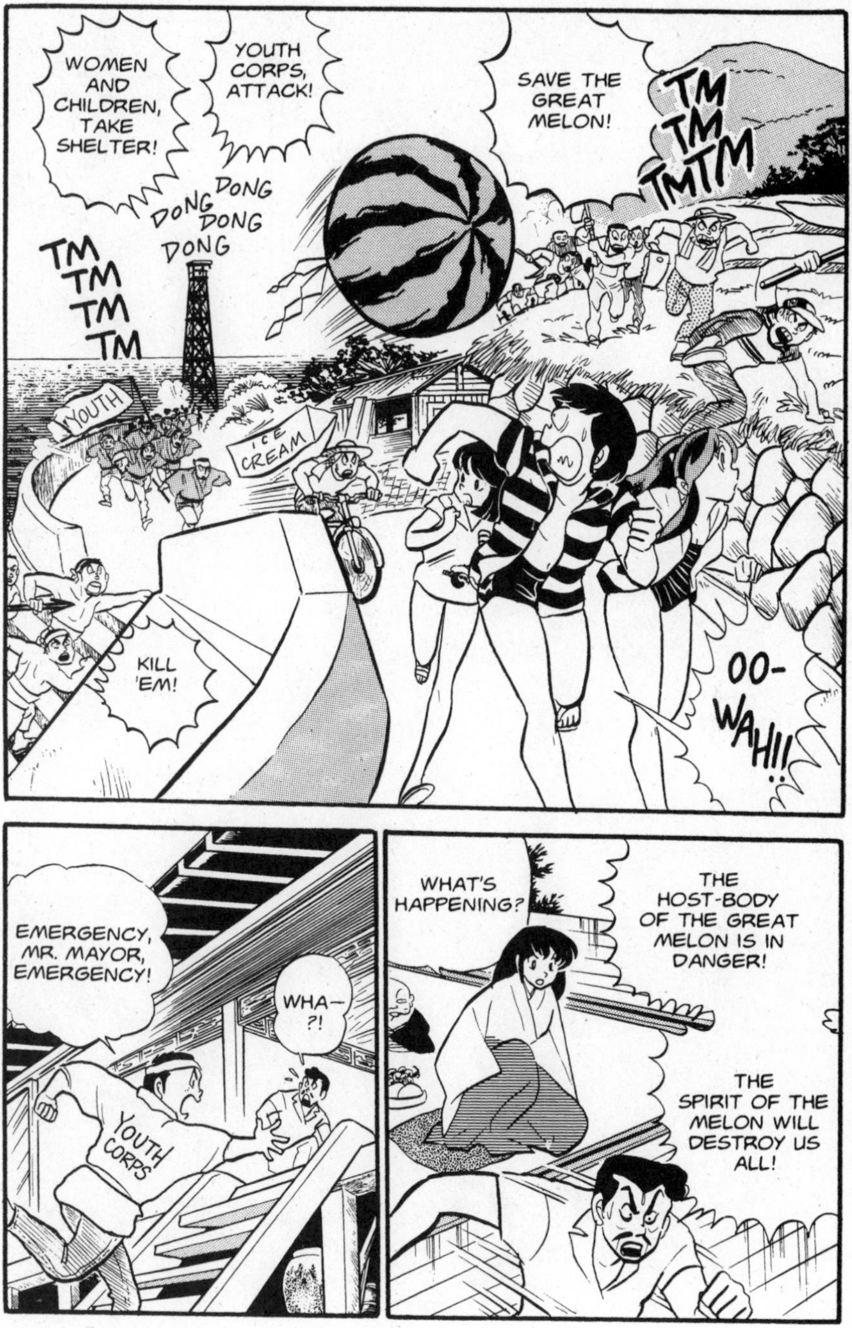
WOMEN AND CHILDREN, TAKE SHELTER!
YOUTH CORPS, ATTACK!
SAVE THE GREAT MELON!
TM TM TMTM
DONG DONG DONG DONG
TM TM TM TM
YOUTH
ICE CREAM
KILL 'EM!
OO-WAH!!
EMERGENCY, MR. MAYOR, EMERGENCY!
WHA— ?!
YOUTH CORPS
WHAT'S HAPPENING?
THE HOST-BODY OF THE GREAT MELON IS IN DANGER!
THE SPIRIT OF THE MELON WILL DESTROY US ALL!

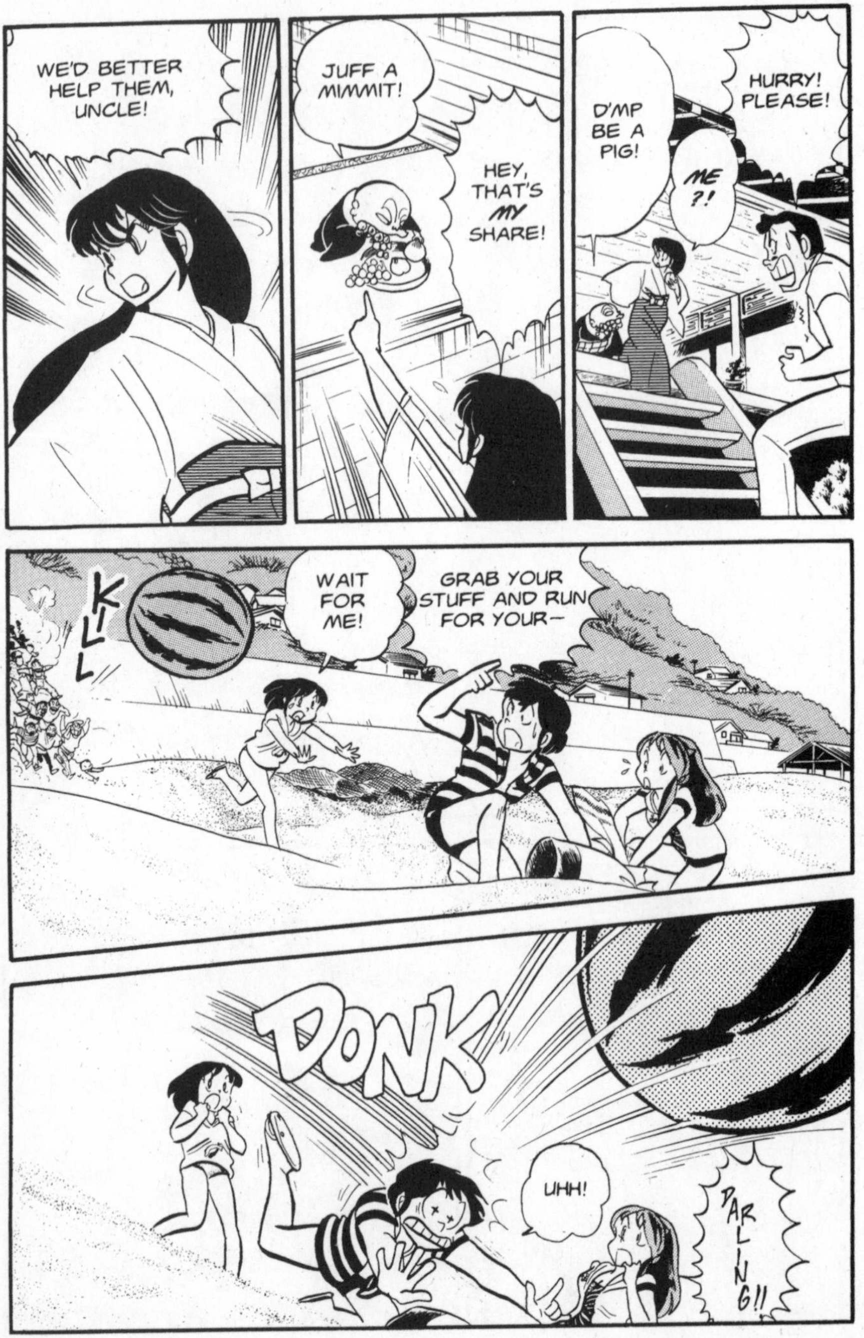

WE'D BETTER HELP THEM, UNCLE!
JUFF A MIMMIT!
HEY, THAT'S MY SHARE!
D'MP BE A PIG!
HURRY! PLEASE!
ME?!
KILL
WAIT FOR ME!
GRAB YOUR STUFF AND RUN FOR YOUR–
DONK
UHH!
DARLING!!

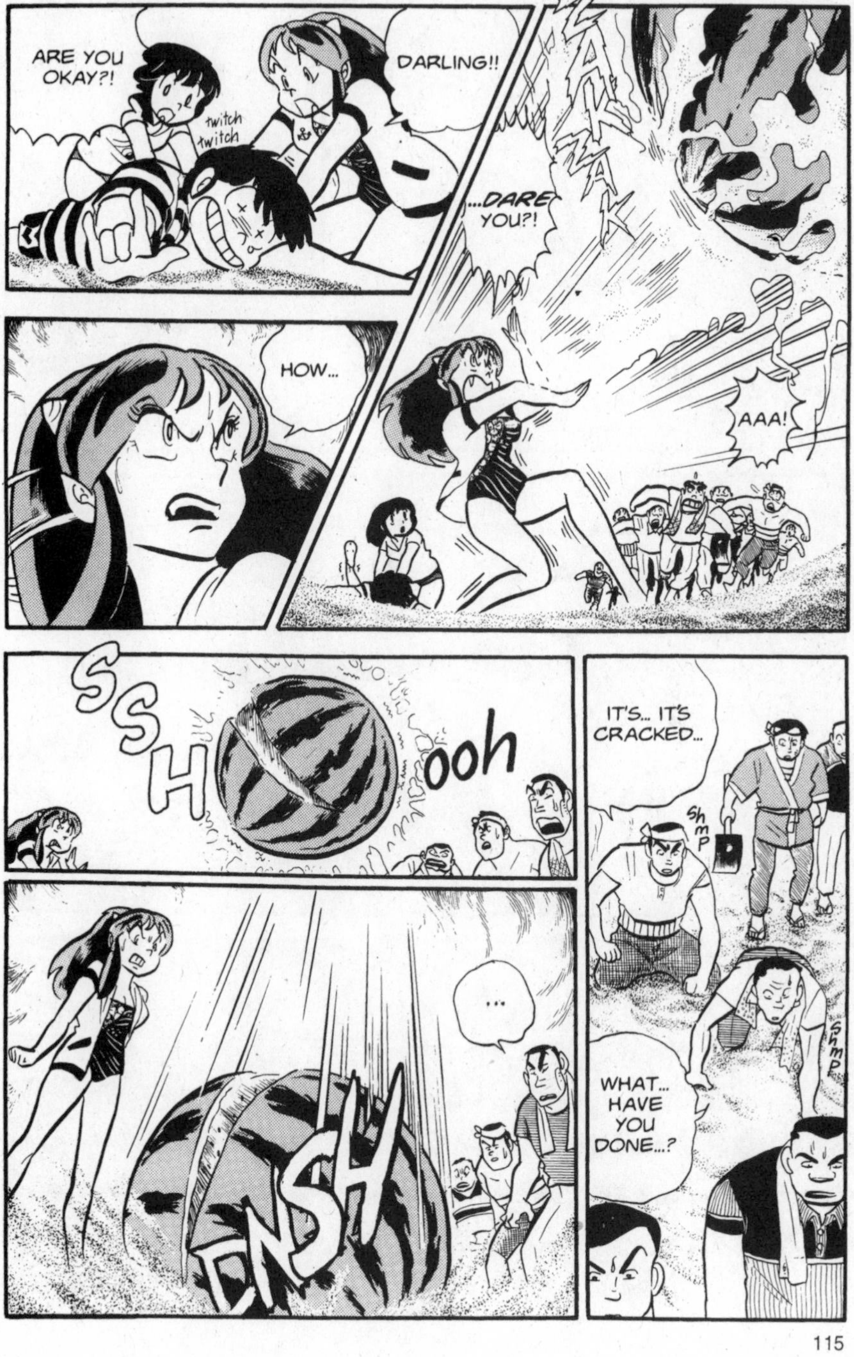
ARE YOU OKAY?!
twitch twitch
DARLING!!
HOW...
...DARE YOU?!
ZAK ZAK
AAA!
SSHooh
...
DNSH
IT'S... IT'S CRACKED...
Shmp
Shmp
WHAT... HAVE YOU DONE...?

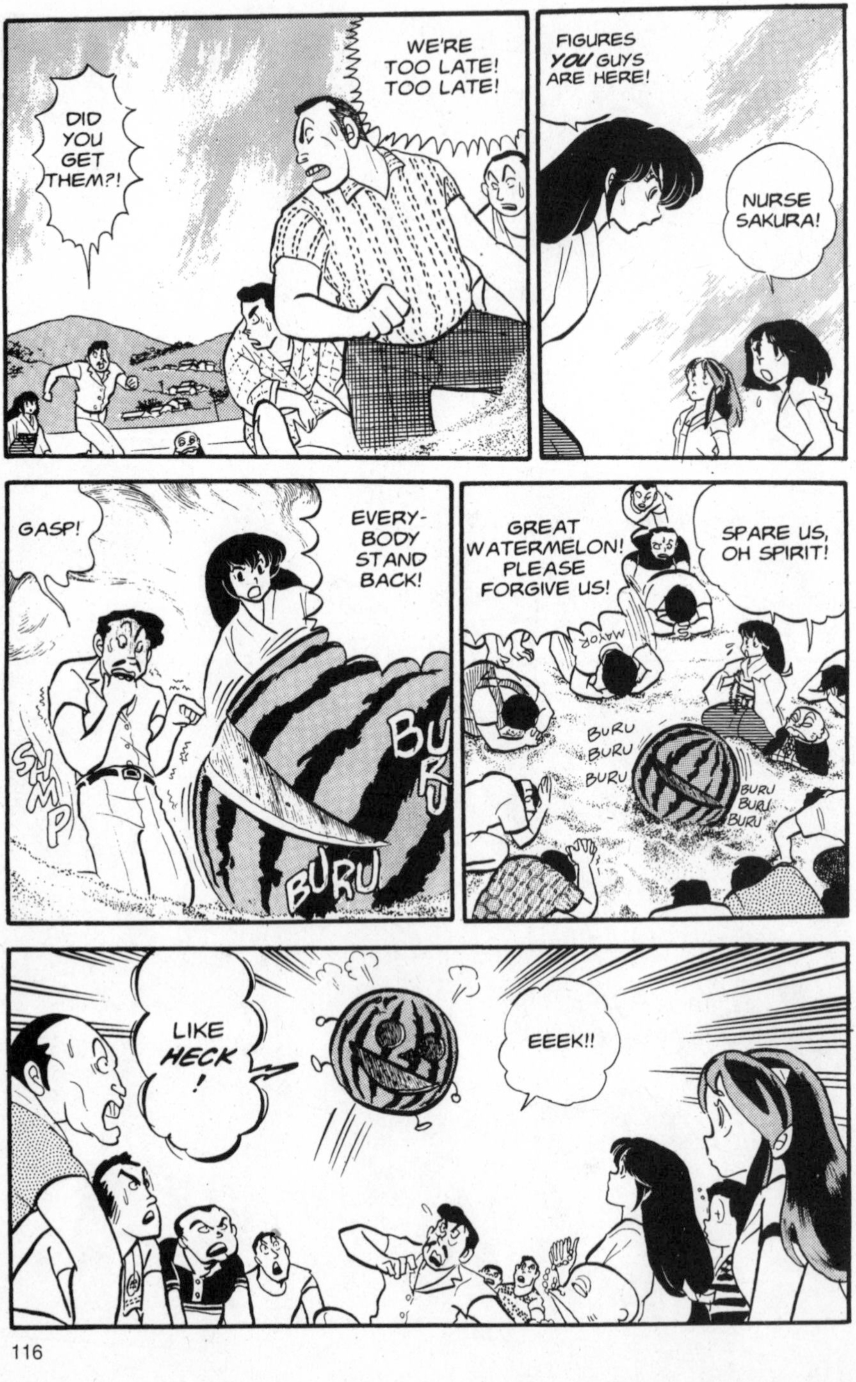

DID YOU GET THEM?!
WE'RE TOO LATE! TOO LATE!
FIGURES YOU GUYS ARE HERE!
NURSE SAKURA!
GASP!
EVERY-BODY STAND BACK!
SHMP
BURU
BURU
GREAT WATERMELON! PLEASE FORGIVE US!
SPARE US, OH SPIRIT!
MAYOR
BURU BURU BURU
BURU BURU BURU
LIKE HECK!
EEEK!!

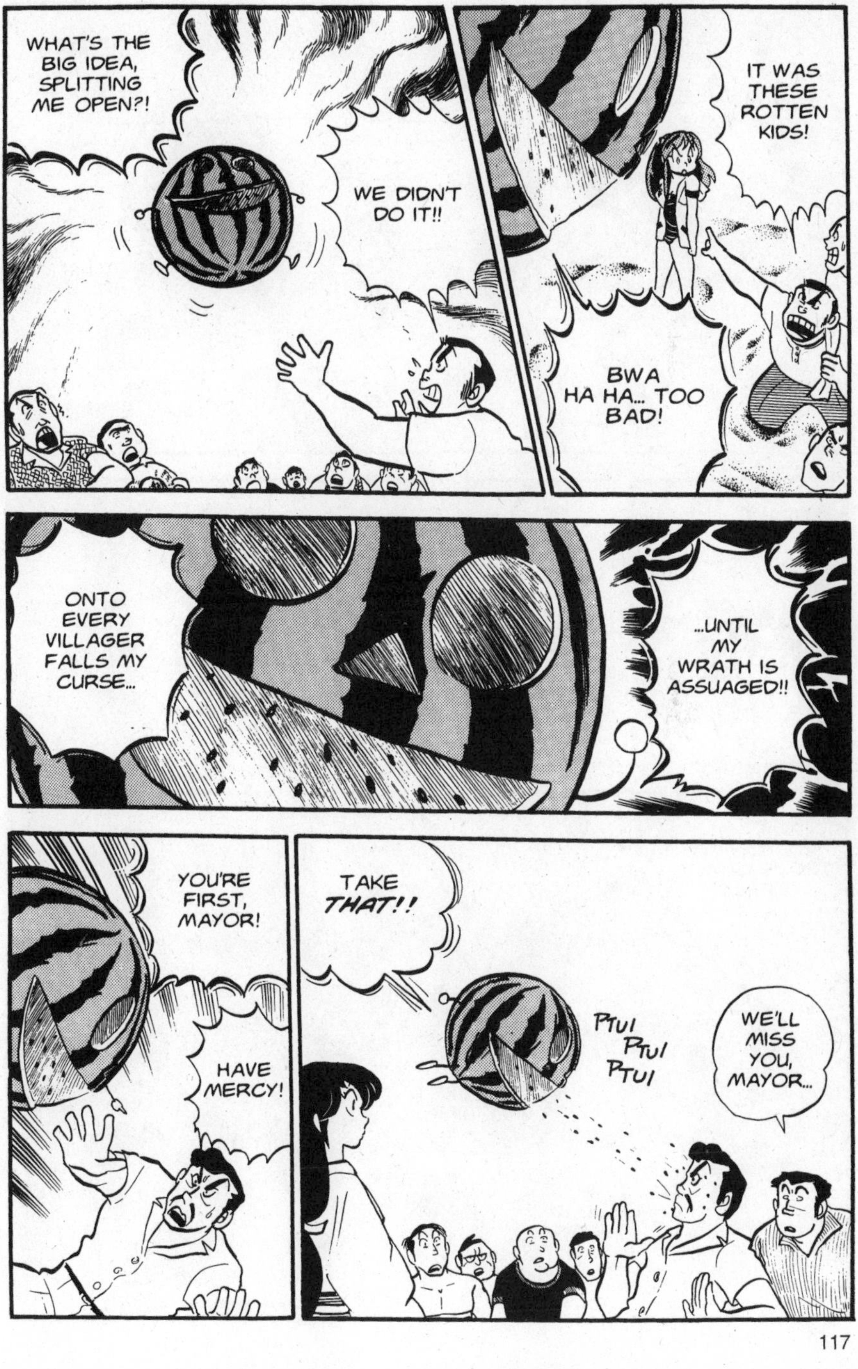
WHAT'S THE BIG IDEA, SPLITTING ME OPEN?!
WE DIDN'T DO IT!!
IT WAS THESE ROTTEN KIDS!
BWA HA HA... TOO BAD!
ONTO EVERY VILLAGER FALLS MY CURSE...
...UNTIL MY WRATH IS ASSUAGED!!
YOU'RE FIRST, MAYOR!
HAVE MERCY!
TAKE *THAT!!*
PTUI PTUI PTUI
WE'LL MISS YOU, MAYOR...

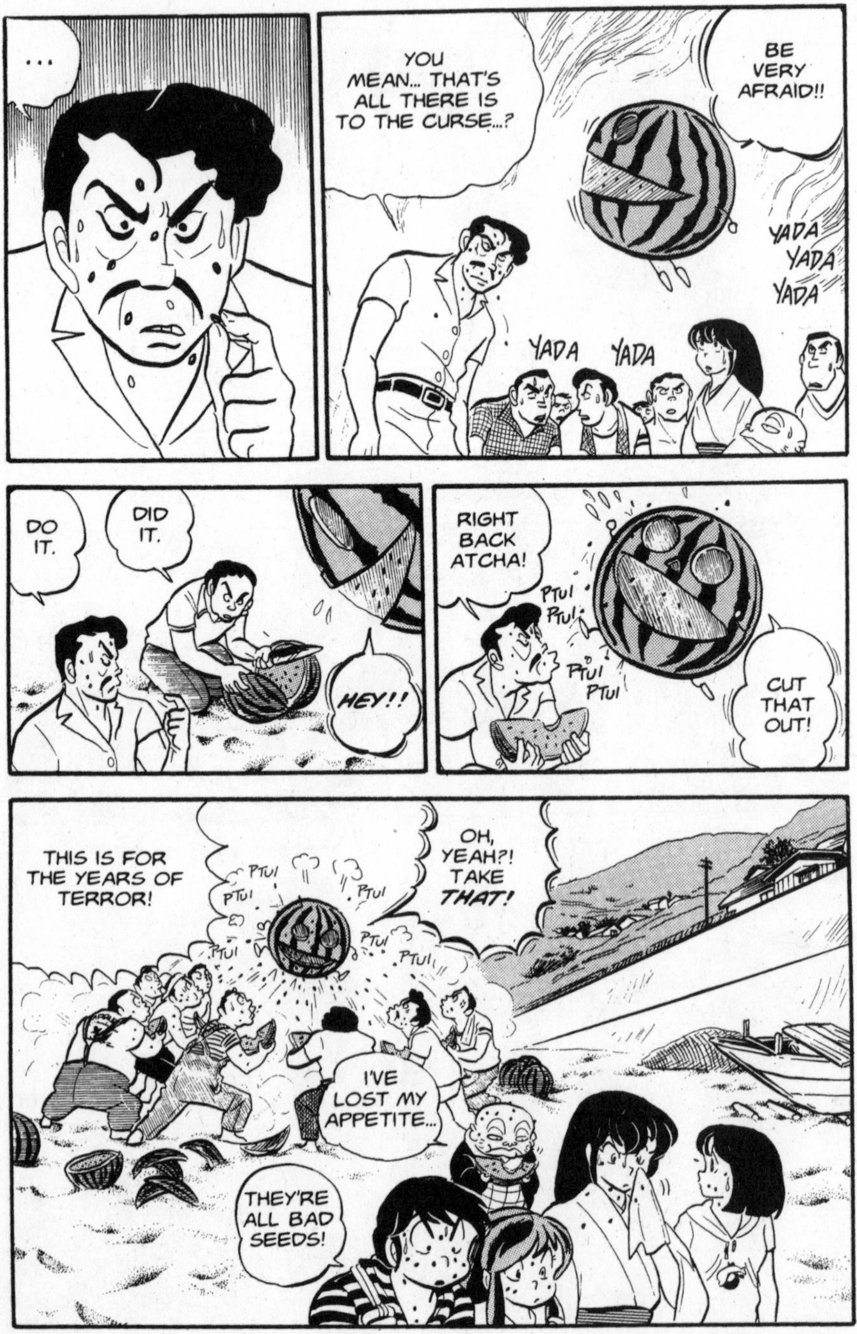
...
YOU MEAN... THAT'S ALL THERE IS TO THE CURSE...?
BE VERY AFRAID!!
YADA YADA YADA
YADA YADA
DO IT.
DID IT.
HEY!!
RIGHT BACK ATCHA!
PTUI PTUI
PTUI PTUI
CUT THAT OUT!
THIS IS FOR THE YEARS OF TERROR!
PTUI PTUI PTUI PTUI PTUI PTUI
OH, YEAH?! TAKE THAT!
I'VE LOST MY APPETITE...
THEY'RE ALL BAD SEEDS!

PART EIGHT

FUN WITH HURRICANES

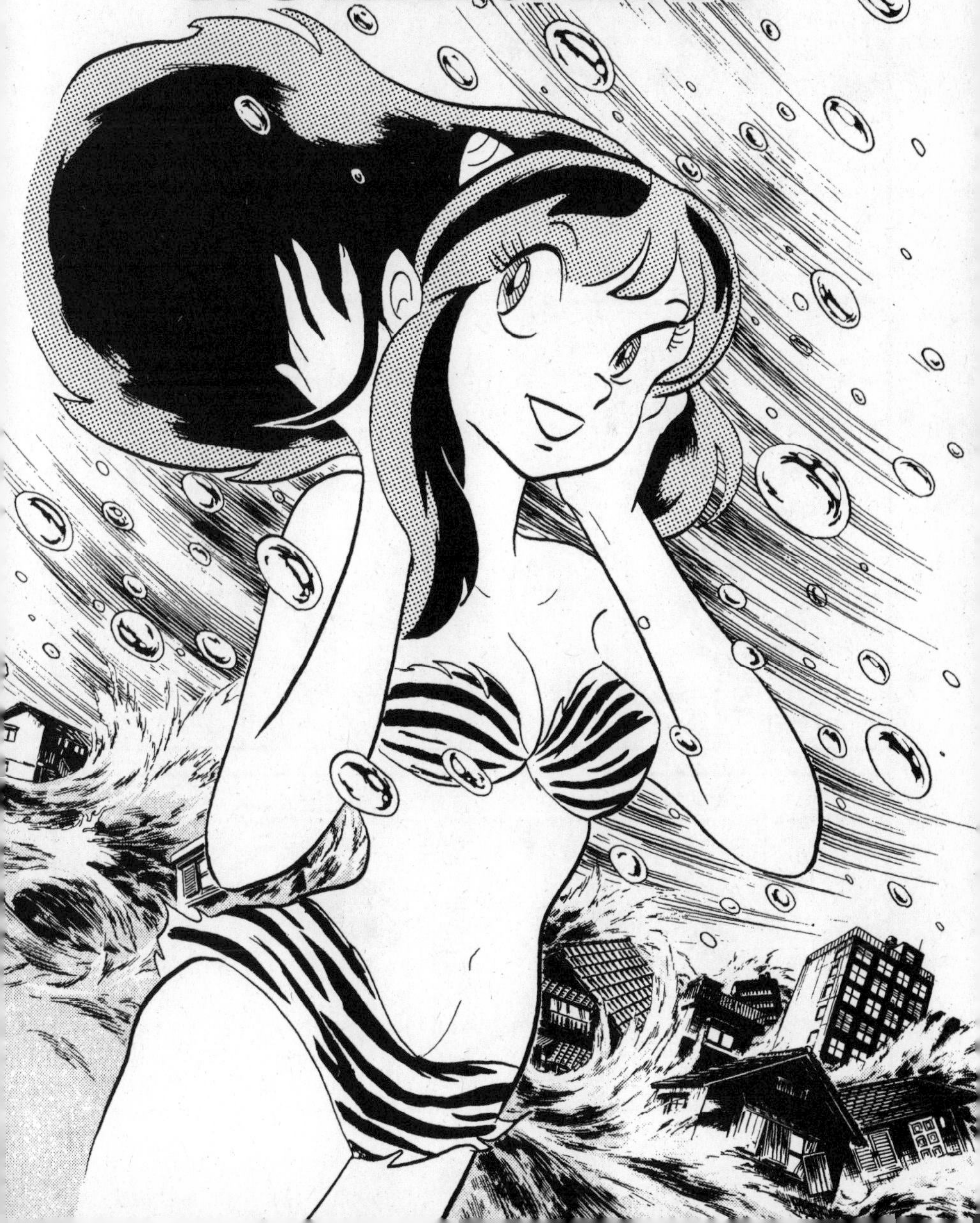

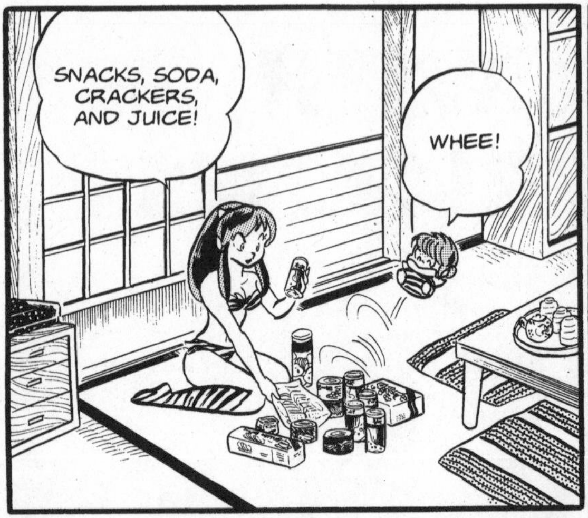
SNACKS, SODA, CRACKERS, AND JUICE!
WHEE!
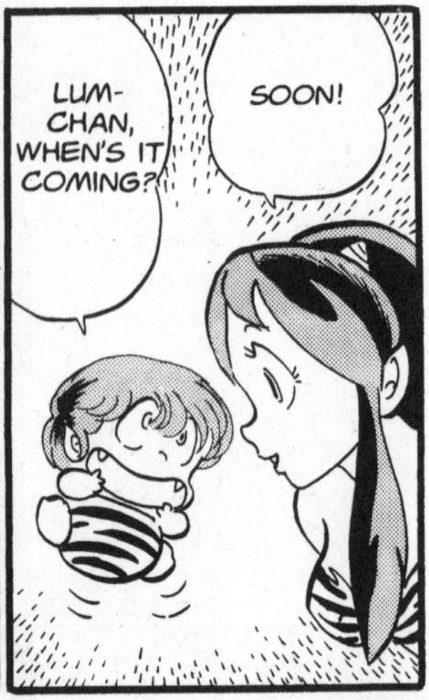
LUM-CHAN, WHEN'S IT COMING?
SOON!
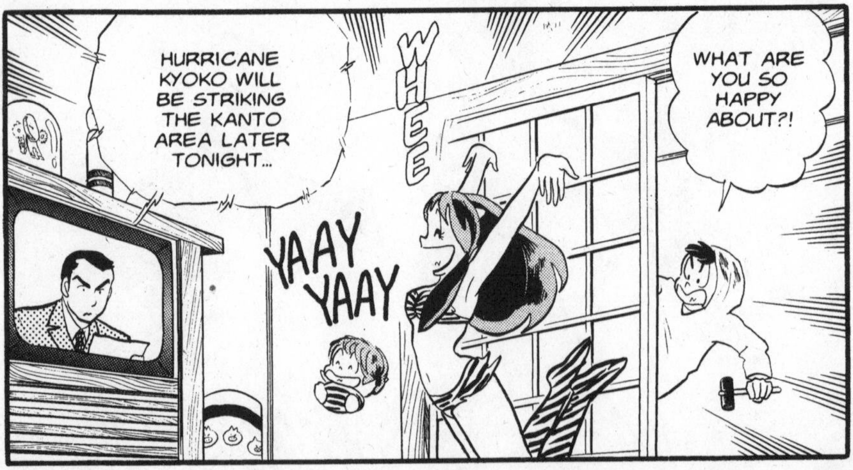
HURRICANE KYOKO WILL BE STRIKING THE KANTO AREA LATER TONIGHT...
WHEE
YAAY YAAY
WHAT ARE YOU SO HAPPY ABOUT?!
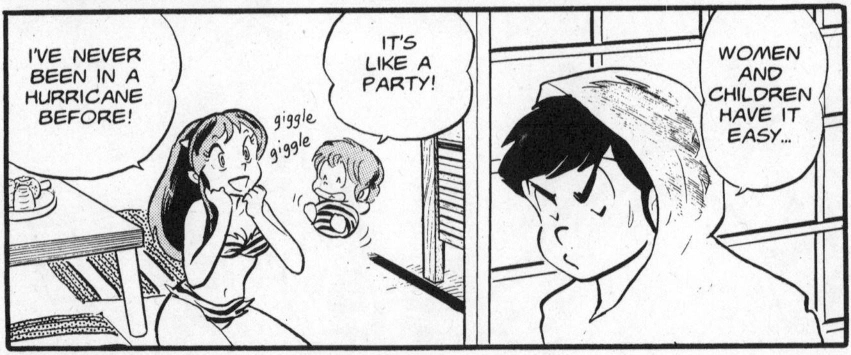
I'VE NEVER BEEN IN A HURRICANE BEFORE!
giggle giggle
IT'S LIKE A PARTY!
WOMEN AND CHILDREN HAVE IT EASY...

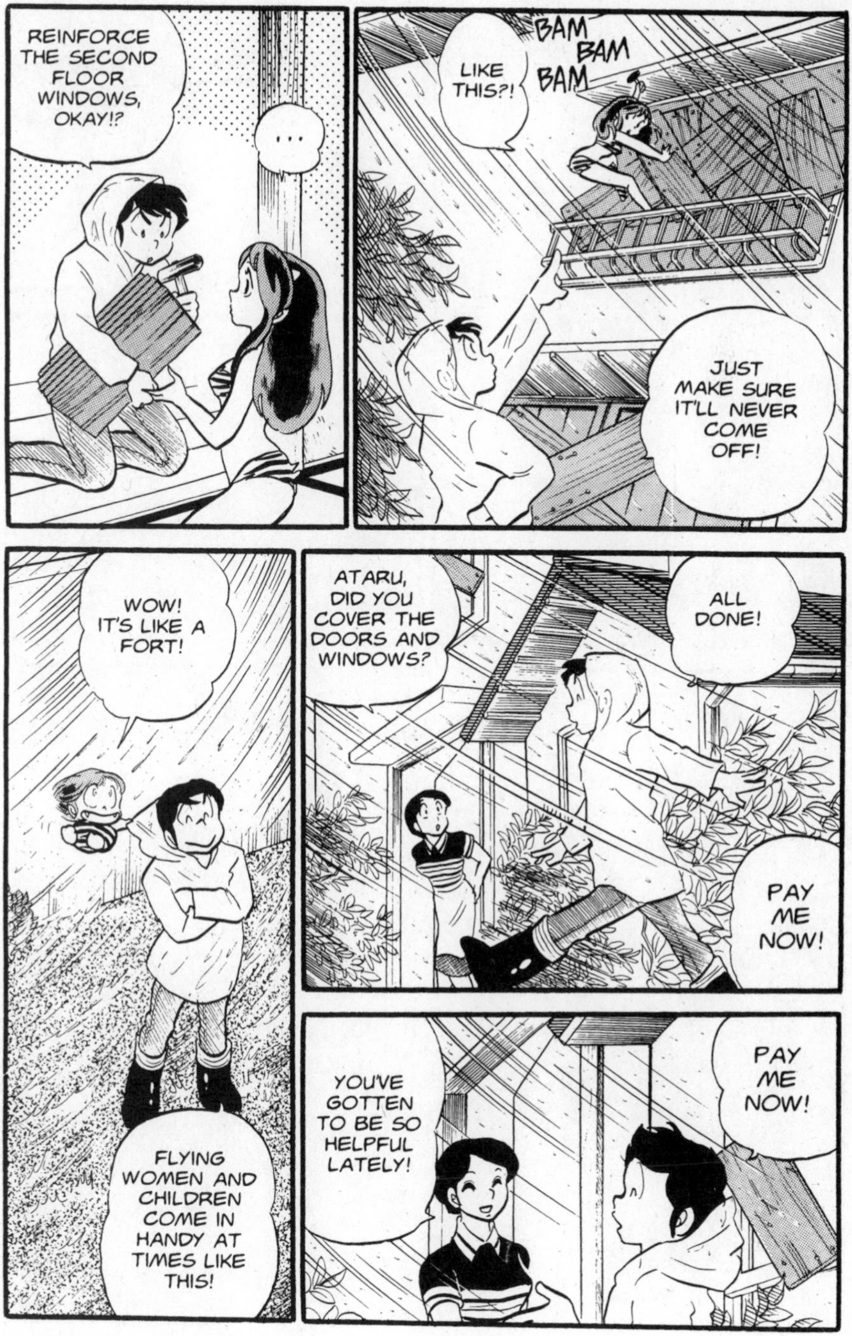
REINFORCE THE SECOND FLOOR WINDOWS, OKAY!?
...
LIKE THIS?!
BAM BAM BAM
JUST MAKE SURE IT'LL NEVER COME OFF!
WOW! IT'S LIKE A FORT!
FLYING WOMEN AND CHILDREN COME IN HANDY AT TIMES LIKE THIS!
ATARU, DID YOU COVER THE DOORS AND WINDOWS?
ALL DONE!
PAY ME NOW!
YOU'VE GOTTEN TO BE SO HELPFUL LATELY!
PAY ME NOW!

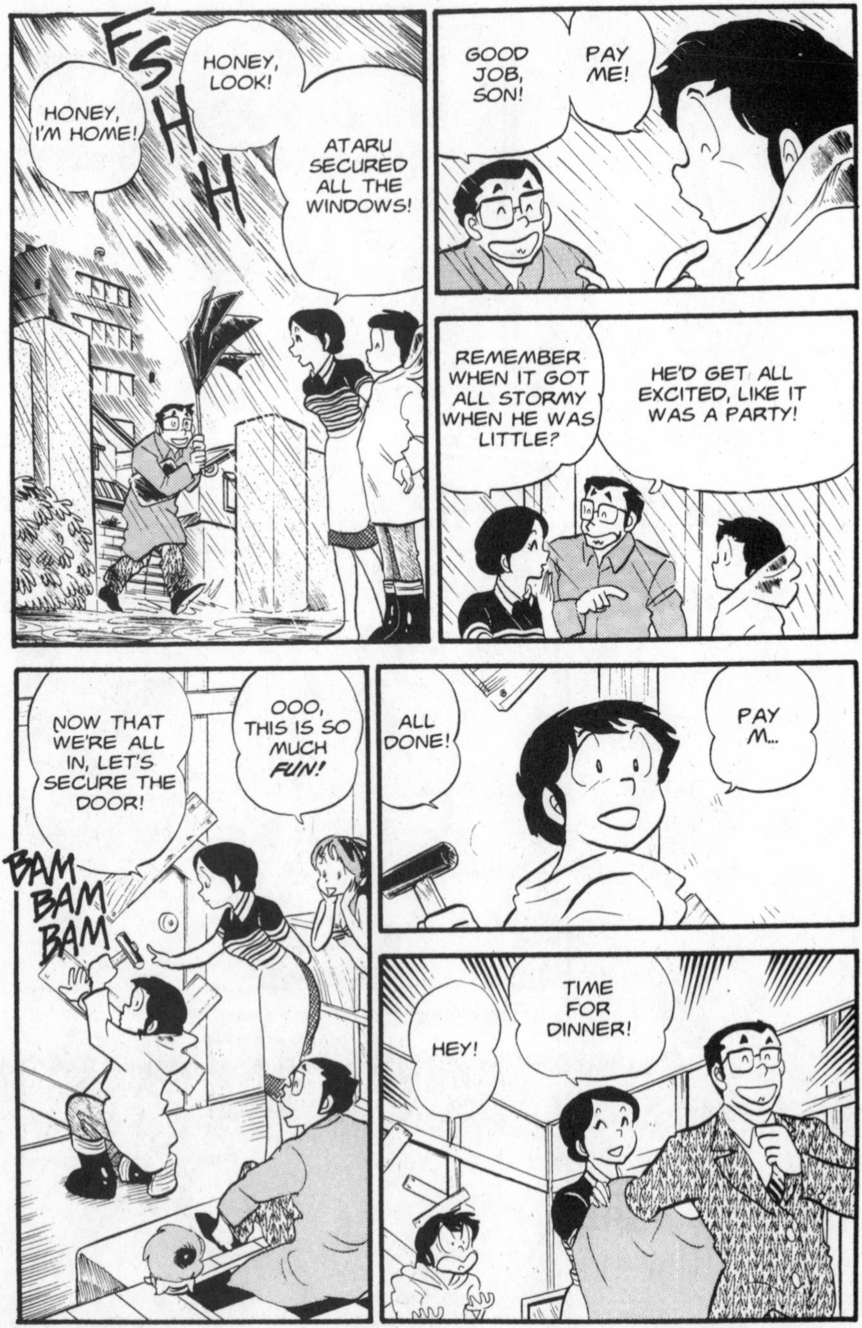
FSHH
HONEY, I'M HOME!
HONEY, LOOK!
ATARU SECURED ALL THE WINDOWS!
GOOD JOB, SON!
PAY ME!
REMEMBER WHEN IT GOT ALL STORMY WHEN HE WAS LITTLE?
HE'D GET ALL EXCITED, LIKE IT WAS A PARTY!
NOW THAT WE'RE ALL IN, LET'S SECURE THE DOOR!
OOO, THIS IS SO MUCH *FUN!*
BAM BAM BAM
ALL DONE!
PAY M...
HEY!
TIME FOR DINNER!

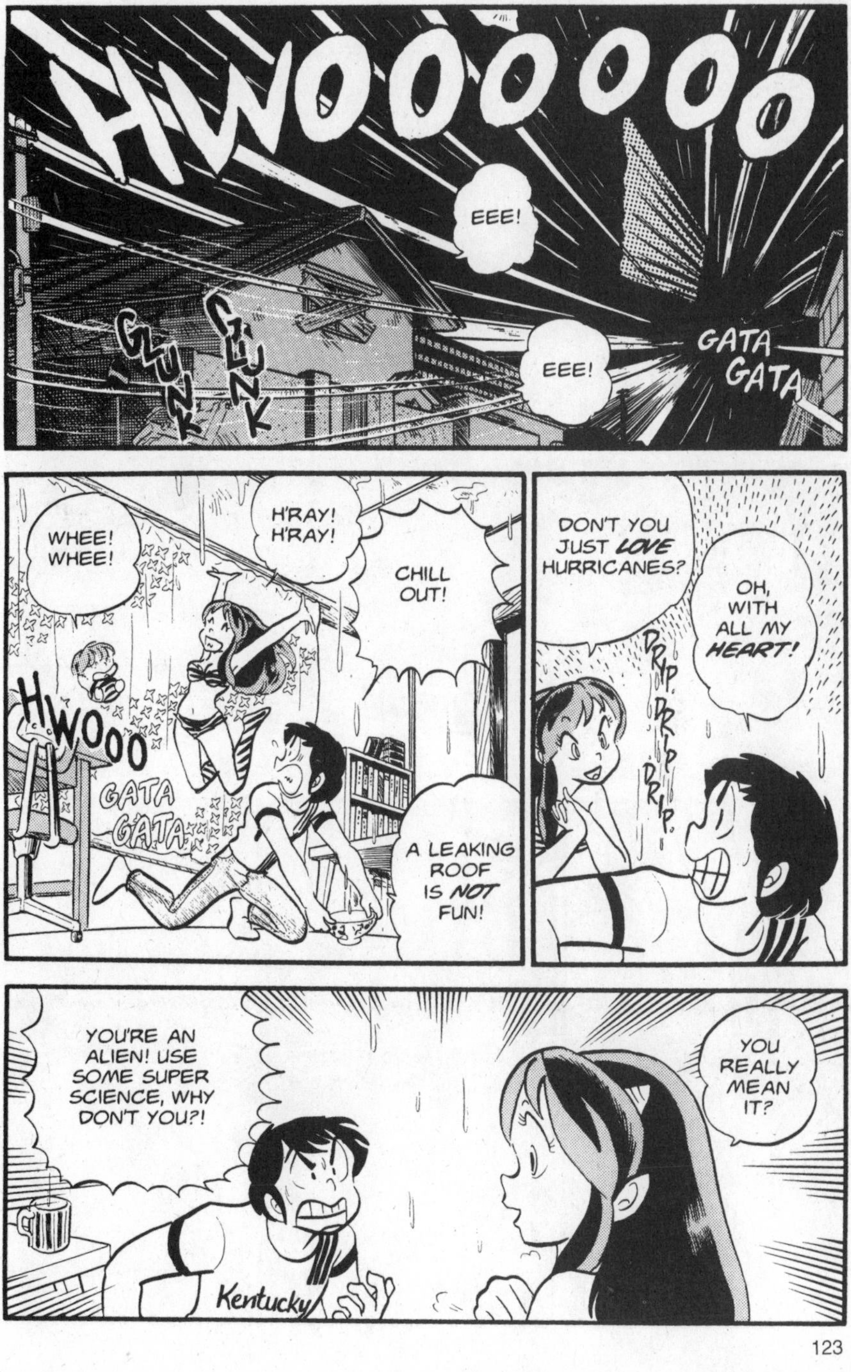
HWOOOOOO
EEE!
EEE!
GLUNK
GLUNK
GATA GATA
WHEE! WHEE!
H'RAY! H'RAY!
CHILL OUT!
HWOOO
GATA GATA
A LEAKING ROOF IS *NOT* FUN!
DON'T YOU JUST *LOVE* HURRICANES?
OH, WITH ALL MY *HEART!*
DRIP. DRIP. DRIP. DRIP.
YOU'RE AN ALIEN! USE SOME SUPER SCIENCE, WHY DON'T YOU?!
YOU REALLY MEAN IT?
Kentucky

HOW ABOUT A GRAVITY CONTROLLER?!

UHH...

JUST DROP IT IN WATER AND WAIT THREE MINUTES!

UHHH...

POINK

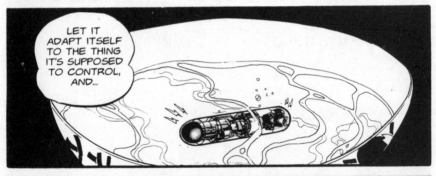

LET IT ADAPT ITSELF TO THE THING IT'S SUPPOSED TO CONTROL, AND...

ACTIVATE!

KREE

DRRIP

WHOA!

PING

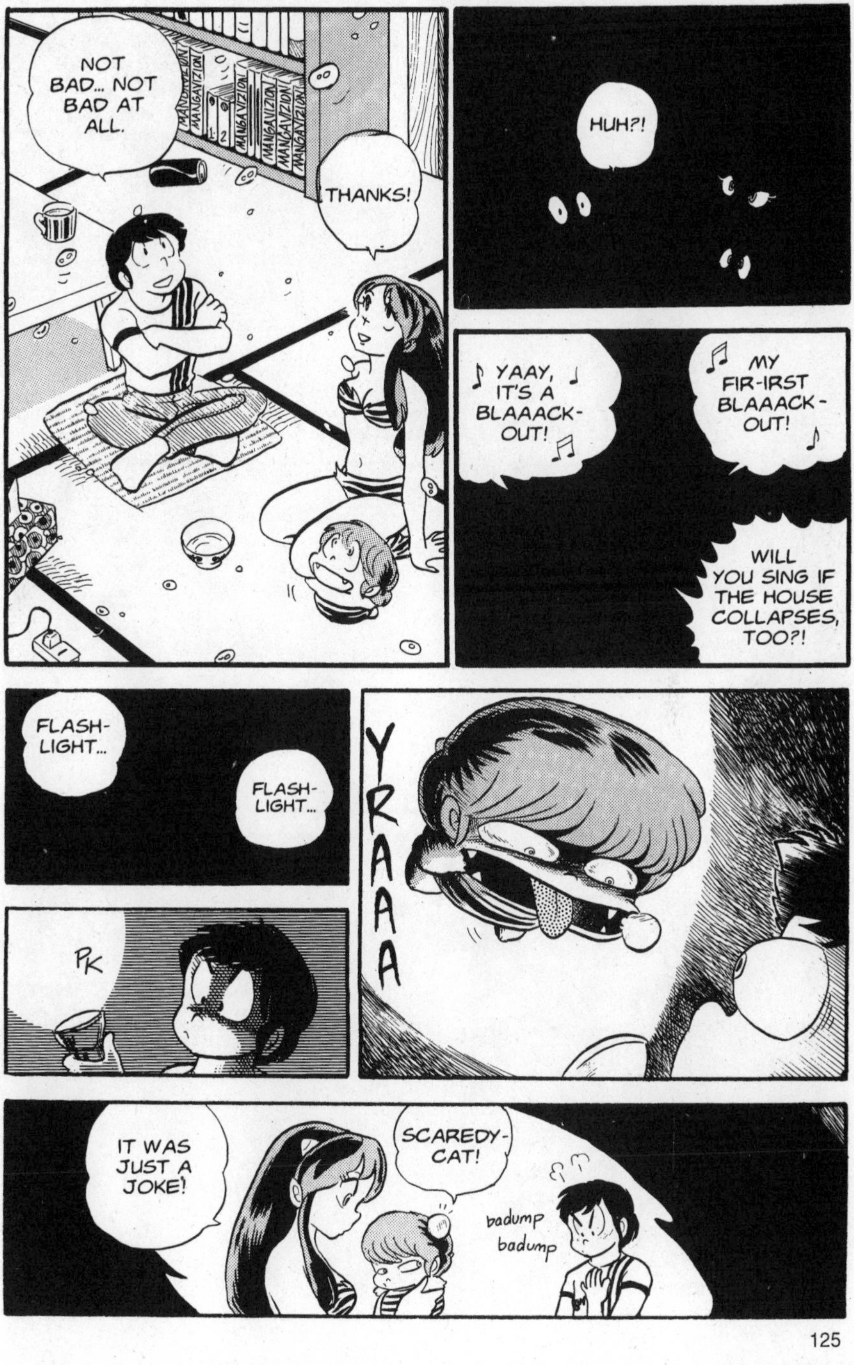
NOT BAD... NOT BAD AT ALL.
THANKS!
HUH?!
YAAY, IT'S A BLAAACK-OUT!
MY FIR-IRST BLAAACK-OUT!
WILL YOU SING IF THE HOUSE COLLAPSES, TOO?!
FLASH-LIGHT...
FLASH-LIGHT...
PK
YRAAAA
IT WAS JUST A JOKE!
SCAREDY-CAT!
badump badump

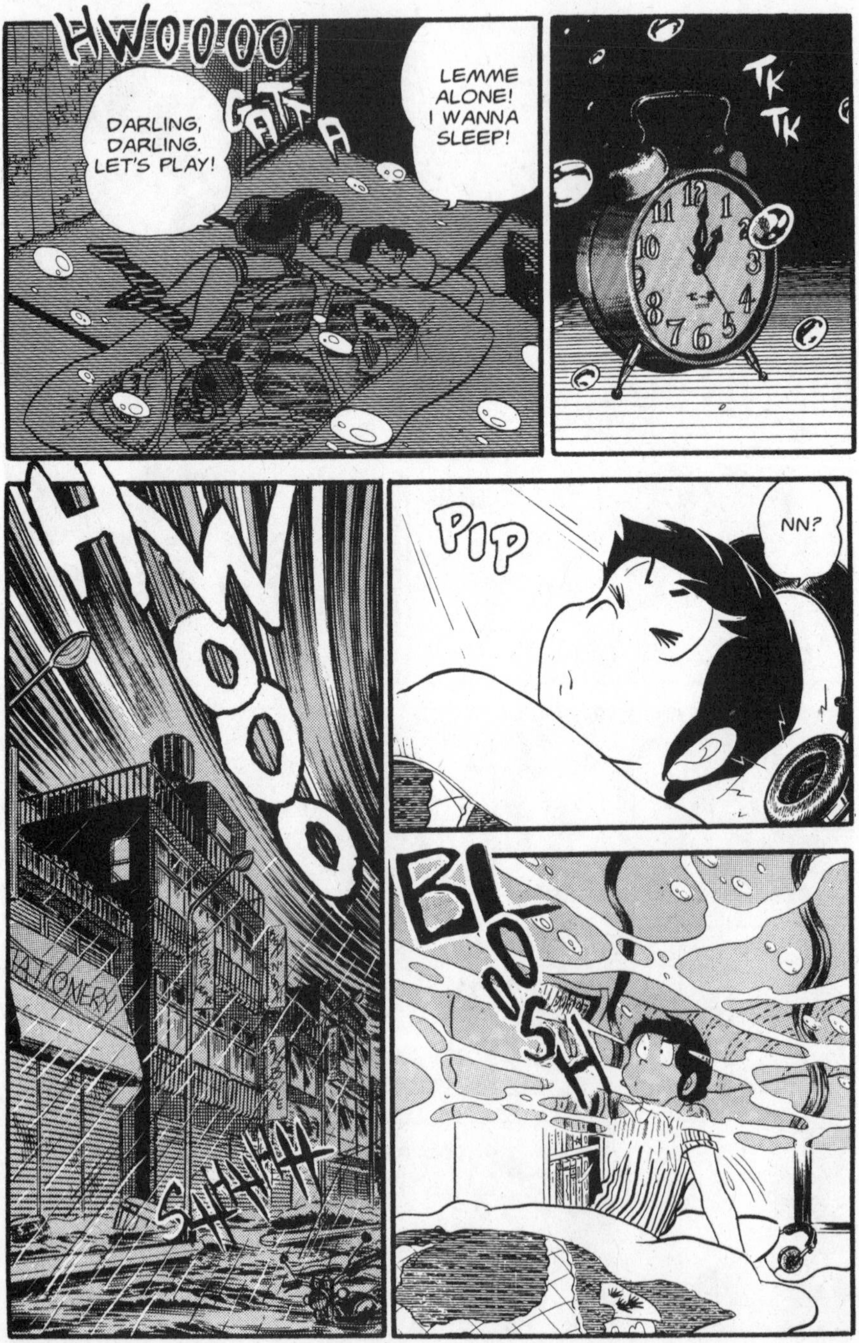
HWOOOO
DARLING, DARLING. LET'S PLAY!
GATTA
LEMME ALONE! I WANNA SLEEP!
TK TK
HWOOOO
SHHHH
PIP
NN?
BLOOSH

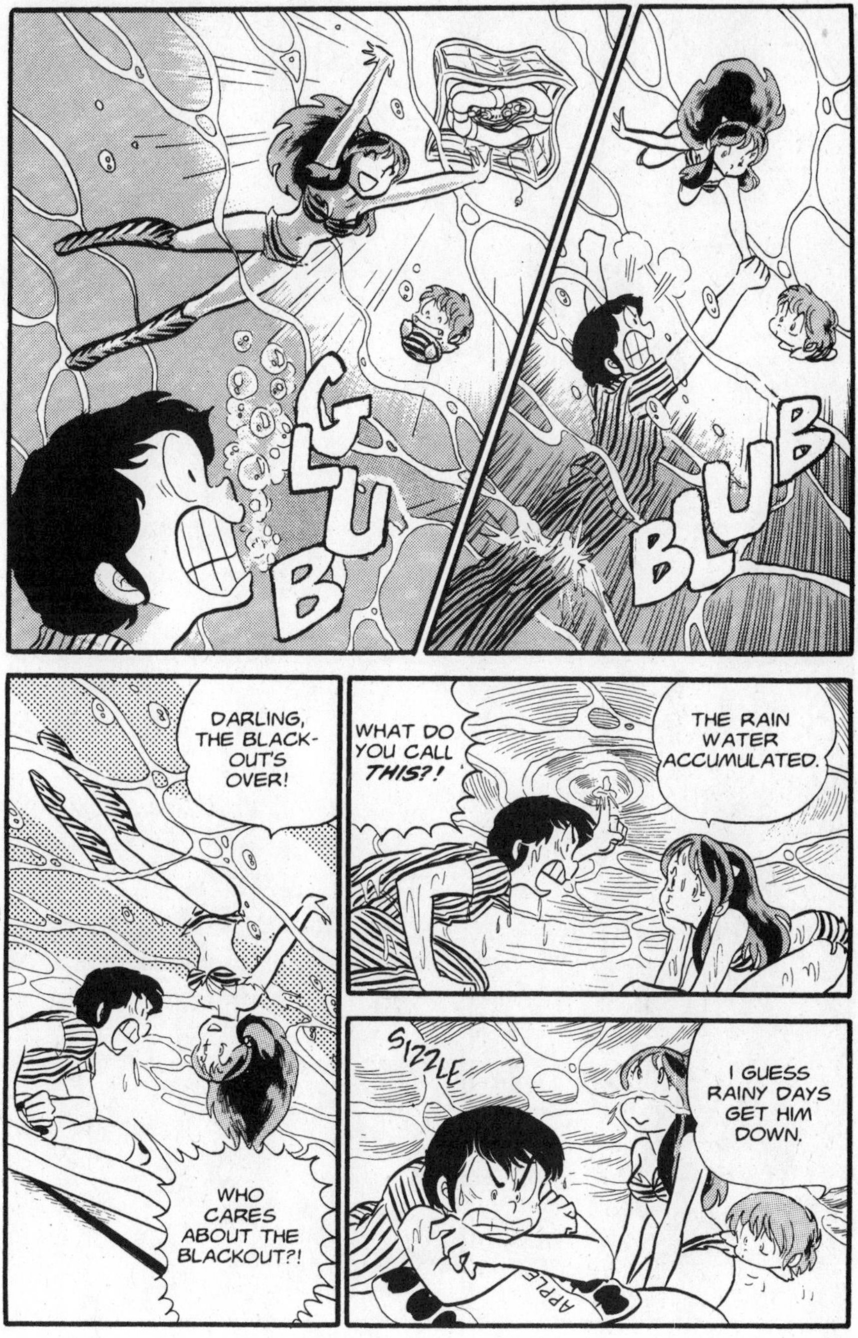
GLUB
BLUB
DARLING, THE BLACK-OUT'S OVER!
WHO CARES ABOUT THE BLACKOUT?!
WHAT DO YOU CALL *THIS?!*
THE RAIN WATER ACCUMULATED.
SIZZLE
I GUESS RAINY DAYS GET HIM DOWN.
APPLE

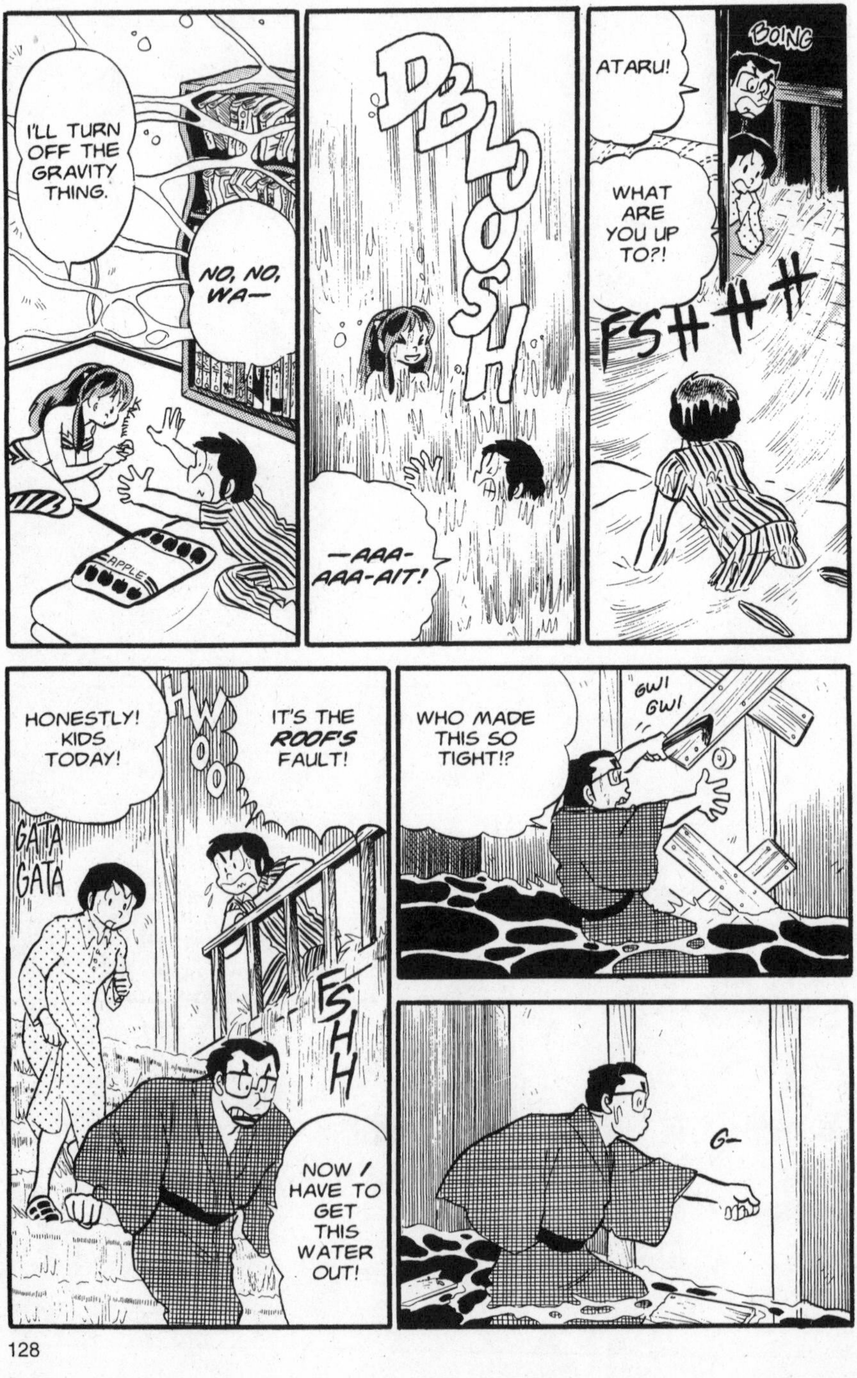
I'LL TURN OFF THE GRAVITY THING.
NO, NO, WA—
APPLE
DBLOOSH
—AAA-AAA-AIT!
ATARU!
BOING
WHAT ARE YOU UP TO?!
FSHHH
HONESTLY! KIDS TODAY!
HWOO
IT'S THE *ROOF'S* FAULT!
GATA GATA
FSHH
NOW *I* HAVE TO GET THIS WATER OUT!
WHO MADE THIS SO TIGHT!?
GWI GWI
G—

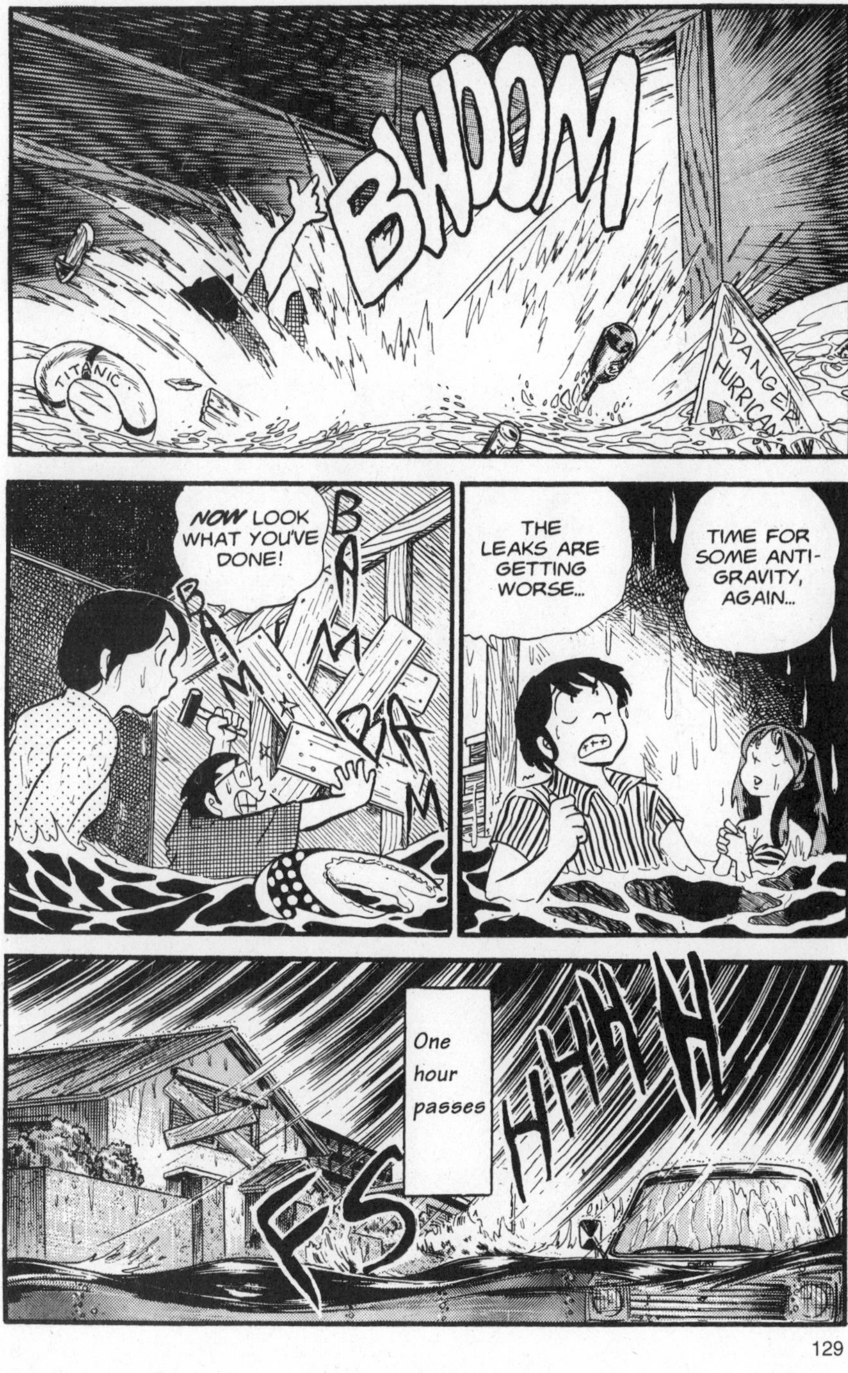
BWOOM
TITANIC
DANGER HURRICAN
NOW LOOK WHAT YOU'VE DONE!
BAM
BAM
BAM
BAM
THE LEAKS ARE GETTING WORSE...
TIME FOR SOME ANTI-GRAVITY, AGAIN...
One hour passes
FS
HHHH

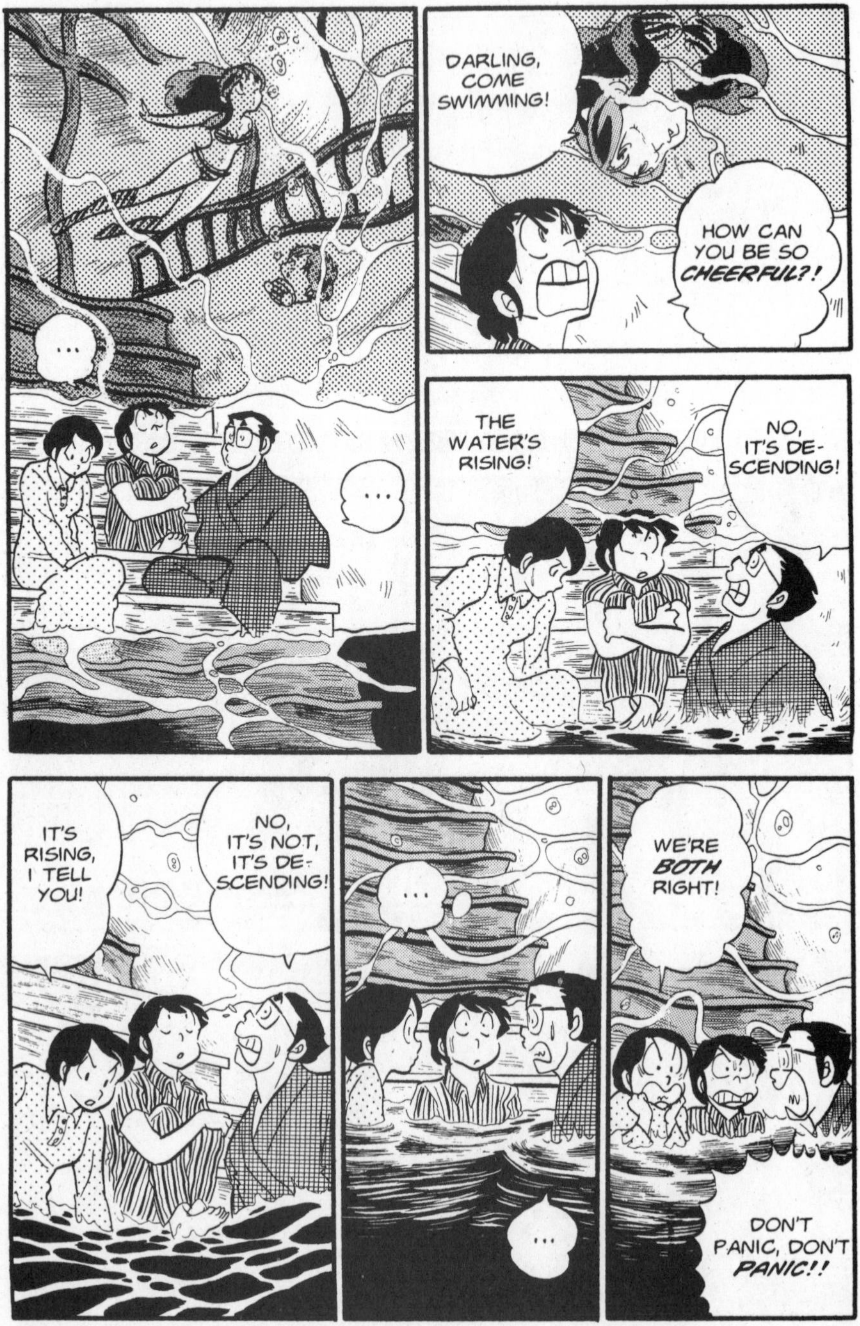
...
...
DARLING, COME SWIMMING!
HOW CAN YOU BE SO CHEERFUL?!
THE WATER'S RISING!
NO, IT'S DE-SCENDING!
IT'S RISING, I TELL YOU!
NO, IT'S NOT, IT'S DE-SCENDING!
...
...
WE'RE BOTH RIGHT!
DON'T PANIC, DON'T PANIC!!

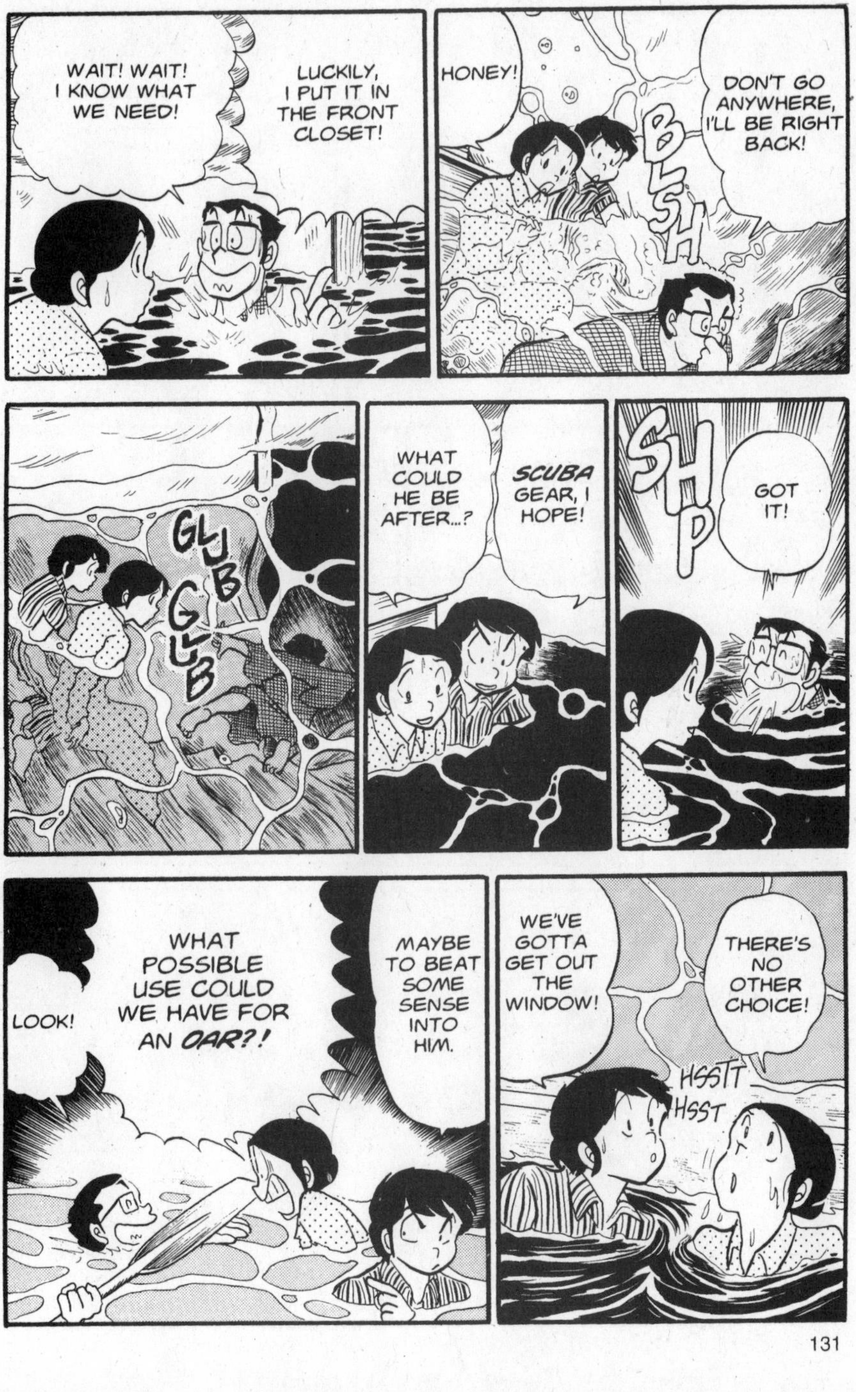
WAIT! WAIT! I KNOW WHAT WE NEED!
LUCKILY, I PUT IT IN THE FRONT CLOSET!
HONEY!
BLSH
DON'T GO ANYWHERE, I'LL BE RIGHT BACK!
GLUB GLUB
WHAT COULD HE BE AFTER...?
SCUBA GEAR, I HOPE!
SHP
GOT IT!
LOOK!
WHAT POSSIBLE USE COULD WE HAVE FOR AN OAR?!
MAYBE TO BEAT SOME SENSE INTO HIM.
WE'VE GOTTA GET OUT THE WINDOW!
HSSTT HSST
THERE'S NO OTHER CHOICE!

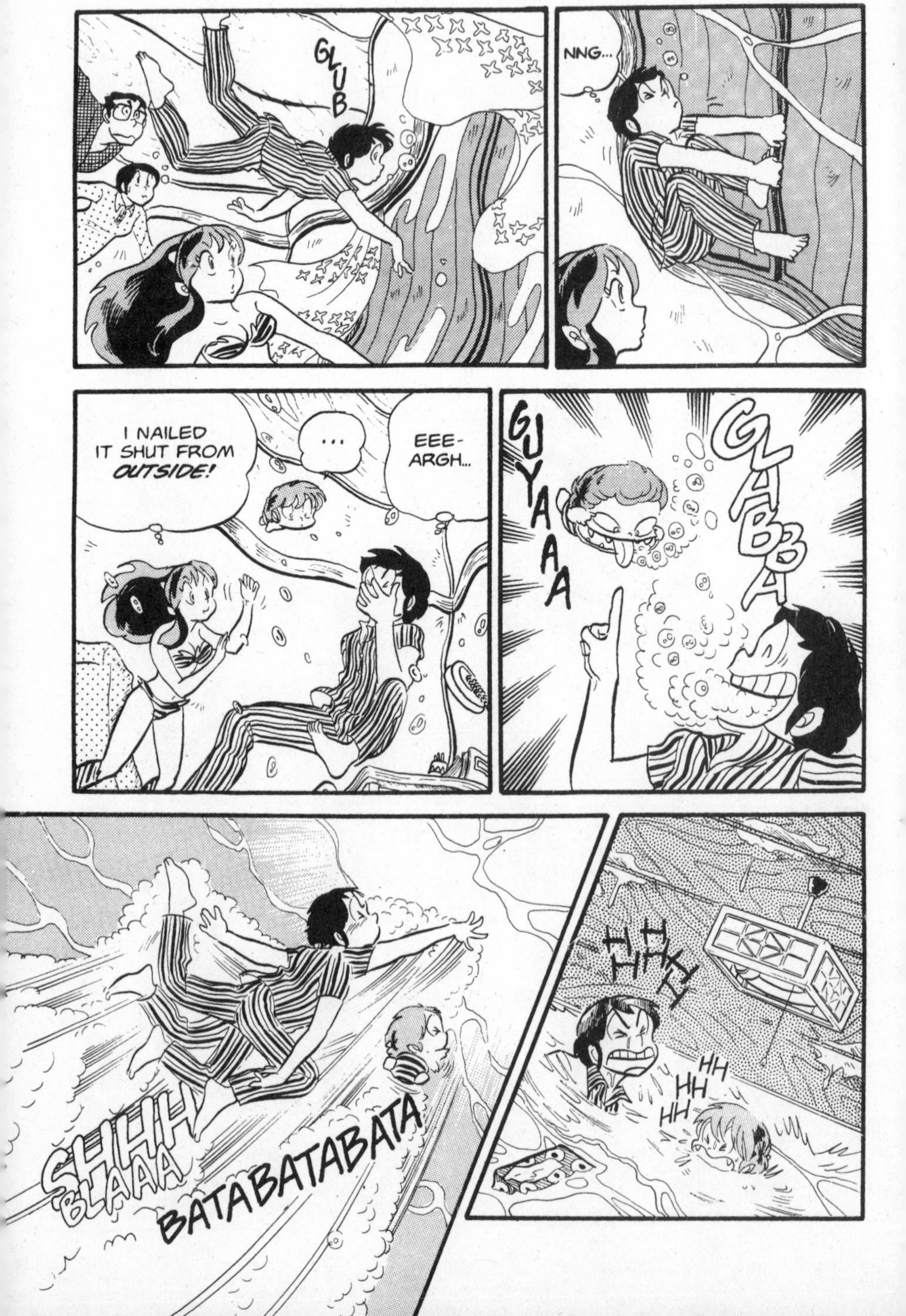
NNG...
GLUB
GUYAAAA
GLABBA
EEE-ARGH...
...
I NAILED IT SHUT FROM *OUTSIDE!*
HH
HH
HH
SHHH
BLAAA
BATABATABATA

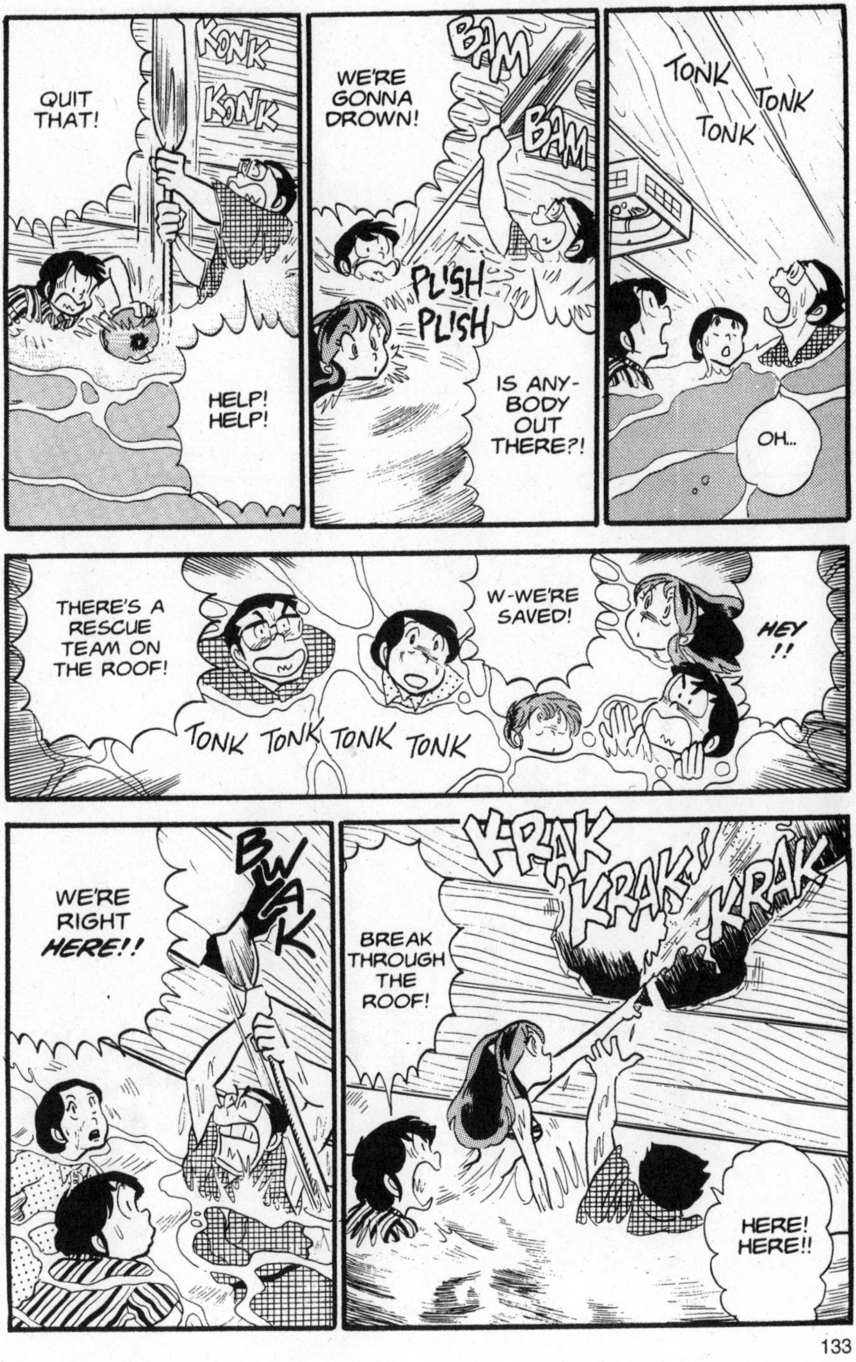
KONK
KONK
QUIT THAT!
HELP! HELP!
BAM
BAM
WE'RE GONNA DROWN!
PLISH PLISH
IS ANY-BODY OUT THERE?!
TONK
TONK
TONK
OH...
THERE'S A RESCUE TEAM ON THE ROOF!
W-WE'RE SAVED!
HEY !!
TONK TONK TONK TONK
WE'RE RIGHT HERE!!
BWAK
KRAK KRAK KRAK
BREAK THROUGH THE ROOF!
HERE! HERE!!

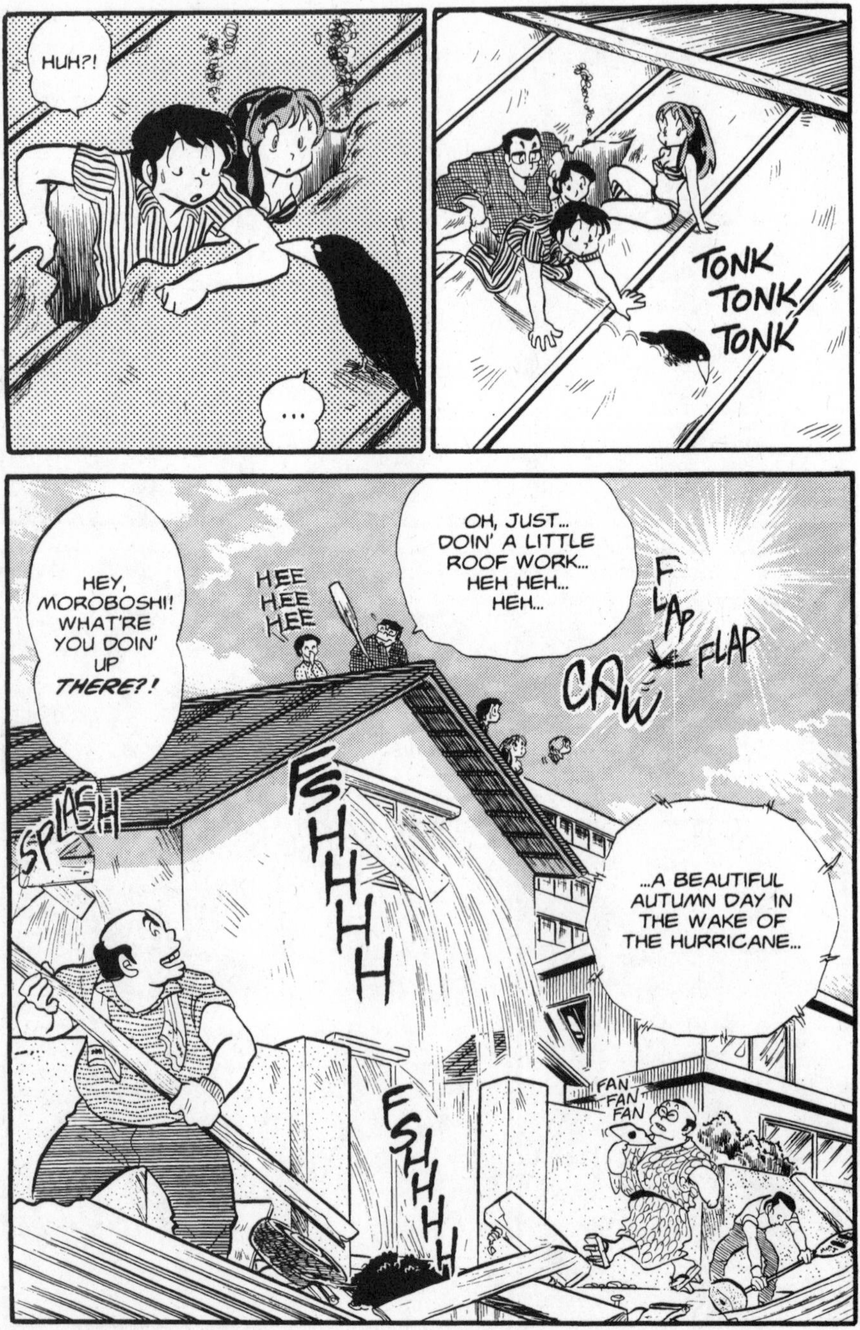
HUH?!
...
TONK TONK TONK
HEY, MOROBOSHI! WHAT'RE YOU DOIN' UP THERE?!
HEE HEE HEE
OH, JUST... DOIN' A LITTLE ROOF WORK... HEH HEH... HEH...
FLAP FLAP
CAW
SPLASH
FSHHHHH
...A BEAUTIFUL AUTUMN DAY IN THE WAKE OF THE HURRICANE...
FAN FAN FAN
FSHHHHH

PART NINE
OPERATION: DATE WATCH

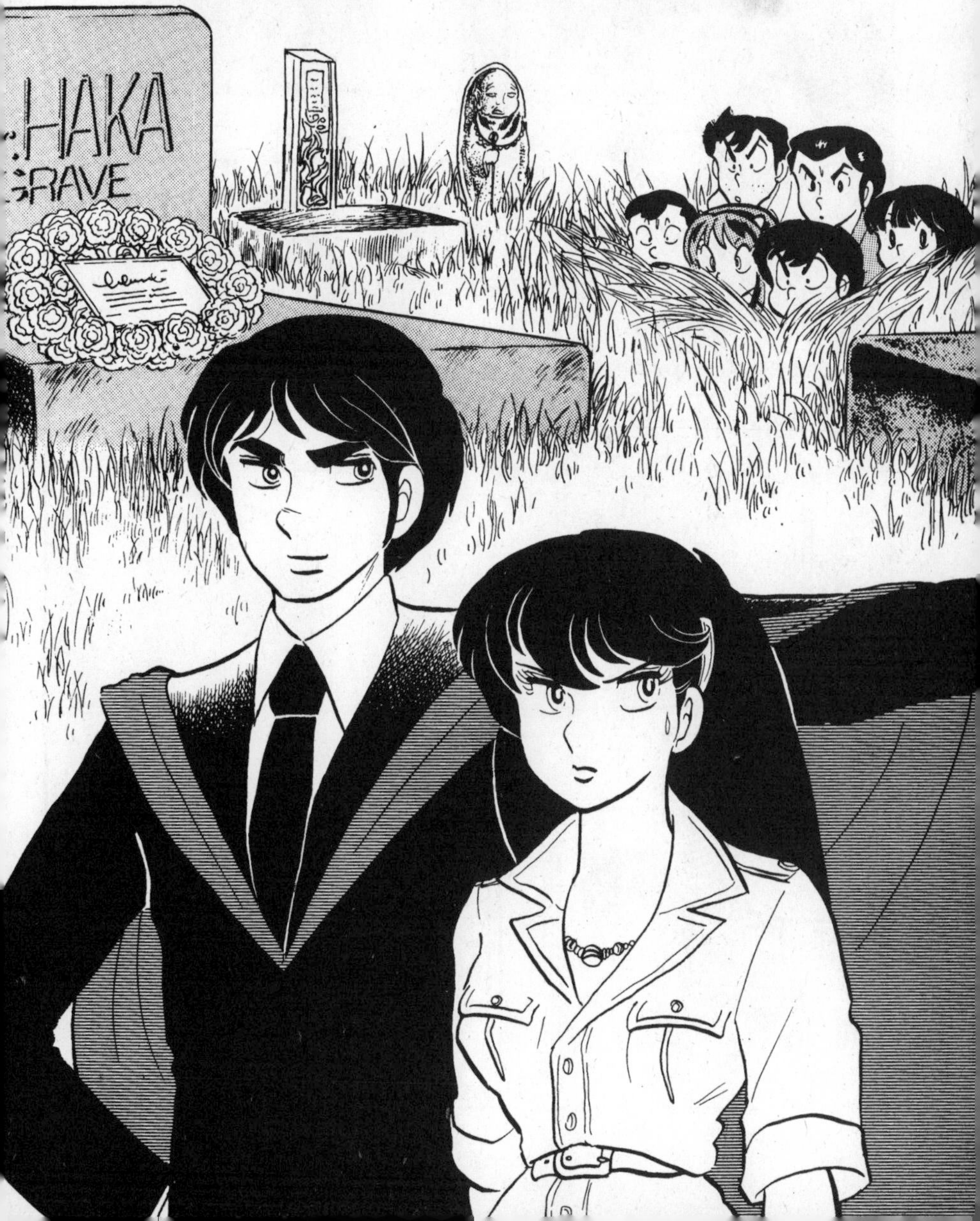
HAKA
GRAVE

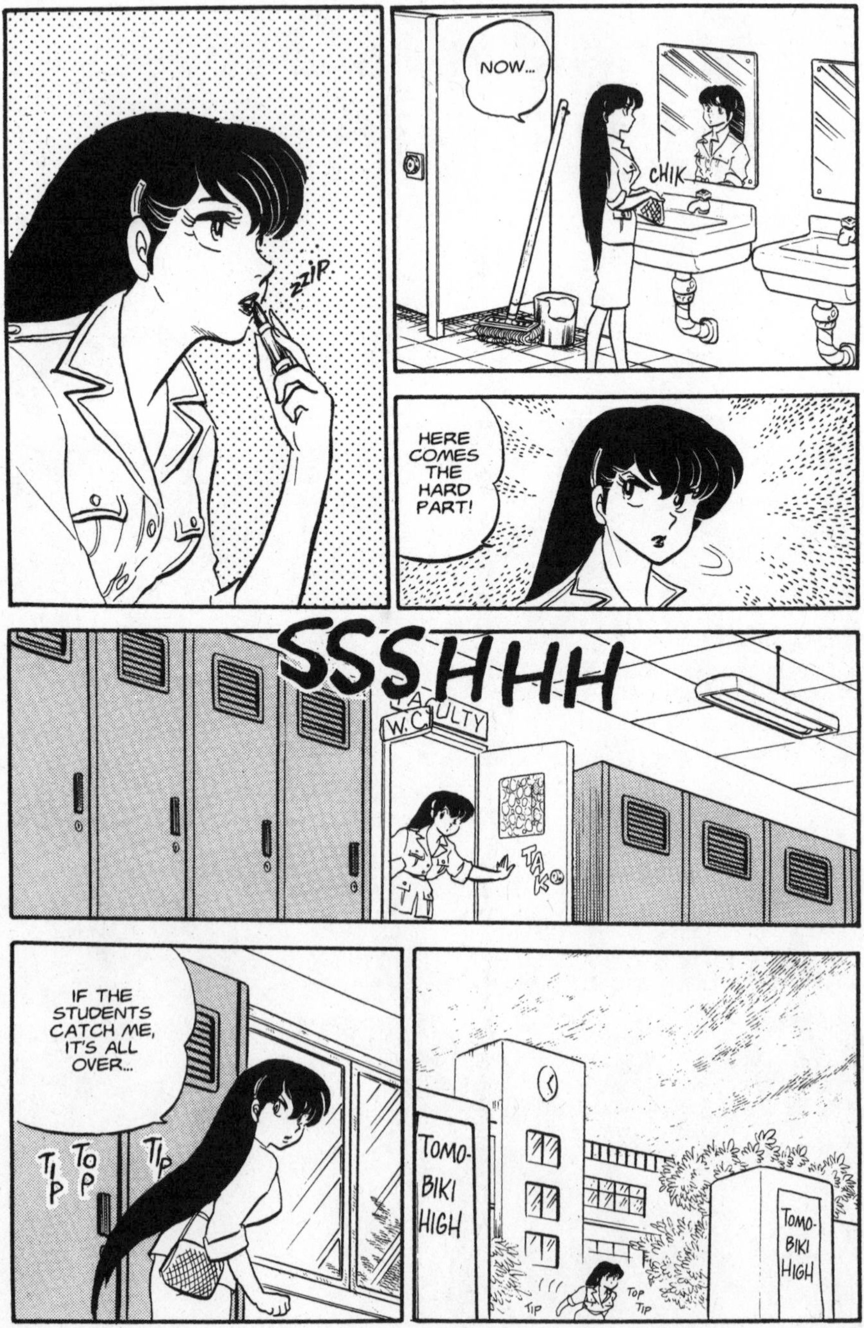
ZZIP
NOW...
CHIK
HERE COMES THE HARD PART!
SSSHHH
FACULTY W.C.
TAK
IF THE STUDENTS CATCH ME, IT'S ALL OVER...
TIP TOP TIP
TOMO-BIKI HIGH
TOMO-BIKI HIGH
TIP TOP TIP

Phew
I MADE IT. I ACTUALLY...
GUMP
THERE SHE IS!
ALL MADE UP!
WOWWW!
PHWEET!
HUBBA HUBBA
GORGEOUS!
SO. OFF ON A DATE?
N-NO... I'M...
DON'T LIE TO US! WHY ELSE WOULD YOU DRESS UP?!
IT MUST BE WITH THAT GUY!
Y'MEAN YOU'VE SEEN IM?!
BZZ BZZ
BLAH BLAH
WHAT'S HE LIKE?!
YADDA YADDA YADDA
DON'T WORRY! YOU'LL SEE HIM SOON!
"SEE HIM SOON" MY MUTTER MUTTER

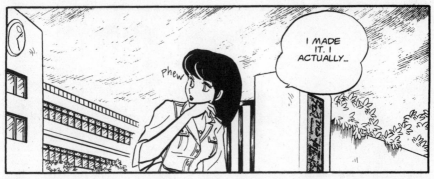

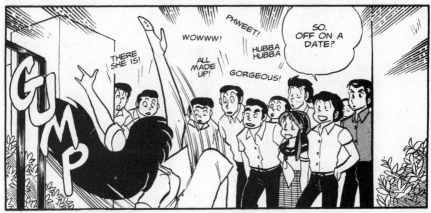

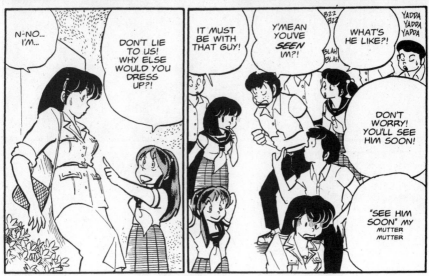

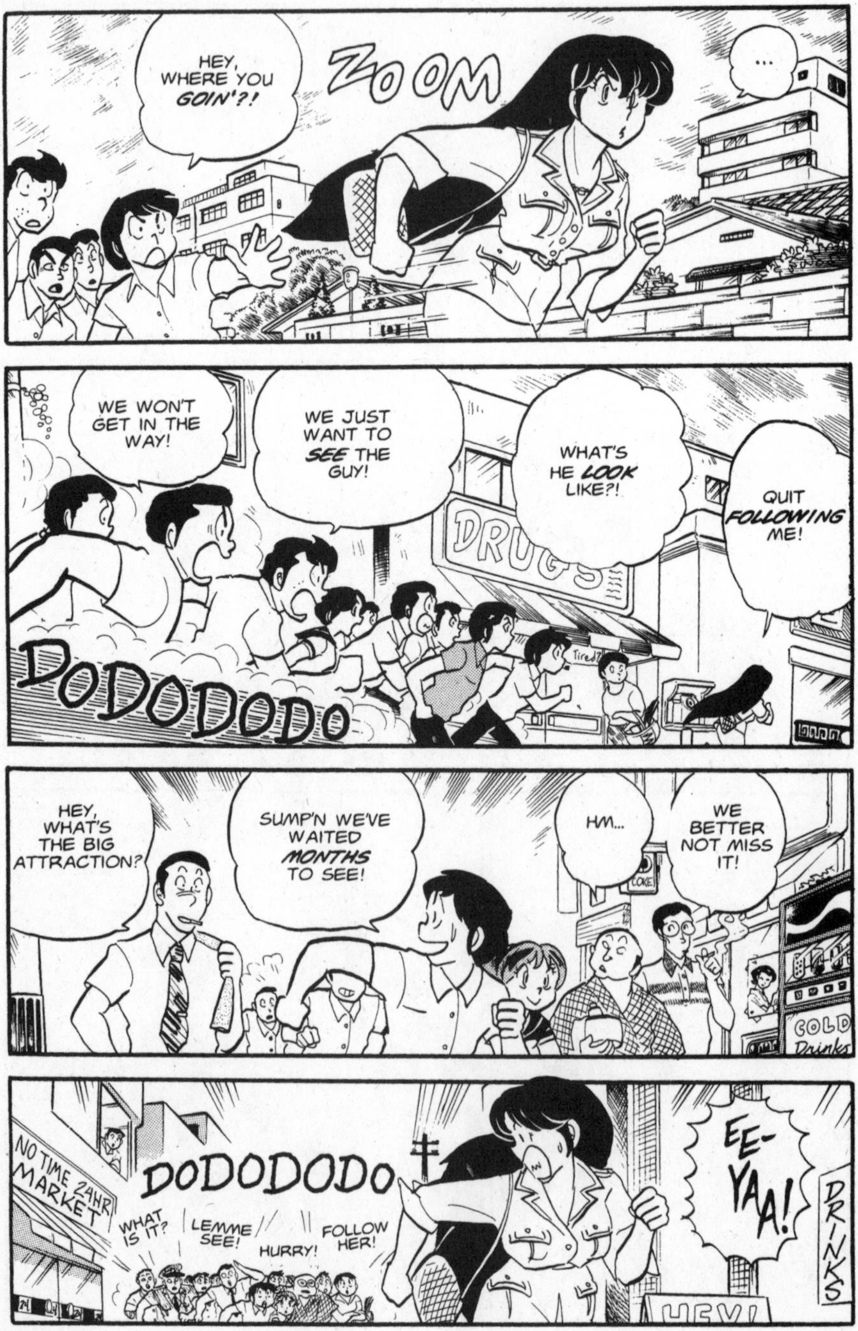

HEY, WHERE YOU GOIN'?!
ZOOM
...
WE WON'T GET IN THE WAY!
WE JUST WANT TO SEE THE GUY!
DRUGS
WHAT'S HE LOOK LIKE?!
QUIT FOLLOWING ME!
DODODODO
Tired?
HEY, WHAT'S THE BIG ATTRACTION?
SUMP'N WE'VE WAITED MONTHS TO SEE!
HM...
WE BETTER NOT MISS IT!
COKE
COLD Drinks
NO TIME 24HR MARKET
DODODODO
WHAT IS IT?
LEMME SEE!
HURRY!
FOLLOW HER!
EE-YAAA!
DRINKS

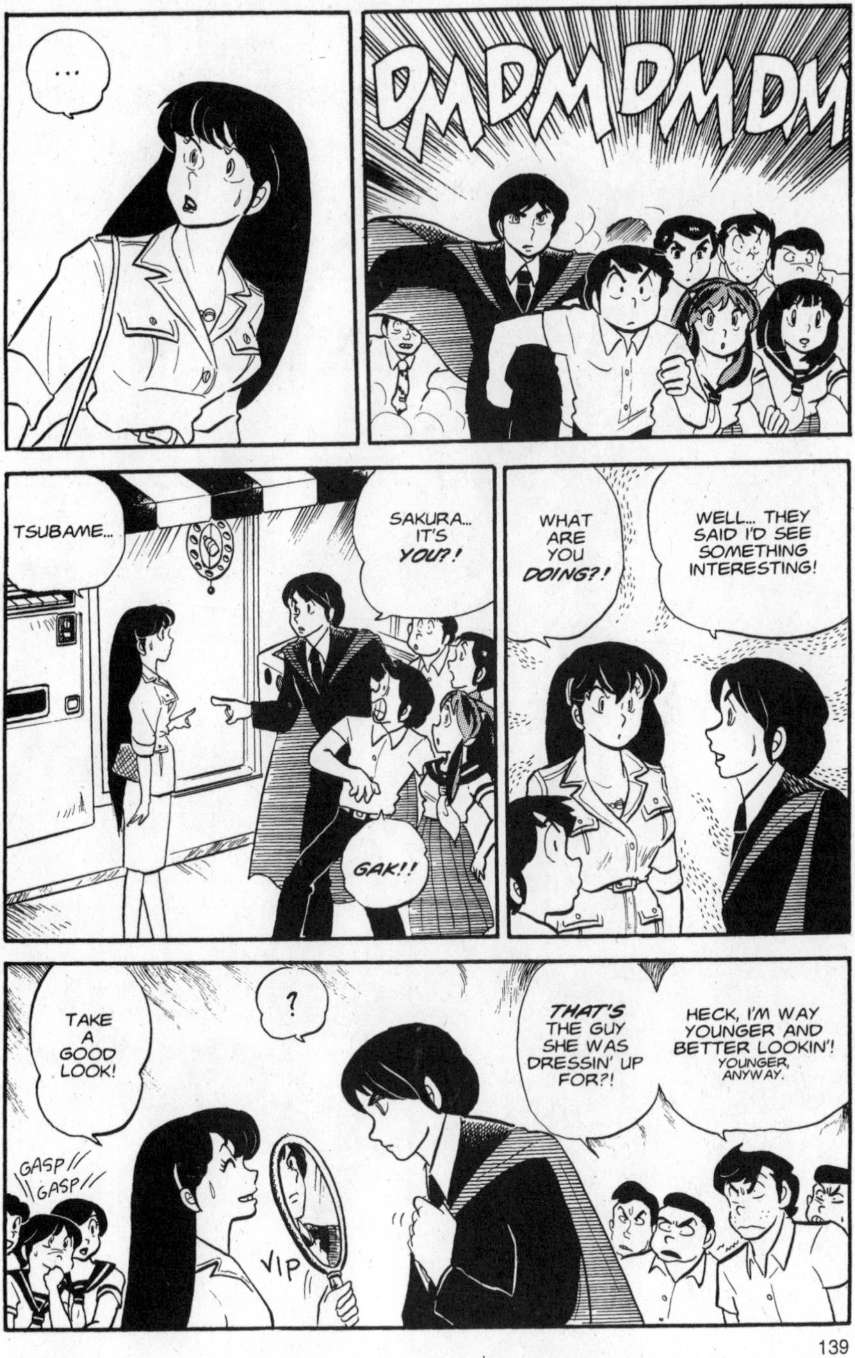
...
DMDMDMDMDM
TSUBAME...
SAKURA... IT'S *YOU?!*
GAK!!
WHAT ARE YOU *DOING?!*
WELL... THEY SAID I'D SEE SOMETHING INTERESTING!
TAKE A GOOD LOOK!
?
GASP// GASP//
VIP
THAT'S THE GUY SHE WAS DRESSIN' UP FOR?!
HECK, I'M WAY YOUNGER AND BETTER LOOKIN'!
YOUNGER, ANYWAY.

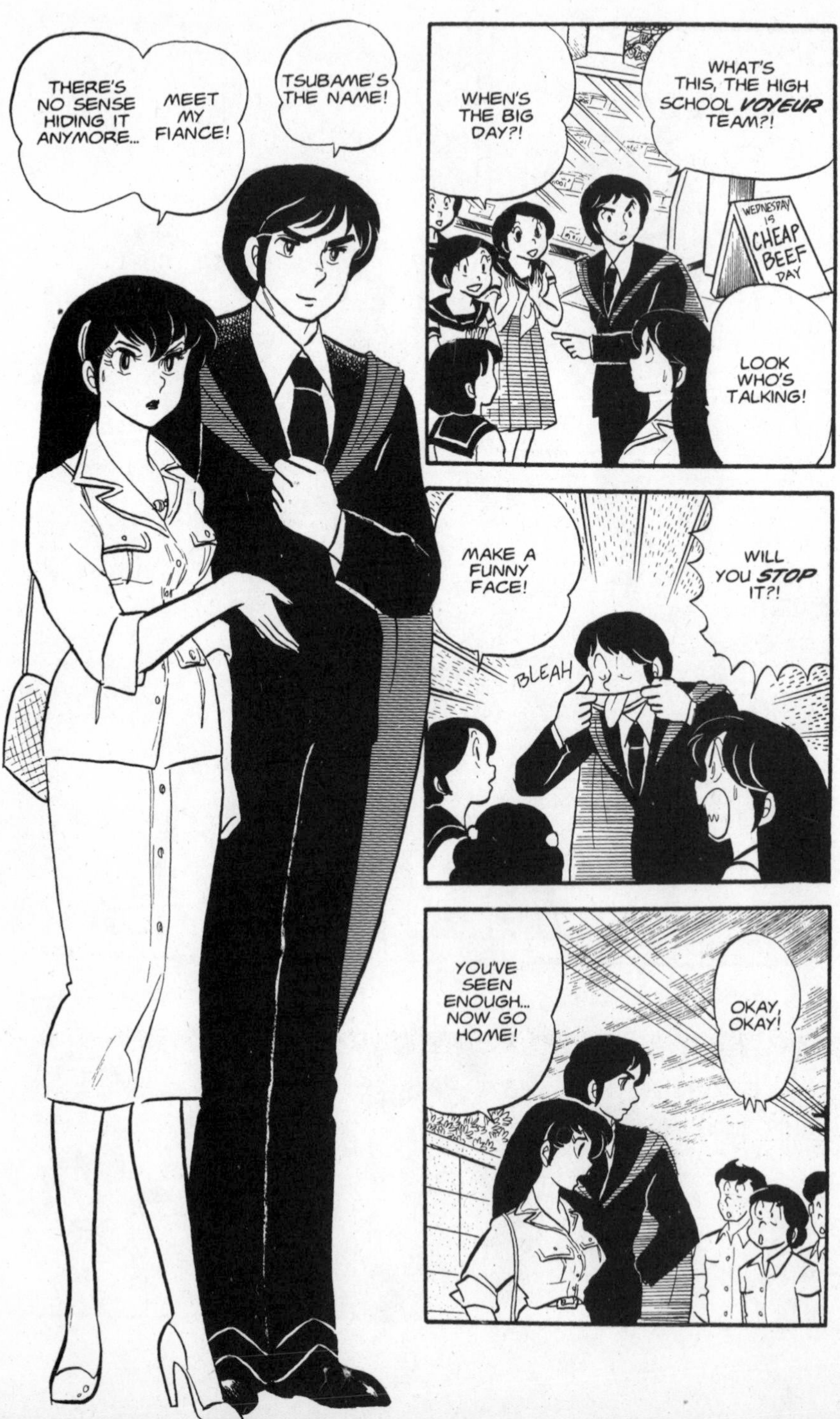
THERE'S NO SENSE HIDING IT ANYMORE...
MEET MY FIANCE!
TSUBAME'S THE NAME!
WHEN'S THE BIG DAY?!
WHAT'S THIS, THE HIGH SCHOOL ***VOYEUR*** TEAM?!
WEDNESDAY IS CHEAP BEEF DAY
LOOK WHO'S TALKING!
MAKE A FUNNY FACE!
WILL YOU ***STOP*** IT?!
BLEAH
YOU'VE SEEN ENOUGH... NOW GO HOME!
OKAY, OKAY!

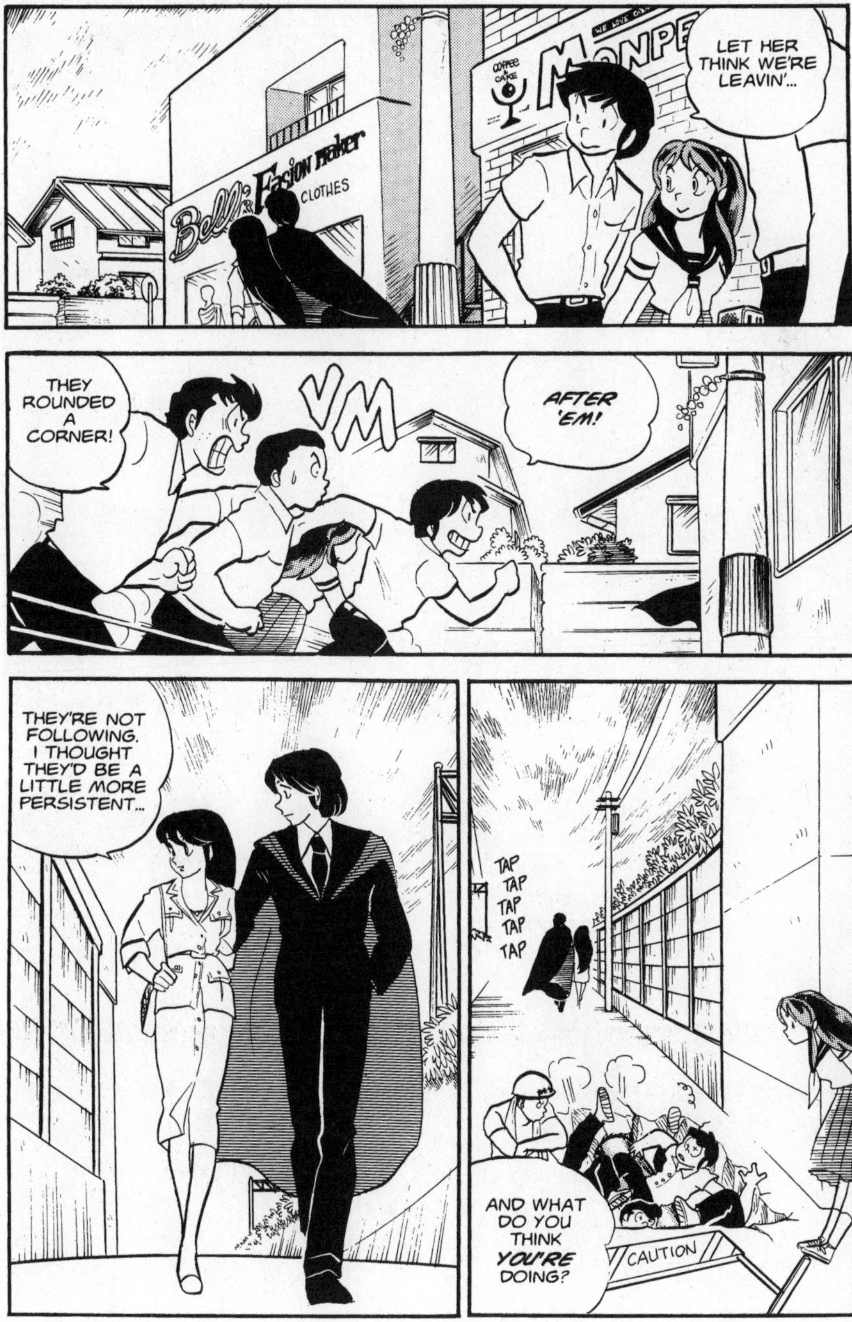
Bell's Fasion maker
CLOTHES
COFFEE & CAKE
MONPE
LET HER THINK WE'RE LEAVIN'...
THEY ROUNDED A CORNER!
VM
AFTER 'EM!
THEY'RE NOT FOLLOWING. I THOUGHT THEY'D BE A LITTLE MORE PERSISTENT...
TAP TAP TAP TAP TAP
AND WHAT DO YOU THINK YOU'RE DOING?
CAUTION

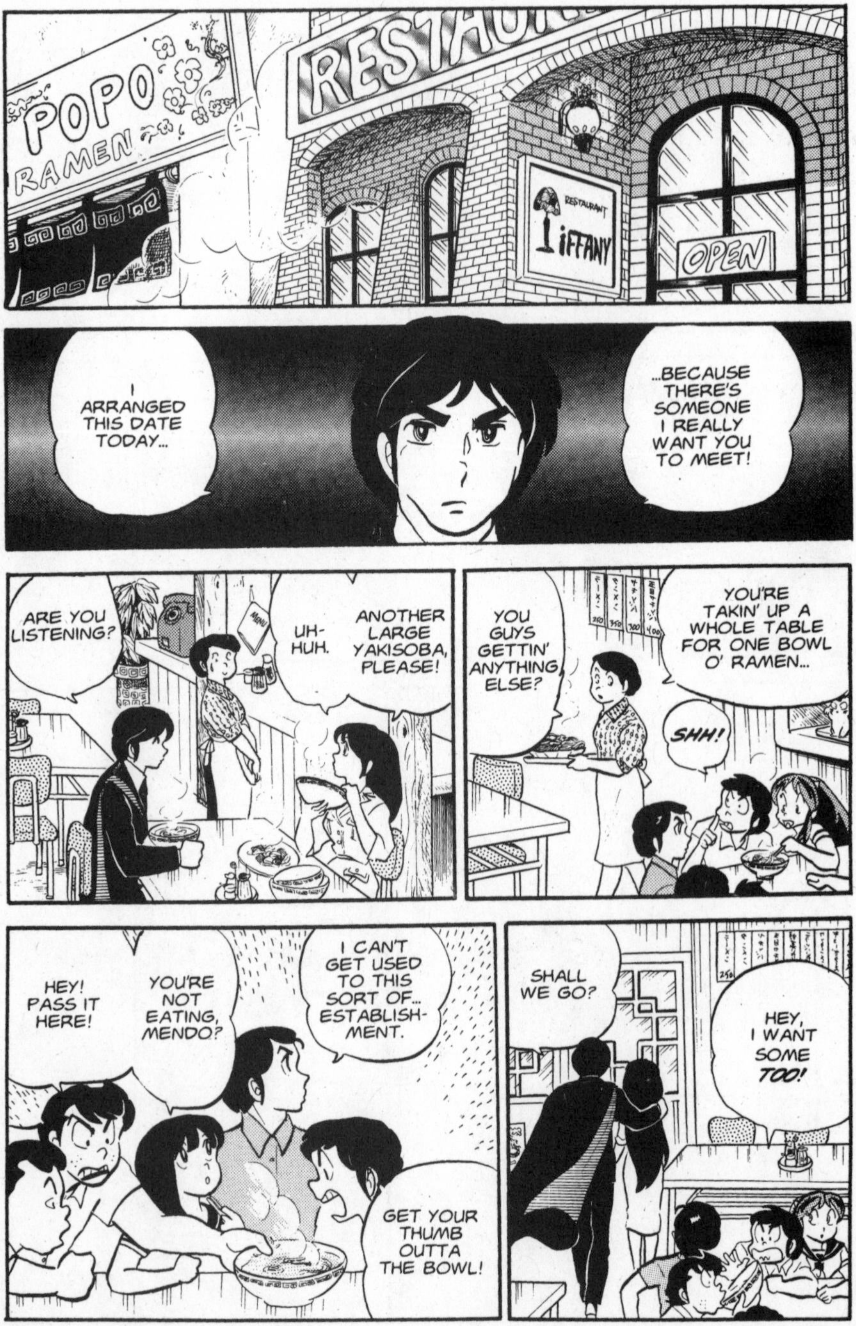
POPO
RAMEN
RESTAU
RESTAURANT
TiFFANY
OPEN
I ARRANGED THIS DATE TODAY...
...BECAUSE THERE'S SOMEONE I REALLY WANT YOU TO MEET!
ARE YOU LISTENING?
UH-HUH.
ANOTHER LARGE YAKISOBA, PLEASE!
YOU GUYS GETTIN' ANYTHING ELSE?
YOU'RE TAKIN' UP A WHOLE TABLE FOR ONE BOWL O' RAMEN...
SHH!
HEY! PASS IT HERE!
YOU'RE NOT EATING, MENDO?
I CAN'T GET USED TO THIS SORT OF... ESTABLISH-MENT.
GET YOUR THUMB OUTTA THE BOWL!
SHALL WE GO?
HEY, I WANT SOME *TOO!*

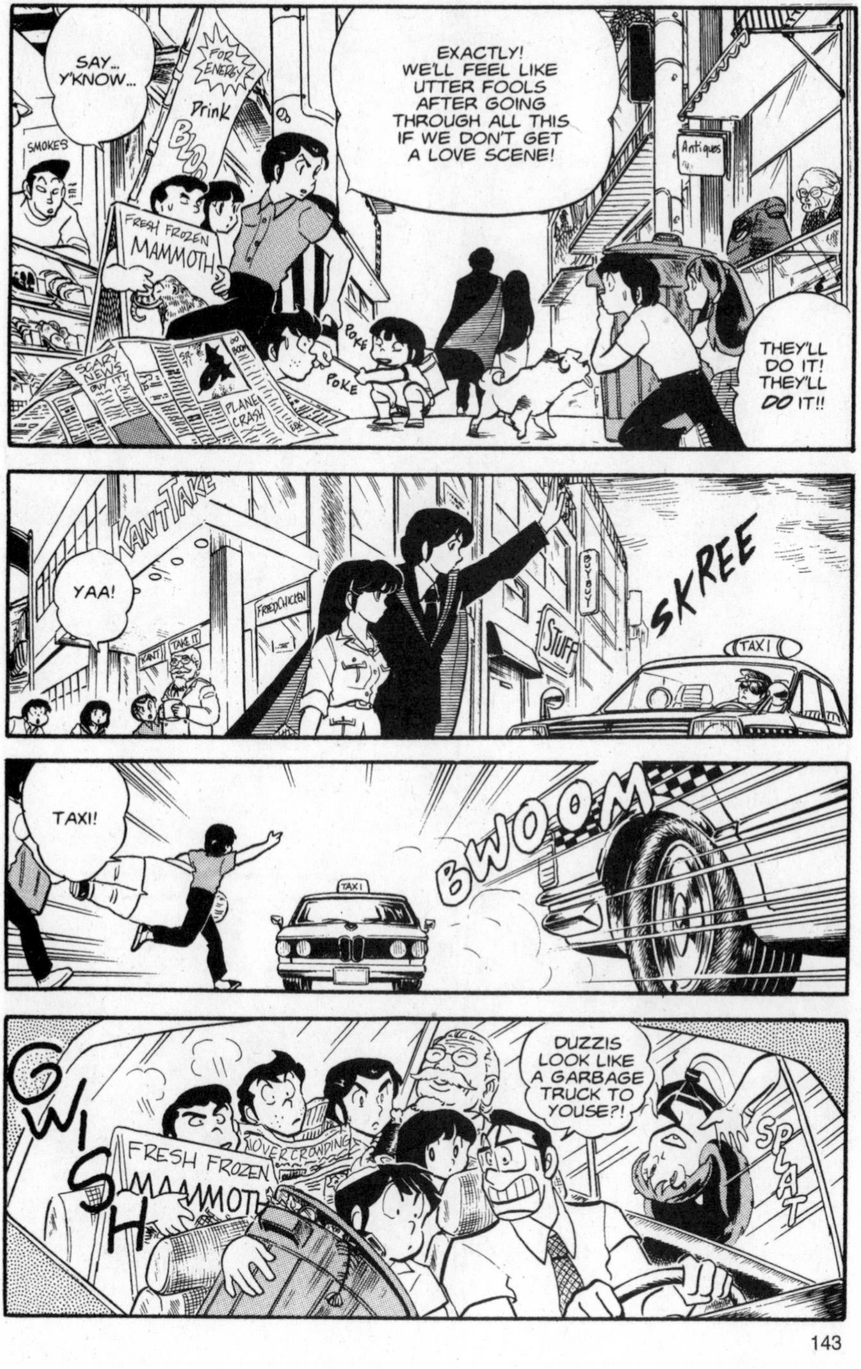
SAY... Y'KNOW...
SMOKES
FOR ENERGY
Drink
FRESH FROZEN MAMMOTH
SCARY NEWS
BUY IT!
PLANE CRASH
POKE
POKE
EXACTLY! WE'LL FEEL LIKE UTTER FOOLS AFTER GOING THROUGH ALL THIS IF WE DON'T GET A LOVE SCENE!
Antiques
THEY'LL DO IT! THEY'LL DO IT!!
KANT TAKE
YAA!
FRIED CHICKEN
KANT
TAKE IT
BUY BUY
STUFF
SKREE
TAXI
TAXI!
TAXI
BWOOM
GWISH
FRESH FROZEN MAAMMOTH
OVERCROWDING
DUZZIS LOOK LIKE A GARBAGE TRUCK TO YOUSE?!
SPLAT

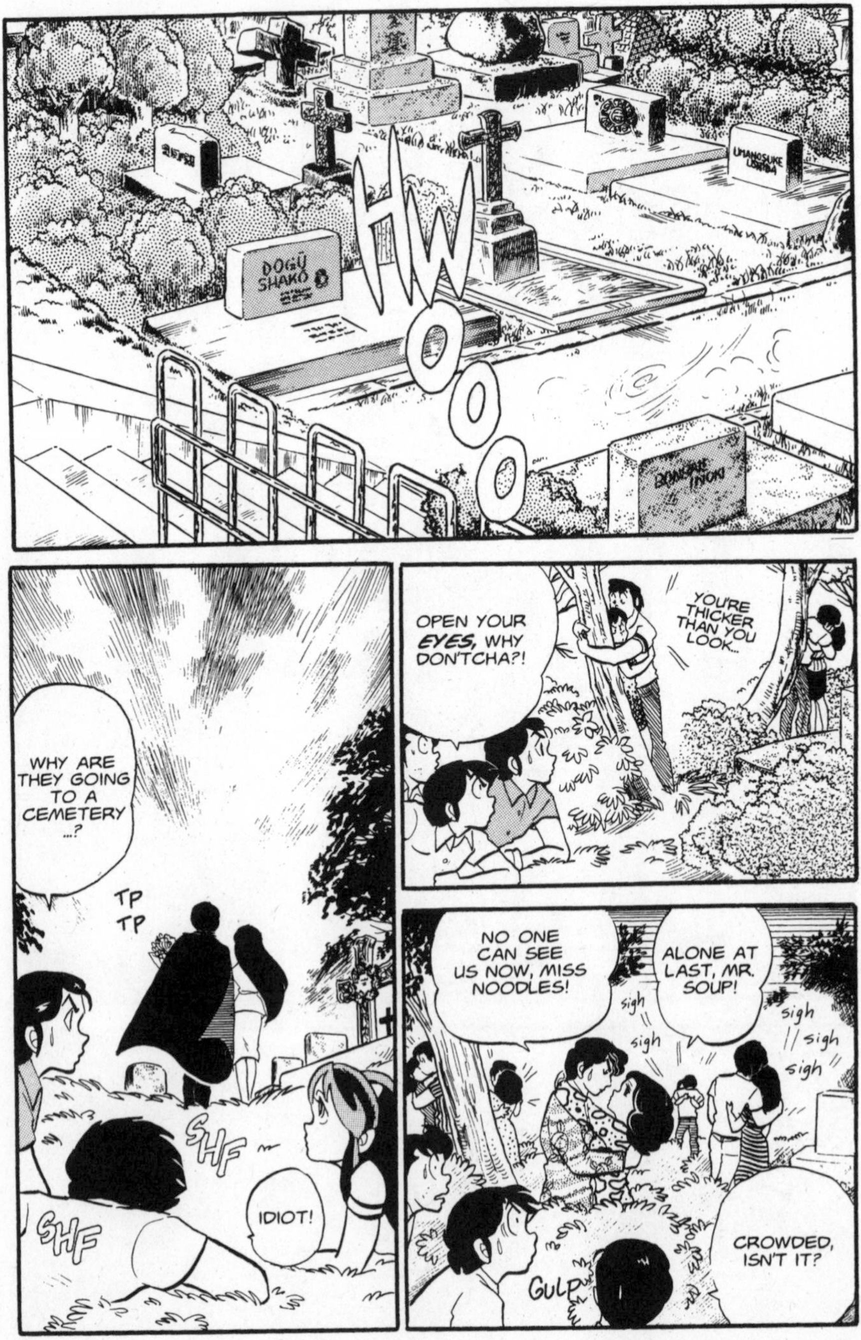
DOGŪ SHAKO
HWOOOO
WHY ARE THEY GOING TO A CEMETERY ...?
TP TP
SHF
SHF
IDIOT!
OPEN YOUR *EYES*, WHY DON'TCHA?!
YOU'RE THICKER THAN YOU LOOK...
NO ONE CAN SEE US NOW, MISS NOODLES!
ALONE AT LAST, MR. SOUP!
sigh
sigh
sigh
sigh
sigh
GULP
CROWDED, ISN'T IT?

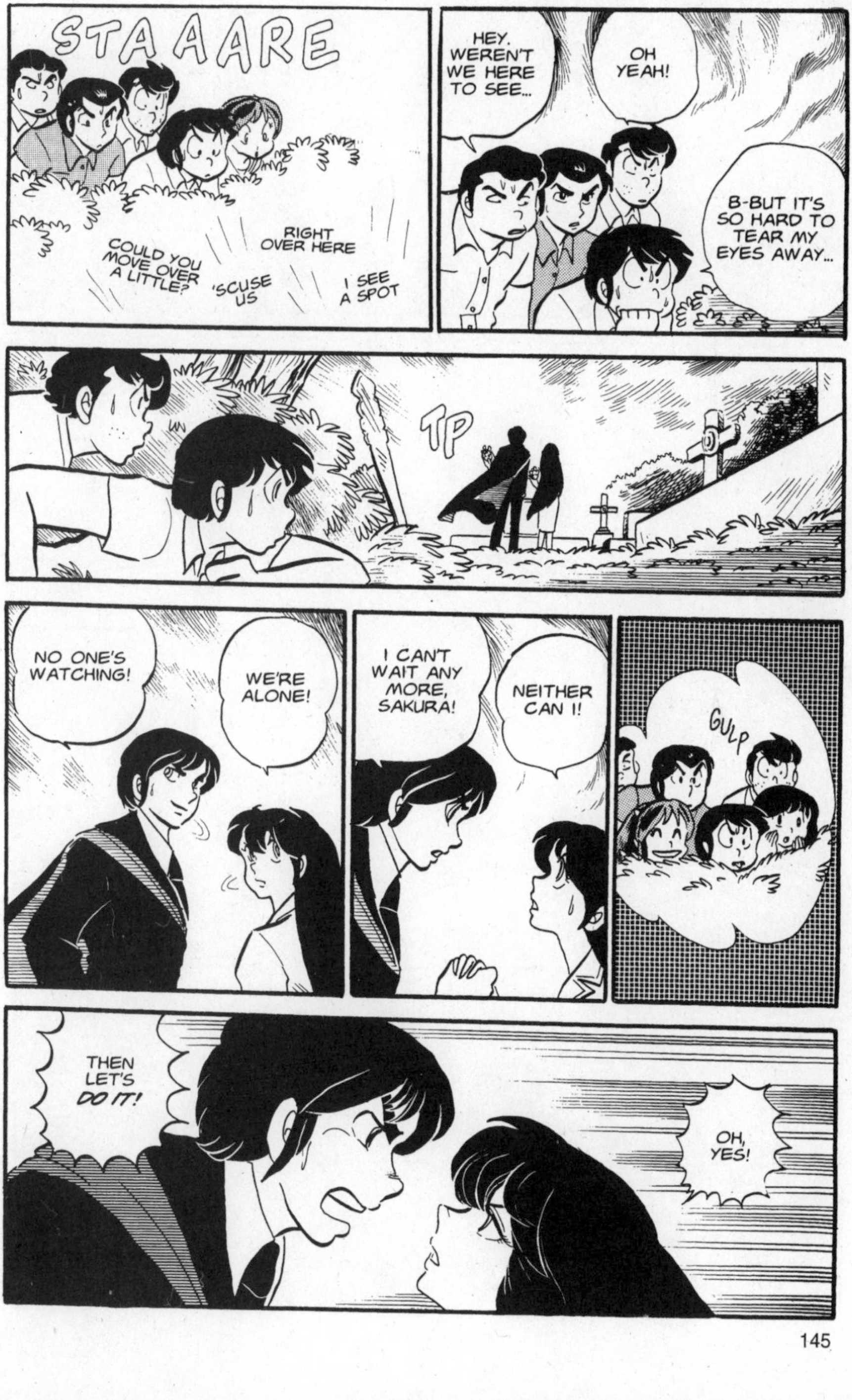
STA AARE
COULD YOU MOVE OVER A LITTLE?
RIGHT OVER HERE
'SCUSE US
I SEE A SPOT
HEY. WEREN'T WE HERE TO SEE...
OH YEAH!
B-BUT IT'S SO HARD TO TEAR MY EYES AWAY...
TP
NO ONE'S WATCHING!
WE'RE ALONE!
I CAN'T WAIT ANY MORE, SAKURA!
NEITHER CAN I!
GULP
THEN LET'S *DO IT!*
OH, YES!

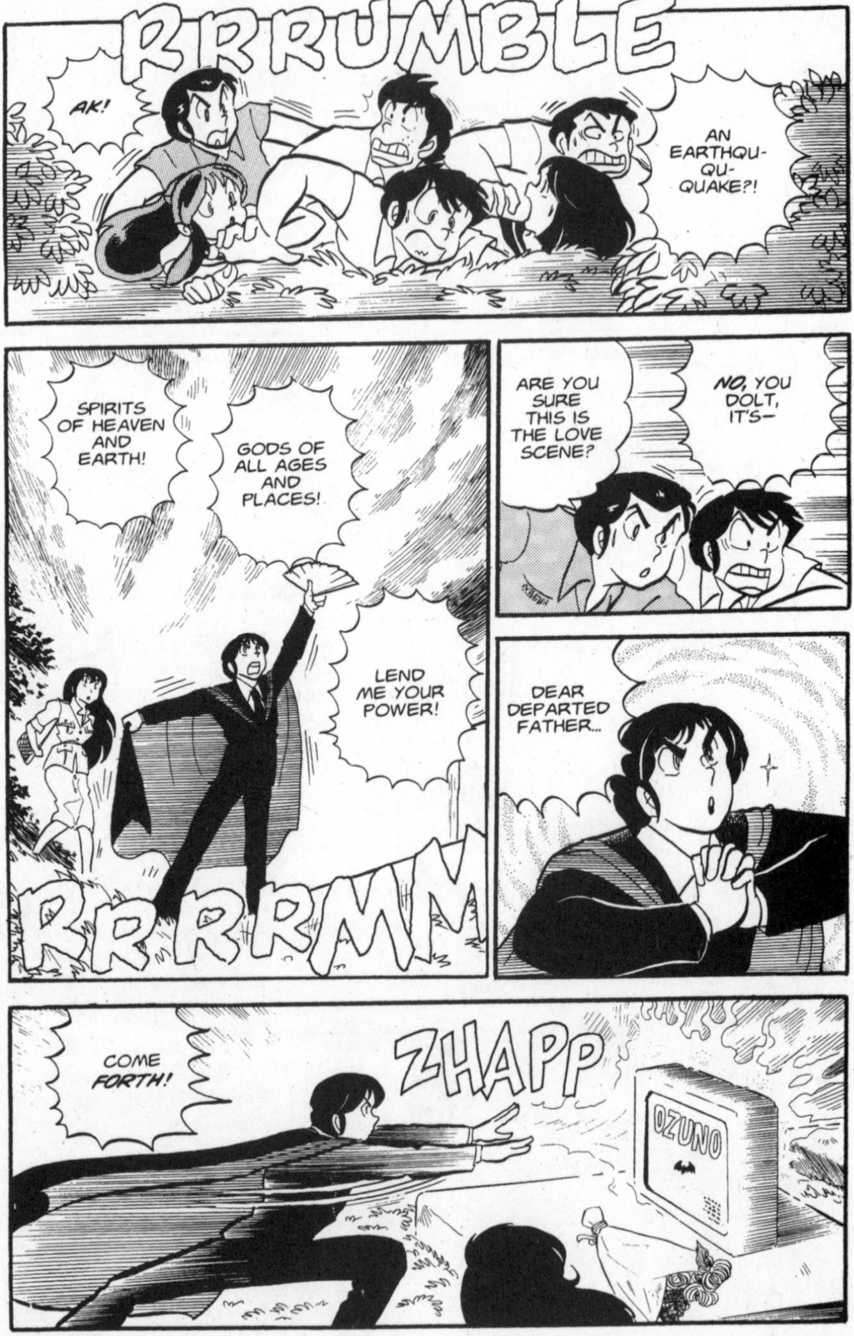
RRRUMBLE
AK!
AN EARTHQU-QU-QUAKE?!
SPIRITS OF HEAVEN AND EARTH!
GODS OF ALL AGES AND PLACES!
LEND ME YOUR POWER!
RRRRMM
ARE YOU SURE THIS IS THE LOVE SCENE?
NO, YOU DOLT, IT'S—
DEAR DEPARTED FATHER...
COME FORTH!
ZHAPP
OZUNO

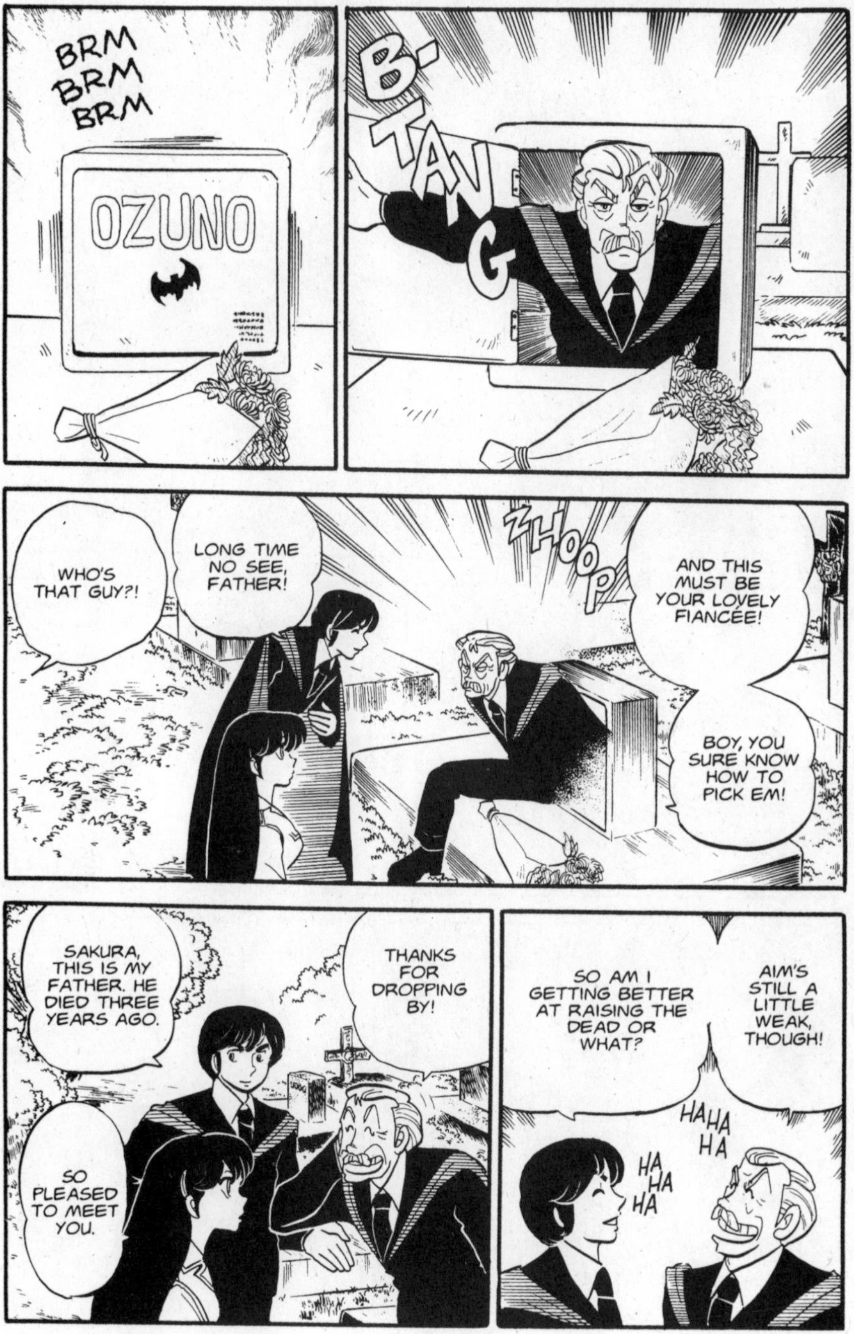
BRM BRM BRM
OZUNO
B-TANG
WHO'S THAT GUY?!
LONG TIME NO SEE, FATHER!
ZHOOP
AND THIS MUST BE YOUR LOVELY FIANCÉE!
BOY, YOU SURE KNOW HOW TO PICK EM!
SAKURA, THIS IS MY FATHER. HE DIED THREE YEARS AGO.
THANKS FOR DROPPING BY!
SO PLEASED TO MEET YOU.
SO AM I GETTING BETTER AT RAISING THE DEAD OR WHAT?
AIM'S STILL A LITTLE WEAK, THOUGH!
HAHA HA
HA HA HA

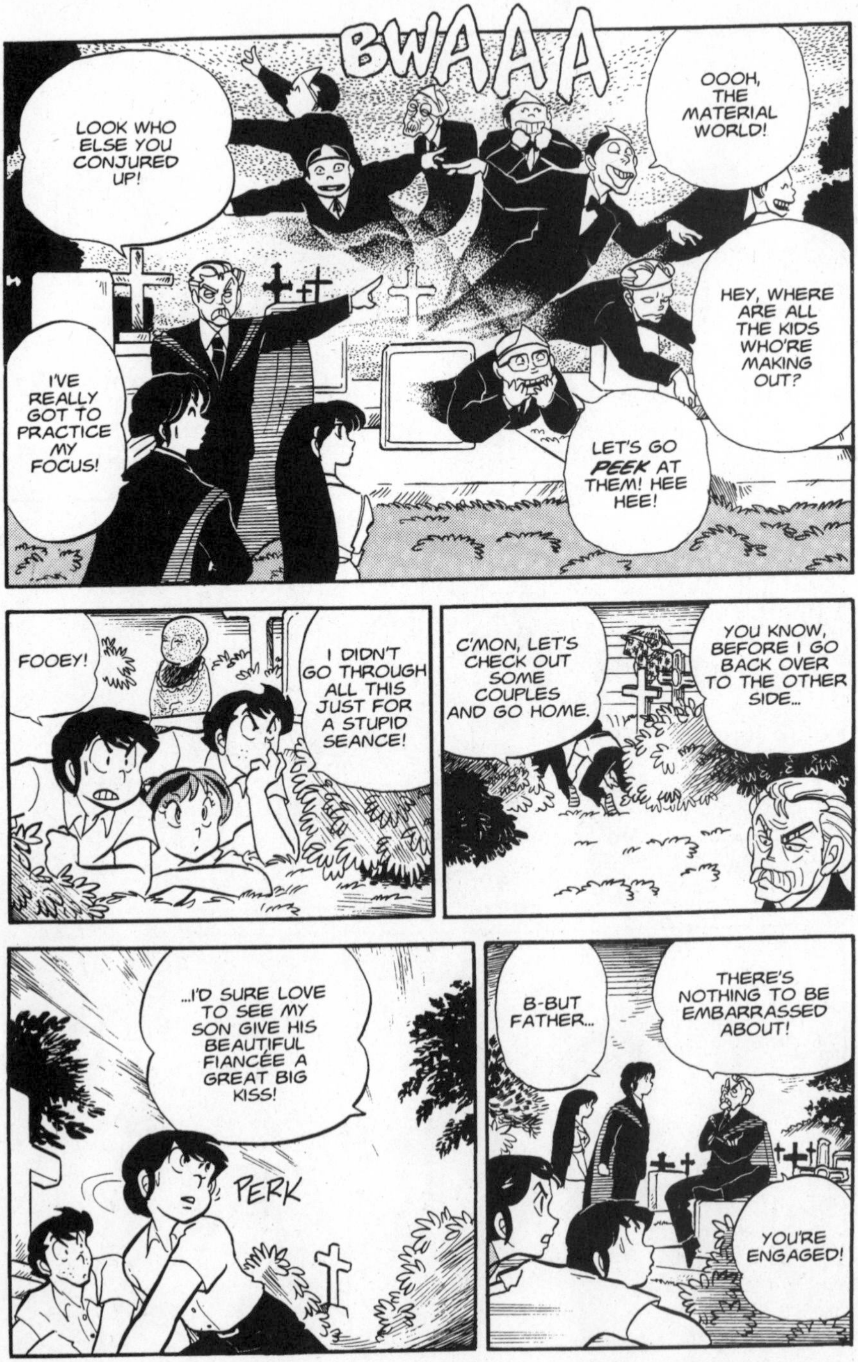
BWAAA
LOOK WHO ELSE YOU CONJURED UP!
OOOH, THE MATERIAL WORLD!
I'VE REALLY GOT TO PRACTICE MY FOCUS!
HEY, WHERE ARE ALL THE KIDS WHO'RE MAKING OUT?
LET'S GO PEEK AT THEM! HEE HEE!
FOOEY!
I DIDN'T GO THROUGH ALL THIS JUST FOR A STUPID SEANCE!
C'MON, LET'S CHECK OUT SOME COUPLES AND GO HOME.
YOU KNOW, BEFORE I GO BACK OVER TO THE OTHER SIDE...
...I'D SURE LOVE TO SEE MY SON GIVE HIS BEAUTIFUL FIANCÉE A GREAT BIG KISS!
PERK
B-BUT FATHER...
THERE'S NOTHING TO BE EMBARRASSED ABOUT!
YOU'RE ENGAGED!

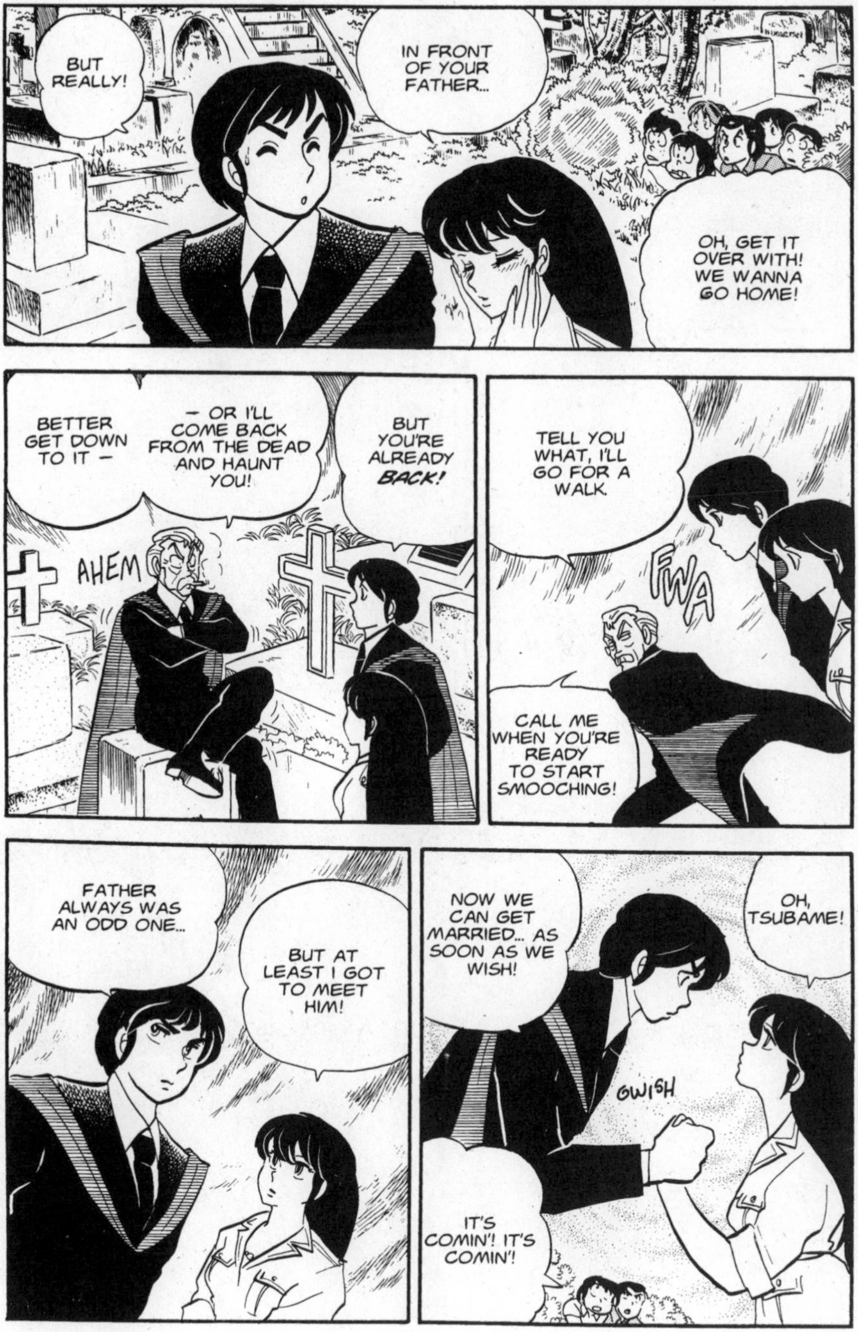
BUT REALLY!
IN FRONT OF YOUR FATHER...
OH, GET IT OVER WITH! WE WANNA GO HOME!
BETTER GET DOWN TO IT —
— OR I'LL COME BACK FROM THE DEAD AND HAUNT YOU!
AHEM
BUT YOU'RE ALREADY *BACK!*
TELL YOU WHAT, I'LL GO FOR A WALK.
FWA
CALL ME WHEN YOU'RE READY TO START SMOOCHING!
FATHER ALWAYS WAS AN ODD ONE...
BUT AT LEAST I GOT TO MEET HIM!
NOW WE CAN GET MARRIED... AS SOON AS WE WISH!
OH, TSUBAME!
GWISH
IT'S COMIN'! IT'S COMIN'!

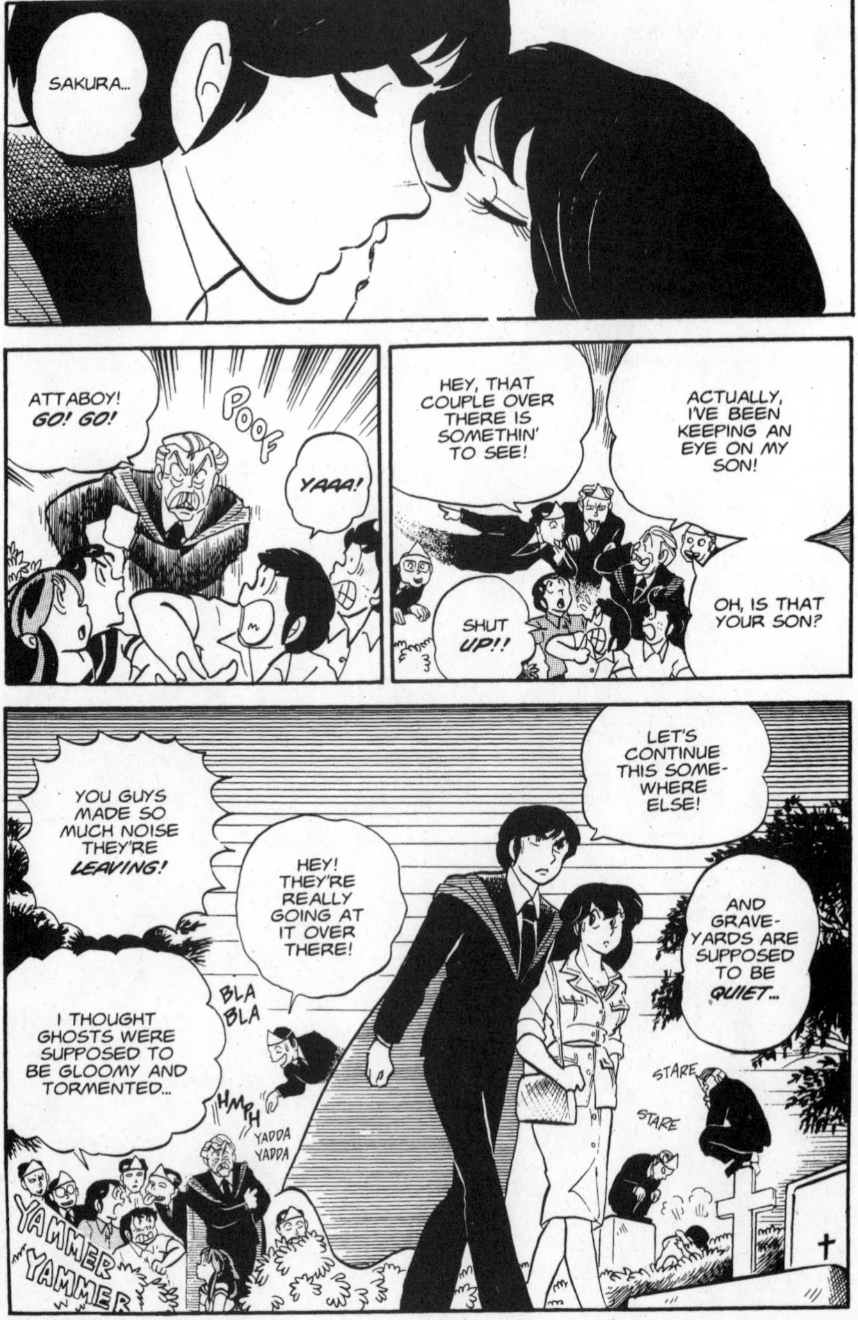
SAKURA...
ATTABOY! GO! GO!
POOF
YAAA!
HEY, THAT COUPLE OVER THERE IS SOMETHIN' TO SEE!
ACTUALLY, I'VE BEEN KEEPING AN EYE ON MY SON!
SHUT UP!!
OH, IS THAT YOUR SON?
YOU GUYS MADE SO MUCH NOISE THEY'RE LEAVING!
HEY! THEY'RE REALLY GOING AT IT OVER THERE!
LET'S CONTINUE THIS SOME-WHERE ELSE!
AND GRAVE-YARDS ARE SUPPOSED TO BE QUIET...
I THOUGHT GHOSTS WERE SUPPOSED TO BE GLOOMY AND TORMENTED...
BLA BLA
HMPH
YADDA YADDA
STARE
STARE
YAMMER YAMMER

PART TEN

CURE FOR THE UNCOMMON COLD

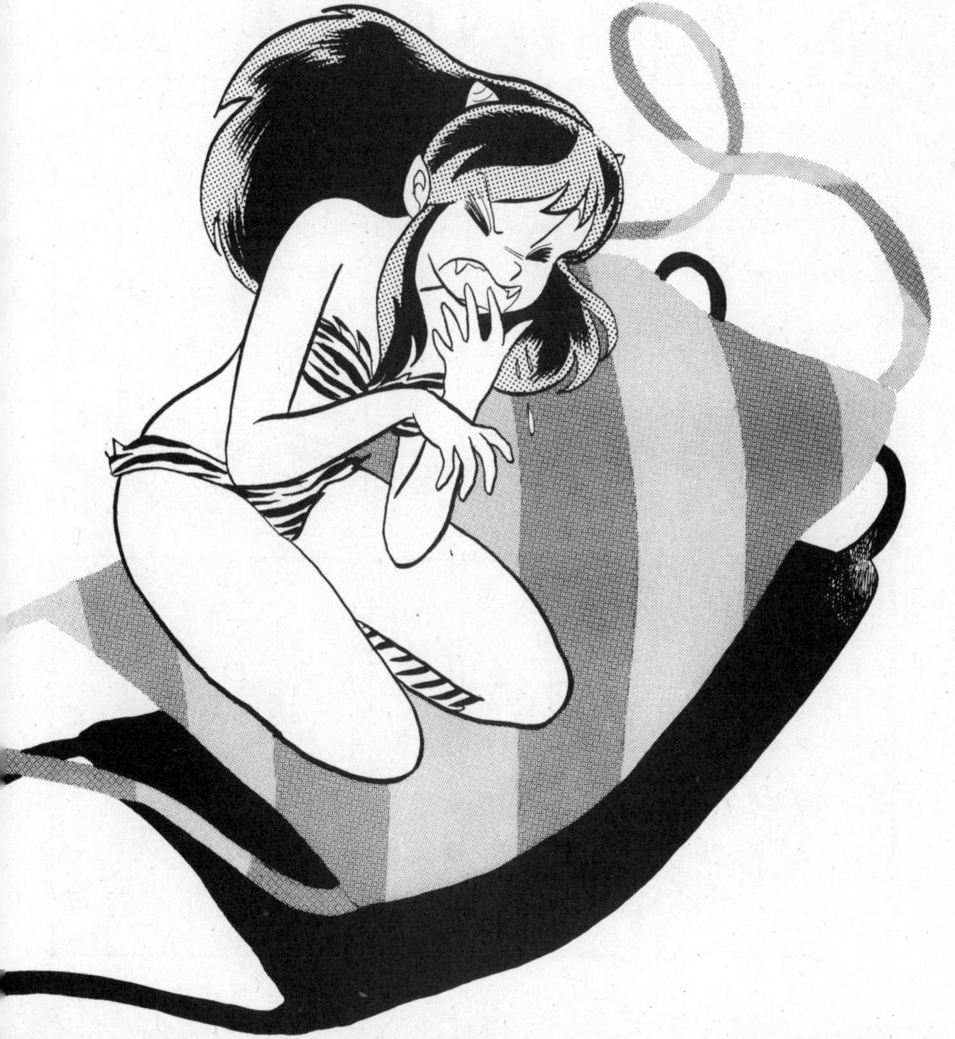

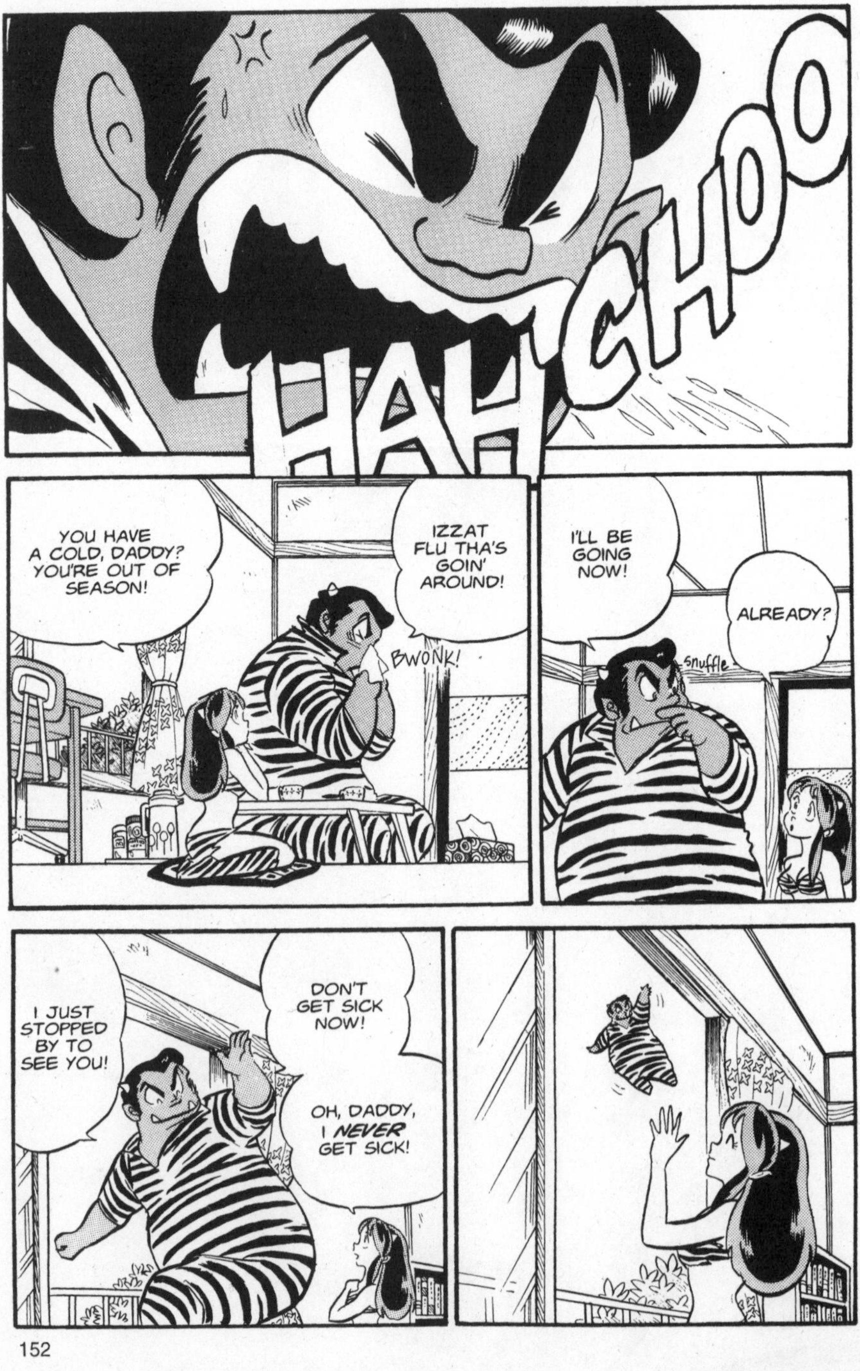
HAH CHOO
YOU HAVE A COLD, DADDY? YOU'RE OUT OF SEASON!
IZZAT FLU THA'S GOIN' AROUND!
BWONK!
I'LL BE GOING NOW!
snuffle
ALREADY?
I JUST STOPPED BY TO SEE YOU!
DON'T GET SICK NOW!
OH, DADDY, I ***NEVER*** GET SICK!

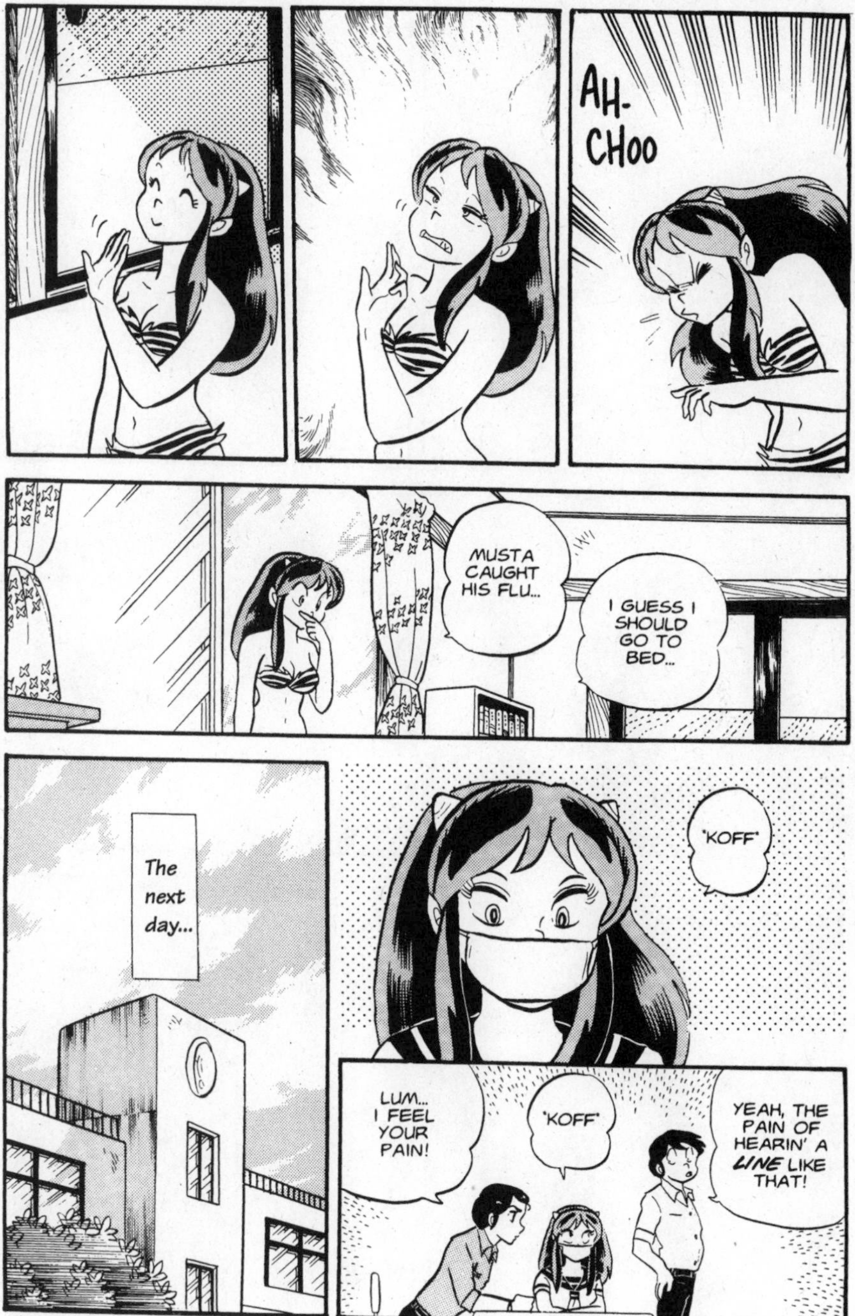
AH-
CHOO
MUSTA CAUGHT HIS FLU...
I GUESS I SHOULD GO TO BED...
The next day...
"KOFF"
LUM... I FEEL YOUR PAIN!
"KOFF"
YEAH, THE PAIN OF HEARIN' A LINE LIKE THAT!

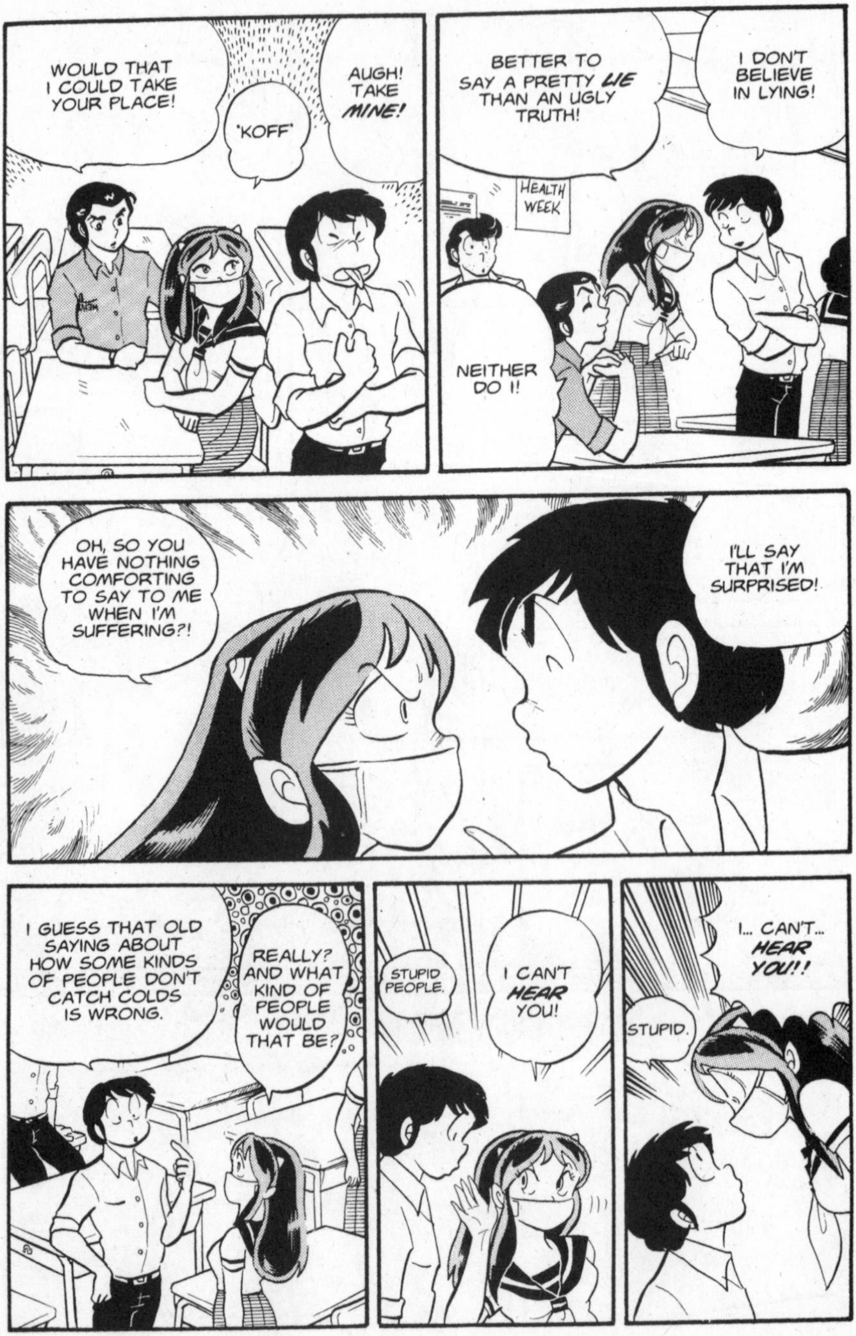
WOULD THAT I COULD TAKE YOUR PLACE!
'KOFF'
AUGH! TAKE MINE!
BETTER TO SAY A PRETTY LIE THAN AN UGLY TRUTH!
I DON'T BELIEVE IN LYING!
HEALTH WEEK
NEITHER DO I!
OH, SO YOU HAVE NOTHING COMFORTING TO SAY TO ME WHEN I'M SUFFERING?!
I'LL SAY THAT I'M SURPRISED!
I GUESS THAT OLD SAYING ABOUT HOW SOME KINDS OF PEOPLE DON'T CATCH COLDS IS WRONG.
REALLY? AND WHAT KIND OF PEOPLE WOULD THAT BE?
STUPID PEOPLE.
I CAN'T HEAR YOU!
I... CAN'T... HEAR YOU!!
STUPID.

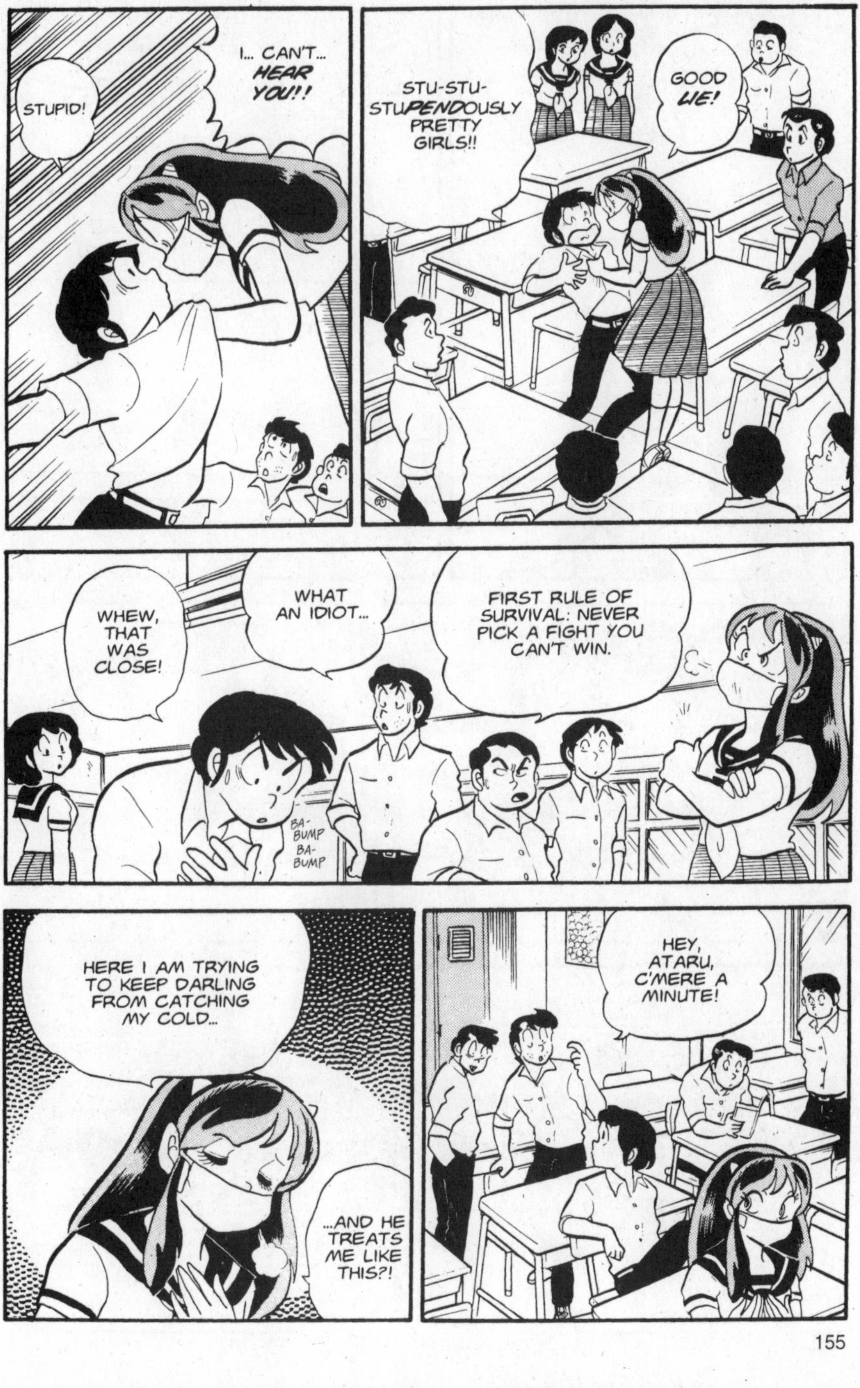
STUPID!
I... CAN'T... HEAR YOU!!
STU-STU-STUPENDOUSLY PRETTY GIRLS!!
GOOD LIE!
WHEW, THAT WAS CLOSE!
WHAT AN IDIOT...
FIRST RULE OF SURVIVAL: NEVER PICK A FIGHT YOU CAN'T WIN.
BA-BUMP BA-BUMP
HERE I AM TRYING TO KEEP DARLING FROM CATCHING MY COLD...
...AND HE TREATS ME LIKE THIS?!
HEY, ATARU, C'MERE A MINUTE!

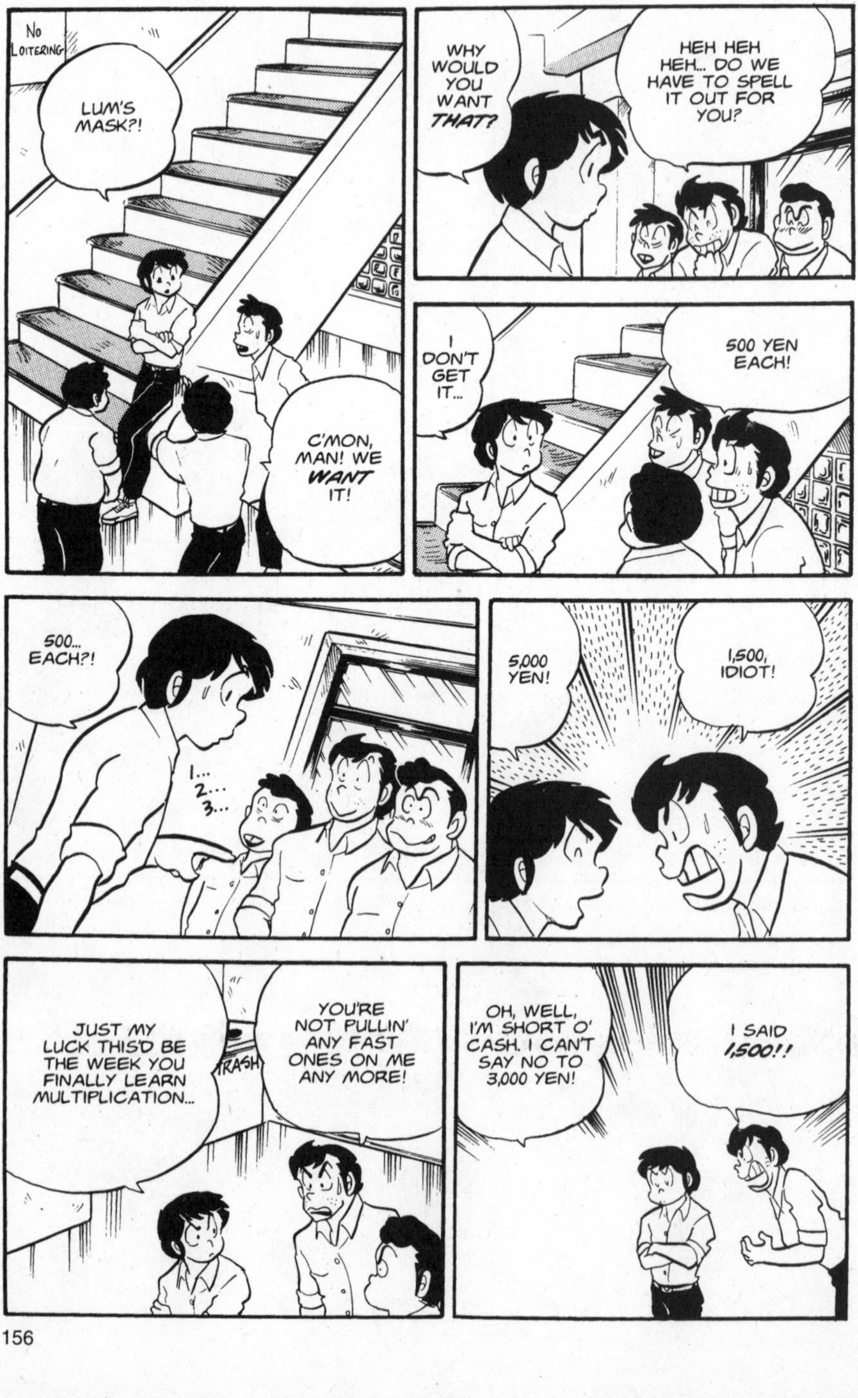
No Loitering
LUM'S MASK?!
C'MON, MAN! WE *WANT* IT!
WHY WOULD YOU WANT *THAT?*
HEH HEH HEH... DO WE HAVE TO SPELL IT OUT FOR YOU?
I DON'T GET IT...
500 YEN EACH!
500... EACH?!
1... 2... 3...
5,000 YEN!
1,500, IDIOT!
JUST MY LUCK THIS'D BE THE WEEK YOU FINALLY LEARN MULTIPLICATION...
TRASH
YOU'RE NOT PULLIN' ANY FAST ONES ON ME ANY MORE!
OH, WELL, I'M SHORT O' CASH. I CAN'T SAY NO TO 3,000 YEN!
I SAID *1,500!!*

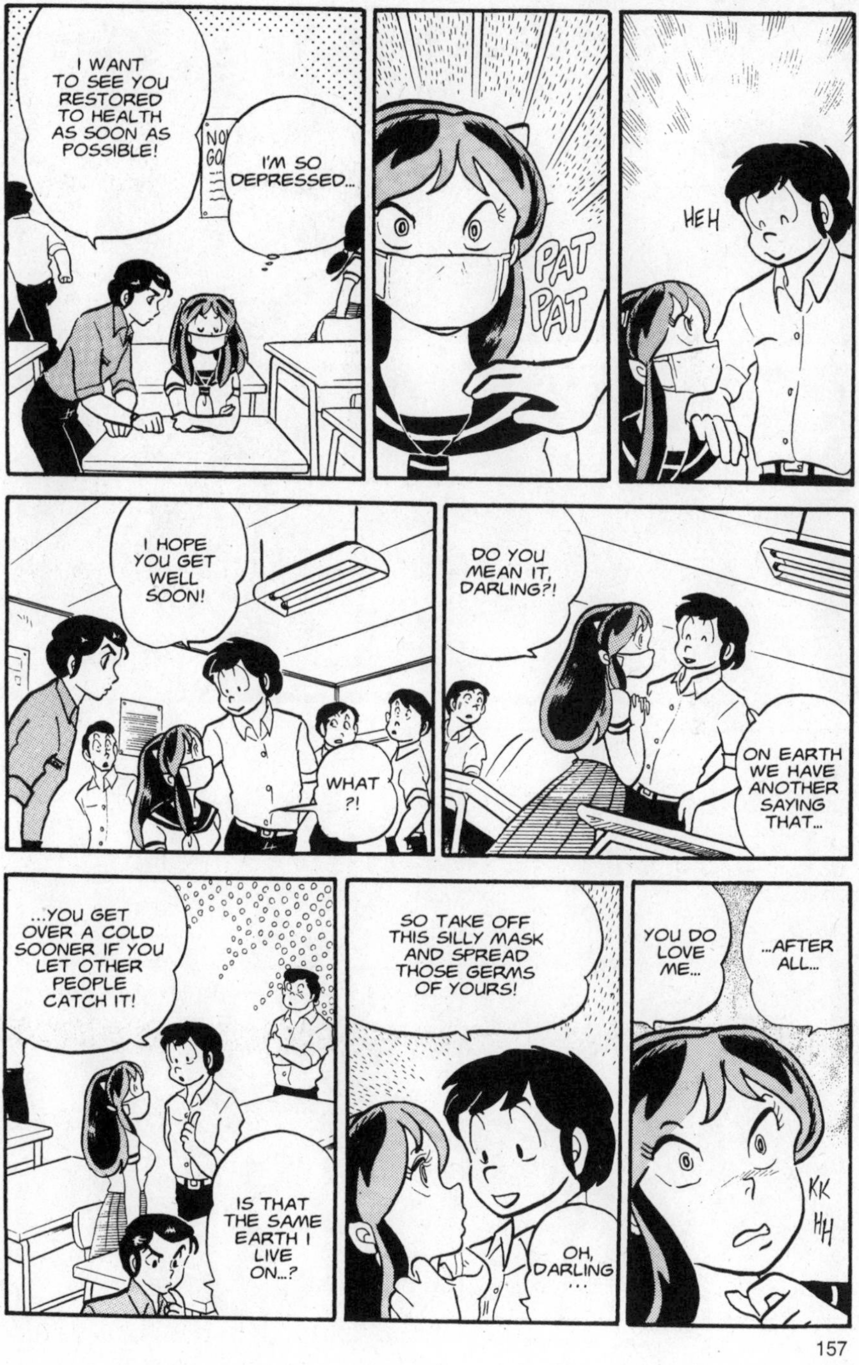
I WANT TO SEE YOU RESTORED TO HEALTH AS SOON AS POSSIBLE!
I'M SO DEPRESSED...
PAT PAT
HEH
I HOPE YOU GET WELL SOON!
WHAT ?!
DO YOU MEAN IT, DARLING?!
ON EARTH WE HAVE ANOTHER SAYING THAT...
...YOU GET OVER A COLD SOONER IF YOU LET OTHER PEOPLE CATCH IT!
IS THAT THE SAME EARTH I LIVE ON...?
SO TAKE OFF THIS SILLY MASK AND SPREAD THOSE GERMS OF YOURS!
OH, DARLING ...
YOU DO LOVE ME...
...AFTER ALL...
KKHH

HACK HACK HACK

HEY!

YOU TRYIN' TO GIVE ME YOUR *COLD*, IDIOT?!

IS IT MY IMAGINATION, OR DID YOUR ATTITUDE SUDDENLY CHANGE?

THIS WEEK'S GOALS:

LATER!

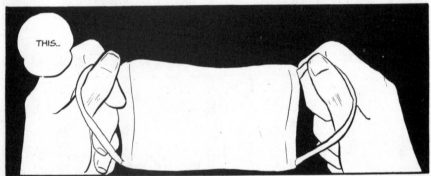

THIS...

...IS LUM-CHAN'S MASK!

HENH! HENH!

INDIRECT KISS, HEE HEE!

ME FIRST!

ME FIRST!

NO, *ME*!

THERE THEY ARE!

GIVE US A SHOT AT IT!

YOW!!

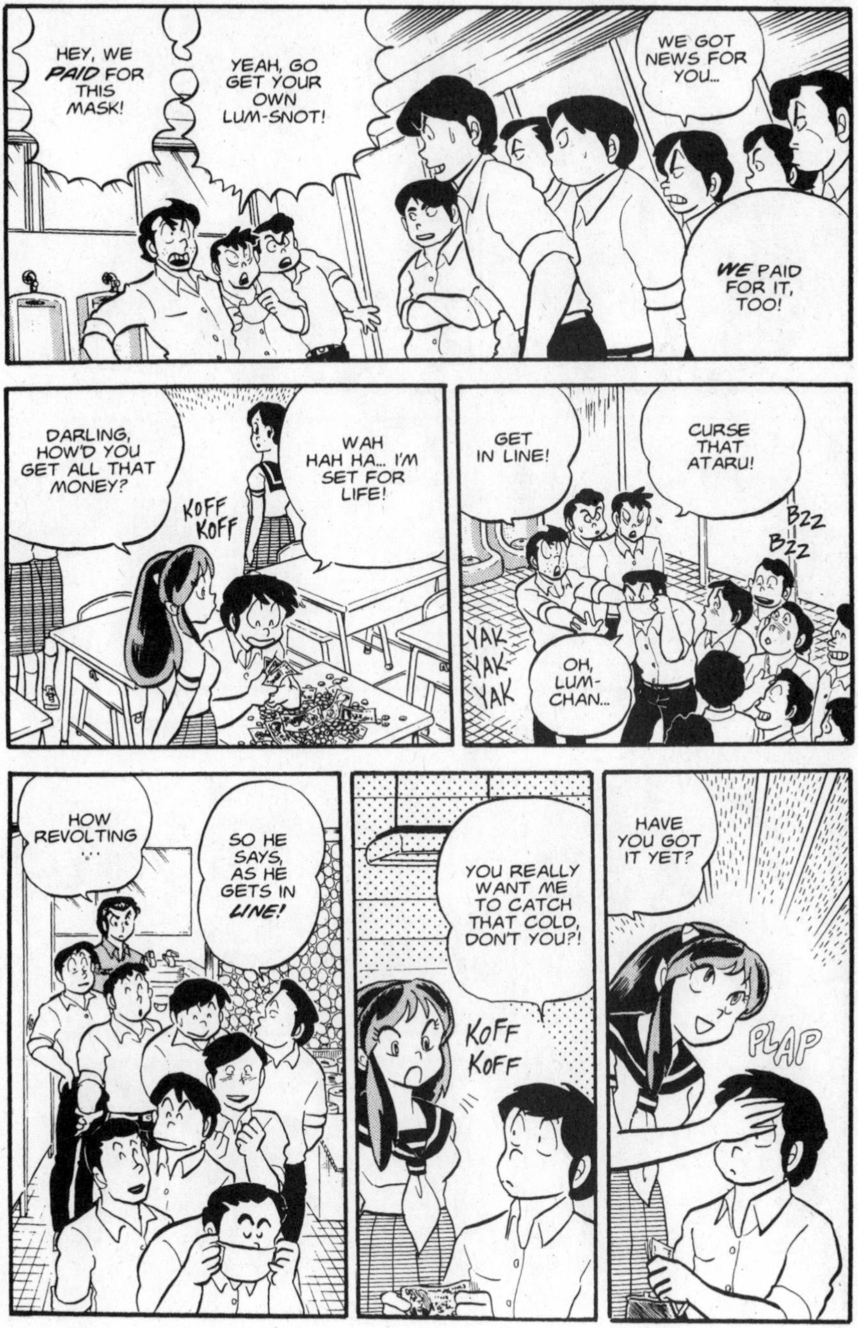
HEY, WE PAID FOR THIS MASK!
YEAH, GO GET YOUR OWN LUM-SNOT!
WE GOT NEWS FOR YOU...
WE PAID FOR IT, TOO!
DARLING, HOW'D YOU GET ALL THAT MONEY?
KOFF KOFF
WAH HAH HA... I'M SET FOR LIFE!
GET IN LINE!
CURSE THAT ATARU!
BZZ BZZ
YAK YAK YAK
OH, LUM-CHAN...
HOW REVOLTING ...
SO HE SAYS, AS HE GETS IN LINE!
YOU REALLY WANT ME TO CATCH THAT COLD, DON'T YOU?!
KOFF KOFF
HAVE YOU GOT IT YET?
PLAP

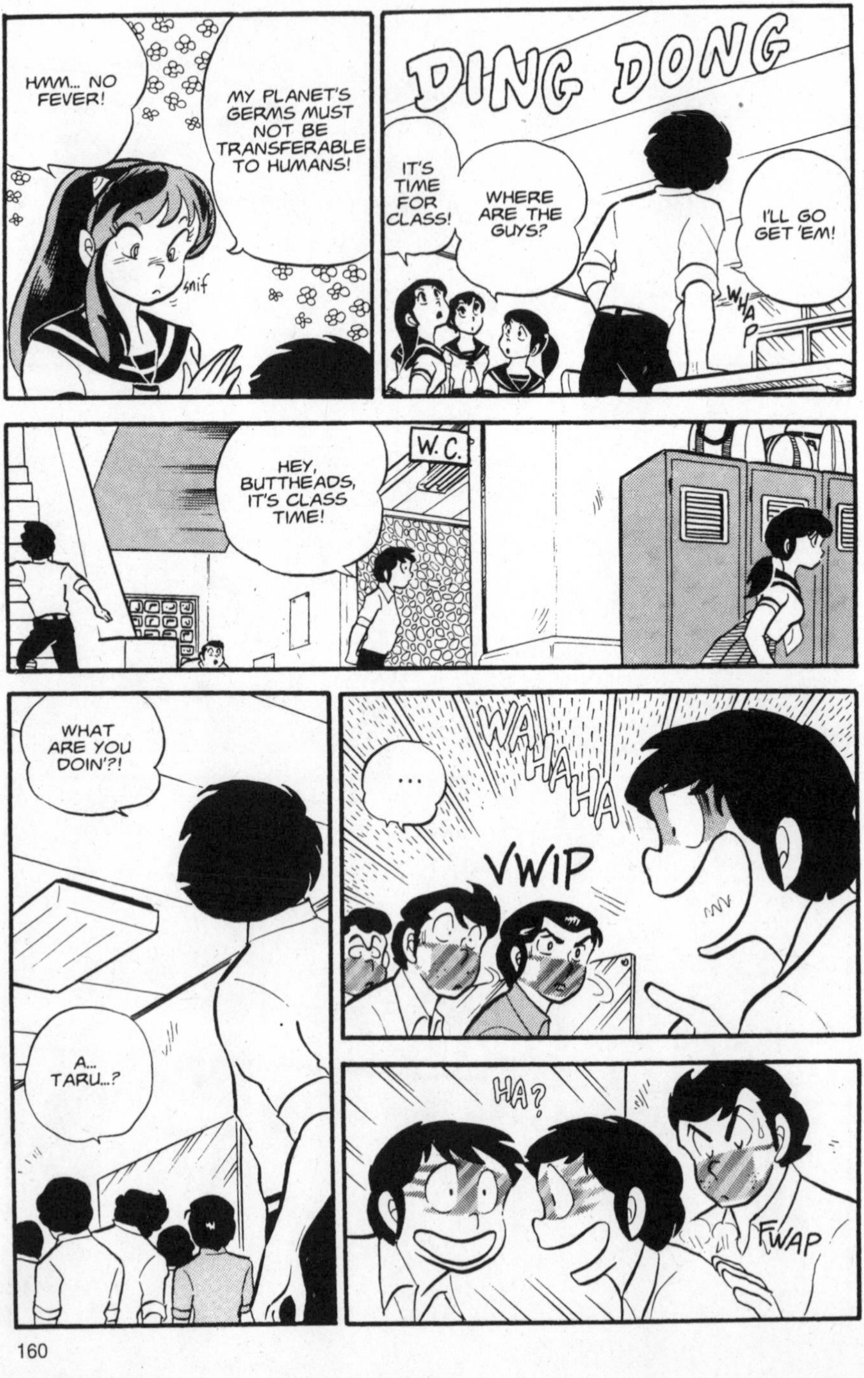
HMM... NO FEVER!
MY PLANET'S GERMS MUST NOT BE TRANSFERABLE TO HUMANS!
snif
DING DONG
IT'S TIME FOR CLASS!
WHERE ARE THE GUYS?
I'LL GO GET 'EM!
WHAP
W.C.
HEY, BUTTHEADS, IT'S CLASS TIME!
WHAT ARE YOU DOIN'?!
A... TARU...?
...
WA HA HA HA
VWIP
HA?
FWAP

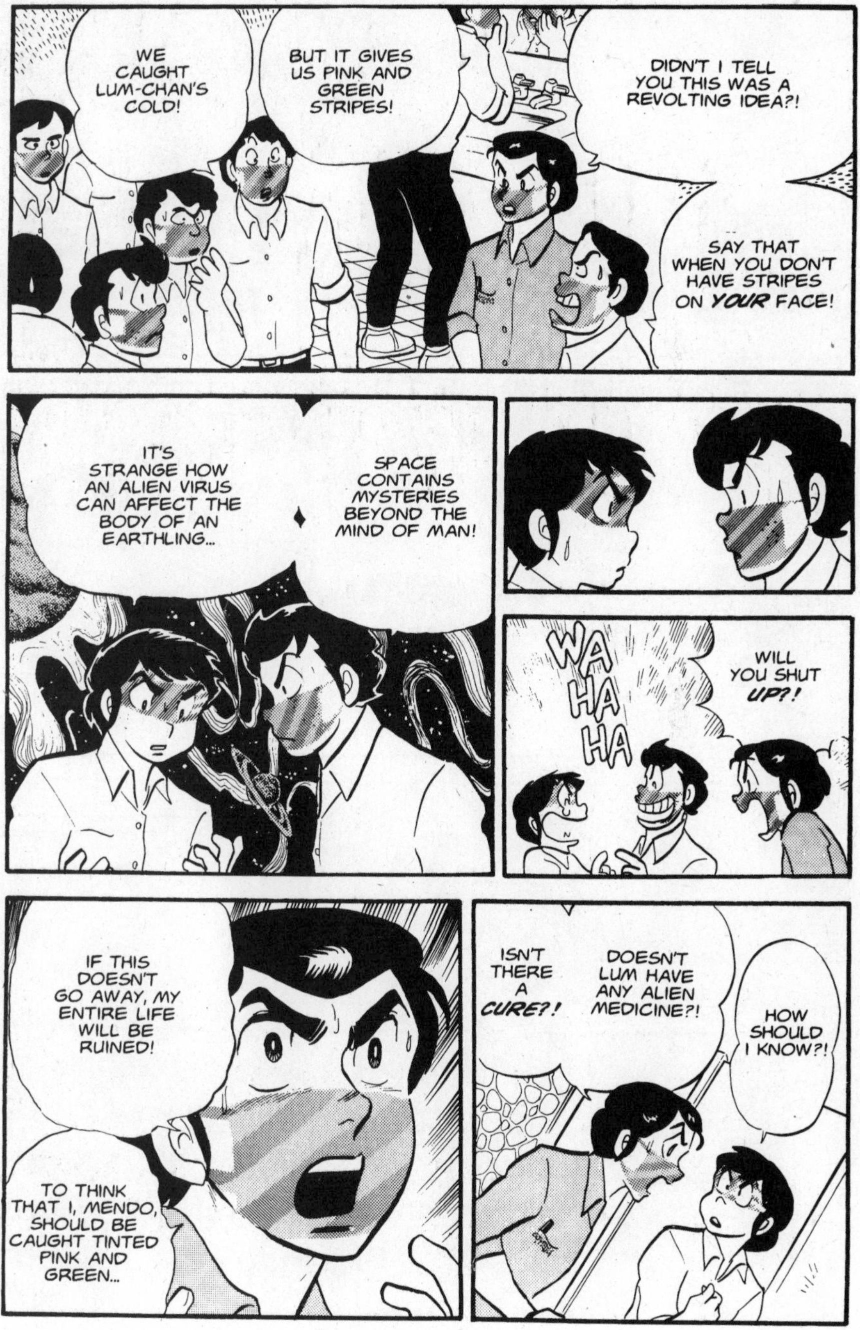
WE CAUGHT LUM-CHAN'S COLD!
BUT IT GIVES US PINK AND GREEN STRIPES!
DIDN'T I TELL YOU THIS WAS A REVOLTING IDEA?!
SAY THAT WHEN YOU DON'T HAVE STRIPES ON *YOUR* FACE!
IT'S STRANGE HOW AN ALIEN VIRUS CAN AFFECT THE BODY OF AN EARTHLING...
SPACE CONTAINS MYSTERIES BEYOND THE MIND OF MAN!
WA HA HA HA
WILL YOU SHUT *UP?!*
IF THIS DOESN'T GO AWAY, MY ENTIRE LIFE WILL BE RUINED!
TO THINK THAT I, MENDO, SHOULD BE CAUGHT TINTED PINK AND GREEN...
ISN'T THERE A *CURE?!*
DOESN'T LUM HAVE ANY ALIEN MEDICINE?!
HOW SHOULD I KNOW?!

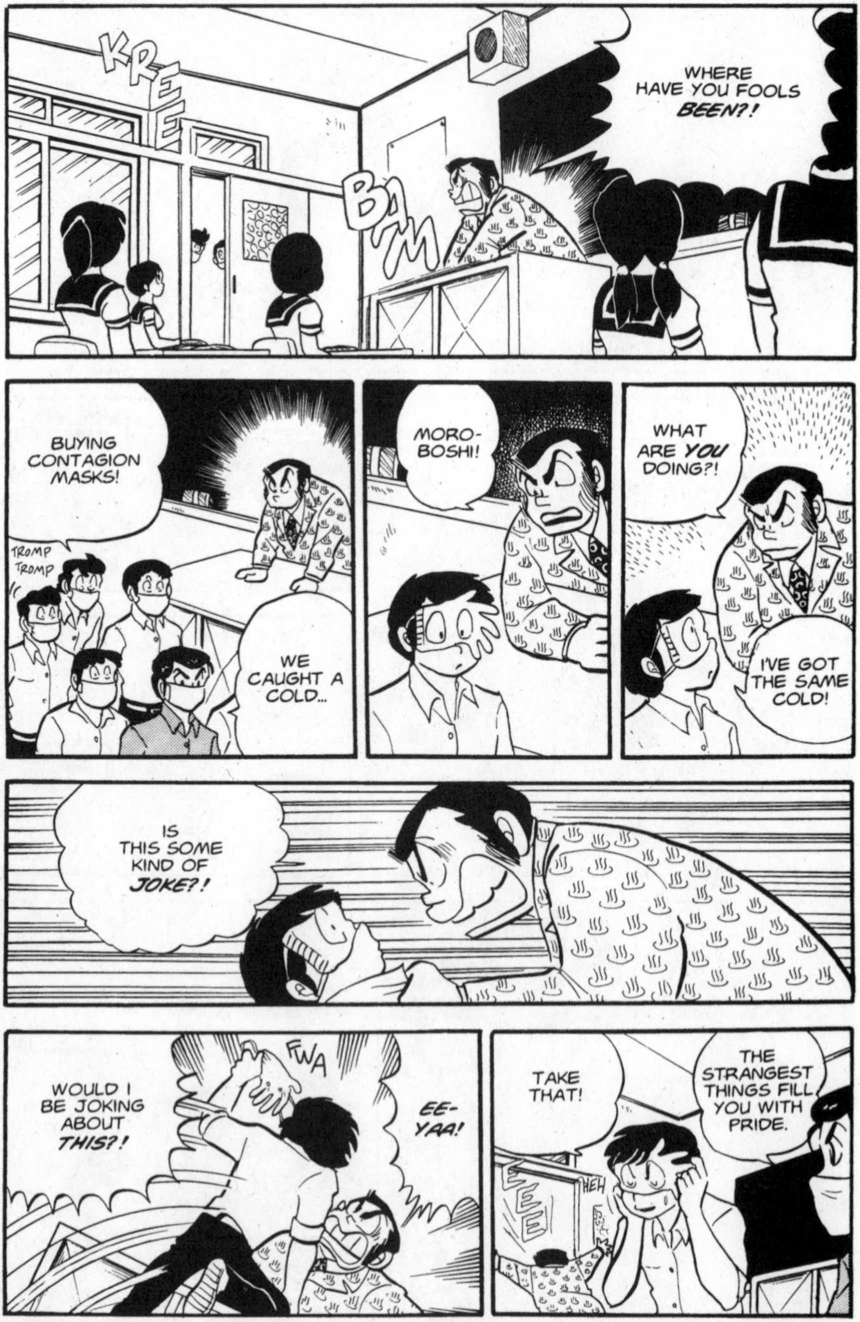
KREE
WHERE HAVE YOU FOOLS BEEN?!
BAM
BUYING CONTAGION MASKS!
TROMP TROMP
WE CAUGHT A COLD...
MORO-BOSHI!
WHAT ARE YOU DOING?!
I'VE GOT THE SAME COLD!
IS THIS SOME KIND OF JOKE?!
FWA
WOULD I BE JOKING ABOUT THIS?!
EE-YAA!
TAKE THAT!
THE STRANGEST THINGS FILL YOU WITH PRIDE.
EEE
HEH

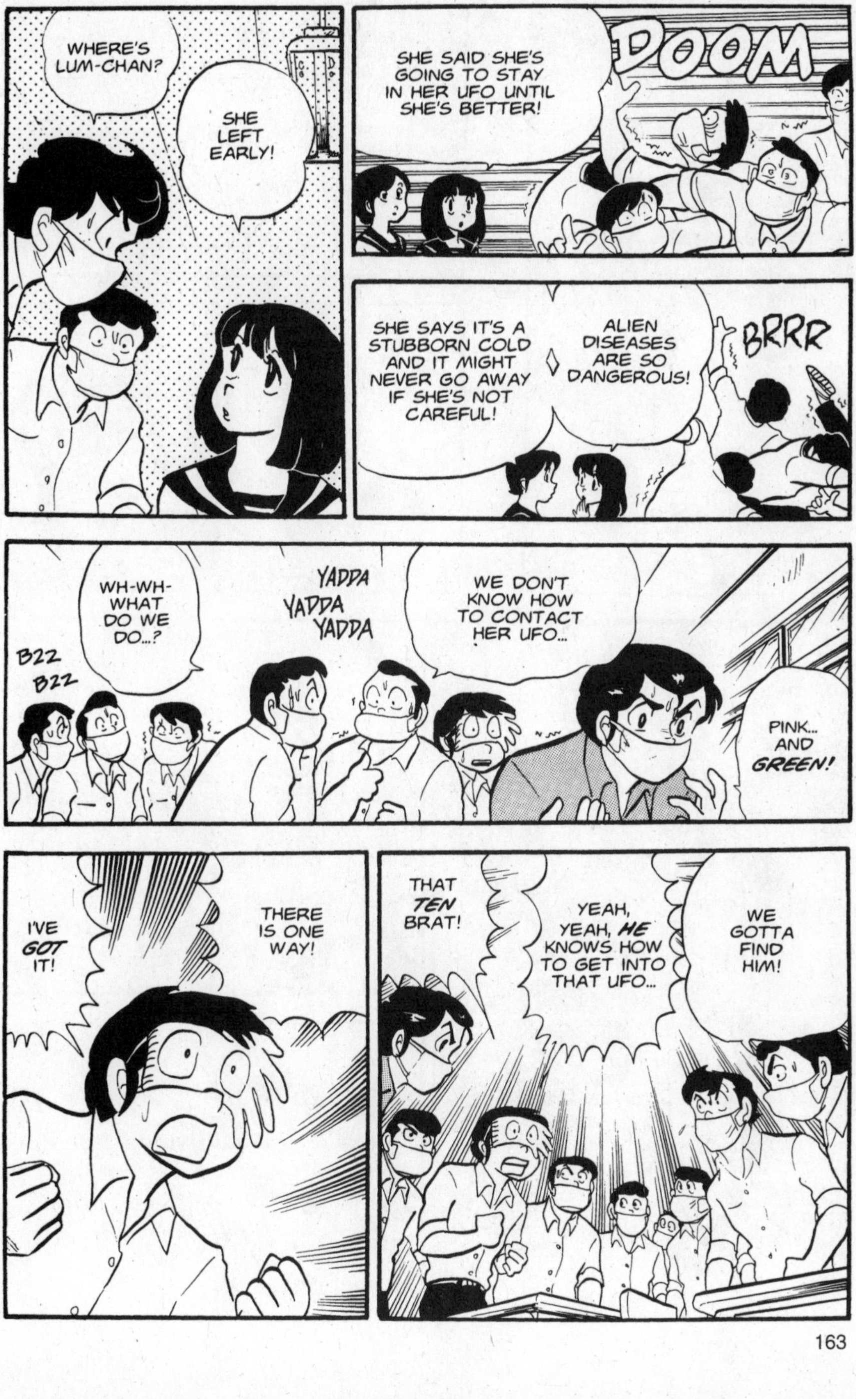
WHERE'S LUM-CHAN?
SHE LEFT EARLY!
SHE SAID SHE'S GOING TO STAY IN HER UFO UNTIL SHE'S BETTER!
DOOM
SHE SAYS IT'S A STUBBORN COLD AND IT MIGHT NEVER GO AWAY IF SHE'S NOT CAREFUL!
ALIEN DISEASES ARE SO DANGEROUS!
BRRR
WH-WH-WHAT DO WE DO...?
BZZ BZZ
YADDA YADDA YADDA
WE DON'T KNOW HOW TO CONTACT HER UFO...
PINK... AND *GREEN!*
I'VE *GOT* IT!
THERE IS ONE WAY!
THAT *TEN* BRAT!
YEAH, YEAH, *HE* KNOWS HOW TO GET INTO THAT UFO...
WE GOTTA FIND HIM!

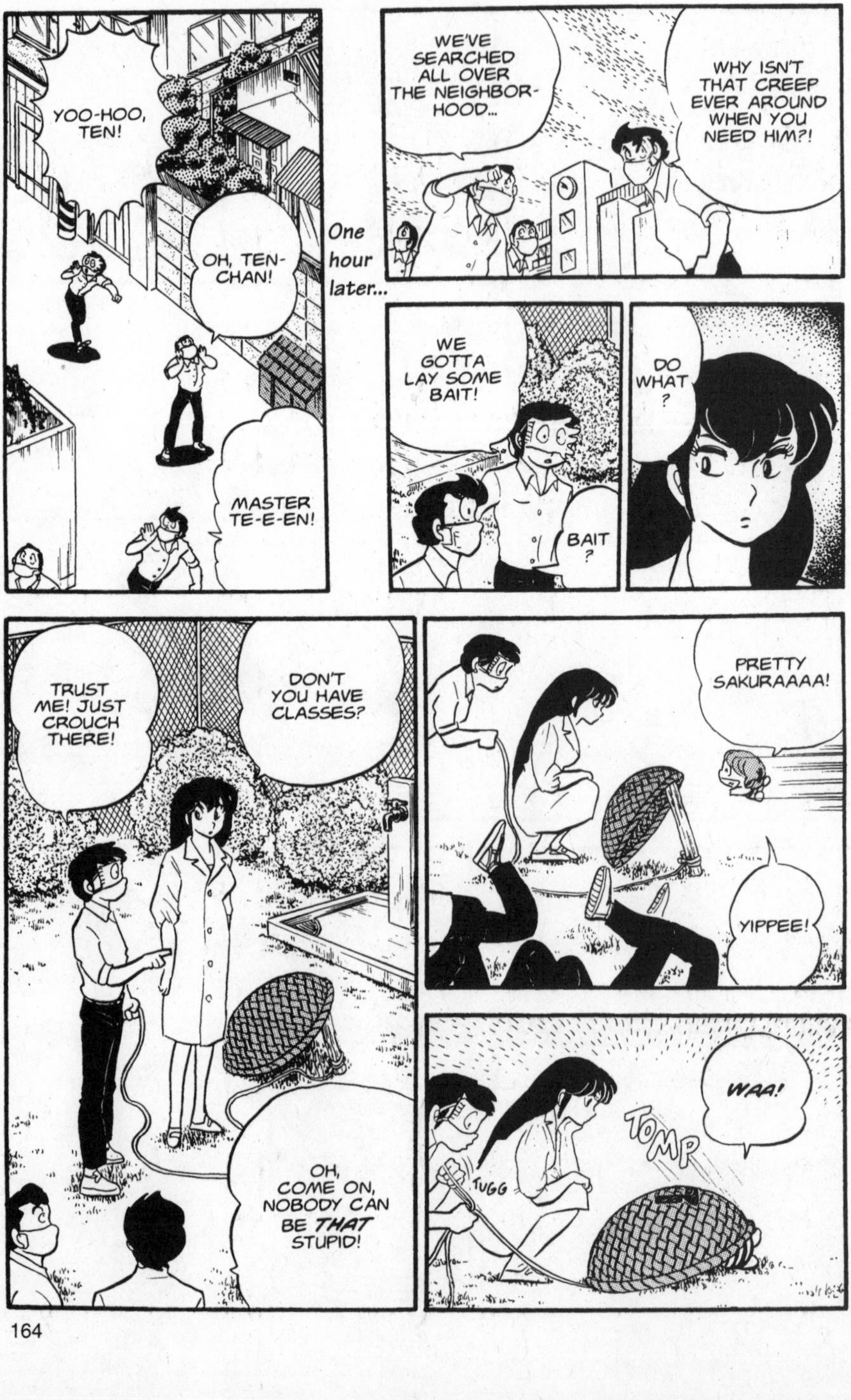
YOO-HOO, TEN!
OH, TEN-CHAN!
MASTER TE-E-EN!
One hour later...
WE'VE SEARCHED ALL OVER THE NEIGHBOR-HOOD...
WHY ISN'T THAT CREEP EVER AROUND WHEN YOU NEED HIM?!
WE GOTTA LAY SOME BAIT!
BAIT?
DO WHAT?
TRUST ME! JUST CROUCH THERE!
DON'T YOU HAVE CLASSES?
OH, COME ON, NOBODY CAN BE *THAT* STUPID!
PRETTY SAKURAAAA!
YIPPEE!
WAA!
TOMP
TUGG

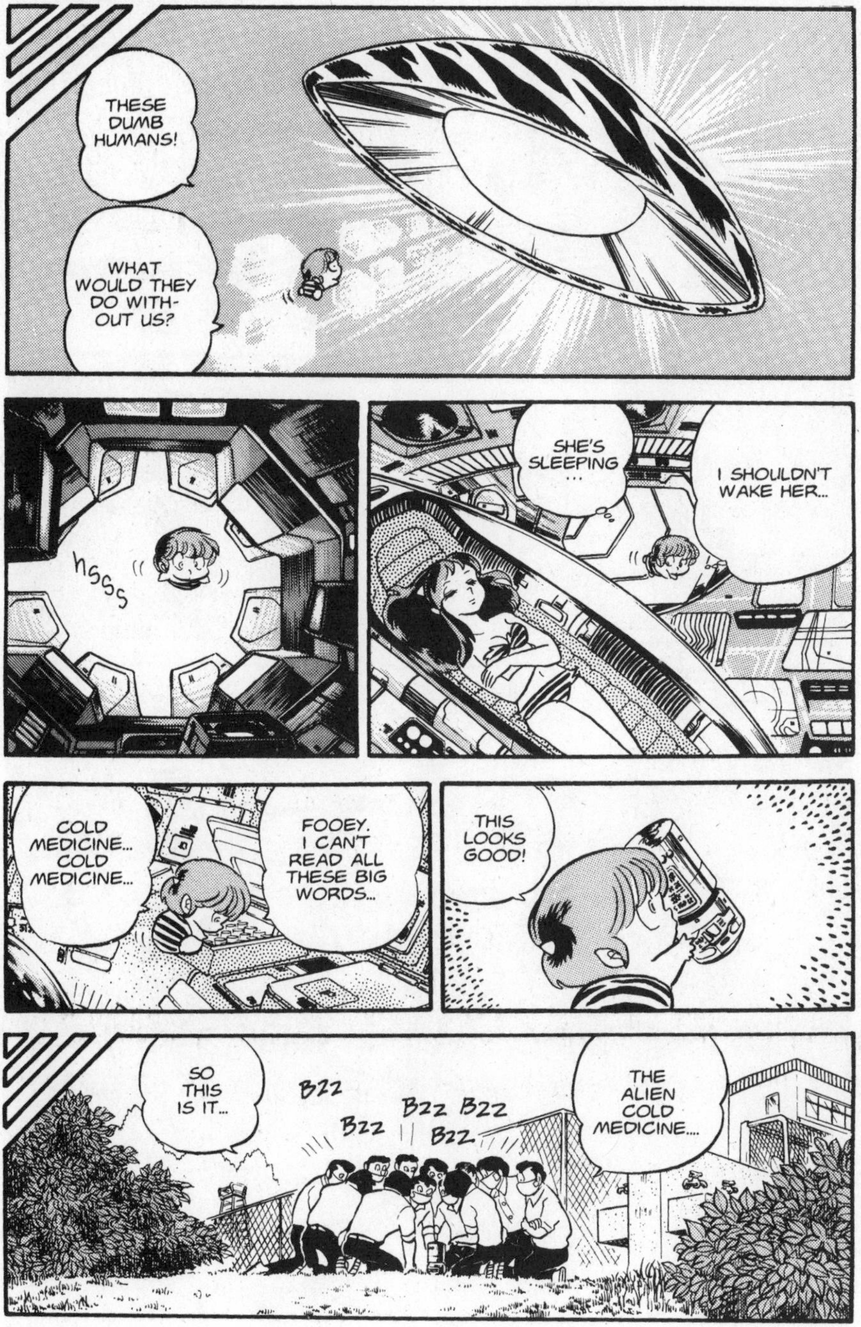
THESE DUMB HUMANS!
WHAT WOULD THEY DO WITH-OUT US?
hsss
SHE'S SLEEPING ...
I SHOULDN'T WAKE HER...
COLD MEDICINE... COLD MEDICINE...
FOOEY. I CAN'T READ ALL THESE BIG WORDS...
THIS LOOKS GOOD!
SO THIS IS IT...
BZZ
BZZ BZZ
BZZ
BZZ
THE ALIEN COLD MEDICINE....

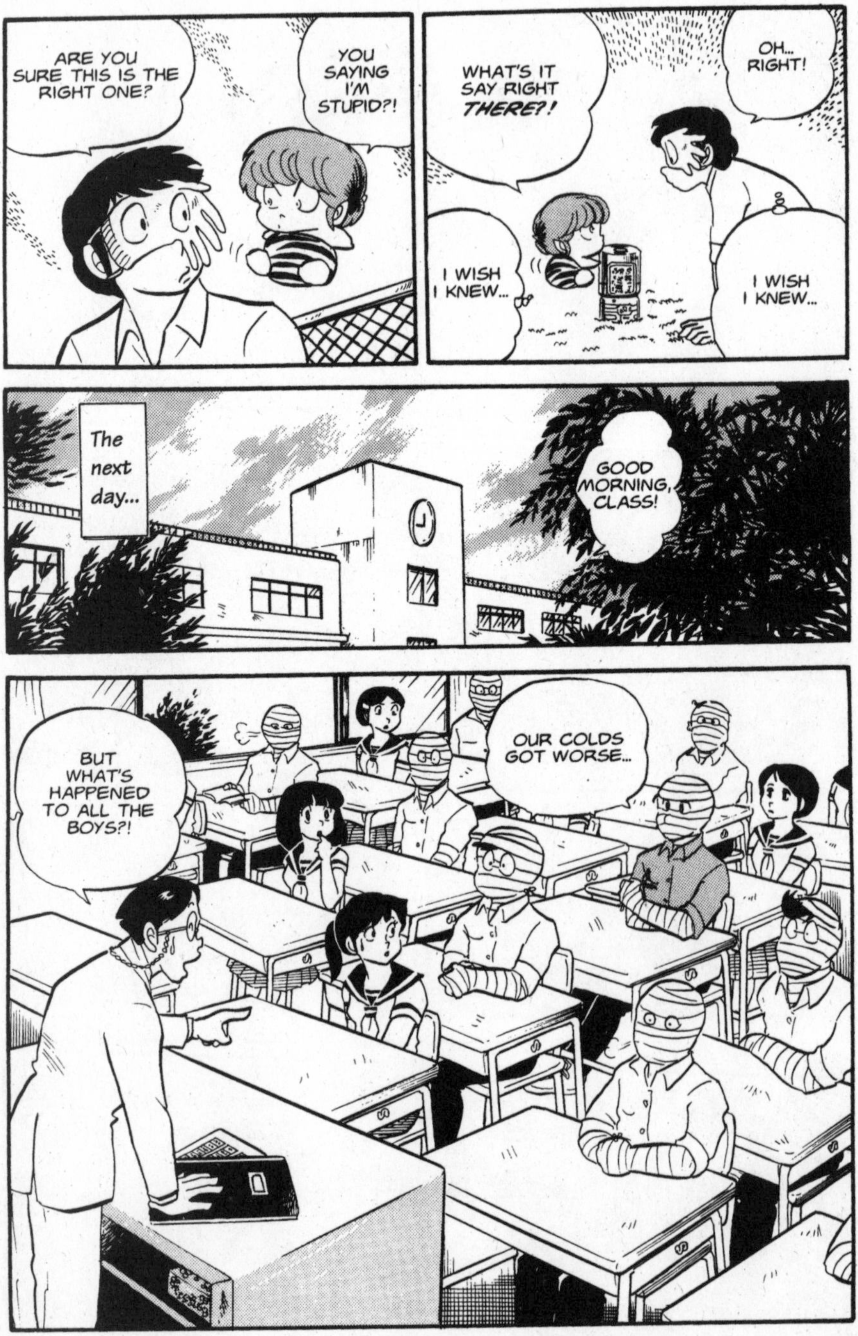

ARE YOU SURE THIS IS THE RIGHT ONE?
YOU SAYING I'M STUPID?!
WHAT'S IT SAY RIGHT *THERE?!*
OH... RIGHT!
I WISH I KNEW...
I WISH I KNEW...
The next day...
GOOD MORNING, CLASS!
BUT WHAT'S HAPPENED TO ALL THE BOYS?!
OUR COLDS GOT WORSE...

PART ELEVEN
DOWN FOR THE COUNT

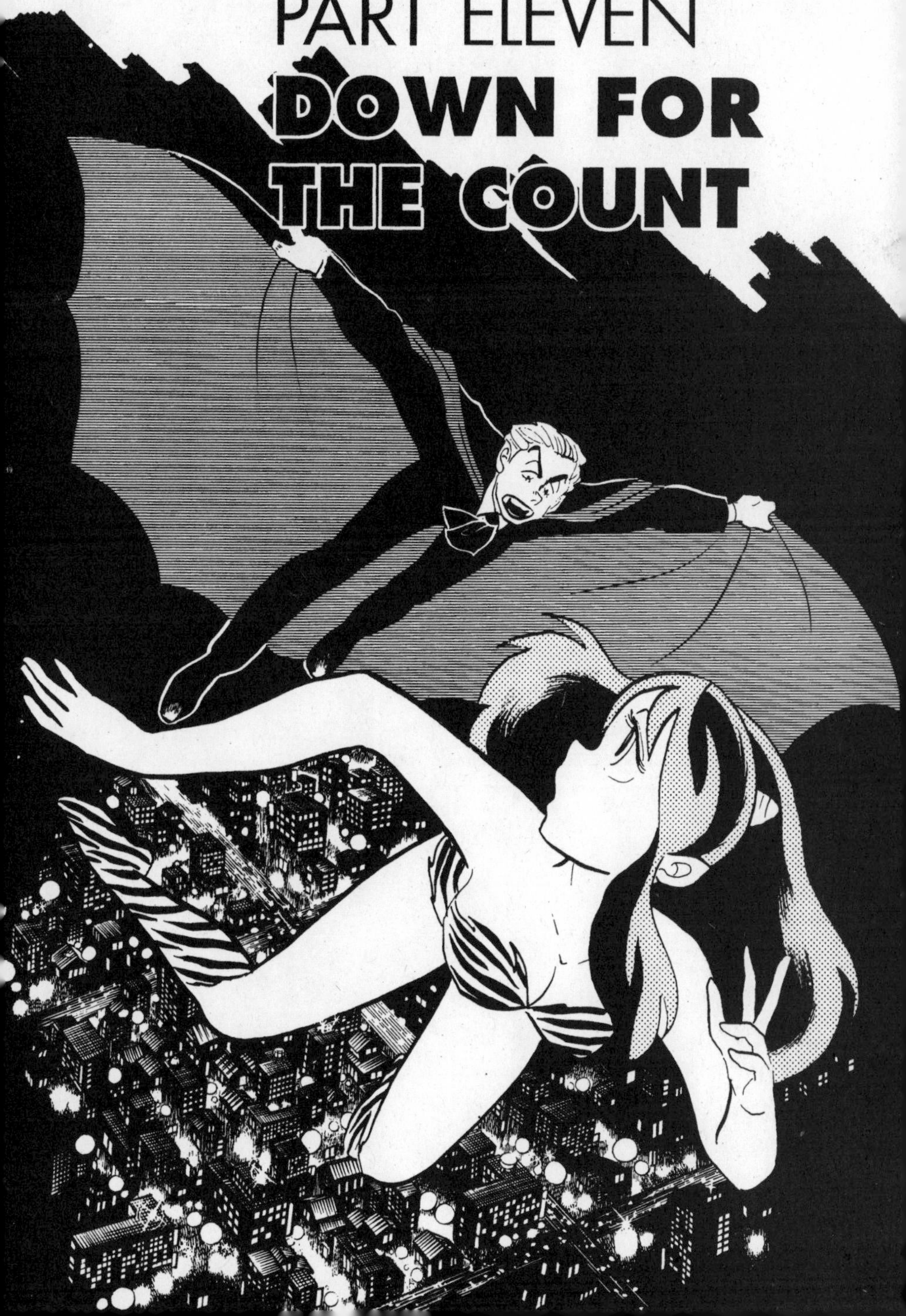

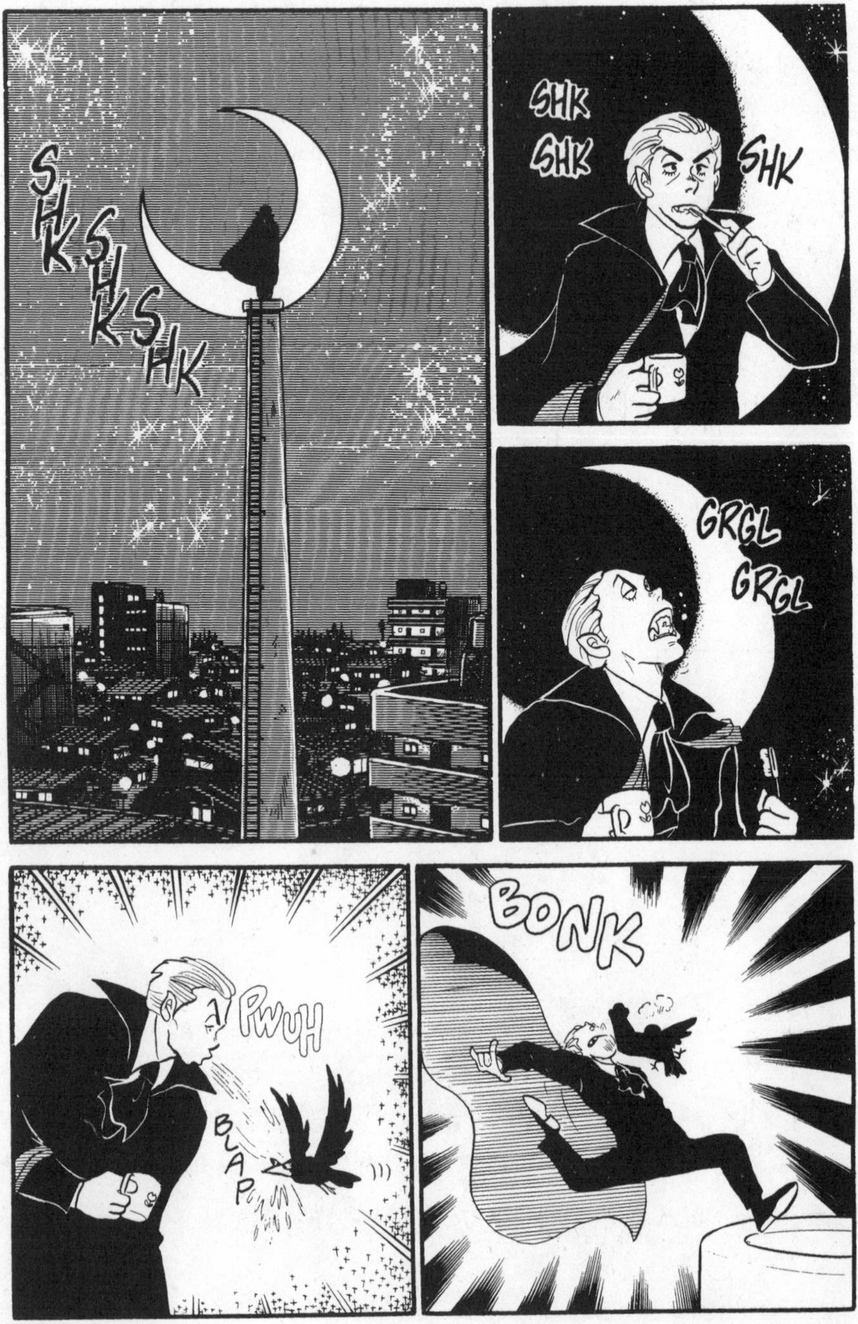
SHK
SHK
SHK
SHK
SHK
SHK
SHK
GRGL
GRGL
PWUH
BLAP
BONK

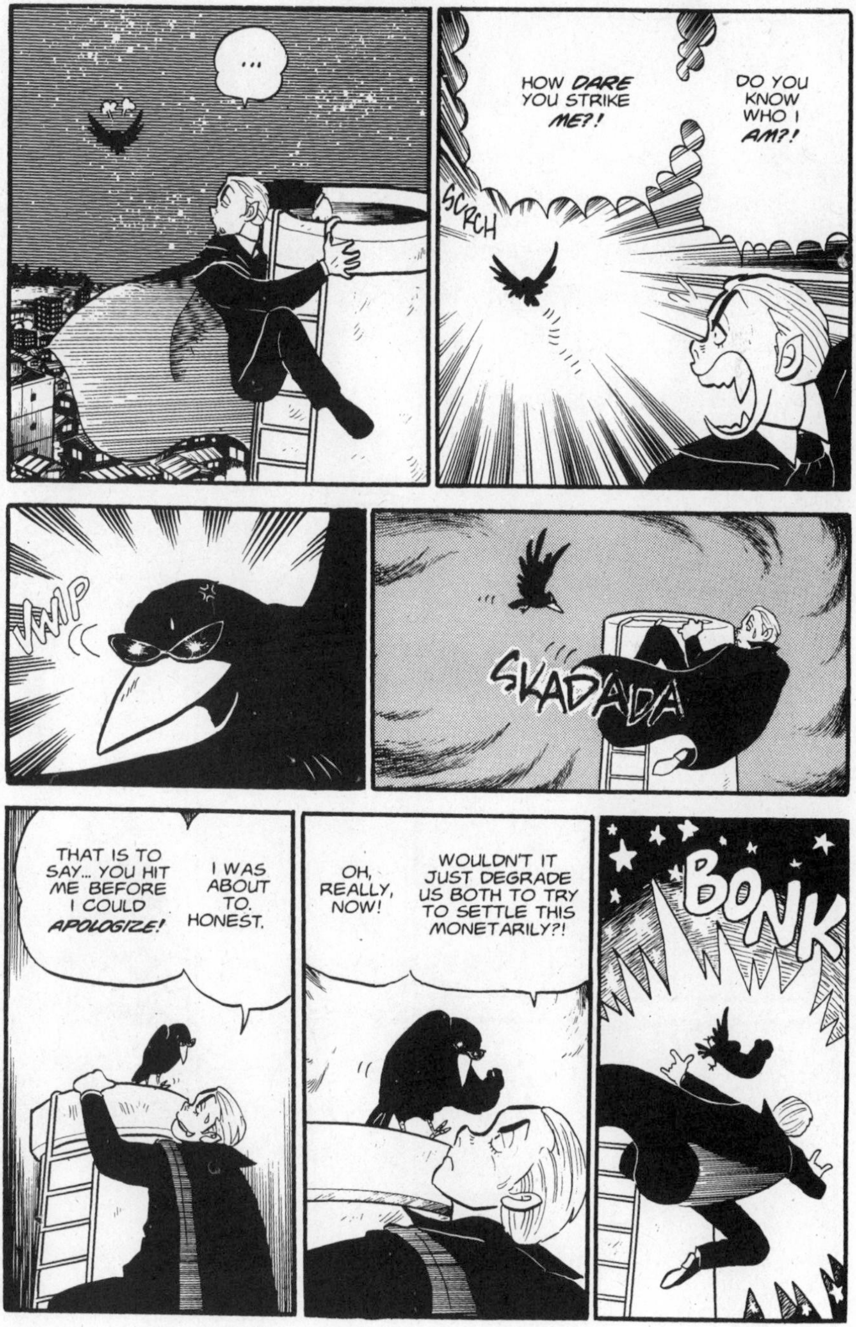
...
SCRCH
HOW DARE YOU STRIKE ME?!
DO YOU KNOW WHO I AM?!
VWIP
SKADADA
THAT IS TO SAY... YOU HIT ME BEFORE I COULD APOLOGIZE!
I WAS ABOUT TO. HONEST.
OH, REALLY, NOW!
WOULDN'T IT JUST DEGRADE US BOTH TO TRY TO SETTLE THIS MONETARILY?!
BONK

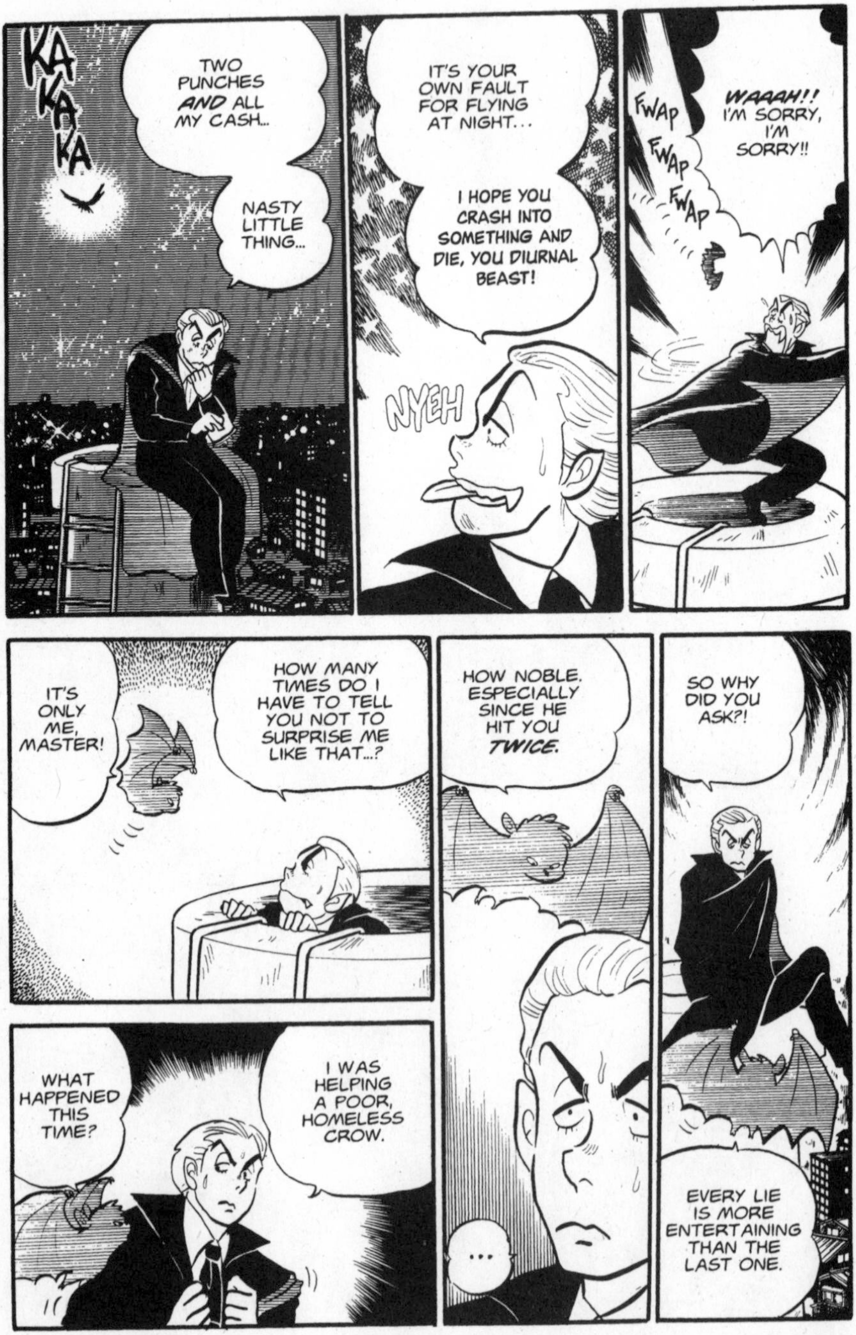
KA KA KA KA
TWO PUNCHES AND ALL MY CASH...
NASTY LITTLE THING...
IT'S YOUR OWN FAULT FOR FLYING AT NIGHT...
I HOPE YOU CRASH INTO SOMETHING AND DIE, YOU DIURNAL BEAST!
NYEH
FWAP FWAP FWAP
WAAAH!! I'M SORRY, I'M SORRY!!
IT'S ONLY ME, MASTER!
HOW MANY TIMES DO I HAVE TO TELL YOU NOT TO SURPRISE ME LIKE THAT...?
WHAT HAPPENED THIS TIME?
I WAS HELPING A POOR, HOMELESS CROW.
HOW NOBLE. ESPECIALLY SINCE HE HIT YOU TWICE.
...
SO WHY DID YOU ASK?!
EVERY LIE IS MORE ENTERTAINING THAN THE LAST ONE.

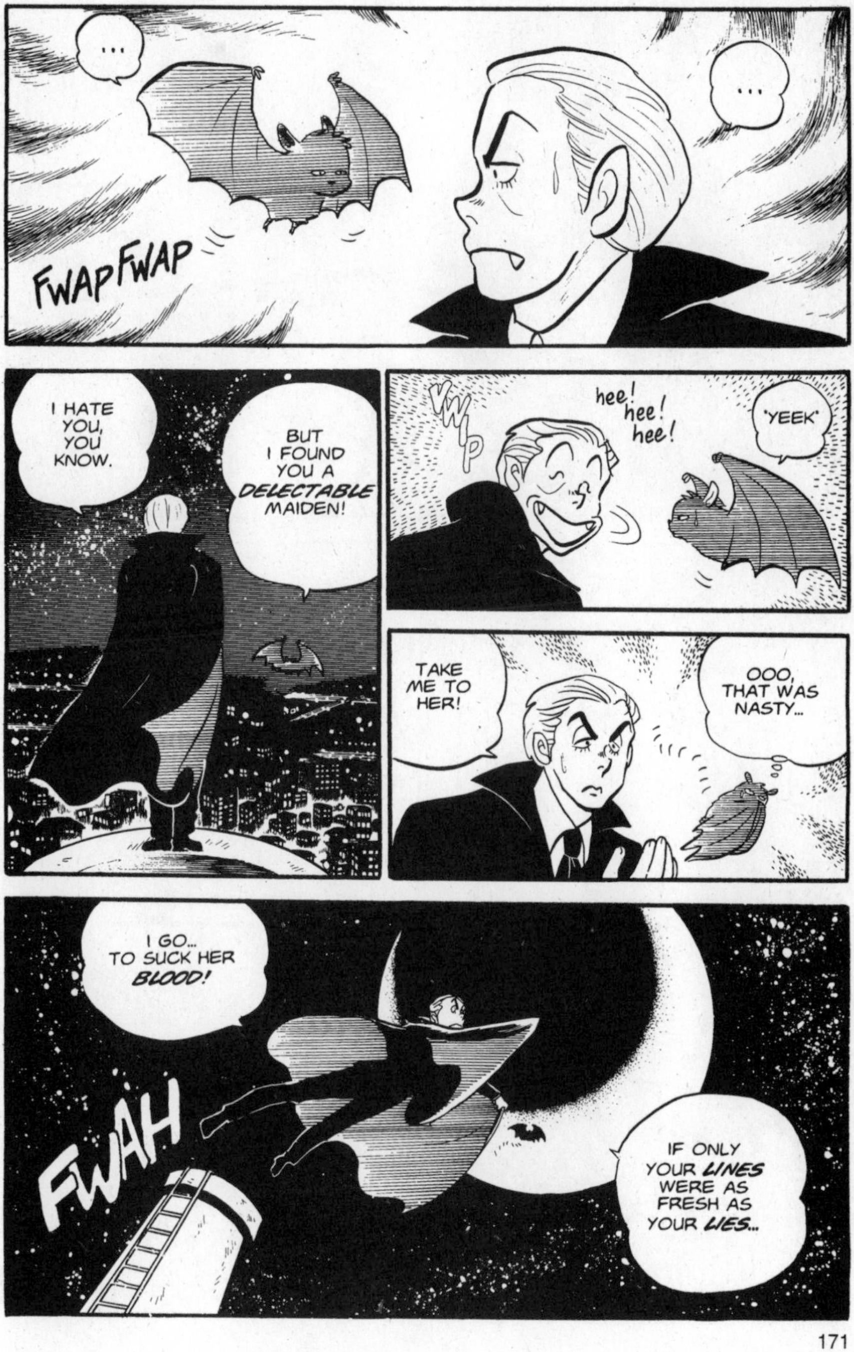
...
...
FWAP FWAP
I HATE YOU, YOU KNOW.
BUT I FOUND YOU A DELECTABLE MAIDEN!
VWIP
hee! hee! hee!
"YEEK"
TAKE ME TO HER!
OOO, THAT WAS NASTY...
I GO... TO SUCK HER BLOOD!
FWAH
IF ONLY YOUR LINES WERE AS FRESH AS YOUR LIES...

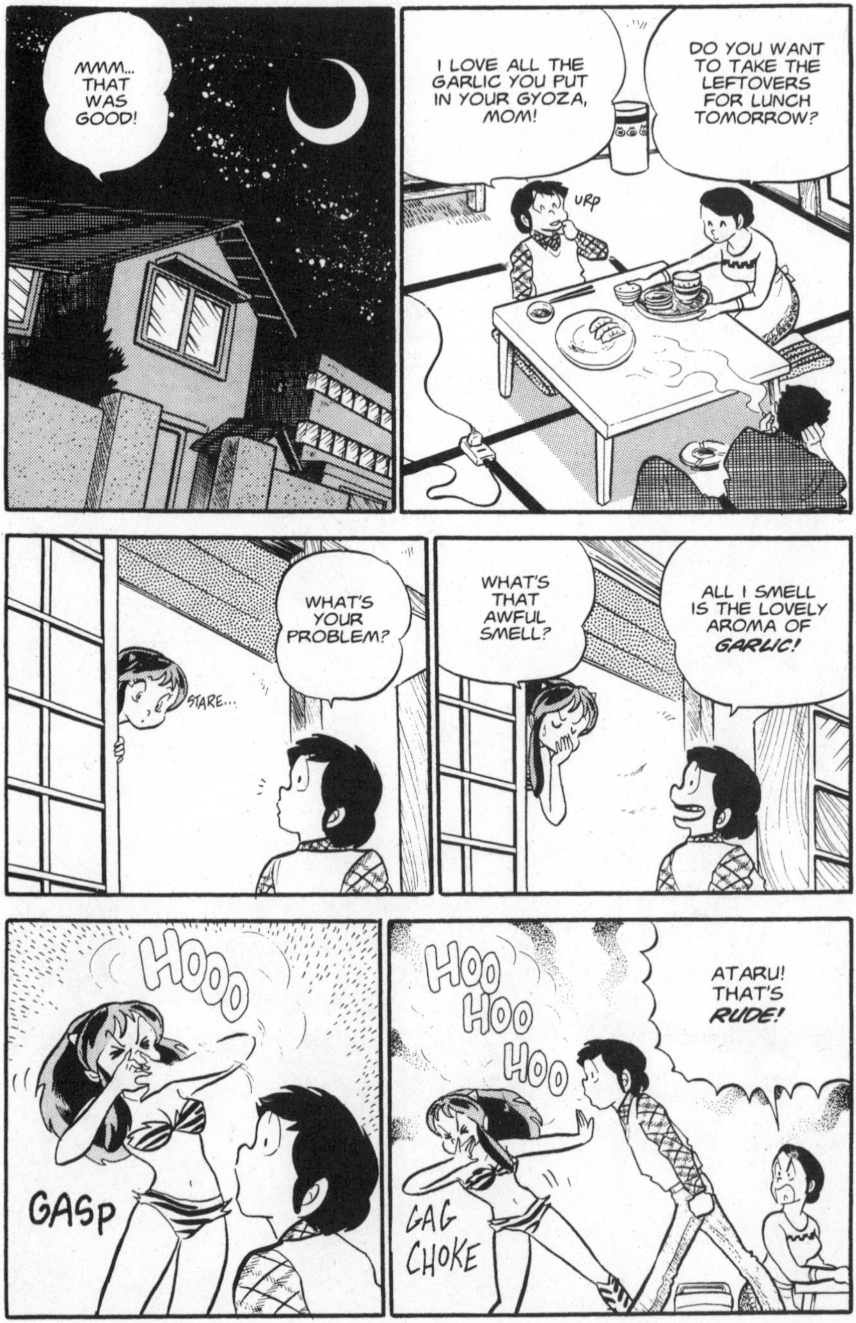
MMM... THAT WAS GOOD!
I LOVE ALL THE GARLIC YOU PUT IN YOUR GYOZA, MOM!
URP
DO YOU WANT TO TAKE THE LEFTOVERS FOR LUNCH TOMORROW?
WHAT'S YOUR PROBLEM?
STARE...
WHAT'S THAT AWFUL SMELL?
ALL I SMELL IS THE LOVELY AROMA OF GARLIC!
HOOO
GASp
HOO HOO HOO
ATARU! THAT'S RUDE!
GAG CHOKE

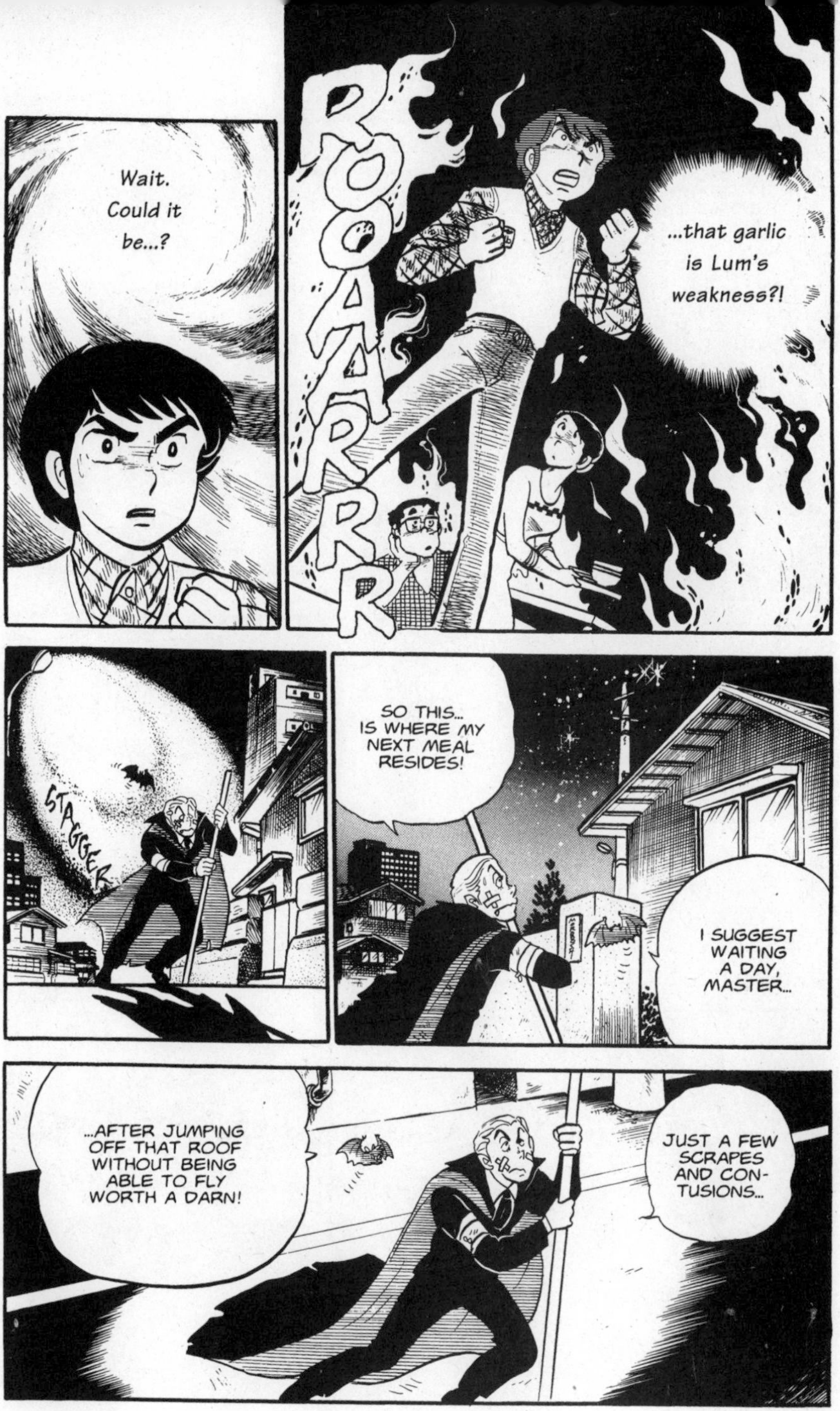
Wait. Could it be...?
ROOAARRR
...that garlic is Lum's weakness?!
STAGGER
SO THIS... IS WHERE MY NEXT MEAL RESIDES!
I SUGGEST WAITING A DAY, MASTER...
...AFTER JUMPING OFF THAT ROOF WITHOUT BEING ABLE TO FLY WORTH A DARN!
JUST A FEW SCRAPES AND CONTUSIONS...

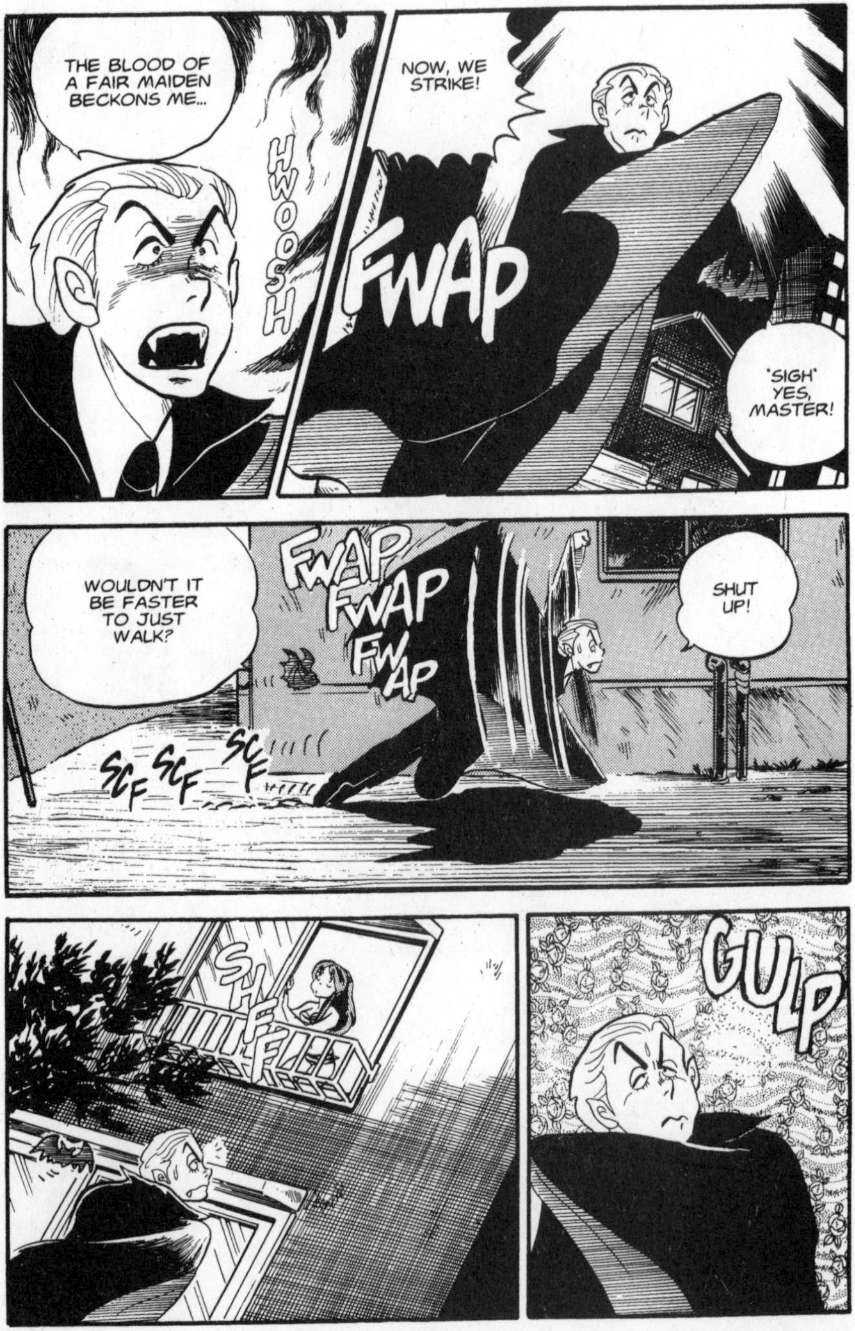
THE BLOOD OF A FAIR MAIDEN BECKONS ME...
HWOOSH
NOW, WE STRIKE!
FWAP
SIGH YES, MASTER!
WOULDN'T IT BE FASTER TO JUST WALK?
FWAP
FWAP
FWAP
SCF SCF SCF
SHUT UP!
SHFF
GULP

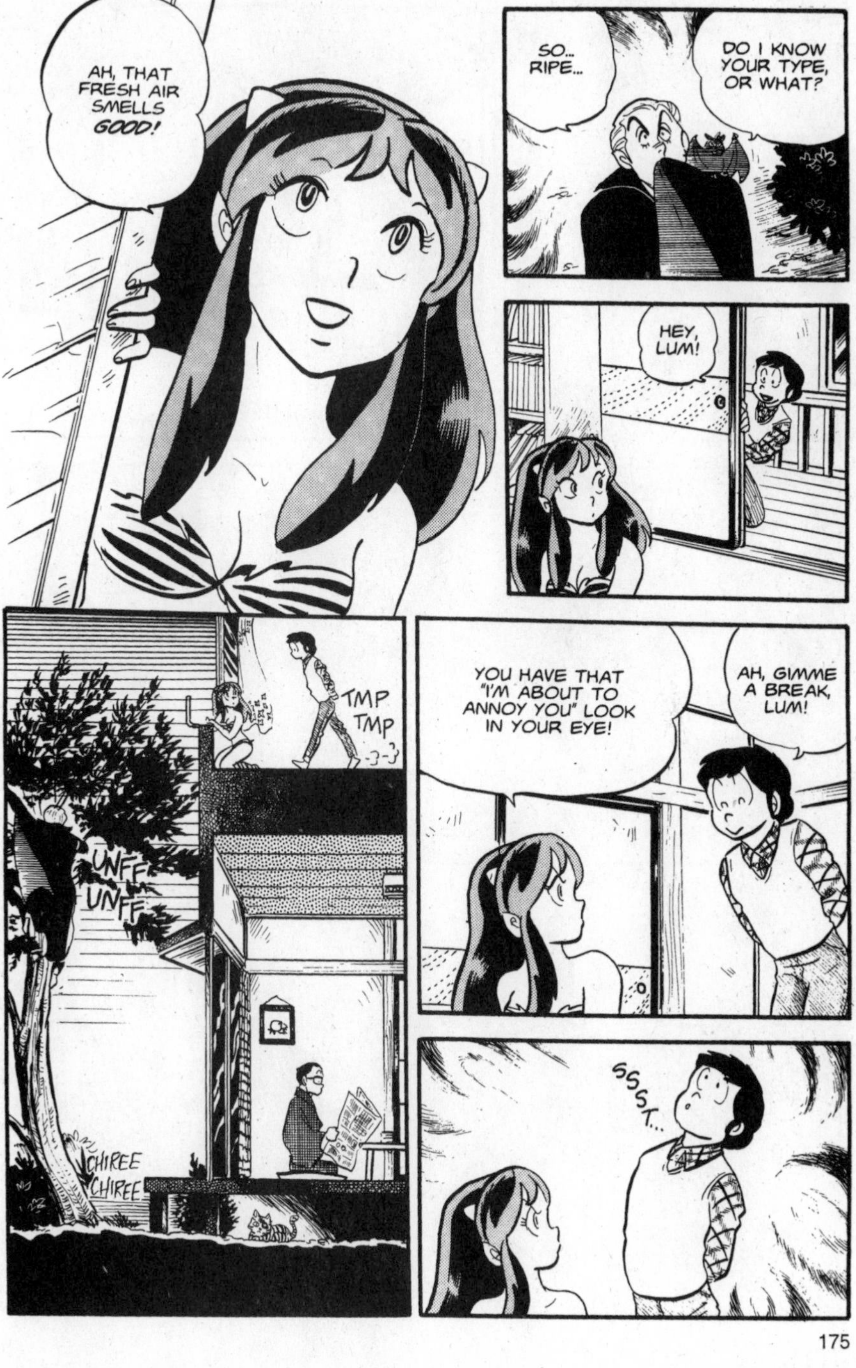
AH, THAT FRESH AIR SMELLS GOOD!
SO... RIPE...
DO I KNOW YOUR TYPE, OR WHAT?
HEY, LUM!
TMP TMP
UNFF UNFF
CHIREE CHIREE
YOU HAVE THAT "I'M ABOUT TO ANNOY YOU" LOOK IN YOUR EYE!
AH, GIMME A BREAK, LUM!
SSSST...

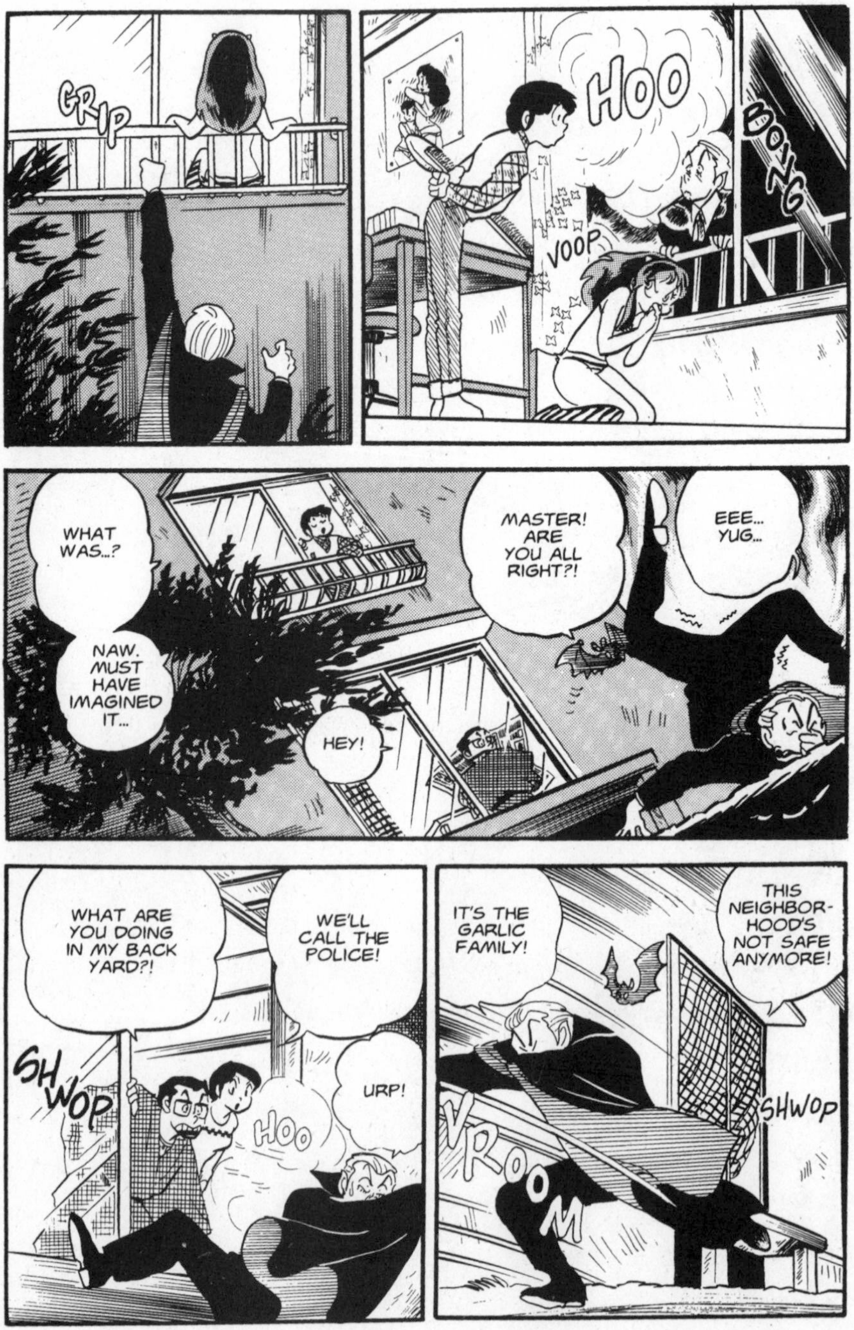
GRIP
HOO
BOING
VOOP
WHAT WAS...?
NAW. MUST HAVE IMAGINED IT...
HEY!
MASTER! ARE YOU ALL RIGHT?!
EEE... YUG...
WHAT ARE YOU DOING IN MY BACK YARD?!
WE'LL CALL THE POLICE!
SHWOP
HOO
URP!
IT'S THE GARLIC FAMILY!
THIS NEIGHBOR-HOOD'S NOT SAFE ANYMORE!
VROOM
SHWOP

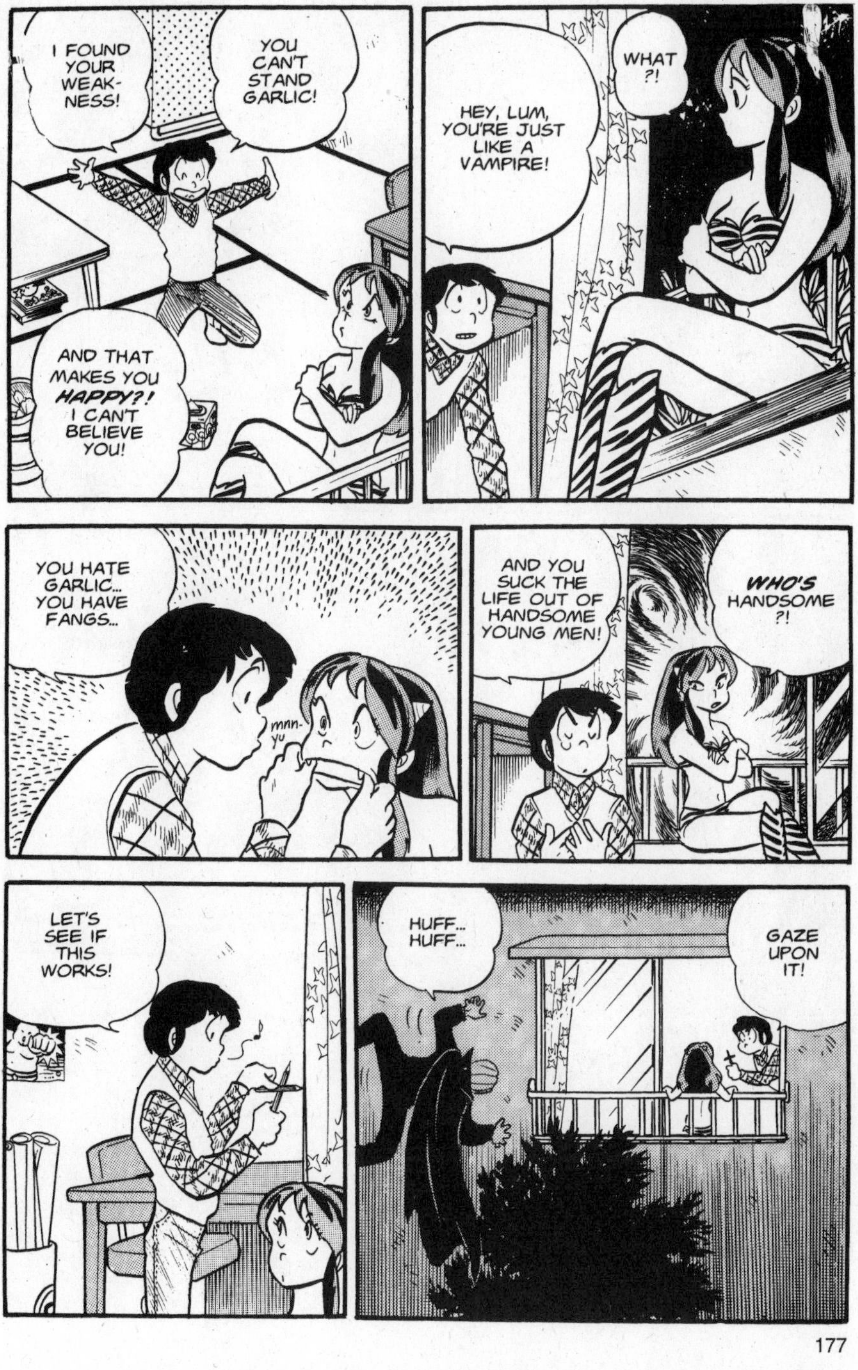
I FOUND YOUR WEAK-NESS!
YOU CAN'T STAND GARLIC!
AND THAT MAKES YOU ***HAPPY?!*** I CAN'T BELIEVE YOU!
HEY, LUM, YOU'RE JUST LIKE A VAMPIRE!
WHAT ?!
YOU HATE GARLIC... YOU HAVE FANGS...
mnn-yu
AND YOU SUCK THE LIFE OUT OF HANDSOME YOUNG MEN!
WHO'S HANDSOME ?!
LET'S SEE IF THIS WORKS!
HUFF... HUFF...
GAZE UPON IT!

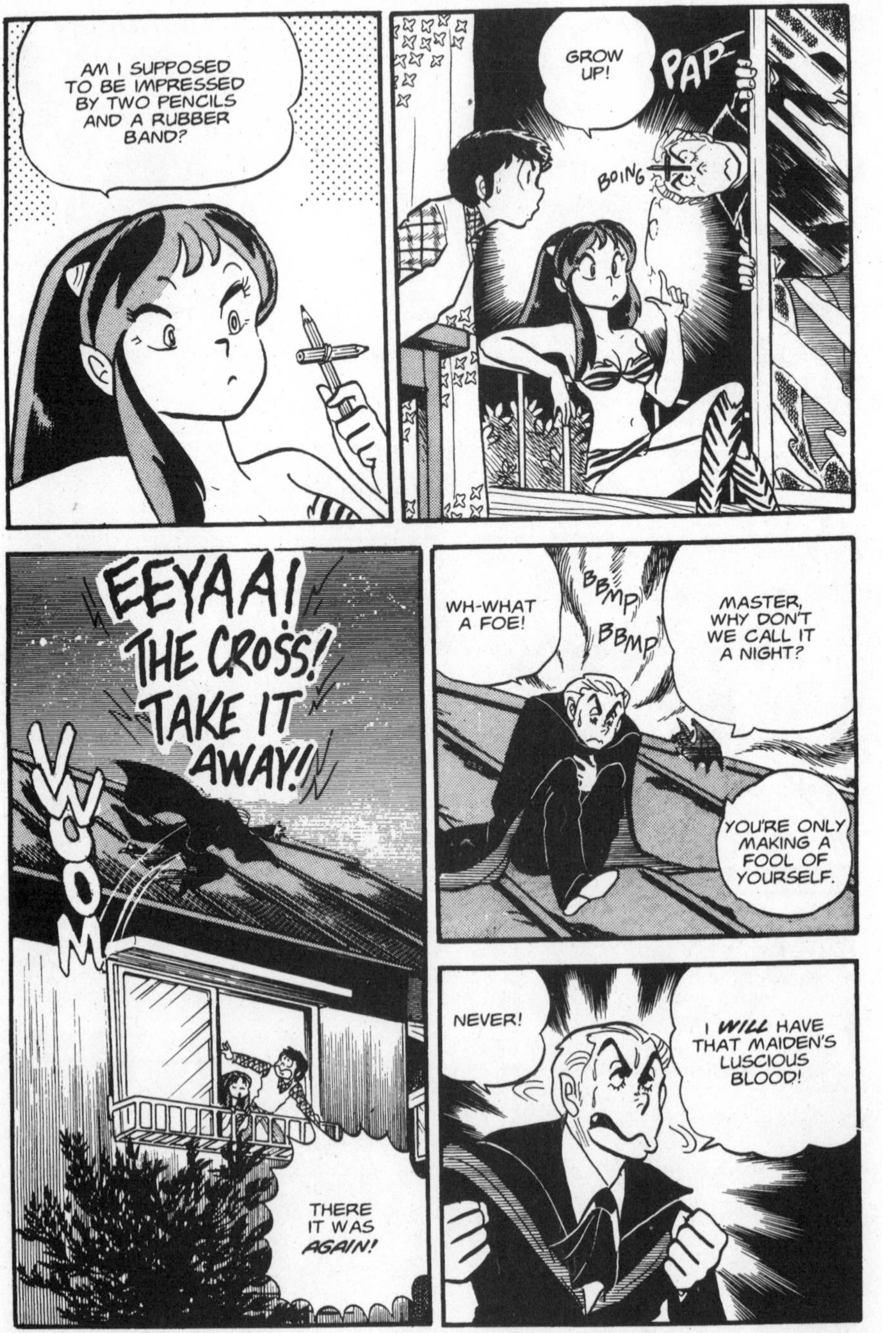

AM I SUPPOSED TO BE IMPRESSED BY TWO PENCILS AND A RUBBER BAND?
GROW UP!
PAP
BOING
EEYAA! THE CROSS! TAKE IT AWAY!
VWOOM
THERE IT WAS AGAIN!
WH-WHAT A FOE!
BBMP BBMP
MASTER, WHY DON'T WE CALL IT A NIGHT?
YOU'RE ONLY MAKING A FOOL OF YOURSELF.
NEVER!
I WILL HAVE THAT MAIDEN'S LUSCIOUS BLOOD!

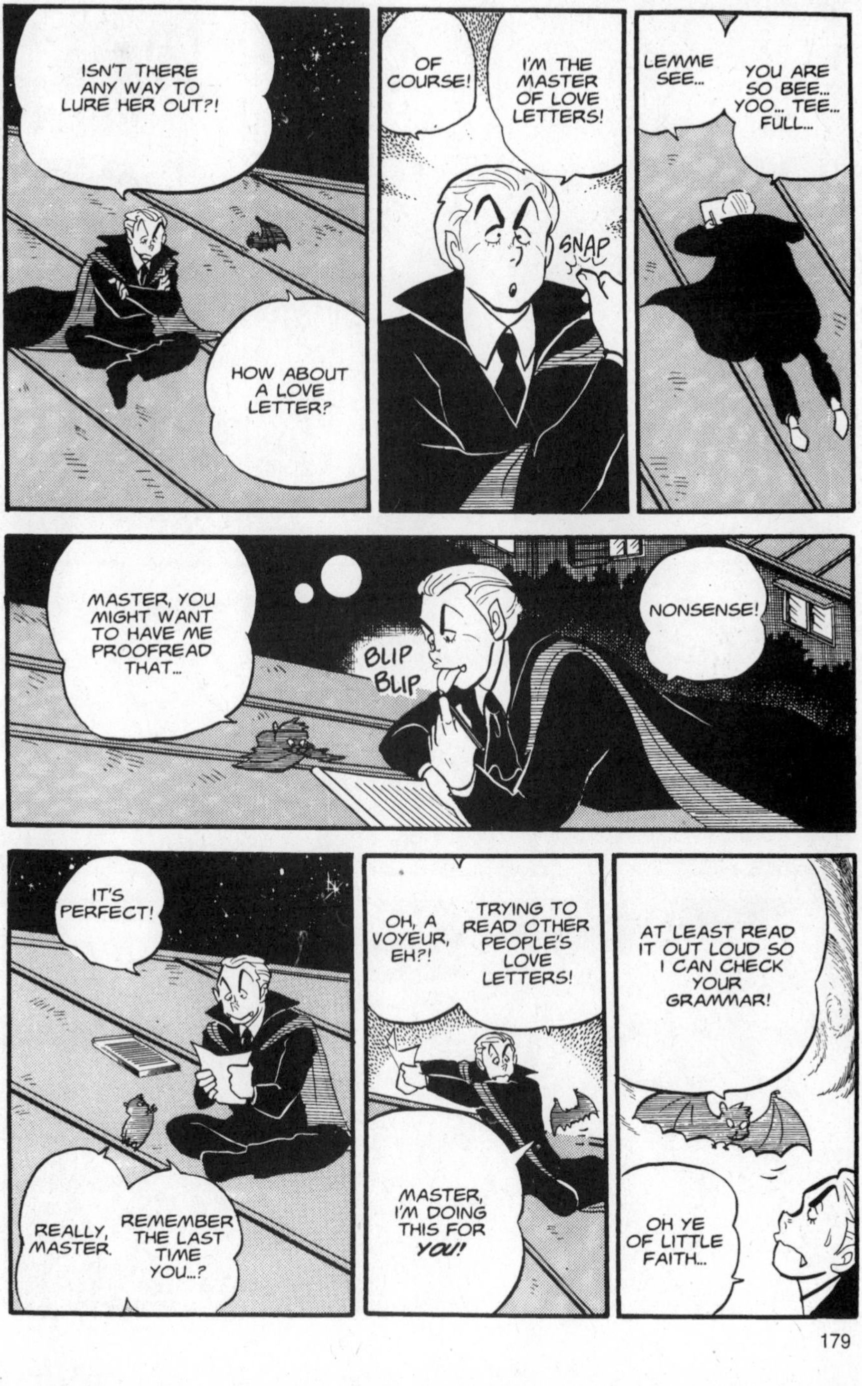
ISN'T THERE ANY WAY TO LURE HER OUT?!
HOW ABOUT A LOVE LETTER?
OF COURSE!
I'M THE MASTER OF LOVE LETTERS!
SNAP
LEMME SEE...
YOU ARE SO BEE... YOO... TEE... FULL...
MASTER, YOU MIGHT WANT TO HAVE ME PROOFREAD THAT...
BLIP BLIP
NONSENSE!
IT'S PERFECT!
REALLY, MASTER.
REMEMBER THE LAST TIME YOU...?
OH, A VOYEUR, EH?!
TRYING TO READ OTHER PEOPLE'S LOVE LETTERS!
MASTER, I'M DOING THIS FOR YOU!
AT LEAST READ IT OUT LOUD SO I CAN CHECK YOUR GRAMMAR!
OH YE OF LITTLE FAITH...

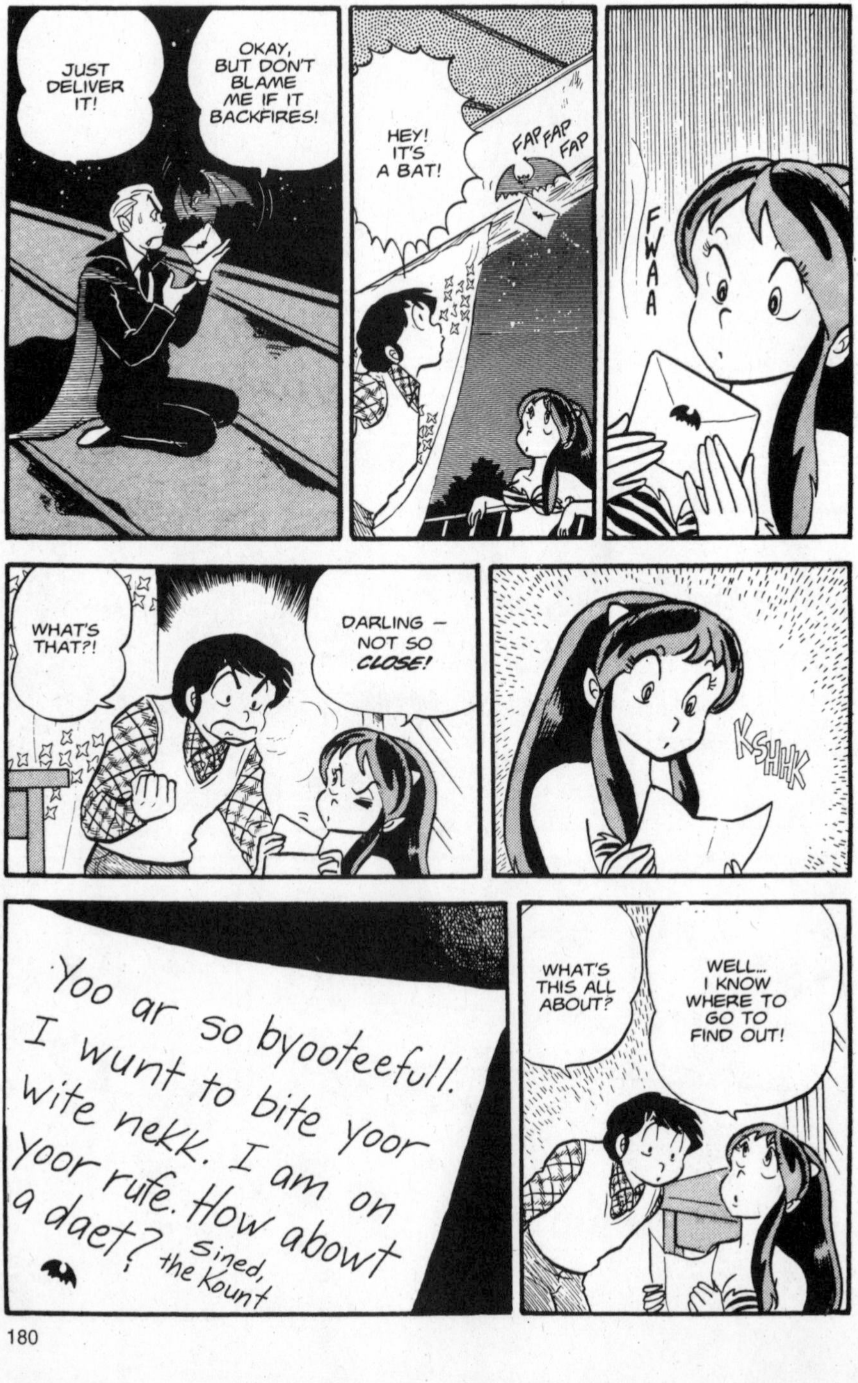
JUST DELIVER IT!
OKAY, BUT DON'T BLAME ME IF IT BACKFIRES!
HEY! IT'S A BAT!
FAP FAP FAP FAP
FWAAA
WHAT'S THAT?!
DARLING — NOT SO CLOSE!
KSHHK
Yoo ar so byooteefull. I wunt to bite yoor wite nekk. I am on yoor rufe. How abowt a daet? Sined, the Kount
WHAT'S THIS ALL ABOUT?
WELL... I KNOW WHERE TO GO TO FIND OUT!

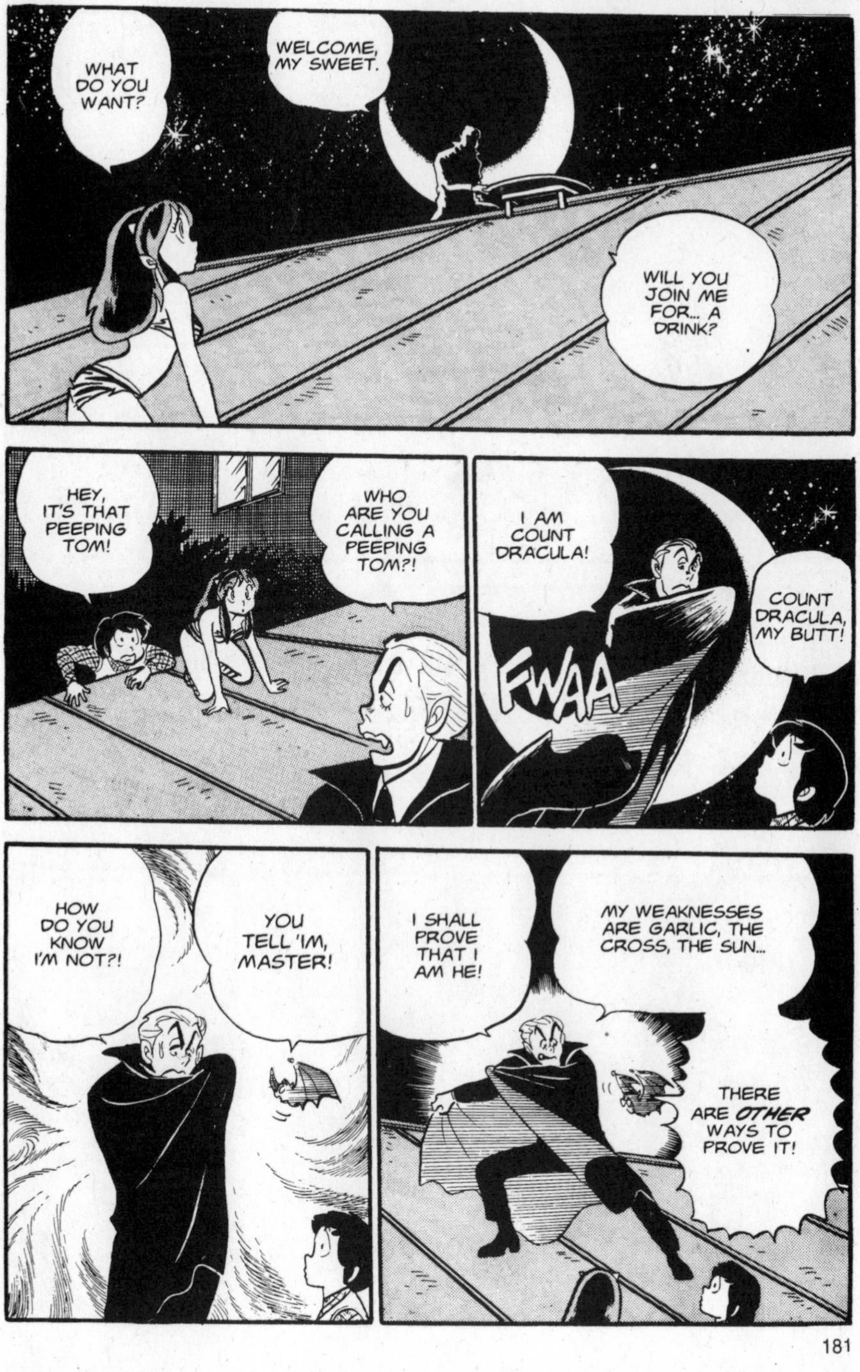
WHAT DO YOU WANT?
WELCOME, MY SWEET.
WILL YOU JOIN ME FOR... A DRINK?
HEY, IT'S THAT PEEPING TOM!
WHO ARE YOU CALLING A PEEPING TOM?!
I AM COUNT DRACULA!
FWAA
COUNT DRACULA, MY BUTT!
HOW DO YOU KNOW I'M NOT?!
YOU TELL 'IM, MASTER!
I SHALL PROVE THAT I AM HE!
MY WEAKNESSES ARE GARLIC, THE CROSS, THE SUN...
THERE ARE *OTHER* WAYS TO PROVE IT!

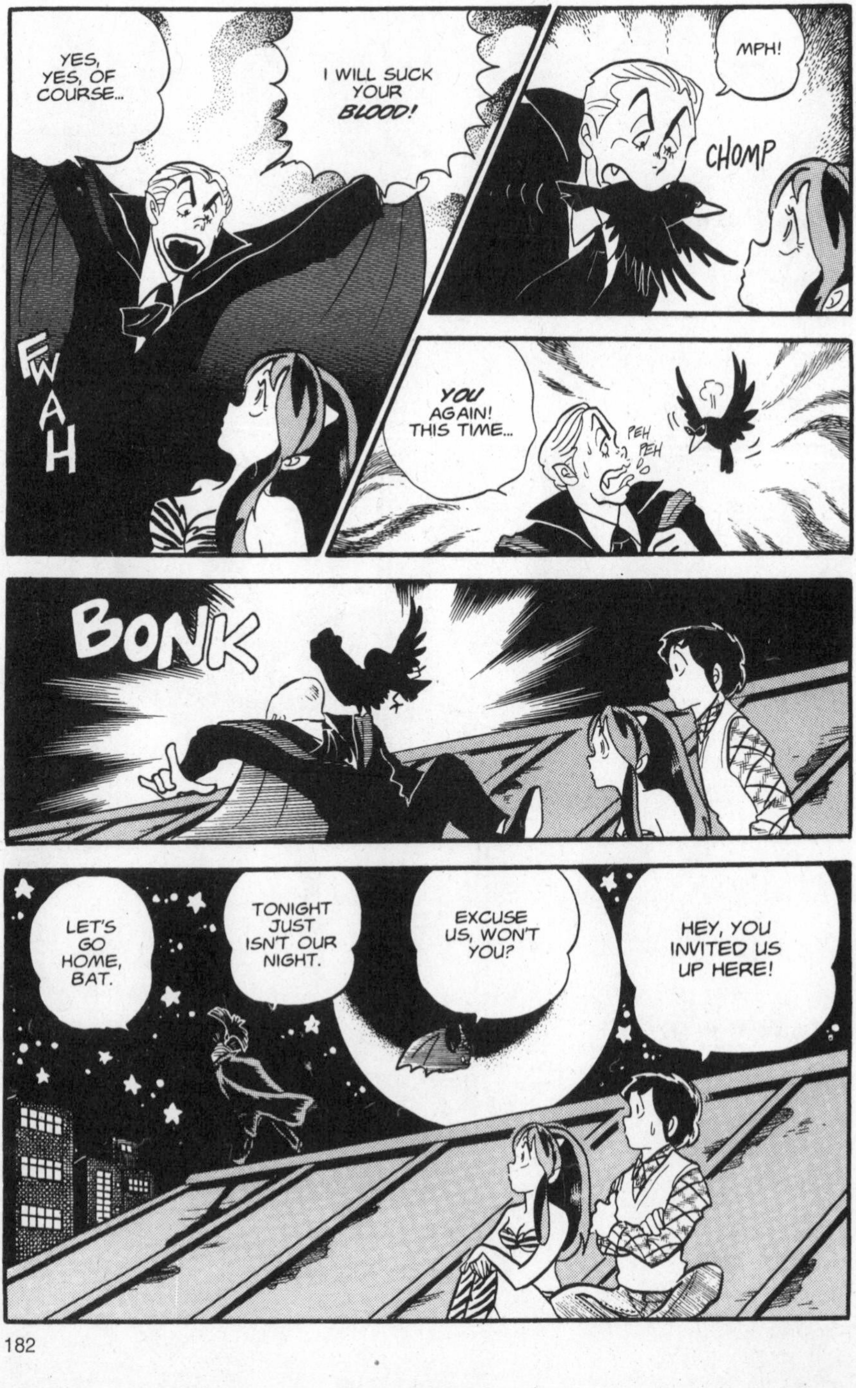
YES, YES, OF COURSE...
I WILL SUCK YOUR BLOOD!
FWAH
MPH!
CHOMP
YOU AGAIN! THIS TIME...
PEH PEH
BONK
LET'S GO HOME, BAT.
TONIGHT JUST ISN'T OUR NIGHT.
EXCUSE US, WON'T YOU?
HEY, YOU INVITED US UP HERE!

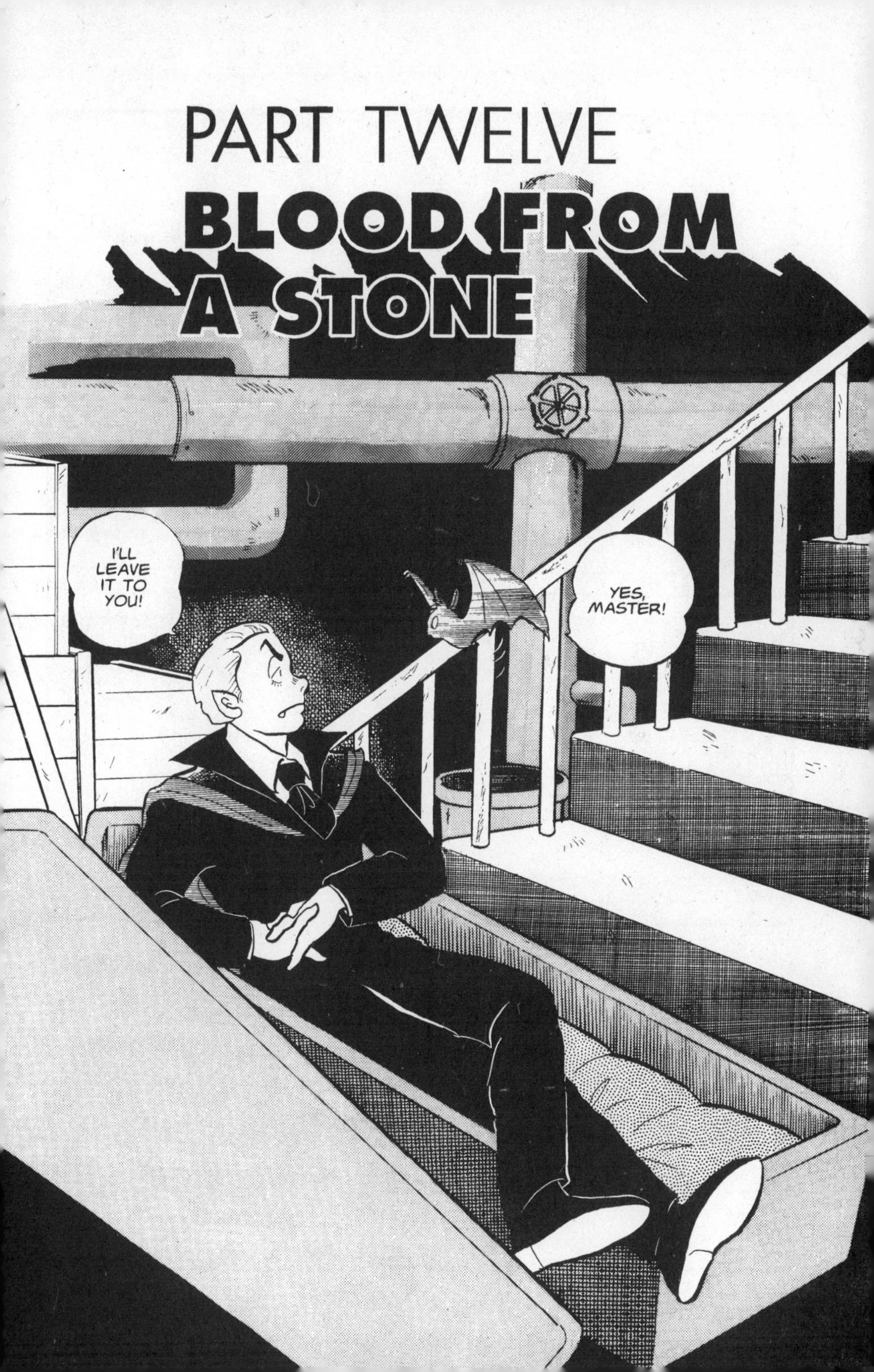
PART TWELVE
BLOOD FROM A STONE
I'LL LEAVE IT TO YOU!
YES, MASTER!

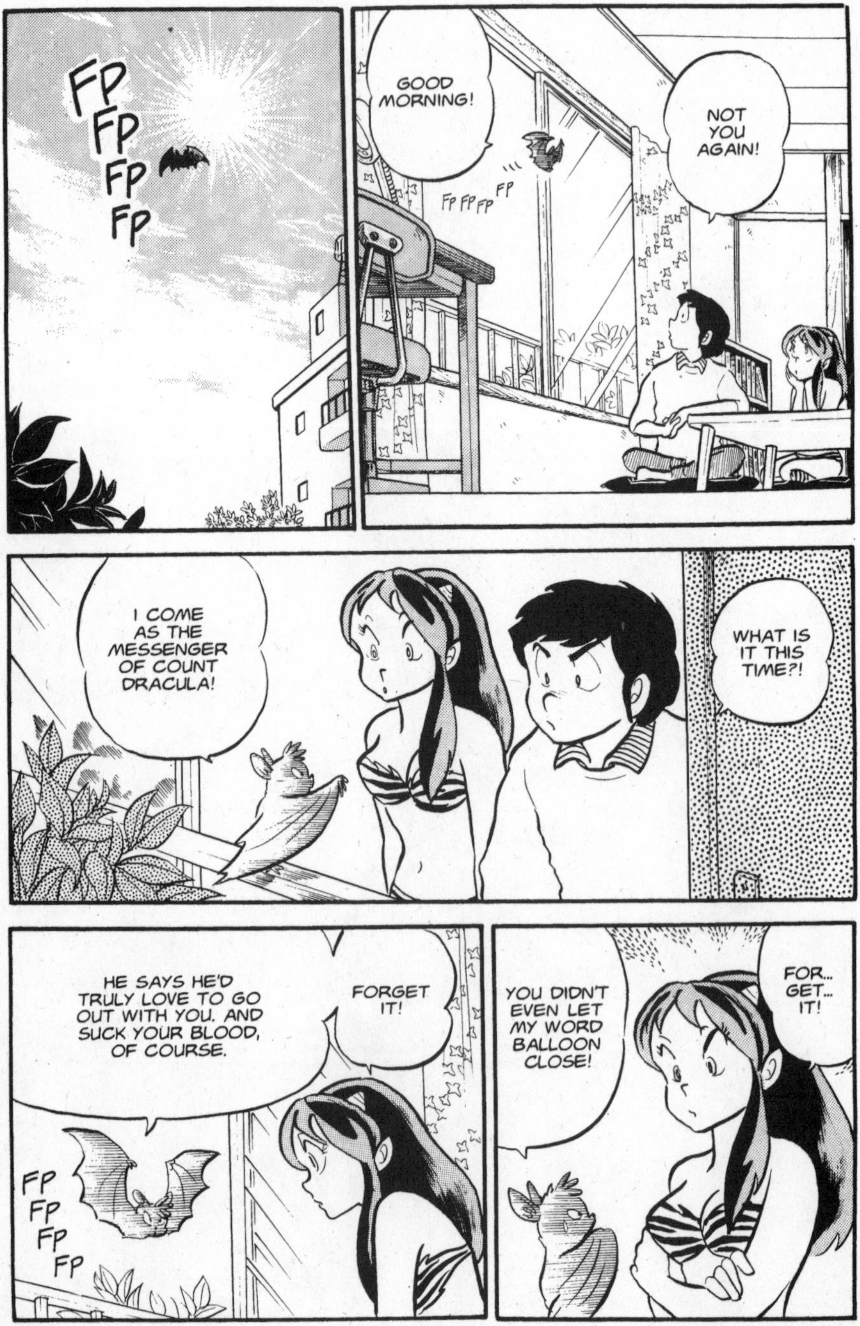
FP FP FP FP
GOOD MORNING!
FP FP FP FP
NOT YOU AGAIN!
I COME AS THE MESSENGER OF COUNT DRACULA!
WHAT IS IT THIS TIME?!
HE SAYS HE'D TRULY LOVE TO GO OUT WITH YOU. AND SUCK YOUR BLOOD, OF COURSE.
FORGET IT!
FP FP FP FP
YOU DIDN'T EVEN LET MY WORD BALLOON CLOSE!
FOR... GET... IT!

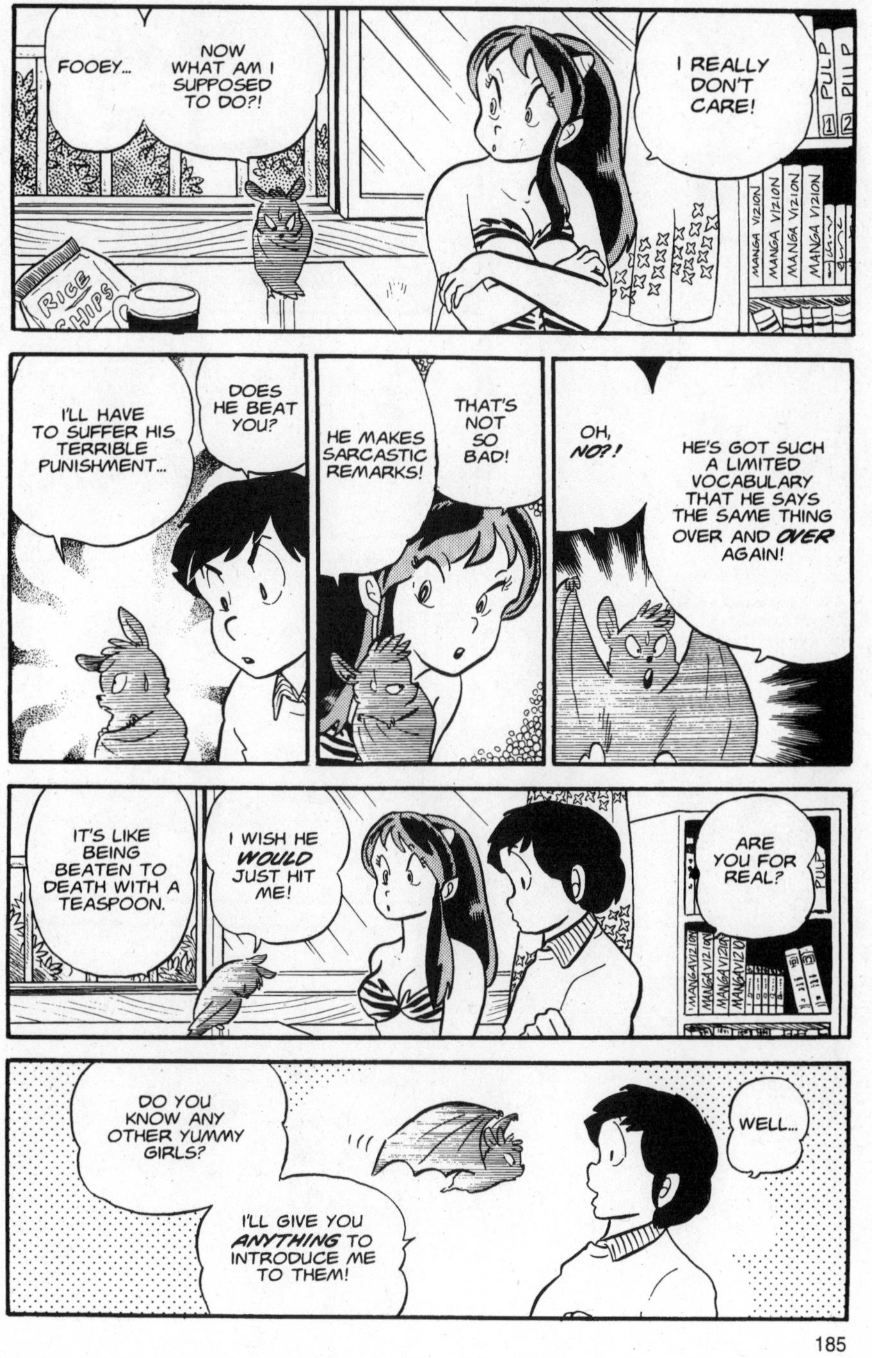
FOOEY...
NOW WHAT AM I SUPPOSED TO DO?!
RICE CHIPS
I REALLY DON'T CARE!
I'LL HAVE TO SUFFER HIS TERRIBLE PUNISHMENT...
DOES HE BEAT YOU?
HE MAKES SARCASTIC REMARKS!
THAT'S NOT SO BAD!
OH, ***NO?!***
HE'S GOT SUCH A LIMITED VOCABULARY THAT HE SAYS THE SAME THING OVER AND ***OVER*** AGAIN!
IT'S LIKE BEING BEATEN TO DEATH WITH A TEASPOON.
I WISH HE ***WOULD*** JUST HIT ME!
ARE YOU FOR REAL?
DO YOU KNOW ANY OTHER YUMMY GIRLS?
I'LL GIVE YOU ***ANYTHING*** TO INTRODUCE ME TO THEM!
WELL...

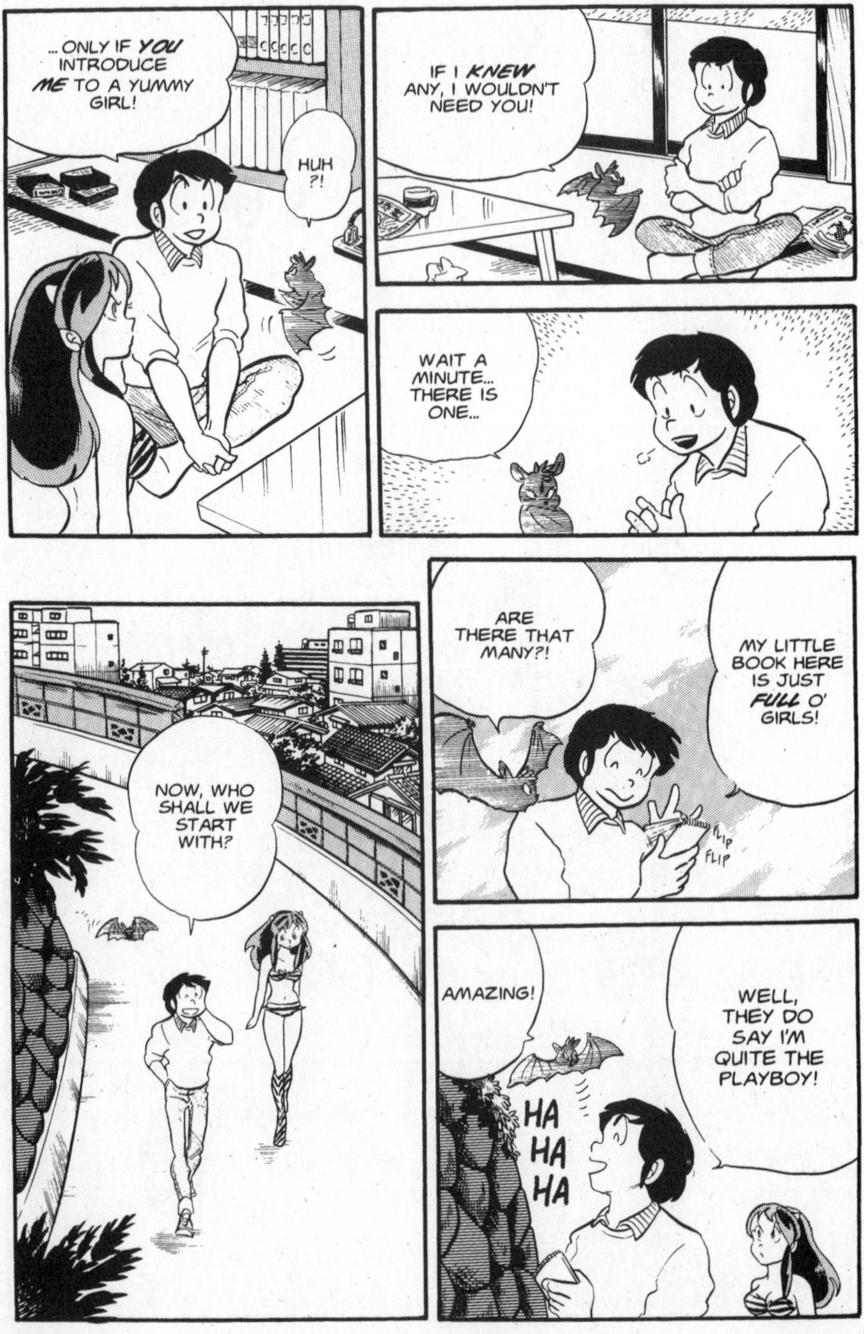

...ONLY IF YOU INTRODUCE ME TO A YUMMY GIRL!
HUH ?!
IF I KNEW ANY, I WOULDN'T NEED YOU!
WAIT A MINUTE... THERE IS ONE...
NOW, WHO SHALL WE START WITH?
ARE THERE THAT MANY?!
MY LITTLE BOOK HERE IS JUST FULL O' GIRLS!
FLIP FLIP
AMAZING!
WELL, THEY DO SAY I'M QUITE THE PLAYBOY!
HA HA HA

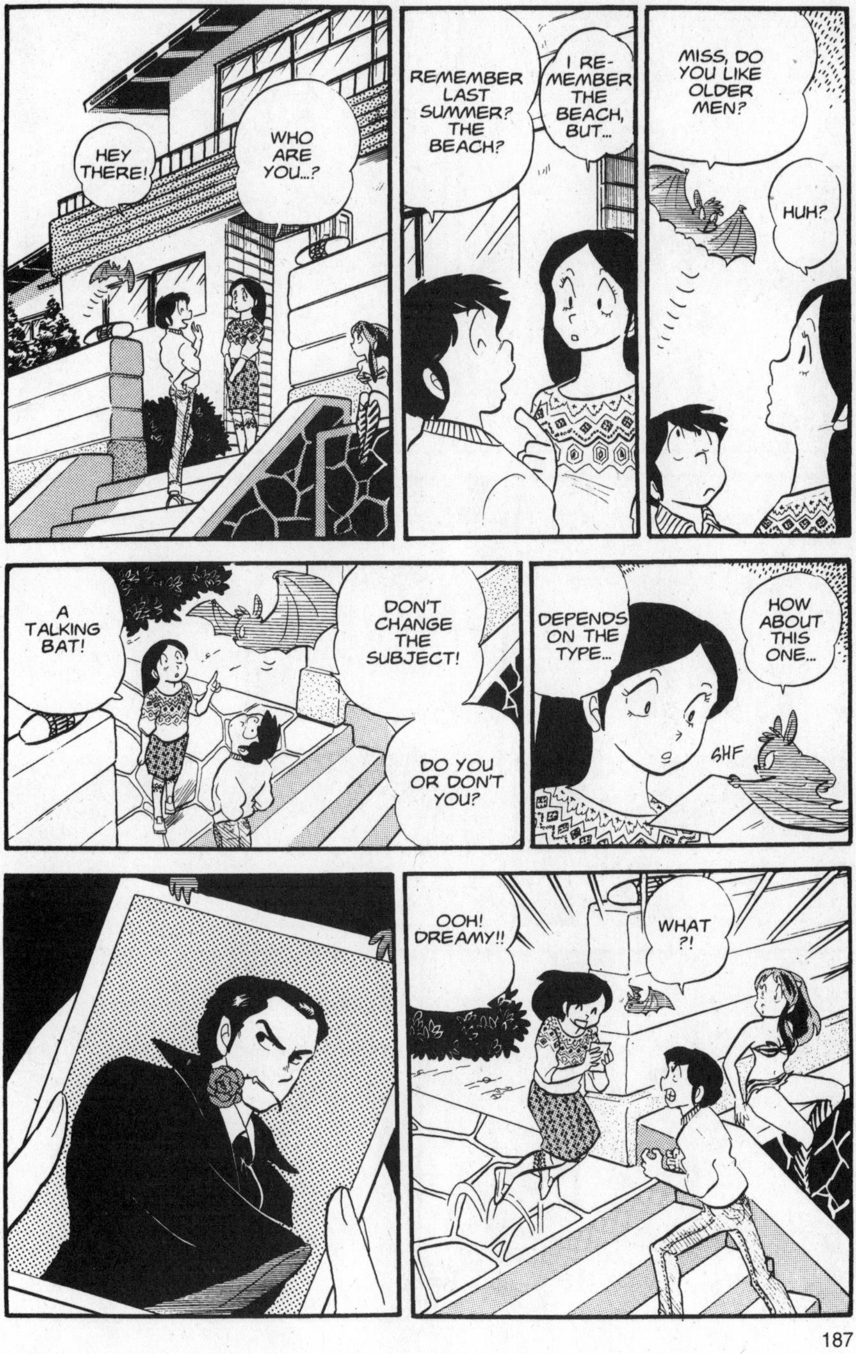
HEY THERE!
WHO ARE YOU...?
REMEMBER LAST SUMMER? THE BEACH?
I RE-MEMBER THE BEACH, BUT...
MISS, DO YOU LIKE OLDER MEN?
HUH?
A TALKING BAT!
DON'T CHANGE THE SUBJECT!
DO YOU OR DON'T YOU?
DEPENDS ON THE TYPE...
HOW ABOUT THIS ONE...
SHF
OOH! DREAMY!!
WHAT ?!

THIS IS...?

IT DOESN'T LOOK LIKE HIM AT ALL!

HEY, STAY OUT OF THIS!

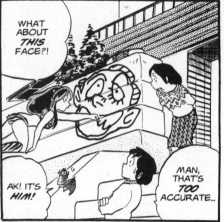

WHAT ABOUT *THIS* FACE?!

AK! IT'S *HIM!*

MAN, THAT'S *TOO* ACCURATE...

THAT WASN'T FAIR...

LYING'S NOT FAIR!

ARE YOU SURE YOU'RE GONNA INTRODUCE ME TO A GIRL?

UH...

WELL?! ARE YOU OR AREN'T YOU?!

I NEVER LIE!

YOU JUST *DID!*

I'M STARTIN' TO WONDER...

IF YOU DON'T BELIEVE ME, I'LL BRING HER RIGHT NOW!

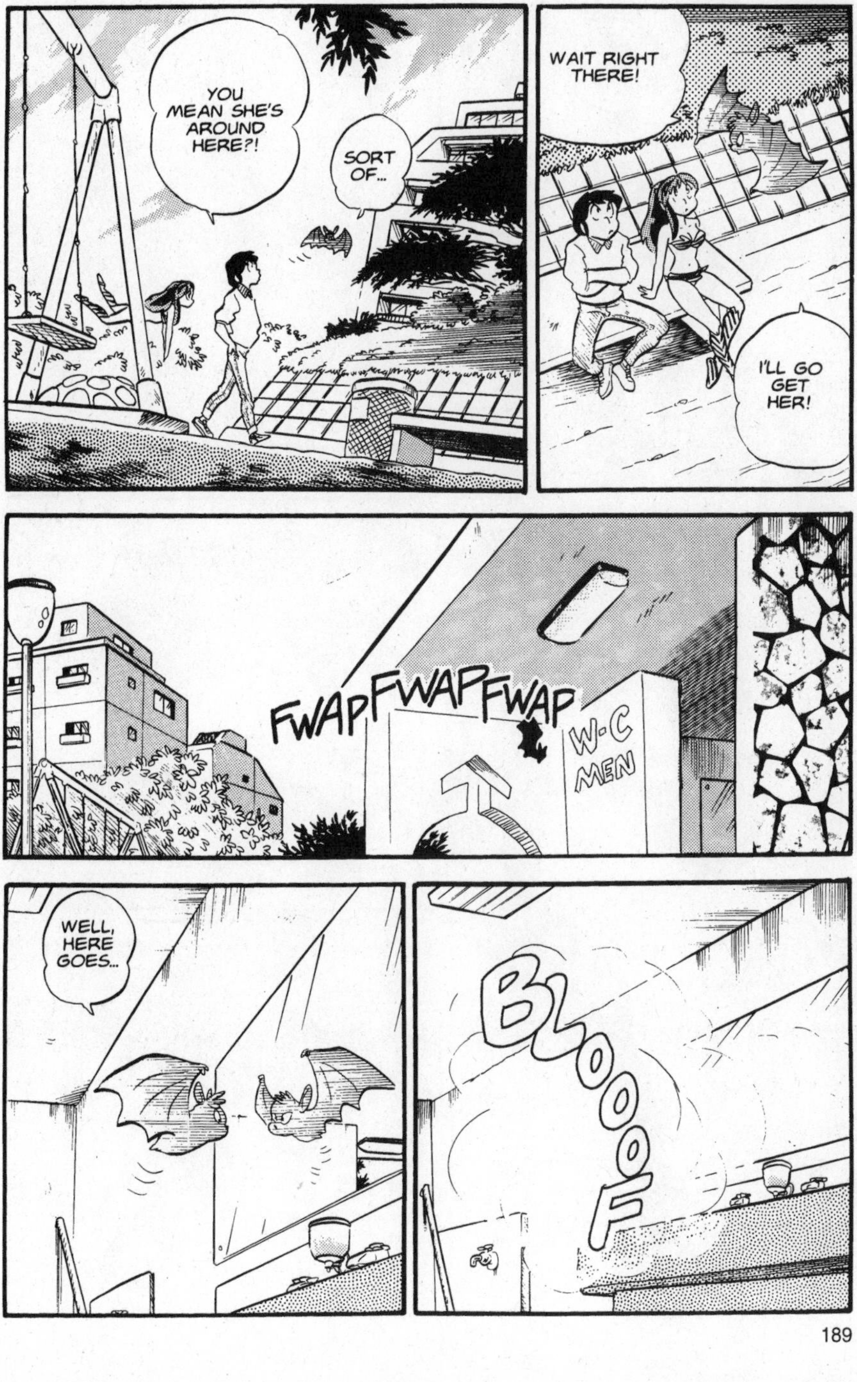
YOU MEAN SHE'S AROUND HERE?!
SORT OF...
WAIT RIGHT THERE!
I'LL GO GET HER!
FWAP FWAP FWAP
W·C MEN
WELL, HERE GOES...
BLOOOOF

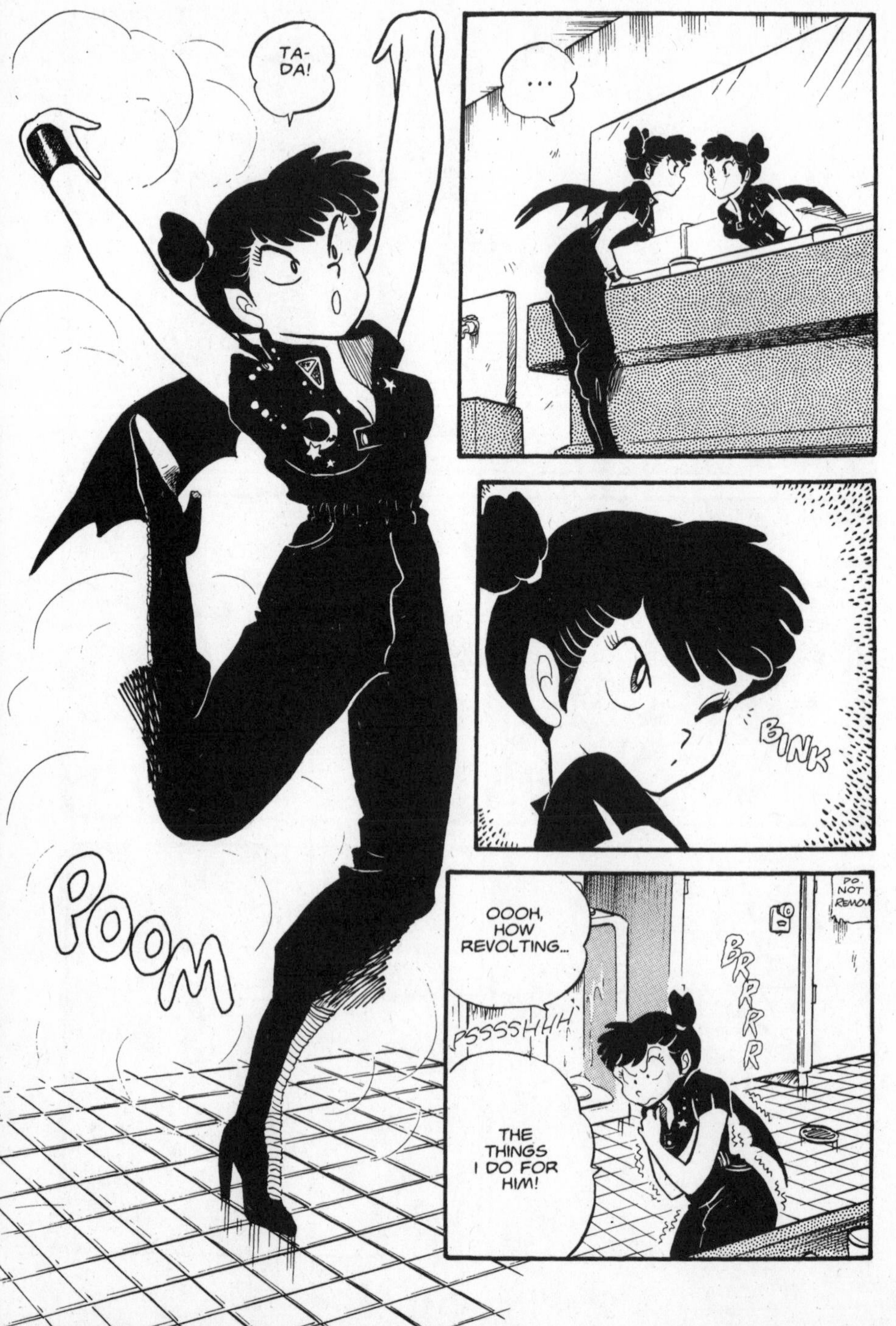
TA-DA!
POOM
...
BINK
OOOH, HOW REVOLTING...
DO NOT REMOV
BRRRR
PSSSSHHH
THE THINGS I DO FOR HIM!

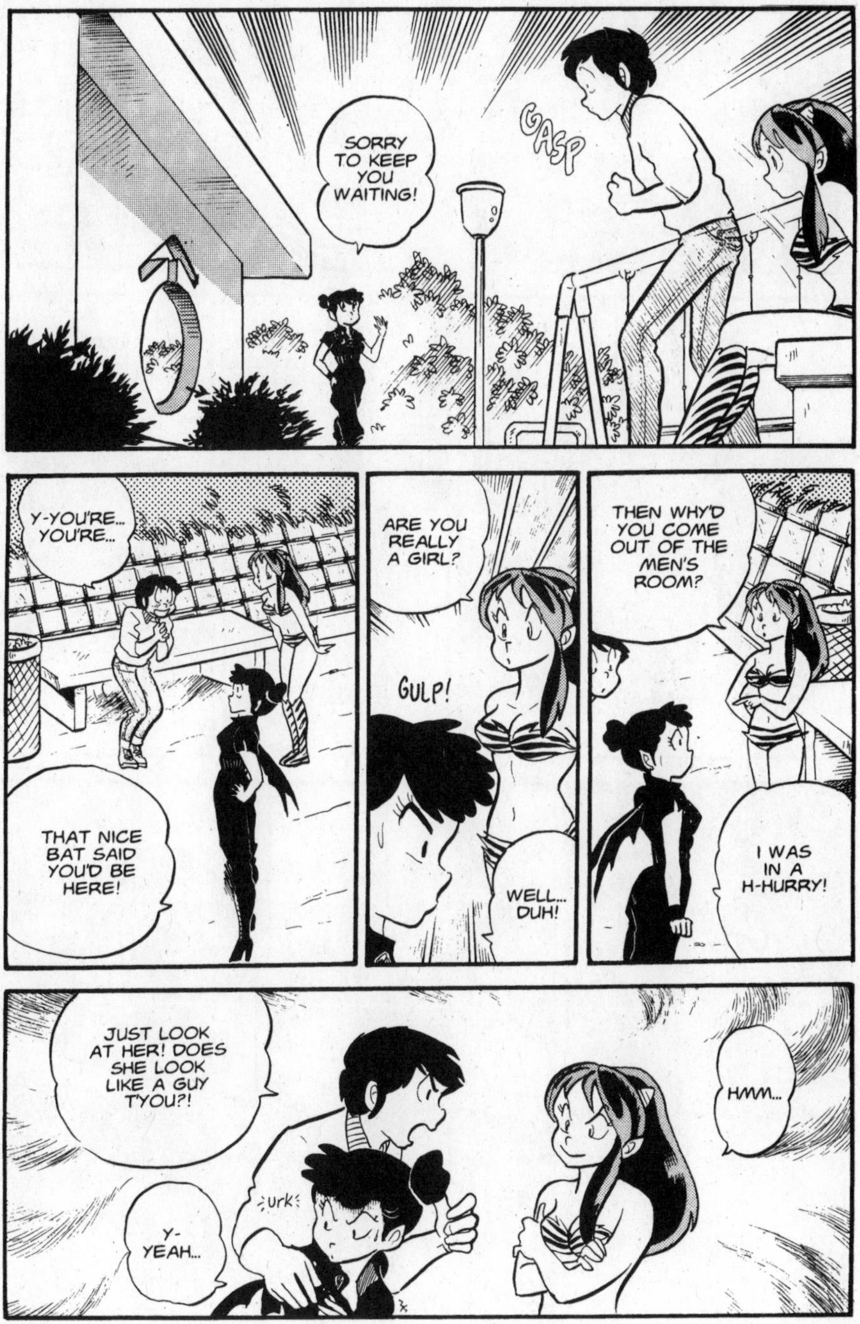
SORRY TO KEEP YOU WAITING!
GASP
Y-YOU'RE... YOU'RE...
THAT NICE BAT SAID YOU'D BE HERE!
ARE YOU REALLY A GIRL?
GULP!
WELL... DUH!
THEN WHY'D YOU COME OUT OF THE MEN'S ROOM?
I WAS IN A H-HURRY!
JUST LOOK AT HER! DOES SHE LOOK LIKE A GUY T'YOU?!
HMM...
urk
Y- YEAH...

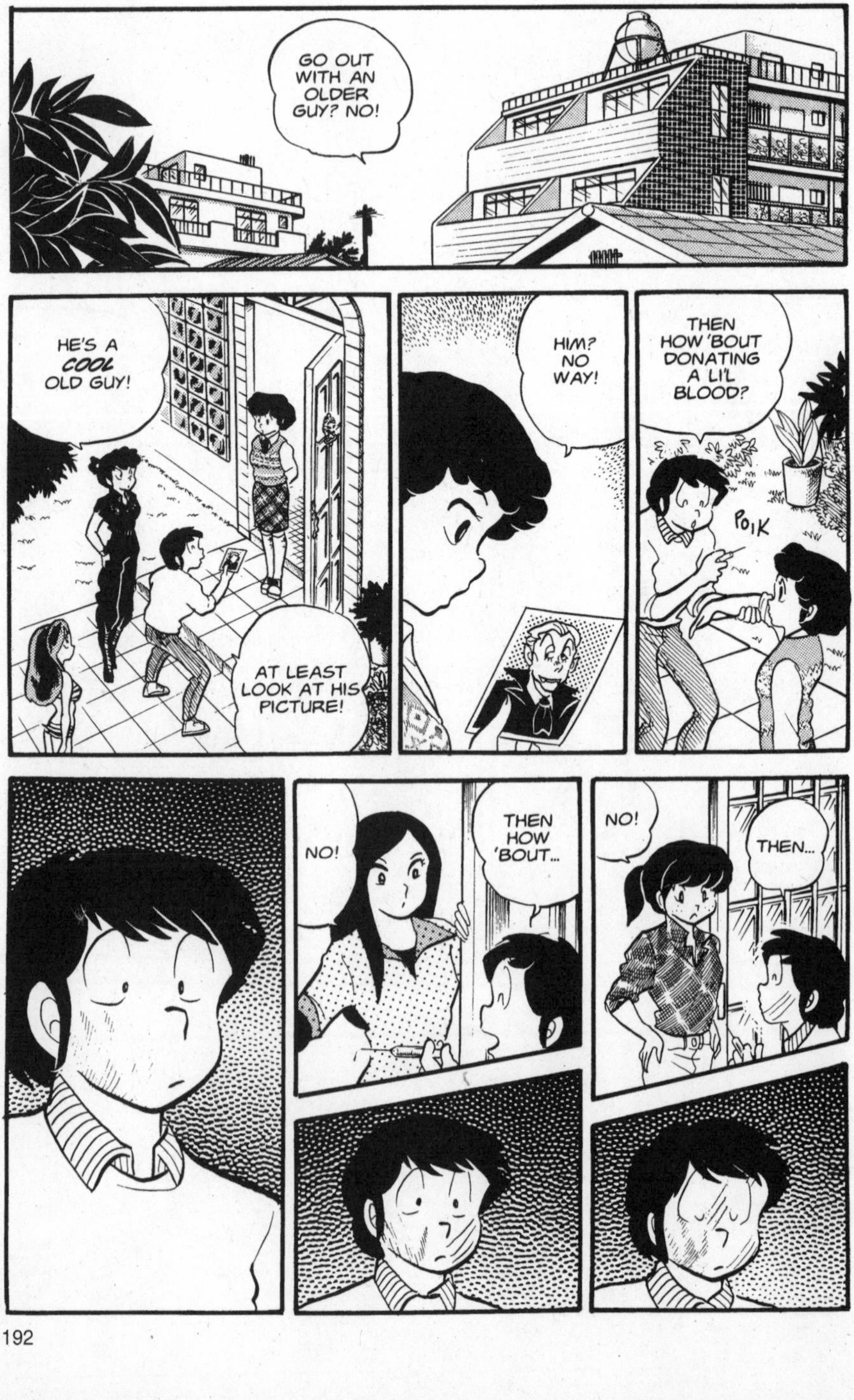
GO OUT WITH AN OLDER GUY? NO!
HE'S A *COOL* OLD GUY!
AT LEAST LOOK AT HIS PICTURE!
HIM? NO WAY!
THEN HOW 'BOUT DONATING A LI'L BLOOD?
POIK
NO!
THEN HOW 'BOUT...
NO!
THEN...

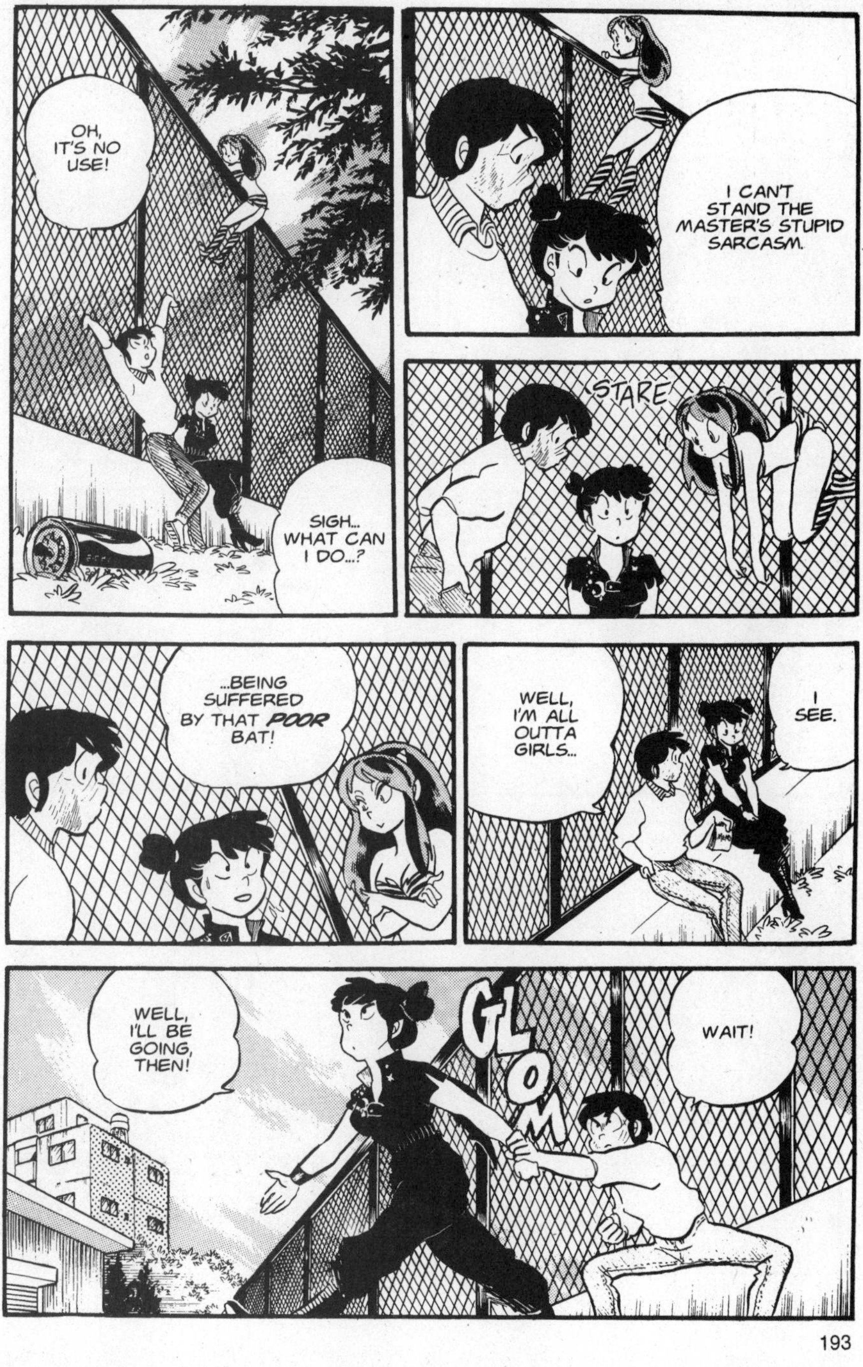
OH, IT'S NO USE!
SIGH... WHAT CAN I DO...?
I CAN'T STAND THE MASTER'S STUPID SARCASM.
STARE
...BEING SUFFERED BY THAT POOR BAT!
WELL, I'M ALL OUTTA GIRLS...
I SEE.
WELL, I'LL BE GOING, THEN!
GLOM
WAIT!

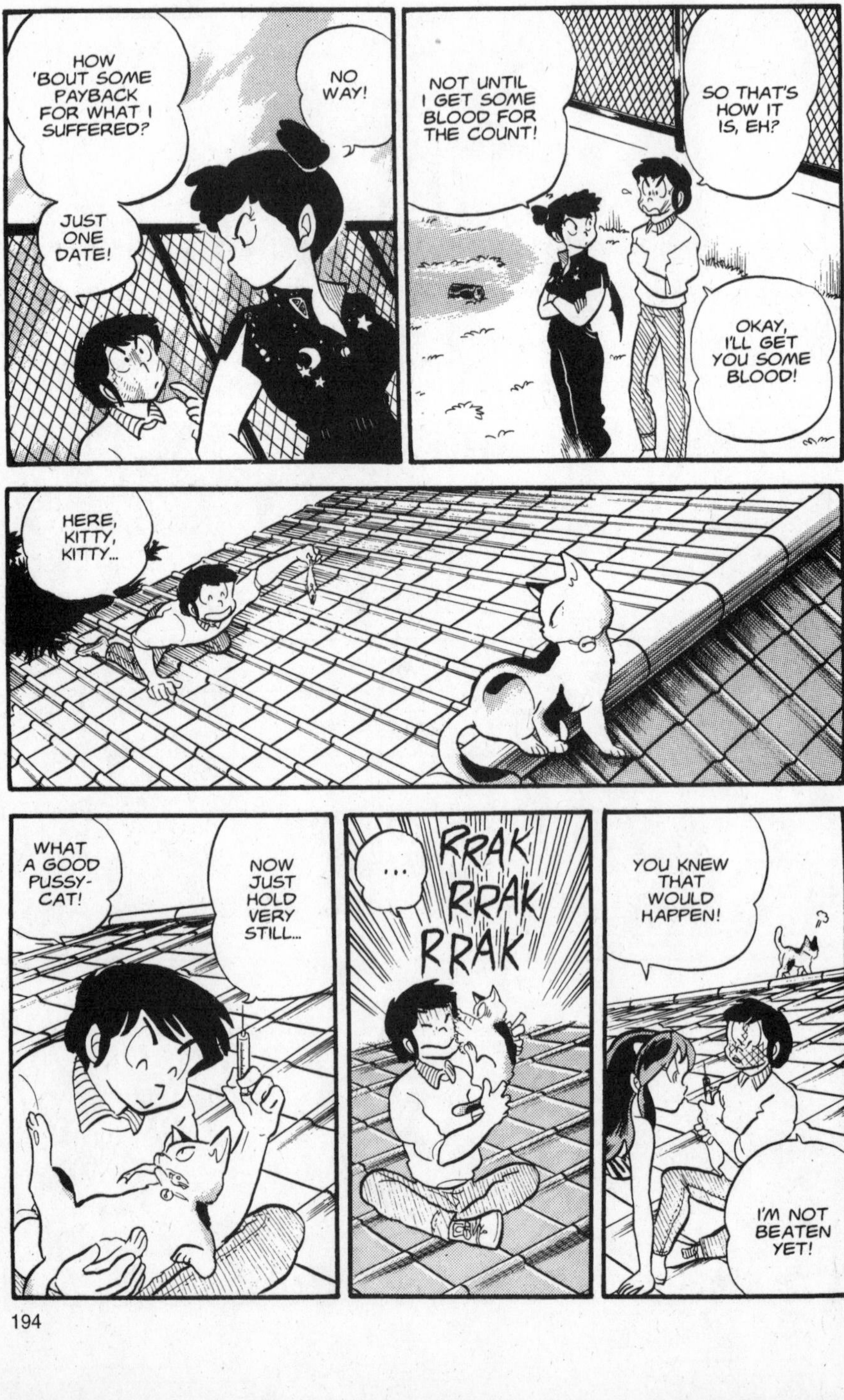
HOW 'BOUT SOME PAYBACK FOR WHAT I SUFFERED?
JUST ONE DATE!
NO WAY!
NOT UNTIL I GET SOME BLOOD FOR THE COUNT!
SO THAT'S HOW IT IS, EH?
OKAY, I'LL GET YOU SOME BLOOD!
HERE, KITTY, KITTY...
WHAT A GOOD PUSSY-CAT!
NOW JUST HOLD VERY STILL...
...
RRAK RRAK RRAK
YOU KNEW THAT WOULD HAPPEN!
I'M NOT BEATEN YET!

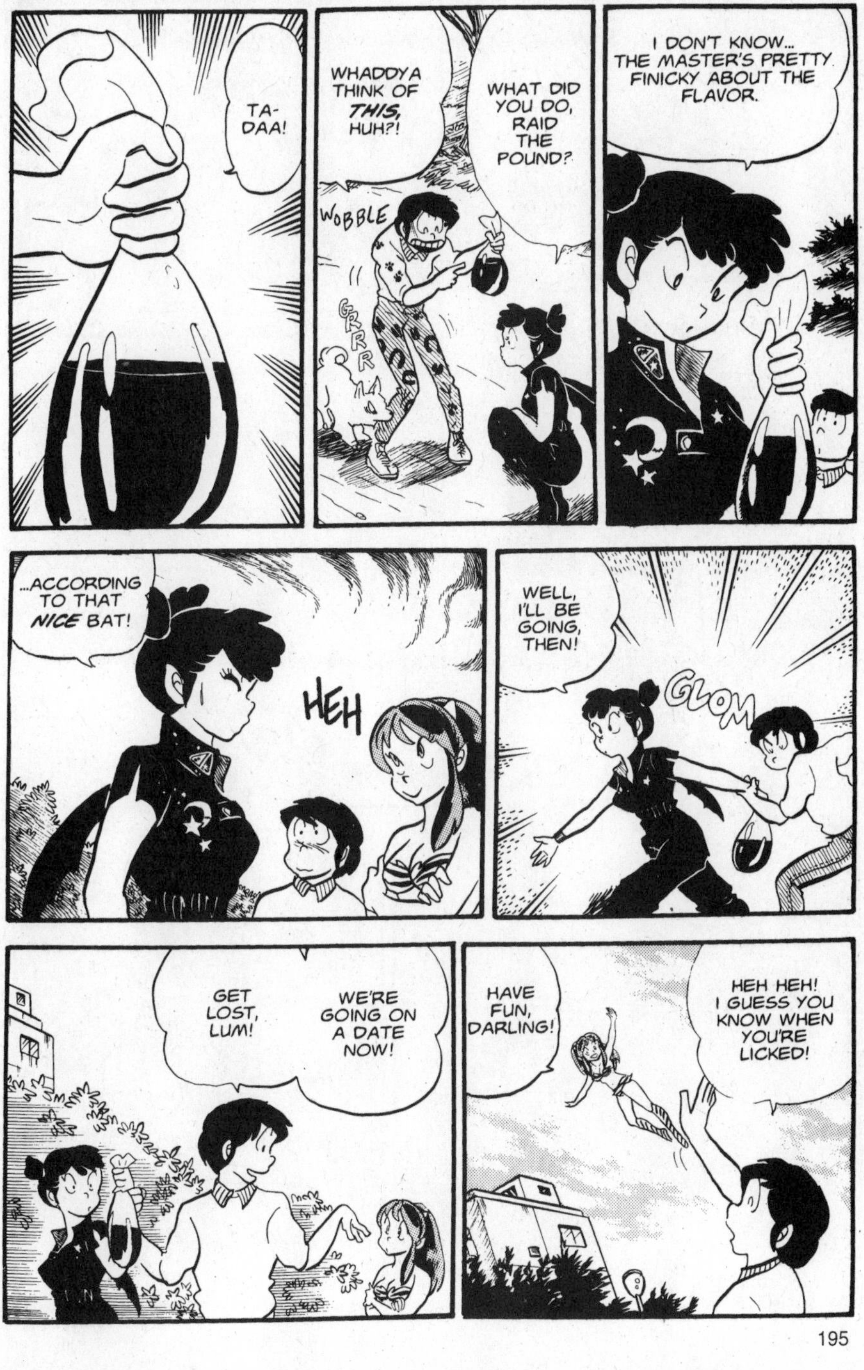
TA-DAA!
WHADDYA THINK OF *THIS,* HUH?!
WHAT DID YOU DO, RAID THE POUND?
WOBBLE
GRRR
I DON'T KNOW... THE MASTER'S PRETTY FINICKY ABOUT THE FLAVOR.
...ACCORDING TO THAT *NICE* BAT!
HEH
WELL, I'LL BE GOING, THEN!
GLOM
GET LOST, LUM!
WE'RE GOING ON A DATE NOW!
HAVE FUN, DARLING!
HEH HEH! I GUESS YOU KNOW WHEN YOU'RE LICKED!

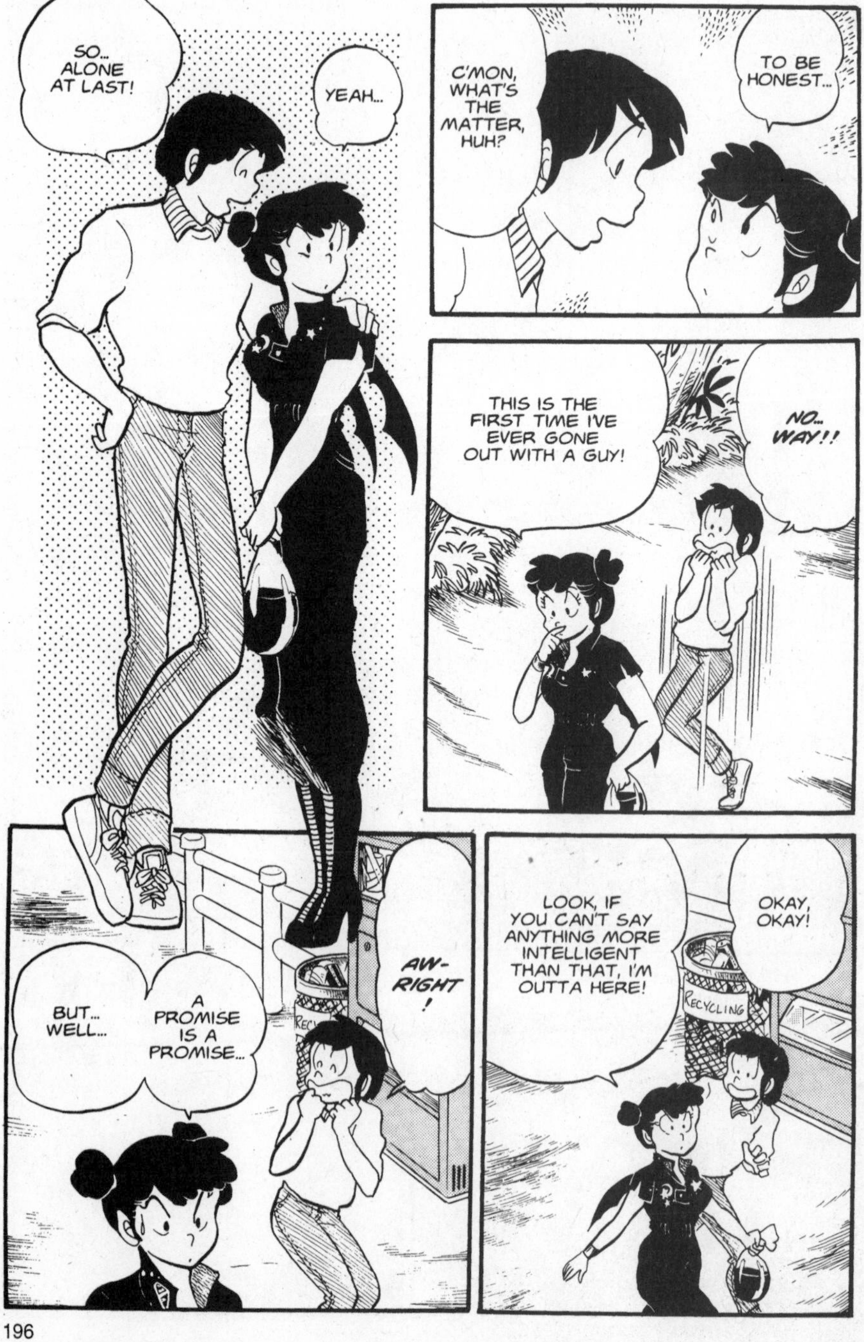
SO... ALONE AT LAST!
YEAH...
C'MON, WHAT'S THE MATTER, HUH?
TO BE HONEST...
THIS IS THE FIRST TIME I'VE EVER GONE OUT WITH A GUY!
NO... WAY!!
BUT... WELL...
A PROMISE IS A PROMISE...
AW-RIGHT!
LOOK, IF YOU CAN'T SAY ANYTHING MORE INTELLIGENT THAN THAT, I'M OUTTA HERE!
OKAY, OKAY!
RECYCLING

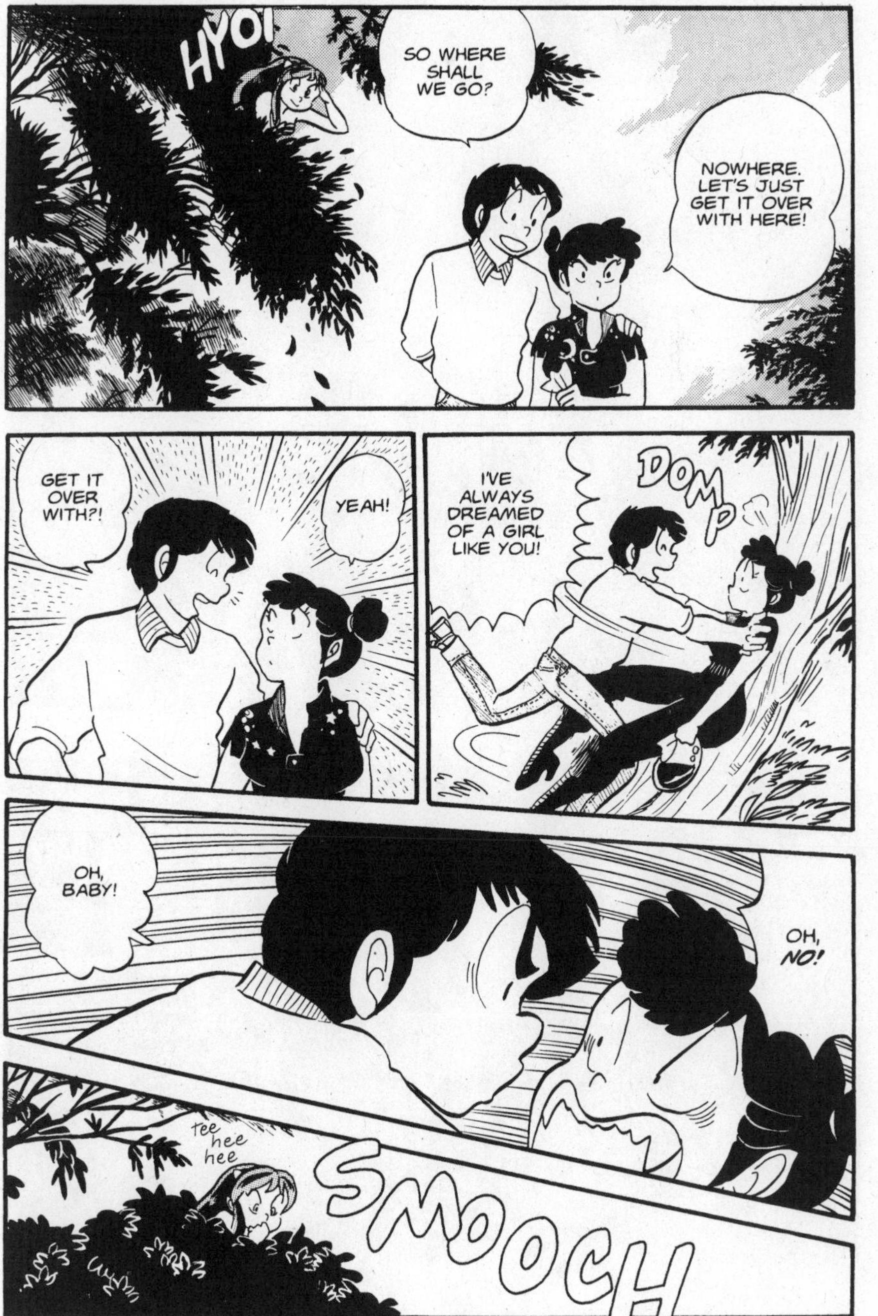
HYOI
SO WHERE SHALL WE GO?
NOWHERE. LET'S JUST GET IT OVER WITH HERE!
GET IT OVER WITH?!
YEAH!
I'VE ALWAYS DREAMED OF A GIRL LIKE YOU!
DOMP
OH, BABY!
OH, *NO!*
tee hee hee
SMOOCH

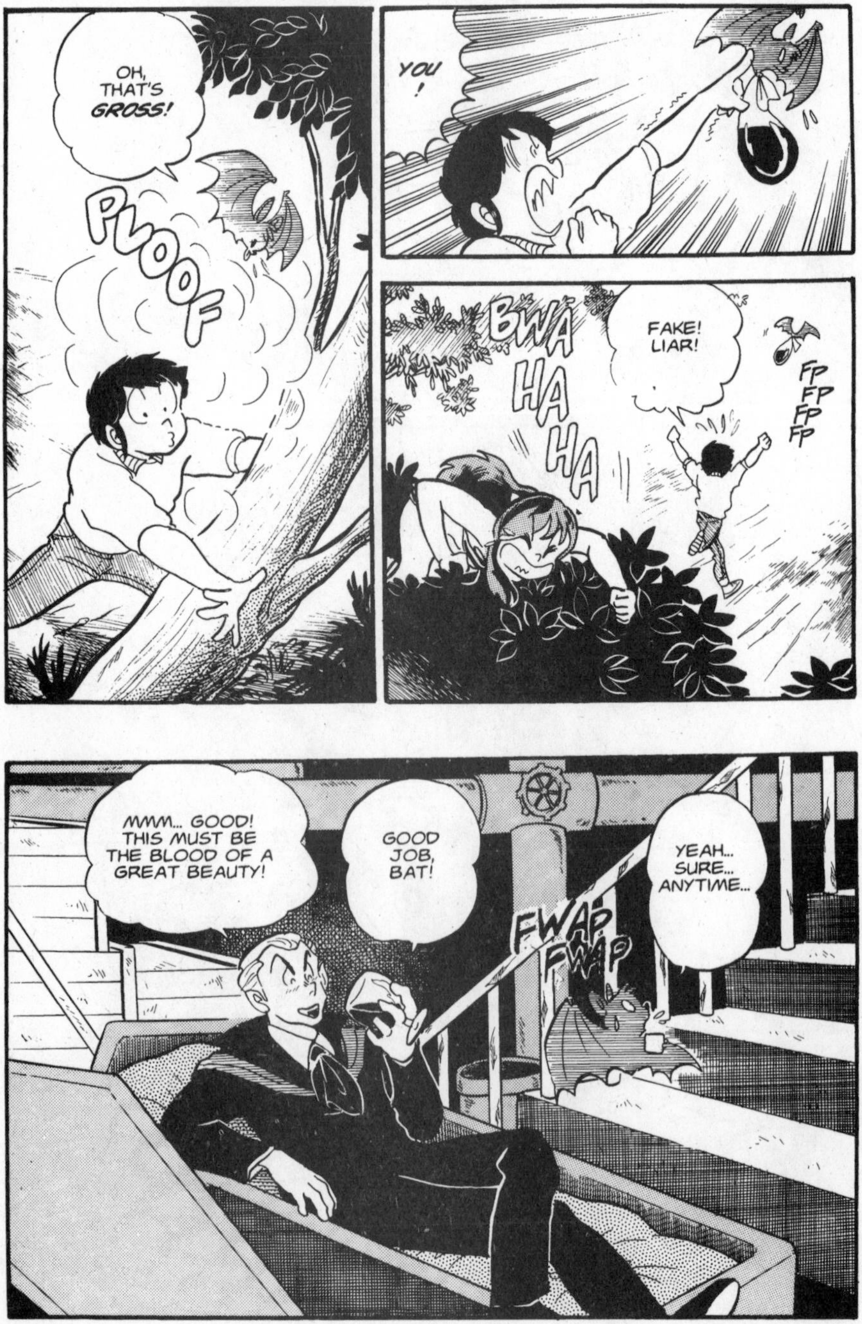
OH, THAT'S *GROSS!*
PLOOF
YOU!
BWA HA HA HA
FAKE! LIAR!
FP FP FP FP
MMM... GOOD! THIS MUST BE THE BLOOD OF A GREAT BEAUTY!
GOOD JOB, BAT!
YEAH... SURE... ANYTIME...
FWAP FWAP

TO BE CONTINUED...